The Wolf and The Lamb

Terry Cloutier

Copyright © 2022 TERRY CLOUTIER

All rights reserved. No part of this book may be reproduced,

in whole or in part, without prior written permission

from the copyright holder.

Books by Terry Cloutier

The Wolf of Corwick Castle Series

The Nine (2019)

The Wolf At Large (2020)

The Wolf On The Run (2020)

The Wolf At War (2021)

The Wolf And The Lamb (2022)

The Past Lives Chronicles

Past Lives (2021)

Jack the Ripper (2022)

The Zone War Series

The Demon Inside (2008)

The Balance Of Power (2010)

Novella

Peter Pickler and the Cat That Talked Back (2010)

The action and adventure continue in the fifth installment of the bestselling Wolf of Corwick Castle series!

Seven years have passed since Lord Hadrack of Corwick defeated the last of the nine and fulfilled his vow to his murdered family. Now a father of four, Hadrack's life has settled into a routine of ruling over his immense lands and swapping lies and tall tales with his two best friends, Baine and Jebido. But, when riders arrive with a plea for help from an old friend, Hadrack finds himself drawn into a bloody war against a group of slavers called the Shadow Pirates and their leader, a monstrosity of a man known only as Captain Bear, who has sworn to kill the Wolf at all costs.

But, more is going on than even Hadrack suspects, as powerful forces inside the Empire of Cardia are also moving against him, with their eyes set on a bigger prize than he can possibly imagine. Hunted at every turn by both pirates and Cardians, Hadrack and the crew of his brand-new ship, Sea-Wolf, must somehow manage to survive against enormous odds, with failure not only death for all on board, but also for the one person who means far more to him than life itself.

Contents

PROLOGUE 7

Chapter 1: Riders 16

Chapter 2: Shadow Pirates 28

Chapter 3: Sea-Wolf 41

Chapter 4: The Overseer 52

Chapter 5: Escape From Blood Ring Isle 65

Chapter 6: The Prophecy 85

Chapter 7: Ascension 99

Chapter 8: Fanrissen 117

Chapter 9: Ravenhold 131

Chapter 10: Storming the Citadel 145

Chapter 11: Alesia 167

Chapter 12: Captain Bear 186

Chapter 13: Battle at Sea 203

Chapter 14: The Lion's Mouth 222

Chapter 15: Bahyrst 239

Chapter 16: Lady Deneux 257

Chapter 17: The Bridge of Betrayal 274

Chapter 18: Not Everything Is What It Seems 289

Chapter 19: Cryptic Message 310

Chapter 20: The Hundred Knives 325

Chapter 21: Return to Blood Ring Isle 339

Chapter 22: Underwater Siege 355

Chapter 23: The Fury Of The Lamb 372

Chapter 24: The Watching Hill 396

EPILOGUE 405

Author's Note 410

PROLOGUE

"Stop fussing over me," I grumbled as my granddaughter, Lillia, fiddled with the pillows propping me up.

"You don't look comfortable, my lord," Lillia said, ignoring my words as she continued to tuck and poke at the stack of frilly, feathered cushions behind me with a fierce look of concentration on her face.

It might have been funny, I thought, if it wasn't for the fact that I was fed up with being treated like a child. I took a deep breath, trying to contain my irritation while she worked. I knew the girl was only trying to help, yet even so, she was wearing down my patience with her constant hovering.

"Don't you think I'm better able to judge how comfortable or not I might be?" I asked.

"Of course you are, my lord," Lillia said, though her expression greatly conflicted with her words. "You're a grown man, after all, so why wouldn't you be?"

"Yes, why indeed," I mumbled, not liking her condescending tone. I might be the Lord of Corwick still, but since I'd awoken from my prolonged bout of unconsciousness, it seemed to be in name only.

"I know what's best for you, lord," Lillia added primly.

I raised an eyebrow. "Do you now?"

"Of course," Lillia said. "So, the sooner you accept that fact and let me do my job, the happier we'll both be."

I sighed. What man stood a chance against a girl like Lillia when her mind was made up? Her grandmother had been just the same. I glanced out the open window near my bed, where I could see blue skies with several puffy white clouds slowly drifting by on a gentle breeze.

"You should be outside, child," I said as Lillia finally finished positioning the pillows—though the overall effect from all that effort seemed no different to me.

She sat on the edge of the bed and tried to button up the top of my sleeping tunic and I pushed her hand away, only to have it return again moments later like a bothersome fly. I glowered at my granddaughter and she glared right back at me in an obvious test of wills. I have fought all manner of men and beasts in my lifetime, charged shield walls and scaled castles with arrows whizzing past my head, but despite all that, I realized I was no match for this slight girl. I finally looked away and relented, ignoring her grin of triumph that I could see out of the corner of my eye as she once again fussed at my collar.

"You should be outside," I repeated, trying to regain some sense of dignity. "Not wasting your life away caring for some foul-smelling old man day in and day out. It's already mid-summer now, child. Winter will be back before you even realize it."

"You know I can't leave you," Lillia said, looking pleased when she finally had my button done to her lofty expectations. She sat back, her expression darkening. "I'll not make that mistake again, lord. If I hadn't left you alone the last time, then maybe I could have done something to help."

"Like what?" I said with a disbelieving snort.

Lillia shrugged. "I would have thought of something." She smiled, pausing to rub my cheek affectionately. "So, like it or not, you're stuck with me until you're better, my lord." She leaned close to me then and sniffed, a twinkle in her eyes now. "Besides, you only smell a little. I can hardly notice it." I chuckled despite myself as she put her hand to my shaved scalp, gently touching an eight-inch puckered scar that ran from the base of my left ear up toward the crown of my head. "How are the headaches today? Any change?"

"Much better," I lied.

"Well, that's good news, at least," Lillia said diplomatically. I guessed by her expression that I wasn't fooling her. "Kieran says the pain should go away any time now, the gods willing."

"Uh-huh," I grunted with little enthusiasm. Kieran Ackler was my physician, and it was he who had come up with the radical idea to cut open my head—though not even he had expected to see what they'd found inside. "Haven't the gods and Kieran done enough to me for one lifetime?" I added, unable to hide the bitterness in my voice. "Maybe it's time they all just leave me be."

Lillia sighed, placing her hands in her lap. "Not this again, my lord. The fact that you're alive at all is a miracle that will be talked about for generations to come. The gods have truly favored you through the brilliance of Kieran Ackler."

"Ha!" I snorted bitterly. "You say they favored me, child, but I know better." I grabbed my granddaughter's wrist, my hand looking like a shrunken claw against her fair, delicate skin. "I was prepared to die, Lillia," I said, harsher than intended. "Don't you see? I wanted it to end, needed it to." I released Lillia's wrist, then lifted my frail arms in helpless despair as I glanced around my bedchamber. "Yet, here I am, still trapped in an old man's body with nothing but memories to keep me company. This is not a miracle, child. This is torture."

"You must not say that, my lord," Lillia admonished. "The gods are listening."

"So, let them hear my words," I snarled. "I'm tired of their constant games and meddling."

Lillia chose that moment to start fussing with my coverings, and I shooed her hands away with an annoyed grunt. I wasn't going to give in this time, I resolved. A man has his pride, even an old one.

"You are a great man," Lillia said, actually respecting my wishes for a change and letting the coverings be. It wasn't much of a victory, but it was something. "The greatest this kingdom will ever know," my granddaughter added, her eyes shining. "The gods have returned you to us for a purpose, my lord. I'm positive about that. This is something that you need to understand."

I laughed dismissively, shaking my head. "It's so easy to be positive of something when you're young and naïve, child. Just wait until you're older, and then you'll see that nothing is what you thought it was."

Both Lillia and I looked up then as a soft knock sounded at the door. I think we were both relieved at the interruption away from our familiar argument.

"Come in," I barked.

The door opened, revealing my physician, Kieran Acker. He strode into the room with a customary smile of greeting on his face and his ever-present brown leather bag in his right hand. I could see my steward, Walice, hovering outside in the corridor uncertainly, his expression hopeful as he peered into my chambers.

"Close the door," I grumbled at the physician, ignoring Walice's disappointed look as Kieran did as I asked. I didn't need any more wet nurses hanging over me this morning. Lillia and Kieran would be more than sufficient for the task.

"So, how are things this morning, my lord?" the physician asked.

"I'm still alive, aren't I?" I grunted.

Kieran laughed good-naturedly as Lillia moved, allowing him to take her place. "Still in good spirits, I see, my lord."

"Why wouldn't I be?" I asked sarcastically. "Thanks to you, I've got a bright future ahead of me. Maybe I'll go climb Mount Halas tomorrow. Or take a swim in Last Gasp Gulch. The possibilities are endless."

Kieran chuckled as he ran his cool, dry hand across my bald pate. "No fever, my lord. That's good. How are the headaches?"

I glanced at Lillia, who nodded to me, her expression clear—tell him the truth, or I will. "Not great," I admitted.

"Ah," Kieran said. He pulled down my left eyelid and peered into my eye, then did the same for the other. "Time will fix that, my lord," he added. Kieran took out a flat, thin piece of wood from his bag. "Open, please, my lord."

I did as he asked, suffering the indignity and trying my best not to gag as the man poked and prodded inside my mouth with his infernal stick. I've learned to despise that horrible little device.

"Excellent," Kieran said, finally removing the stick. I swallowed and then coughed while the physician fished in his bag. He drew out a small box covered with a thin glass cover.

"What's that?" I asked, curious now. I'd never seen anything like it.

"I took the liberty to have the castle carpenter make it for you," Kieran said. He placed the box in my lap. "I thought you might like to have it."

I stared down at the box's contents in surprise. Inside lay the source of all my health issues over the last few years. It still seemed hard to imagine.

"We measured it before putting it in there," Kieran said, shaking his head. "Almost seven inches long. It's a wonder you were able to function as long as you did, my lord."

"Indeed," I said as I studied the pale, thin tapeworm that had burrowed into my brain and almost killed me.

Kieran had told me I'd likely ingested the worm's larvae from raw pork at some point, though truthfully, I couldn't remember ever eating any. The physician had guessed the damn thing had been living and growing inside me for years. I felt a sudden blackness settling over me as I stared through the glass at the worm. *Too bad you failed in your mission,* I thought in annoyance before I tossed the box on the bed beside me.

Kieran frowned. "Did I do wrong, my lord?"

I waved a hand. "No, not at all. It's not the stupid worm. I'm just tired of lying here day after day, I suppose."

Kieran's face brightened. "Well, then you're in luck, lord." He paused, waiting as I just stared at him. Finally, the physician glanced at Lillia and winked. "Your granddaughter tells me you've been restless, so, to that end, I've agreed to her request to let you go outside."

I could feel my eyes widening with sudden hope.

"But only for an hour or so, lord," Kieran cautioned. "We mustn't overdo it, you see." He glanced up at the door. "Walice?"

The door swung open instantly, revealing the steward, who pushed a two-wheeled contraption into the room that I hadn't seen in many years. It was the moveable chair that Haverty had built for me almost fifty years ago after I'd broken my leg during the Battle of Silver Valley.

"It can't be," I said, shaking my head in wonder. "How?"

Kieran stood up. "It isn't the same chair, my lord," he said. "I found Physician Haverty's drawings and built it myself." He smiled modestly. "With a few minor modifications from the original design, of course."

Two burly castle servants came in after Walice, and together, they lifted me out of bed, sitting me on the end of it while Lillia took off my sleeping tunic and dressed me. I didn't fail to notice one of the servants staring at my white, emaciated body riddled with old scars in fascination before he saw my gaze on him and hastily looked away.

"So," Kieran said once I was ready, his hands behind his back as he studied me with a faint smile on his lips. "Where would you like to go for your first time out, my lord?"

I paused for less than a heartbeat. There really was only one place I needed to be. "The Watching Hill," I whispered, the words catching in my throat.

Kieran nodded, not looking surprised as Lillia squeezed my shoulder. "Then The Watching Hill it is, my lord."

Forty-five minutes later, I sat at the peak of a large hill a half-mile east of the castle in my new, padded chair. I could feel the warmth of the sun on my face for the first time in many months as a gentle breeze tugged playfully at the collar of the heavy coat Lillia had insisted that I wear. The morning was already quite warm, but in truth, I was thankful for the coat, for I was always cold. Tall trees with purple flowers ringed the hilltop, giving off a heady scent that I'd never expected to smell again. I took a deep breath, enjoying the moment as birds sang and bees and brightly colored hummingbirds moved among the flowers.

"Do you want to be alone?" Lillia asked me. "Uncle Hughe, Uncle Taren, and Aunt Kalidia should be here shortly. I can wait below until they arrive if you wish?"

I glanced downward where Kieran, Walice, and the two servants waited at the point where the road from the castle broke to either side of The Watching Hill before heading west again on the other side. A crowd of curious onlookers had traveled the short distance from the castle, whispering to each other as they watched me. I could see more people coming from the market town of Camwick to the east, as word of my outing spread. I guessed I must look quite the sight up on the hill, like a ghoul risen from one of the graves.

I looked up at Lillia. "No, child. Stay. I think your mother and grandmother would want you here with me."

Lillia nodded but said nothing, both of us turning inward as we focused on the stone grave markers lined up in a row along the hill's crest. I studied each one, seeing a familiar face in my mind for every name.

Jebido Grayerson

My mentor, my father, my friend. I still awoke every morning, expecting to see him and hear his familiar voice. I fought back tears as I moved on.

Baine of Corwick

My dear, dear friend and brother, always with a smile on his face, unless you crossed him. Oh, how I miss you, old friend, I thought with infinite sadness.

Lady Alline Corwick

My beautiful daughter and Lillia's mother. If I close my eyes, I can still hear her musical laughter. Alline had been so much like her mother, inheriting not only Shana's breathtaking beauty, but her intelligence and sense of humor as well.

Finally, I turned my gaze on the middle stone, saving it until the end, tears rolling unashamedly down my cheeks.

Lady Shana Corwick

My wife, my friend, my lover, and my life. I started to weep harder then, with the blue skies above me, a throng of people watching, and my granddaughter by my side as she wept along with me. We stayed that way for a long time, before finally I looked up as a shadow crossed over me. It was my eldest son, Hughe, with my daughter, Kalidia, beside him.

"Father," Hughe whispered, his voice catching in his throat as he dropped to his knees beside me. I noticed his beard was more grey than black now, although he looked just as big and powerful as ever. When had that happened? "I'm sorry I'm late, lord."

Kalidia moved to my other side, taking my hand. "You should have told us about this, Father," she scolded in a low, yet firm voice. "I will have words with both Walice and Kieran later."

I kissed the back of her hand. Always the worrier, my little Kalidia. It was a trait earned honestly by all the Corwick women. "None of that, now, child," I said to my daughter, my voice hoarse and cracking. Kalidia was more like me than her mother, always ready for conflict if needed. "This was my idea," I added. I looked around, realizing that someone was missing. "Where's Teran?" I asked.

"Gone to settle a dispute in Ashwick, Father," Hughe answered. "I've sent for him. He should be here soon."

"Good," I said with a nod.

I took one last look at the gravestones, letting the grief of what I'd lost wash over me before finally, I signaled to Hughe that it was enough. I had lost much to the next world, it was true, but there were still those I loved and who loved me back in this one. It was something that I needed to remember.

"Take me back," I said, looking into the faces of my two children. "Take me back to my rooms. It's time to tell you what happened to your mother." I glanced at Lillia, letting her see the love I felt for her. "And you as well, child. It's time for you all to know the truth, even if you despise me for it afterward."

Chapter 1: Riders

My opponent was fast. Much faster than I'd expected. His thin face was etched in serious concentration, his eyes glowing with determination as he advanced on me with his weapon poised to strike. I shifted my feet carefully with my own sword balanced easily in front of me in both my hands. My foe would have to get past my defenses first if he wanted to get to me, and I had no intention of letting him do that. I heard shouts of encouragement rising all around me and I frowned with displeasure—for I knew none of those shouts of support were intended for me.

My adversary suddenly darted forward, trying to skewer me with a sudden, unexpected lunge. I wasn't fooled, having expected it. I twisted away, mindful to swipe at my attacker's backside as he charged past me. The flat of my sword whacked solidly against vulnerable flesh, provoking an exclamation of outrage and pain. I heard instant boos and shouts of disapproval fill the courtyard, and I took a moment to doff my hat and bow to the unhappy crowd.

"Stop showing off, you damn bully!" I heard a familiar voice call out.

I turned, focusing on Jebido where he sat at the back of an open cart, his legs dangling over the edge. Baine sat beside him, cuddling with one of Corwick Castle's many female servants. I couldn't remember which girl it was this time, having lost track of Baine's many conquests years ago.

"Perhaps you'd care to take a turn?" I called to Jebido mockingly. "It's been a while since you've had your arse slapped like that, old man."

"What?" Jebido grunted in outrage, his eyes widening. He jumped down to the ground, dropping his hand to the hilt of his sword. "Old man, is it now, Hadrack? I've half a mind to teach you some proper manners."

"Half a mind sounds about right," I countered with a laugh. "I understand that particular infirmity comes with advanced age."

"Don't press your luck, Hadrack," Jebido growled. "I'm not so addled in the head just yet that I don't remember how pathetic with a sword you once were. Where would you be now if not for me and my teachings?"

I chuckled, about to respond when I felt something crack painfully off my shoulder. I grunted, turning as my six-year-old son, Hughe, dodged away from me before he thrust his wooden sword in the air in victory.

"I got him! I got him! I won! I can't believe I won!"

The crowd cheered while I grudgingly rubbed my shoulder through my tunic where Hughe's wooden sword had struck me. The boy was strong for his age, I reflected ruefully, glad he hadn't broken anything. I knew I'd have a nasty bruise there later, though.

"Do I get the horse now, Father?" Hughe asked breathlessly as he skipped circles around me, careful not to get too close. "Huh? Huh? Do I?"

"Well," I said gravely as the repetitious sounds of a hammer ringing on steel echoed from the smithy nearby.

Hughe's face darkened immediately into a pout that I knew well. "But you promised if I could hit you that I'd get a horse all of my own."

I glanced at Jebido as he grinned in satisfaction, aware now that he'd deliberately distracted me. "Maybe your Uncle Jebido should be the one to decide that," I said. My friend's pleased expression turned to sudden confusion as my son's young face brightened with hope. "Since he's the one that said he'd provide the horse if you won," I added, giving Jebido a challenging look.

"Really?" Hughe gasped, turning to stare at Jebido in surprise. "He did?"

"He sure did," I nodded. "Well, Jebido, what's it to be? The boy won fairly, did he not?"

"Please, Uncle Jebido, please let me have a horse!" Hughe cried as he ran over and pulled at my friend's arm. "Please, Uncle Jebido! Please!"

"Thanks a lot," Jebido grunted at me.

I shrugged. "You started this, old—" I hesitated as Jebido's eyes narrowed. "Old friend," I finished with a chuckle.

Jebido pursed his lips, shaking his head in disgust as Hughe continued to jump and skip around him, pleading for a horse. Finally, he put his hands on his hips, glaring down at the boy. "Have you been a good lad, young Master Hughe? Do you even deserve a horse, I wonder?"

Hughe hesitated, his eyes suddenly turning cautious. "What do you mean by good, Uncle Jebido? Holy House good, or just regular good?"

Jebido struggled not to smile as laughter rang out from the crowd. He raised one bushy silver eyebrow. "Is there a difference, lad?"

"Oh yes," Hughe said, his face twisted in serious concentration. "Being Holy House good means always saying your prayers and never having bad thoughts."

Jebido folded his arms over his chest. "Is that so?" he said. "And being regular good is what, then?"

Hughe shrugged his already heavy shoulders. "Oh, you know, like not putting horse dung in your sisters' beds or hitting your brother for no good reason. That kind of thing."

"Ah," Jebido said in understanding, giving me a quick look. I rolled my eyes at my friend, amused by his serious face. "And which good have you been, young Master Hughe?"

Hughe straightened his shoulders proudly. "I said my prayers this morning and didn't forget one word, Uncle Jebido. And I ain't had one bad thought all day, I swear."

"Not one?" Jebido asked in mock wonder. "Really?"

"Uh-uh," Hughe said, shaking his head. "Not one. Does that mean I get a horse now? Can I have your mare? The pretty white one with the circle around her eye? Huh?"

Jebido scratched at his grey beard. "Well, I don't know, lad. What about the other kind of good? There's still that to consider. How have you been doing there?" Hughe opened his mouth to answer just as Jebido lifted a warning finger. "Keep in mind, young Master Hughe, that I saw Teran just this morning by the stables. Your little brother didn't look so good to me."

Hughe's mouth formed a round circle, his eyes widening with sudden, guilty dread. "He fell," the boy hurried to say. "That's all, Uncle Jebido. He fell all by himself and hit his nose, I swear."

"Is that right?" Jebido grunted. "And what about your sister, Alline, then? How did her nice long hair get covered in all that axel grease yesterday?"

Hughe looked down at the ground, rubbing a foot in the dirt. "I don't know, Uncle Jebido. Honest. Maybe Clayfor Prest did it."

I chuckled to myself. Clayfor Prest was the youngest son of Wiflem, the captain of my guards. Hughe and Clayfor were arch-enemies right now, so it was no surprise to me that Hughe would try to pin the mischief on him.

"I'll tell you what," Jebido said. "Today is Sunday, right?" Hughe nodded slowly, looking unsure of himself. "If you can go a week without causing any trouble, I'll give you a horse of your own. How does that sound?"

Hughe blinked, looking confused. "A week?" he said. "How long is that?"

"Seven whole days," Jebido answered.

"You can do it, Hughe, my boy!" Baine shouted in encouragement, his hands cupped around his mouth. "It'll be over before you know it, lad!"

Hughe glanced briefly at Baine, his face filled with doubt. "That's an awfully long time, Uncle Jebido."

"Yup," Jebido agreed. He bent down, his hands on his knees. "But you have to do it to get that horse. No fighting with any of the boys in the castle or Camwick, and no picking on your sisters or your brother." Jebido stuck out his hand. "Is it a deal, young lad?"

Hughe took a quick glance at me over his shoulder. I had to fight not to burst out laughing at the look of despair on his face. Even at six, the boy already knew his limitations.

Finally, Hughe turned back to Jebido. "How about one day of being good, and you give me a pony?" he suggested.

Jebido snorted and shook his head as he straightened. "Your boy is a natural negotiator, Hadrack," he called to me. "He'd do well at the king's court, this one."

"That he would," I agreed as I made my way toward my son and friend. I waved my wooden sword at the watching crowd. "All right, everyone, that's it for today. Back to your chores." I stopped beside my son and put my hand on his shoulder, turning him to face me. "You will abide by the original agreement, Hughe," I said down to him. "No fighting for a week, just as Uncle Jebido said, and you will leave your sisters and brother alone."

"But, Father—" Hughe began.

I squeezed his shoulder just hard enough to make him gasp. "The Lord of Corwick has spoken," I said gruffly. "Do not talk back, boy. Do as you're told."

Hughe dropped his eyes. "Yes, Father."

"Good," I grunted as I spun my son around and gave him a light tap on his backside. "Now go and find your mother. I'm sure she'll have some chores for you to do to keep you out of trouble."

Hughe trudged away, looking dejected before he spun around and pointed at Jebido. "Better get that mare groomed for me, Uncle Jebido. I'll be coming for her in seven days!"

With that, the lad took off, racing around the smithy and out of sight as my blacksmith, Hekmar Lorain, continued to hammer away at his forge with intense concentration.

"That lad's going to be a handful," Jebido said with a sigh. He glanced at me, looking me up and down. "Just like his father was, I expect."

I chuckled. "Well, you set me straight fast enough when I was near his age, as I recall."

"That I did," Jebido grunted. "That I did." He sighed again. "How long do you think the lad will last?"

I looked up at the midday sun. "Maybe until dusk," I said as Jebido laughed. "If he's lucky."

"My Lord!"

I turned to see my steward, Finol, rapidly approaching with his assistant, Hanley, limping along beside him. The old man's face was pinched with worry, which in the old days might have given me concern. Now though, I'd come to realize that it was an expression the steward wore every day from the moment he arose in the morning to the moment he went to bed at night. I imagined he even worried in his sleep.

"My Lord," Finol said again as he stopped beside me, looking out of breath. "I've just received word that a force of riders has been seen several miles from Lestwick."

I raised an eyebrow. Maybe the old man had a reason to worry this time after all. It had been years since anyone had ridden onto my lands without permission. "How many riders?" I asked. I noticed Baine kiss his girl on the cheek, then send her off as he jumped nimbly down to the ground to join us.

"Perhaps forty," Finol answered. He hesitated. "Initial reports suggest they might be Piths."

I paused at that, surprised. After the war between the Piths and Ganderland, the savage tribes had returned to their lands and a wary truce had fallen between the two traditional adversaries. That truce, I knew, was mainly due to the revelations in the codex, which the Piths had reluctantly accepted. Those startling revelations, however, still had not come to Ganderland after almost seven years, as only a few select people even knew about them here.

I had intended to tell King Tyden and the First Daughter about the codex once Pernissy Raybold fell at Silver Valley and the threat to Ganderland was over. But circumstances led to it ending up in the hands of the House Agent, Malo, instead, who disappeared right afterward, taking the only proof of the lie with him. Nothing had been seen of the man since, and with First Daughter Gernet, First Son Oriell, and both sides of the Holy House always in a constant state of disagreement, we few who knew the truth had agreed to say nothing until Malo and the codex were found. But that, unfortunately, had proven easier said than done.

After three unsuccessful forays over the last seven years to find Malo, I was beginning to think that the man had died long ago and that the codex was once again lost, leaving me in a quandary about what to do. The truth about the Master and the First Pair needed to come out eventually, I knew. I just didn't know how to make that happen without potentially setting off another civil war. Without the codex as proof, I doubted either side of the House would believe me that the Master had created our world and that The Mother and The Father were actually his children. I know I wouldn't have.

"Who saw these so-called Piths?" Jebido asked, sounding unconvinced.

"Osbeth Prader," Finol answered.

I nodded as Jebido's expression changed to one of thoughtfulness. Osbeth had been just a youth when I'd become the Lord of Corwick, but he'd since followed in his father's footsteps to become my master hunter. The man was tough, competent, and smart, so if he thought the riders might be Piths, then Jebido knew as well as I did that the chances were good that they were.

"Which way were these riders heading?" I asked.

"According to Osbeth, due north directly toward us, my lord," Finol answered.

"And they have attacked no one along the way?"

"Not according to Osbeth, lord, no."

"Where is he now?"

"I sent him back out to watch their progress, my lord," Finol replied. "He and his brother will track these men. If they change direction, one of them will return to inform us."

"Do you think it's a raiding party?" Baine asked me, looking skeptical.

"I doubt it," I said. "Alesia gave me her word the last time I saw her that no Pith would ever come north again to raid after that mess in Windacre."

A group of ten Pith youths eager for war had gone against their tribe's wishes and had crossed the border into Ganderland several years ago, where they had laid waste to a tiny village called Windacre. It had been a stupid, bloody affair, and only by diplomacy and my personal assurances that it would never happen again had I been able to stop the lord of that holding from riding south to exact revenge.

Today seemed like something other than just simple youths, though, and I couldn't help but be reminded of what had happened with Lorgen Three-Fingers' son, Nedo, and the chain of events that he'd set off by riding onto my lands in a similar way years ago. I could only pray the Piths' intentions this time were peaceful.

"Maybe it's Einhard and Alesia come to visit," Jebido said hopefully. He shrugged. "I know he swore never to set foot in Ganderland again, but things might have changed since then."

Finol shook his head. "No, Osbeth said they were all warriors and riding light. No wagons, just spare mounts."

"Sounds like a raiding party to me," Baine muttered. He shrugged. "Well, even if that's who they are, there aren't that many of them." He grinned. "We're not the easy target we were the last time they came this way. If they hurt even one person, we'll make them pay for it."

I thought of my friend, Einhard. I had ridden to the land of the Piths several times in the ensuing years since we'd parted at Land's End, visiting him along with Alesia and their five children in the stronghold they were building along the Western Sea. The fact that the Piths would even consider staying in one place and living behind walls still astonished me even today.

Alesia had been pregnant once again the last time I'd seen her, and I'd finally had to concede to Einhard that he'd won regarding how many offspring we could each produce. Shana had borne four children for me without complaint. But she had stated emphatically after my youngest daughter, Alline, was born three years ago that that was enough, no more babies—my competition with Einhard be damned. I was still hoping to change Shana's mind about that, but, having been married to her now for more than eight years, I knew my hopes of that happening had little chance of bearing fruit.

"It's not Einhard," I grunted, knowing in my gut that it was true.

I could tell the last time we'd met that my friend still felt a great deal of bitterness over what had happened during the short but bloody war between the Piths and Ganders seven years ago. In his eyes, victory had been snatched away from him at the last minute by a book filled with *chicken scratches,* as he'd called them. And while I knew Einhard cared for me deeply, I believed that a part of him also hated me. First for besting him on the battlefield at Land's End, then for turning the Pathfinders against him to end the war and send him home. But even so, I knew nothing could bring the Sword of the Queen back here. Unless it was for war, I thought, feeling suddenly uncomfortable with my assurances.

"Then, if not him, who is it?" Baine asked.

"Let's go and find out," I said.

Three hours later, Baine, Jebido, Wiflem, and fifty of my men—all mounted on horses— waited on the crest of a hill overlooking a field cut by a narrow dirt road. I could see Osbeth and his brother, Hubeth, galloping down the road toward us, identifiable by the small white wolf banner that Hubeth held up, tied to the blade of his sword.

"They're about a mile behind us, my lord," Osbeth said when the two men reached the hilltop. He paused to pat his mare's neck, which I saw was lathered with sweat.

"Still riding hard?" I asked.

"Fast but steady, lord," Osbeth said.

"You're certain they're Piths?" Jebido asked.

"No question about it," Hubeth said. He was bigger than his brother, with sun-darkened skin and flat features.

"Did they see you?" I asked.

"Yes, my lord," Osbeth said. "I showed myself on purpose to see what they would do."

"Which was?'

"Nothing, lord. They just kept riding at the same pace."

I stroked my beard as I thought, while beneath me, Angry pawed at the ground restlessly. "Rather odd, don't you think?" I said to no one in particular.

"Should I have the Wolf's Teeth dismount and take up defensive positions, my lord?" Wiflem asked, looking as though he already knew the expected answer.

I glanced behind me at the serious faces of my men as the creak of leather, horses stamping their feet, and jingle of metal bits echoed across the hilltop. I'd brought twenty-five seasoned men-at-arms with me, along with an equal number of archers. Those archers wouldn't do much good with their oversized bows on horseback, but I was convinced I wouldn't need them now.

"No," I finally said with a shake of my head. "I don't think that will be necessary, Captain."

Wiflem frowned. "Are you sure that's wise, my lord?" he said. "These are Piths, after all."

"I am aware of that, Wiflem," I muttered.

I studied the empty road below me. Whatever this was about, it didn't seem to me like aggression. Something was wrong. That was clear to me if Piths were here. But whatever that something was, I was positive it was not the beginnings of an attack.

"May I respectfully ask that I be allowed to deploy the horses along the hill in formation at least, my lord?" Wiflem asked, his body held stiffly with disapproval.

I sighed. "Very well, you may do so, Wiflem," I grunted, giving in.

My captain was right, of course, from his perspective, anyway. Always be prepared for any situation because the enemy will use every opportunity at their disposal to surprise or trick you. The question was, which Piths were coming down that road— enemies or friends?

It didn't take me long to find out, as first a cloud of dust appeared on the road, then a blurred mass of horses that quickly came into focus as they drew nearer.

"They must have seen us by now," Jebido muttered, squinting against the sun that had come out from a bank of clouds and was now in our eyes.

From a strategic position, the hilltop was sound, with nothing but flat fields below my force, giving us the advantage of the high ground. The sun in our eyes was another matter, and I prayed that my instincts were right and this wouldn't go wrong for us.

"They have seen us," I said as the horses came on, not slowing. "They just don't seem all that bothered by it." I gestured with a hand and one of my men rode forward, unfurling my wolf's head banner and letting it snap and crackle in the wind. "If they had any doubts before," I added. "Then now they know who they're dealing with. So, let's see what they do about it."

Below, I could see individual riders now, then an answering bright banner fluttering from the end of a lance. I let out a lungful of air in relief, unaware that I'd been holding my breath. It was a rearing bear with huge teeth and wicked claws. The Piths below us were Amenti.

"Stay with the men, Wiflem," I commanded my captain. "Baine, Jebido," I grunted. "Come with me."

The three of us rode down the hill, where we waited on the road at the base. The mass of Amenti horsemen started to slow, then came to a halt in a cloud of dust thirty yards away. Three riders kept coming on at a trot, with the man in the center looking very familiar to me. He was older now, of course, with some grey in his beard, but it was unquestionably Saldor.

I grinned as the three warriors paused their horses six feet from Jebido, Baine, and me. "It's good to see you again, Saldor," I said. I felt the grin fade at the look on my old friend's face.

"I wish it were under better circumstances, Chieftain," Saldor said gravely.

I felt a thud in my gut. "What's happened?"

"It's Einhard," Saldor said, his face dark and unreadable. "He's dying and needs your help, Chieftain."

Chapter 2: Shadow Pirates

Einhard was dying. It was a concept that I still found hard to believe hours after learning of it. I stood in my solar, my hands behind my back, thinking about my friend and waiting as Saldor ate alone at the long table in front of me. The Amenti chieftain looked as if he hadn't had anything to eat in days—which, after what he'd told me of his long, hazardous journey here, I guessed was probably true.

Several female servants arrived with trays laden with beer, and they began handing the full mugs out to my men where they sat on benches lining the walls. One of the women nervously placed a cup by Saldor's hand, looking thoroughly frightened of him, though the Pith warrior barely noticed her as he continued to shovel food into his mouth like a starving wolf. I had made arrangements for the rest of Saldor's men to be fed as well and to have their horses cared for while they waited down in the outer bailey.

Initially, the appearance of forty savage Pith warriors entering the castle had caused widespread panic and apprehension among the inhabitants. But, after I had assured my people that they had nothing to fear from the Amenti, a sort of uneasy calm had settled over the castle. I knew that calmness could be easily broken, however, as all it would take was one harsh word spoken in anger or a single dark look given at the wrong moment. To ensure that didn't occur, I had Wiflem post armed men to keep the Piths and Ganders separated until I'd had a chance to talk to my inner circle and make plans.

"My lord," Shana said, appearing at the entrance to the solar wearing an elegant blue dress with flared sleeves that hung almost to the floor. She had a gold belt cinched around her waist with a blue, stuffed circlet on her head that had a see-thru train attached to it flowing down her back. An oversized Blazing Sun pendant hung around her neck on a golden chain. I thought, as always, that she looked radiant.

Every man in the room except for Saldor automatically stood as Shana entered, bowing to her.

"Thank you for coming, my dear," I said. I moved to the table and pulled out a chair opposite Saldor so that she might sit.

"Of course," Shana said. Her voice was flat and even, almost disinterested sounding, yet I could tell by the set line of her jaw that my wife was on edge, as were we all.

The Amenti paused in his eating to study Shana curiously, the two having never met before. "So," he finally said, returning to gnawing on a turkey leg. "You would be the woman who took my Chieftain's heart, then?"

Shana nodded her head and smiled politely. "I am. As did he, mine."

Saldor tossed the now stripped bone onto his plate, then pushed it away, having filled his belly to his satisfaction. "Now I understand why he chose you over the Amenti," the Pith grunted in admiration. He took a long drink of beer from his mug, wiping foam from his beard, then burped before turning his eyes to me. "So, my Chieftain, what say you? Will you help?"

I glanced around the room at my men. Baine, Wiflem, and Jebido already knew everything that had happened, but Shana, along with the rest of my inner circle, Putt, Niko, Berwin, Tyris, Finol, and Hanley, only had an inkling so far.

"Tell your story again from the beginning, Saldor," I said, crossing my arms over my chest. "I want everyone to hear it from your lips before we decide what to do."

The Amenti chieftain let his eyes roam around the room. "For the last five months, strange men have been coming from the Western Sea to raid our villages along the coast. They sometimes arrive in just one ship, sometimes in many. They strike hard and fast and then leave, with nothing but destruction and death left behind them."

"Are they Cardians?" Niko asked from behind Saldor.

The Amenti half-turned to look at him. "No, these men are different from those turd-suckers. We have not seen their kind before."

"Afrenians, perhaps?" Tyris asked doubtfully.

"Afrenians are traders first and mercenaries second," Jebido grunted. "They rarely bother with raiding." He shook his head. "This doesn't sound like their way of operating to me."

"They are not Afrenians either," Saldor confirmed. "We have dealt with those people in the past, as you well know, Chieftain."

I nodded. Einhard had contracted some Afrenian mercenaries to build siege engines for him when he'd invaded Ganderland. Those men, while unscrupulous, were not likely to raid random villages like Jebido had said and even less likely to do so against their occasional allies, the Piths.

"Describe these raiders to my men please Saldor," I said.

Saldor sat back in his chair. He shrugged. "They're strange-looking creatures with painted white faces and black armor. None wear helmets and their hair is long, shaggy, and covered in white powder." He grimaced, his voice now filled with grudging respect. "They never speak when they attack and seem more like beasts than men. But even so, they are strong and fearsome fighters."

"Tell us about the ships," I said.

Saldor stood and stretched, looking weary now as the food settled deeper into his belly. "They only come at night," the Pith said as he glanced around him at the seated Ganders. "Their crafts are long and low to the water, with the hulls painted black and fearsome heads of animals rising at the prow."

"Sounds like Cardian longboats to me," Putt said with a frown.

"The ships are similar to those," Saldor conceded. "Yet somehow different." He shrugged. "I do not have the words to explain."

I saw Baine's face turn thoughtful as he rubbed at his chin. My friend was going beardless these days, having shaved off his facial hair after losing a bet with Tyris. Baine had decided he rather liked his new look, thinking it made him appear younger and more handsome, though I found he seemed more menacing without the beard somehow.

"I think I may have heard about these ships before," Baine said. He glanced at me. "Do you remember I told you about that family who saved me after I was swept off *Sea-Dragon*?"

I nodded. Baine had floated for days in the Western Sea after a storm had nearly capsized our ship many years ago, with only *Sea-Dragon's* broken rudder keeping him from sinking into the depths. A young girl and her father who were out fishing had eventually found Baine. They'd dragged him from the water more dead than alive and had nursed him back to health. I'd been convinced Baine had perished beneath the waves back then, and I can still feel an ache in my heart every time I think about how close I'd come to losing my friend that terrible day.

"They told me a story about a similar ship to what Saldor is describing," Baine said. He shook his head, looking reluctant now. "Only, it's kind of a strange tale, Hadrack. I'm not sure now that it's even worth mentioning."

"You already started telling us," I said with a shrug. "So you might as well finish the job."

"Well, don't blame me if you don't believe it, then," Baine said. He leaned back against the wall and crossed his arms over his chest. "According to Nelsun Merklar, the man who saved me, the ship is said to be manned by the corpses of shipwrecked sailors who escaped The Father's burn pits." Baine paused as Tyris chuckled and rolled his eyes. My friend gave the tall blond archer a dark look before continuing, "These creatures are known as Shadow Pirates, and they sail the Western Sea only at night, looking for children to steal from their beds."

"Why?" Niko asked, his thin face twisted with superstitious dread. "Why children?"

"It's said that if a Shadow Pirate eats the heart of a child untainted by sin," Baine answered. "Then their own sins are forgiven, and they are released from the ship to be reborn again in the world of the living."

I could see all my men except for Tyris glancing at each other nervously as silence filled the room. I snorted to break the tension, though I could feel a tingling going up and down my spine. "That's just some old wives' tale used to frighten children," I said dismissively. I pointed at Saldor. "These men bleed like any other. Just ask him."

"That is true," Saldor grunted. "Beneath the paint and powder, they are just flesh and blood. Not easy to kill, I grant you, yet mortal just the same." He sighed, glancing at Baine. "But perhaps there is some truth to what this man says, for strangely, many of our children have been taken these past months."

"Which brings us to the reason why Saldor has come to see me," I said in a grave voice. I moved to put my hand on Shana's shoulder, drawing some much-needed strength from her as she rested her slim hand on top of mine. "Three weeks ago, these so-called Shadow Pirates attacked Einhard's stronghold at Clendon's Reach. Most of the Peshwin warriors were away for the summer hunt when they came, which I'd wager they must have known. The remaining Piths fought back, of course, but there were too many of the enemy and they were overwhelmed. Unfortunately, the stronghold was burned to the ground, and almost everyone inside of it was slaughtered." I squeezed Shana's shoulder as I fought to say the last words. "When Saldor arrived several days later, he found Einhard badly burned and barely clinging to life in the rubble." I hesitated, my voice catching. "He may have died by now, for all we know. All we can do is pray to The Mother that that is not the case."

"What of Alesia and the children, my lord?" Shana asked into the stunned silence. Her startling blue eyes were filled with pain and sorrow as she looked up at me. "What has become of them?"

"A woman who survived the attack claims she saw Alesia and her oldest son, Einrack, being herded onto one of the ships, which then sailed away," I answered.

"And her other children?"

I shared a grim look with Saldor, then focused back on my wife. "Many of the Peshwin elders and some of the children were burned alive in the fire, Lady. The others were taken. From what Saldor and his men could tell, it looks like the rest of Einhard's family were inside the keep when it collapsed. Einhard tried to rescue them and was burned in the process."

A single tear escaped Shana's right eye at that news, and then her expression abruptly hardened with steel-like resolve. "What are you going to do?" she asked, although I could tell my wife had already anticipated the answer I would give and was in favor of it.

"I'm going to get Alesia and Einrack back," I growled as I looked around at the grim faces of my men. "I'm going to get them back, and then I'm going to kill every one of the bastards who did this."

Ten days of hard riding later, Jebido, Baine, and I, escorted by Saldor and his men, arrived at Clendon's Reach, where Einhard and Alesia had built their stronghold at the end of a narrow peninsula jutting out into the Western Sea like a curled finger. It was a good location, though the fortress had been nothing much to look at the last time I'd been there two years before—just four wooden palisade walls built around a central keep of wood and stone with some minor outbuildings surrounding it. The Pith stronghold was a far cry from the massive stone castles of Ganderland, I remembered thinking at the time, but at least it was a step in the right direction and could always be improved.

Now, whatever improvements may have been added since my last visit were gone, with nothing but blackened, charred ruins left behind to indicate that anything had been there. Not even the central keep that I remembered stood anymore. Faint tendrils of smoke still rose into the air from the unrecognizable rubble of what was once that main building, only to be whisked out to sea by the swirling wind and then consumed by the vast open space. Foaming white water washed along the banks of the peninsula below me to the south and west with steady precision, sending spray leaping into the air with every wave. Seeing the tide pounding against the dark stone of Clendon's Reach with relentless tenacity reminded me greatly of the island castle of Calban.

I finally paused Angry where the peninsula joined the mainland, while my companions and I continued to stare in dismay at the devastation the Shadow Pirates had wrought. I could feel a deep sorrow rise in me at the needless waste of what might have one day been something special. Would the Piths rebuild the stronghold after this, or was the great experiment over? It was a question that I didn't have an answer to just yet. The Piths had always considered living inside walls beneath them in the past. But, having seen the benefits of fortified defenses during their invasion of Ganderland, many of the old ways of thinking and of doing things had begun to change. Would this devastating tragedy end that new way of thinking, or would it just galvanize the Piths into further changes?

Einhard was probably the most stubborn and pigheaded of all the Pith leaders, I thought, but, despite that, he was no fool. Nor was Alesia. They both had recognized that if they wanted the Piths to flourish in this ever-changing world, the tribes would have to continue building the strong, united nation that Alesia's father had begun. To that end, the Piths had made inroads in trading with other kingdoms in recent years, like the Afrenians, Parnuthians, and even the vile Cardians, though so far, they had shunned any contact with Ganderland. I had little doubt that had everything to do with the codex and its unpleasant truths.

"Come," Saldor finally said gravely, leading us away from Clendon's Reach. "If the Master is willing, then Einhard yet waits for us in the land of the living."

The Peshwin had made camp half a mile south of the ruined stronghold, where we found Trak the Serious, the Ear of the Queen, waiting for us in front of a central tent. I'd learned with relief that Einhard indeed still lived, although his condition was described as dire.

"Greetings, brother," Trak said to me as I jumped down from Angry's back.

The Pith held out his hand, which I warmly accepted as we locked forearms. "Greetings, brother," I replied, unable to keep the anxiety I felt from my voice. "How is he?"

"Not good," Trak grunted, nodding to Saldor. "Any other man would have long succumbed by now, but the Sword is not just any other man." Trak glanced at me with appraising eyes. "Einhard says that he must wait to talk to the Wolf first before he can walk the final path." The Pith motioned that Saldor and I should enter the tent ahead of him, stopping me with a rough hand just as I started to pull back the tent flap. "A word of caution, Wolf. If you have a weak stomach, then prepare yourself, for the sight you are about to see will not sit well with you."

I took a deep breath, steeling myself for the unknown horrors within, then stepped through the opening, where I paused in the gloom to let my eyes adjust. A strong odor instantly filled my nostrils, a noxious mixture of burnt charcoal, piss, shit, and rot. The first thing that I saw was a bent old woman standing over a central hearth, stirring a pot. I recognized her immediately as she stared at me, first in surprise, then with relief.

"Hadrack of the Peshwin," the old woman whispered, staggering toward me with her spindly arms held out. "Thank the Master you have come."

"Of course I've come, Wise Mother," I said. "Nothing could have kept me away." I embraced the woman gently, knowing she was almost a hundred years old and that her bones were brittle and easily broken. Her name was Thora, and she was Clendon the Peacemaker's mother and Alesia's grandmother.

I could see Einhard lying on a cot at the back of the tent, and I felt my stomach start to churn. Despite Trak's words, a part of me had hoped the Pith had been exaggerating about Einhard's wounds. Those hopes were now dashed as I stared at the naked, blackened husk of what had once been my friend.

Einhard's face was mercifully turned away from me, and I could see his badly-burned chest rising and falling erratically. A bald, purple-robed Pathfinder stood over him, chanting softly as he swung a smoking incense pot slowly back and forth. Two women knelt by the cot, one to either side of it, using cloths to gently squeeze small amounts of water onto Einhard's ravaged skin. I could see raw, cracked streaks of oozing red flesh through the charred blackness of that skin, with clusters of giant, angry boils weeping green and yellow fluid all along his legs, stomach, and shoulders.

Thora clutched at my arm as I started to go to Einhard. "You must help us, Hadrack of the Peshwin! You must get our Queen back!"

I nodded, reluctantly tearing my gaze away from Einhard as I patted Thora's wrinkled hand. "You have my word, Wise Mother. I will get her back. I will get everyone back."

Einhard moaned then, perhaps hearing me talking or sensing that I was there. He turned his head to stare in my direction with his good eye. The leather patch that he'd worn over the other was gone now, leaving a jagged, red-rimmed hole where the eye had once been.

"Puppy?" Einhard croaked. "Is that you, my friend?" He lifted a shriveled arm, the once-great muscles that had flexed and rippled there now burned away to the bone as he gestured for me to come closer. "Come to me, Puppy. Come, let me look at you."

I moved slowly toward the cot, trying to keep the horror I felt at what I was seeing from showing on my face.

"Go, Malakar," Einhard whispered to the Pathfinder. "Leave me be with my friend."

"But—" Malakar started to protest.

"It's all right," I said, putting my hand on the bald priest's shoulder. Malakar and I had first met years ago during the Battle of Land's End. He and I were not friends, although we both had a wary respect for one another. "You don't have to go far, Wise One."

Malakar studied me, as always warring with his ingrained dislike of Ganders and his reluctant acceptance that I was a Peshwin. I was surprised to see a hint of sorrow in his eyes, for he and Einhard had rarely gotten along over the years.

"Very well, Wolf," Malakar finally said, bowing his head. The Pathfinder motioned for the two women to stand, and together, they moved away, joining Thora and Saldor by the hearth.

I turned my eyes back to Einhard, suddenly at a loss for words as I stared down at the man who'd meant so much to me over the past eleven years.

"Don't look so sad, Puppy," Einhard wheezed. "All men are fated to die, even me." He lifted a hand then, his ravaged face filled with need. I stared at that hand, which was really nothing more than a claw now, almost unrecognizable as human. Einhard's fingernails were burnt away, with most of the flesh on the backs of his thumb and fingers missing, revealing stark white bone. "Take it," Einhard almost pleaded. "Take my hand, Hadrack, and let me feel your warmth and strength one last time before I walk the final path. Please, old friend."

I knelt by the cot, glancing at his hand again, reluctant to touch it—not out of revulsion, but out of fear that it would only add to Einhard's pain.

The Sword must have sensed my concerns, for he attempted to smile, though his lips had long since burnt away, leaving a permanently grinning skeleton behind. "Do not worry so, Hadrack. There is little pain left for me now." He grunted then, which I realized was meant to be a chuckle. "The worst is behind me. I think all the nerves in my body have finally died, for I feel nothing anymore."

Only slightly reassured, I tentatively took Einhard's hand in mine, gently at first, then with more force as he clasped his skeletal fingers tightly around me. His expression turned fierce then, made worse by the flame's merciless devastation of his once handsome face. "You made a vow to me once, Puppy," he rasped. "Do you remember it?"

I nodded. "Of course I do." I smiled, thinking back to our first meeting so long ago. "That day when I almost killed you at Father's Arse."

"Ha!" Einhard grunted in amusement. "You must be getting old, Puppy, for your memory is clearly fading along with your sword arm. It was I who almost killed you, remember?"

"Well, we'll never know for sure what would have happened, now will we?" I said, doing my best to make light of things. The words weren't what I wanted to say at that moment, but I knew Einhard would be grateful for the familiar camaraderie.

"No, I suppose not," Einhard agreed. "Yet either way, you swore to serve me in all things that day. Does your fading memory recall that?"

"Yes," I said, trying to keep my face blank. Inside, I could feel a crushing weight of despair bearing down on me, getting heavier with every heartbeat that thudded within my chest. As strange as it may seem, a part of me had been clinging to the hope that somehow Einhard would find a way to live through this—that his legendary strength, stubbornness, and tenacity would be enough to overcome even death. But now, as I looked at Einhard lying broken and shattered in front of me, I knew that hope had been misguided. He was going to die, and there was nothing that I or anyone else could do to change that. "And I honored that vow to you, old friend," I finally said, my voice catching in my throat.

"That you did," Einhard agreed, squeezing my hand. "That you did." He paused then, searching my face and looking suddenly desperate and perhaps a little frightened, I thought. "I told you once that I had never met a man with more strength and honor than you, Hadrack," Einhard continued. "And I meant that back then and even more right now." He closed his eye as tortured air rattled in his chest. Then he looked at me again. "But now I need another vow from you, old friend. I need you to swear that you will find my wife and son. That you will go to the very ends of the world if need be to bring them home. Swear that to me, Hadrack, so that I can be free to go to the Master knowing that it will be done."

I bowed my head, not ashamed as tears started to roll unchecked down my cheeks, where they clung briefly to my beard before dropping to the floor. I took a deep breath, remembering another vow I'd pledged over two graves when I was just a young, frightened boy. I had never stepped back from that vow until it was completed, regardless of the cost, nor, I knew, would I do so with this one, either.

"I, Hadrack of the Peshwin, the Lord of Corwick, and your friend," I said formally. "Pledge to you, Einhard, Sword of the Queen, that I will fulfill this vow. I will find your son, Einrack, this, I swear. I will find your wife and Queen, Alesia, this, I also swear. And I will find whoever did this to you and your family and make them pay for it with their lives. Nothing and no one in this realm or any other will stop me until that task is done. This, I swear to you, my Peshwin brother, before the Master and The First Pair."

Einhard sighed, his grip slowly loosening on my hand as his eye fluttered, then slowly closed again. "Thank you, my dear friend," he whispered so faintly that I barely heard it. "You have given me great peace. I only wish that I could be there to fight by your side one last time, for I think that it will be a great adventure."

I sat then for long minutes, holding Einhard's hand in mine and listening to his ragged breathing, until eventually, there were no breaths left for him to take.

Einhard the Unforgiving—equal parts my friend, my enemy, my teacher, and my brother, was dead.

Chapter 3: Sea-Wolf

Jebido and I stood at the edge of a towering sandstone cliff overlooking the Western Sea, peering northward at the outline of a tiny ship that seemed to be crawling along the coast far in the distance. We'd been observing the vessel for over an hour already, and it seemed to me that it was no closer to our position now than it had been when we'd first started watching it. I could feel a deep restlessness swirling inside me, with the almost insatiable need to be doing something eating away at me ever since Einhard's death twelve days before. It had been perhaps the longest, saddest, and most frustrating twelve days of my life, as I'd had nothing to do but wait and reflect on the gaping hole in me that Einhard had left behind when he'd died.

"Your eyesight is much better than mine, Hadrack," Jebido said, cutting into my thoughts. He shielded his eyes from the sun overhead. "Which one is it, do you think?"

"I can't tell yet," I grunted moodily. "They're still too far away. It might be *Sea-Wolf* by her size, or maybe *Sea-Dragon*, assuming it's even one of ours. It's hard to say from way up here."

"It's *Sea-Wolf*," Jebido said with an air of confidence. "I can feel it. The Mother is watching over us, Hadrack, you'll see."

"Uh-huh," I muttered, unconvinced.

I'd built two ships similar to *Sea-Dragon*—the great cog that I'd taken from the Cardians—in the last few years, naming them *Sea-Wolf* and *Sea-Spirit*. *Sea-Wolf* was the newest and biggest of the three boats, completed just six months ago, while *Sea-Spirit* was much smaller and more agile than the others, designed to traverse the many narrow rivers that crisscrossed Ganderland. I dearly hoped that Jebido was right and that it really was *Sea-Wolf* down there, for the big ship was more suited than the other two for the kind of fighting that I expected to see soon.

When they weren't out on trading expeditions—which were frequent—all three of my ships were docked at Calban, so I'd sent Putt, Niko, and Tyris to the great island fortress in the hopes that at least one of those ships would be in port when they got there. I hadn't even wanted to consider what I would do if none of them were. The Piths didn't have any boats to speak of other than small, one-manned fishing crafts, and after what Saldor had told me, I knew if I had any hopes of exacting revenge on the pirates and finding Alesia and Einrack, then I would need one of my cogs.

More than three weeks had gone by since I'd first ridden out from Corwick Castle with Saldor, with each passing day since we'd arrived at Clendon's Reach reminding me that the chances of finding Alesia and Einrack had become that much slimmer. Knowing that, yet helpless to do anything about it until my ship arrived—if it did at all—had torn and gnawed at the pit of my stomach day and night like razor-sharp teeth from a pack of starving wolves.

After the first week of doing nothing, I'd become moody and uncommunicative and had taken to camping out alone on the clifftop, wanting to be away from the others as I stared ever north, willing sails to appear. I had made a vow to Einhard on his deathbed that I would find his family and bring them home—a solemn, unbreakable oath that I was determined to fulfill at all costs. But I couldn't do that without one of my ships, which I now conceded might have finally come, though it appeared as if the gods had decided to toy with me a little while longer by dangling it just out of reach.

"What in the name of The Mother are they doing out there?" I exploded, lifting my hands in exasperation after five more long minutes of watching. If anything, it looked to me as if the sailing vessel was going backward now.

"Patience, Hadrack," Jebido said soothingly from beside me. "Shouting won't make that ship move any faster." He stood now with his hands behind his back while a warm breeze swept over the clifftop, making the branches on the trees in the forest behind us dance as it whipped and played with my friend's long silver hair and beard.

"My patience was used up days ago," I snarled as I started to pace. I paused to glance at the ship again, then snorted. "Don't those fools know how urgent this is?"

"I'm sure they are doing their best, Hadrack," Jebido said in a resigned voice. I could tell by his tone that he thought I was being an ass. He was right, of course. I was being an ass—I just didn't care who knew it. "The winds can be tricky close to land," Jebido added. "Chances are Putt is dealing with some hidden shoals, too. Better he be cautious than run aground, no?"

"Then why doesn't he just go further out?" I snapped in irritation, more at my friend's infuriating calmness, I think, than anything else.

Jebido sighed. "Because you told him to stay close to the coast so that he could see our signal, remember?"

I took a deep breath, knowing that Jebido was right. I had told Putt to do just that. I hadn't known at the time what I might find at Clendon's Reach, nor where we might be when Putt eventually arrived, so I'd told him to continue south along the coast if we weren't at the demolished stronghold and watch for a signal fire.

"How much longer before he gets here, do you think?" I asked, slightly mollified now as I tried hard to keep my tone civil.

Jebido took a moment to study the approaching ship. "Depends on the winds, I suppose. An hour, perhaps. Maybe a bit more if they need to use the oars."

"Damn," I grunted, feeling the familiar anger return with a vengeance. I kicked at a small rock in frustration, watching as it skittered away across the weathered reddish-brown sandstone before disappearing over the cliff edge. It actually made me feel somewhat better.

"Maybe we should try sparring for a while?" Jebido suggested, glancing at me with one eyebrow raised. "It would kill some time and maybe get rid of that aggression of yours."

"We do that, and I'm likely to kill you by accident instead," I growled, not joking. I cared too much for Jebido to chance crossing swords with him right now in my frame of mind. I'd been itching for some kind of action for a while now, and when it finally came, I pitied the man foolish enough to get in my way.

"Ah," Jebido said with a weak grin as he thought about that. "A good point, Hadrack. No sparring, then. I've grown rather fond of my handsome head where it sits upon my equally handsome neck, so let's just forget that I mentioned anything, shall we?" Jebido sighed when I didn't react to his attempt at humor, muttering softly to himself.

We both turned moments later when Baine, dressed in his usual black attire, appeared along a faint trail through the trees behind us. "Is it ours?" my friend asked anxiously as he peered north toward the ship.

"It is," Jebido confirmed.

"Maybe it is," I corrected, sounding pessimistic even to me. I knew in my gut that it had to be Putt down there, for who else would hug the coastline like that if they didn't have to? I just wasn't ready to let go of my black mood yet. "I think they've decided to stop and take a swim," I added as if to prove it. "Clearly, *they're* in no hurry."

Jebido shook his head at Baine's confused look, and I didn't fail to notice my older friend roll his eyes while a silent message passed between the two of them.

"Well, the bonfire is ready whenever you are, Hadrack," Baine finally said. "Just give me the word."

I took a deep breath, willing myself to calm down and try to find some patience. Baine and Jebido wanted to rescue Alesia and Einrack just as badly as I did, and taking my frustrations out on them did none of us any good. "We'll light the fire when the ship passes around that promontory over there," I said, pointing to the southwest where a kidney-shaped mass of rock rose from the sea near the coastline. My voice had sounded almost cheery, I thought, proud of myself.

We'd located an inlet five miles south of Clendon's Reach, where Putt could safely bring whichever of my three ships he'd sailed from Calban close to land so that we could board. Unfortunately, the water around the peninsula where Einhard and Alesia had built the stronghold was too treacherous for large boats. It was teeming with unpredictable tides and hidden reefs that would tear open a ship's hull in less time than it took to speak of it. Saldor and twenty hand-picked Peshwin and Amenti warriors were waiting a quarter mile away to the south on the inlet's sandy beach with enough fresh water and supplies to last us for at least a month. I hoped that we wouldn't need them and would find the Shadow Pirates well before then.

"You sure bringing Piths on board a ship is a good idea, Hadrack?" Baine asked. He took a knife from his boot and began twirling and flipping it in a dizzying array of speed and prowess. My friend's incredible skill with a blade never ceased to amaze me.

"You heard Saldor," I grunted, thinking about the impassioned plea the Amenti chieftain had given me days ago. "He has as much right to revenge as we do. Maybe more. How could I say no?"

"But they're not sailors," Baine pointed out as he flicked the knife in the air, spun in a circle, and then caught the blade by the base of the handle in his open palm, where it stood straight up, balanced perfectly. My friend always was something of a showoff. "They've never been off land before, you know. It might not go well, Hadrack."

"They're Piths," I said with a shrug. "They'll adapt. Besides, who would you rather have by your side in a fight than them, whether it's on land or water?"

"A fair point," Baine conceded.

"Hadrack," Jebido cut in, pointing north. "The ship has turned. I can see her lines clearer now." He glanced at me and grinned triumphantly. "It's *Sea-Wolf*, all right, just like I said it would be."

I looked north again, shading my eyes. It was indeed *Sea-Wolf*, I saw with relief, able now to make out the familiar outlines of her giant hull and the cut of her sails.

Jebido put his hand on my shoulder and squeezed. "So, maybe now it's time to finally wipe that dark look off your face and go kill us some of these phantom pirates, eh? What do you say?"

"I say I think you're right," I growled to my friend, my hand automatically dropping to the hilt of Wolf's Head. "And woe to the bastards when we finally find them," I added grimly.

Once I'd pulled myself up the rope ladder and onto *Sea-Wolf's* deck, the first thing I noticed was that Putt and Niko were waiting for me. The second thing I noticed was that both of them looked terrified.

"What's this?" I grunted. Behind me, I could hear Jebido wheezing with effort as he climbed the ladder. I turned and reached down, helping him over the gunwale before focusing back on Putt and Niko.

"We didn't have a choice, my lord," Putt said, wringing his hands. "Please don't be angry with us."

"Truly we did not, lord," Niko added, bobbing his head up and down.

Baine appeared over the gunwale just then, pausing with his arms supporting his weight on the wooden railing as he peered first at me, then at Putt and Niko. "What's going on?" he asked curiously.

"That's what I'm wondering," I muttered.

"Ah, shit," I heard Jebido grunt beside me. I turned to follow his gaze, understanding now why Putt and Niko had been so afraid. I felt instant anger surge through me, knowing they had a right to be.

"Hello, my lord," Lady Shana said, appearing from the cabin doorway beneath the towering aftercastle in the stern. She paused there in the entrance for a moment, dressed in a man's pair of dark leather trousers and a white tunic. Shana had her hands on her hips and a combative look that I, unfortunately, knew all too well. Her long black hair was pulled back and tied in a braid, and I saw that she wore a short sword on her hip.

"What the blazes is this?" I exploded. "What are you doing here?" I turned on Putt and Niko, who shrank away from my fury even as Jebido put a hand on my arm to hold me back.

"Easy, Hadrack," Jebido said softly. He glanced at Putt and Niko, his expression hardening. "I'm sure these gentlemen have a reasonable explanation for why they've lost their damn minds."

"It's not for them to explain," Shana said, striding forward confidently with her head lifted in challenge. "They only did what they were told."

Shana paused three paces from me as I glanced around at the crew of *Sea-Wolf*, who'd all stopped their chores to watch in nervous fascination. I saw Tyrus leaning against the railing in the forecastle, his expression grim as he looked down at us. I met his eyes and he nodded to me, then half-shrugged in apology. It did not help my mood in the least.

"Well?" I demanded, turning on Putt. "You were in charge," I growled, advancing on the red-bearded, former outlaw. "What do you have to say for yourself?"

Putt glanced helplessly at Shana, who stepped between us, putting a hand on my chest. "These are your men, are they not, Lord Hadrack?" she asked calmly. The question and her demeanor threw me off, and I hesitated. "Well?" Shana prodded, her blue eyes bright, almost glowing as her gaze bored into mine. "Are these, or are these not your men, my lord?"

"They are," I grunted in assent. I paused to glare at the crew around me one by one. None would meet my eye, not even Tyris. "But now that they've disobeyed my wishes," I finally added, raising my voice so all could hear clearly. "I don't think they are anymore."

I heard murmurs of dismay ring out as Shana snorted. "Disobeyed you how?" she asked. "Did you not tell your men that when I speak, my words are to be obeyed as if they'd come from you?" I pursed my lips, not having an answer to that as Shana smiled in triumph. I had said those very words several years ago before heading out after some poachers who'd killed some of my sheep. "So, when I told Putt that I would be accompanying him to Calban," Shana continued, "was this not, in fact, an order issued by his lord that he dared not disobey?"

"You're twisting things around," I growled, annoyed at her game. I could see Putt and Niko relaxing in my peripheral vision, and I fixed them with a baleful look, satisfied to see their discomfort return full force. I pointed to the two men. "I left strict orders that my wife was to be protected above all else," I snarled. "You have failed me."

Niko looked positively sickly now, and I took a small amount of pleasure from that fact, while Putt's face was beaded with nervous sweat and flushed almost as red as his beard. They would soon look much worse, I vowed.

"Failed you, great lord?" Shana said, her hands back on her hips again. "How exactly did they do that? Do I look injured or unwell to you?"

"That's not the point," I said. "You were to stay in Corwick where it's safe, and they knew that."

"Did you order your men to keep me there, lord?" Shana asked. "Locked up, perhaps, in the White Tower like a common criminal until your return? Is that how it was to be?" I paused, staring at my wife in befuddlement as she smiled at me. "Well, my lord?" Shana prompted.

"Of course not," I said through gritted teeth. "It was implied when I left that you needed to stay in Corwick."

"I see," Shana said thoughtfully. She sighed, changing tactics now as she continued in a softer, more conciliatory tone, "I do understand how upsetting this must be for you, lord. Please don't be angry with me."

I mentally groaned. Shana was a master at reading my moods and nibbling away at my defenses with precision strikes, as the many arguments that I'd lost to her over the years could attest. She began to gently rub her hand along my forearm, another one of her many weapons.

"I need to be with you this time, my love," Shana said when I remained silent. "I have sat idly by more times than I care to remember while you risk your life for others, and to do so again would have driven me mad. I could not stay behind our stone walls, safe and at ease, knowing that Alesia and Einrack desperately needed help and I was doing nothing. Surely you can see that?"

I knew what my wife was doing, of course, but like a leaf in a waterfall, I was helpless to resist the sheer force of her. I found my anger lessening despite my trying to hold onto it, the tension in my limbs receding as she continued to knead me in a slow, almost hypnotic rhythm.

"It's not safe here, Lady," I finally protested weakly, my anger replaced now with resignation. I never could resist Shana from the moment I laid eyes on her.

"Am I not at my safest when you are there to protect me, lord?" Shana asked.

"That's not what I meant," I grunted. "And you know it." I perked up at a sudden thought, hoping to swing the battle back in my favor. "What of the children, lady? Think of the baby, if nothing else. Surely Alline needs her mother right now?"

"Alline was weaned many months ago, my lord, and is a baby no longer," Shana said. "As for the care of the children during my absence, I have given that task to Hamber and Hesther, who, as you know, the children adore."

I made a sour face, my last wall of defense crumbling. Hamber and Hesther were Shana's ladies-in-waiting, unmarried twin spinsters that were inseparable from each other and loved by my children. I knew my sons and daughters wouldn't even miss us.

"So you see, my lord," Shana said. "Our children are truly in good hands, and there is nothing to fear." She lifted her chin boldly, well aware that she'd won. "Now, are there any other concerns you still have, lord?"

I pursed my lips. "We have a long journey ahead of us, lady," I said, throwing out the last of my reserves. "It will be a long, dangerous one with much fighting undoubtedly waiting at the end of it. I can't have you with us when that happens. For this reason, you must return to Ganderland."

"Must I?" Shana asked, one finely plucked eyebrow arched. "And how will you achieve my return, lord? Will you sail north now, all the way back to Calban, and lose precious weeks on the journey? Or will you simply send me by horse through treacherous lands filled with Pith warriors where all manner of foul things might happen to me along the way?" Shana patted my arm at the look of dismay on my face. "No, I think not. We both know time is of the essence right now, my lord. So, rather than stand here all day in the hot sun making a spectacle over this, why not just accept that which cannot be changed and move forward?"

I glanced sideways at Jebido, who had suddenly found something on one of his boots to keep his interest, then behind me at Baine, who remained propped up on the gunwale. My friend just grinned at me lopsidedly and shrugged, knowing, as I did, that the battle had been lost the moment I had set foot on the ship. All that was left for me now was accepting that fact and then making as dignified a retreat as I could muster.

"Very well," I grunted as Shana smiled in victory. "You may stay. But you will obey me from now on and do as I say, or I swear, I will send you back even if you have to swim all the way."

"Of course, my lord," Shana said, lowering her eyes.

I could see a faint smile playing across her lips and I suppressed a curse, glancing around at my men instead. "All right, you worthless dogs, back to work! The sooner we sail, the sooner we find those bastards and kill them all!"

I turned away as my men cheered, grabbing hold of Shana's arm at the elbow. I leaned in close to her. "As for you, my lady," I said, lowering my voice. I prodded her toward the open cabin door. "I think we need to talk privately, you and me."

"Of course, my lord," Shana said, her tone meeker now, though I did not fail to notice her wink at Jebido before we entered the cabin and I closed the door firmly behind us.

Despite my brave words, however, the conversation that followed fared no better for me than the previous one had, perhaps actually going even worse. I was known as the Wolf of Corwick to my friends and enemies alike, renowned from sea to sea for my fierceness, tenacity, and fighting prowess. But against my beloved Shana, as always, I was as helpless as a newborn babe.

If only I had not given in to her that day. If only I had set aside my vow to Einhard for a time to take Shana home first, then the horrors that we would all soon face would never have happened.

If only...

Chapter 4: The Overseer

According to Daril—a gnarled and leathery-skinned Parnuthian sailor who was part of my crew of six that had come with Putt from Calban—our island destination was known as Blood Ring Isle. It was apparently named that due to the treacherous reefs that surrounded the island on three sides—reefs that Daril assured me had been the cause of hundreds of shipwrecks over the years. There was only one safe approach to the island, that on the leeward side, which he'd described as a narrow inlet surrounded by high cliffs that opened into a roomy, crescent-shaped bay.

That single approach was guarded by two stone watchtowers at the peak of the cliffs, I saw once we were less than half a mile out from the island. I studied those towers with the eyes of a seasoned warrior, knowing they would be a problem if trouble came. I could see mounds of large rocks positioned along the ledges overlooking the inlet, having no illusions about their purpose. It was a cheap and simple way of protecting the island that I knew would undoubtedly be quite effective. I hoped I wouldn't have to put those defenses to the test, for even *Sea-Wolf's* stout decks would surely crumble if those rocks were ever to rain down on her.

Daril had assured me that the men stationed in those towers were watching us right now and that the island's Overseer, a man named Quilfor Wentile, would have already been informed of our approach. No boat entered Blood Ring Isle or left it, for that matter, without the Overseer's knowledge or permission. Nor would one be allowed to take harbor within the bay without first agreeing to pay a docking fee. Failure to pay that fee would mean automatic seizure of the vessel and the crew sold into slavery. It was a rule that, while somewhat harsh, no doubt ensured complete compliance from anyone who wished to enter the Isle's protective waters.

The Parnuthian had warned me to be cautious around the Overseer, for he was known to be a hard, uncompromising man, only softened by the promise of gold or silver paid on top of the cost of the docking fee. Luckily, I'd had the foresight to bring a substantial amount of coin, which I hoped would buy me the information I needed.

"What do you think?" I asked Jebido.

We stood together on the forecastle, studying the island dominated by barren, rocky cliffs that overlooked equally rocky shores. Below us, great sheets of spray shot upward from *Sea-Wolf's* bow while white gulls circled in the air overhead, shrieking their odd cries. I glanced down at the wooden battle ram affixed to our hull with its thick covering of metal plating, watching as it cut through the water effortlessly. The idea and design for the ram had come from Hanley, whose incredible imagination and innovations always left me shaking my head in amazement. I wondered how long it would be before Hanley's creation was actually needed. *Sea-Wolf* and her ram had yet to be tested in any kind of battle situation, but even so, I had every confidence that she would not fail me when the time came.

"I think we're putting our necks out by going in there," Jebido grunted, always the cautious one. "It's too risky." He motioned to the island moments later as if to say I told you so as several sleek longboats with billowing sails slipped out from the inlet, heading directly toward us. I could see both ships were filled with armed men. "Looks like we've got ourselves some unwelcome company," Jebido muttered bitterly.

"Our escorts, no doubt," I said with a shrug as I watched the sleek crafts skim over the water.

"Or our executioners," Jebido grumbled pessimistically.

I chuckled at the dark look on my friend's face, although his fears weren't completely lost upon me. I watched the approaching longboats for a moment longer, then moved to the inner railing, where I saw Saldor down on the main deck. I made a gesture to him and he nodded before barking commands to his Pith archers, who hurried to take up positions in the aftercastle. I doubted their arrows would be needed, but like Jebido always liked to say, *"Being cautious costs you nothing, but being dead costs you everything."*

"This Wentile fellow might realize who you are, Hadrack," Jebido continued when I returned to his side. "And just in case it slipped your mind, let me remind you that Cardians have little love for you."

"Nor do I for them," I grunted, turning to smile at my friend. "But the bastards do appreciate gold, now don't they?"

Blood Ring Isle was officially a joint Cardian and Parnuthian outpost. However, Daril told me the Parnuthians gave it little thought anymore, leaving the management of the place to the Cardians. The island was one of several supply ports on the long journey west to the continent known as Aramtala, where the kingdom of Cardia, among others, could be found. I dearly hoped that was not where my hunt for the pirates would lead me, but if it was, I was resolved to go there regardless of the risk.

"Those bastards do love their gold, Hadrack," Jebido admitted. He glanced at me out of the corner of his eye. "But I'd wager my last Jorq that they hate you even more."

I laughed at that, though inside, I knew my friend had a fair point. I had done much to earn that hate from the Cardians. As much, I suppose, as they had done to earn mine. "Well," I said, spreading my arms out to my sides. "Daril insists that this is the best place to learn about the pirates' movements, so I don't see a choice in the matter."

An hour later, *Sea-Wolf* lay safely nestled within the protection of the island's many cliffs, tucked in smartly along a pier that stretched entirely around an enormous bay. I could see hundreds of small fishing crafts also moored neatly in place, along with sleek Cardian longships and bulky Afrenian traders, all of them rolling in unison on the gentle tide that lapped at the giant pilings supporting the docks. There was even a Parnuthian galley with its double banks of oars. I had no idea how it could have gotten this far out to sea without a sail.

Only one ship in the bay came close to matching *Sea-Wolf* in size. A cog just like mine with a high fore and aftercastle and well-maintained hull. I studied that hulking vessel where it sat moored alone at a smaller wharf on the far side of the bay, wondering who it belonged to. I could see several men standing in the ship's forecastle, examining us with as much curiosity as I had for them, while around me, my crew hurried to ready *Sea-Wolf* for inspection.

A rather short and fat official with a bald head and imperious air about him had come down the wharf at our approach ten minutes before and had shouted to us that we should expect to be boarded and inspected. Now, that man stood waiting for our gangplank to be lowered with his arms crossed on top of his impressive belly and a look of utter boredom on his face. Five soldiers dressed in red capes and pointed black boots stood behind him, their faces mostly hidden by their rounded helms and cheek guards. Our armed escorts who'd guided us into the bay were now floating fifty yards away in open water, watching us with hawk-like intensity as the Amenti and Peshwin archers, along with Tyris, stared back at them from the aftercastle.

"Do you recognize that banner over there?" I asked Jebido as I pointed across the bay toward the other cog. The pennant was bright yellow and triangular, snapping in the wind at the peak of the big ship's single mast. I squinted, certain that I could just make out an orange sun transfixed by a pair of swords.

"Never seen it before," Jebido grunted. He glanced at Baine, who was leaning over the gunwale beside us, staring down into the crystal-clear water at a swarm of small, brightly-colored fish. "What about you?"

Baine looked up, shading his eyes as he studied the cog. Then he shrugged. "No, that's a new one to me."

"Travelers," the fat official on the dock called, his voice now filled with impatience. "My time grows short. You are not my only arrivals today, so make haste, I say."

"My apologies for the delay, my good man," I said down to him pleasantly. "The splendor of your island just overcame me for a moment."

The bald man took a deep breath as he fiddled with a gold medallion hanging from his neck by a silver chain. "A common occurrence, traveler," he finally acknowledged. "The beauty of Blood Ring Isle is legendary." He lifted the medallion for me to see. "My name is Lennart Farimin, and I am the island's dockmaster. Now, if you would kindly allow me on board for the inspection, then we can get these proceedings over with as quickly as possible."

"Certainly, Dockmaster," I said, nodding graciously. I turned, motioning to Putt, who had several crewmembers roll out the wooden gangplank.

Farimin came waddling up the ramp when it was in place, his Cardian entourage following close behind. I met them on the main deck with Jebido and Baine while my crew and the Piths watched warily from the upper decks. Shana was in our cabin, where I'd told her to stay out of sight for now. I hadn't noticed before, but one of the Cardian soldiers was carrying an odd-looking device with a metal bar supporting a bronze bucket the size of my hands on either end. I realized that it was a type of scale, though I couldn't fathom its purpose.

Farimin's inspection took almost an hour as he went over every square inch of the ship, including the hold and the cabin, surprising me with his thoroughness after his earlier impatience. The short official had seemed startled to find Shana within the cabin, and I could tell by the way he reacted to her with great deference that he was quite taken by her beauty. It was a common response that most men had when first setting eyes on my wife.

"So, Lord Grayerson," Farimin said to me when the inspection was finally concluded and we stood again on the main deck together.

Grayerson was the name that I'd given the official as my own, although it was actually Jebido's last name. I'd only learned that a year ago during a drunken outing that he, Baine, and I had taken to one of my northern holdings. It's funny, but it had never occurred to me in all the years that I'd known Jebido to ask him if he had a last name, as my friend had always been tight-lipped about his childhood and family.

"Everything seems to be in order here, I am pleased to inform you," Farimin said. "All that remains now is the payment of the docking fee. Once that is complete, you and your crew will be free to disembark and partake of the Isle's many pleasures for one day. After that, if you choose to stay longer, another docking fee will be assessed."

"That sounds quite reasonable," I said with a smile, thinking the opposite. I certainly had no plans on staying one minute longer than I needed, let alone another day. "And what might that fee be, Dockmaster?"

Farimin took several moments to study *Sea-Wolf's* decks with an experienced eye. "We charge by gross weight, lord," he finally said. "Including cargo, which strangely, I see you have little of." He stared at me, his eyes narrowing. "It seems like a long and rather pointless journey to make, lord, coming from Ganderland with an empty hold."

"Ah, indeed," I said with a grimace, thinking quickly. "I'm actually on my way to Parnuthia to purchase wine. I had expected to have fifty bales of cotton to trade when I arrived there, but alas, my supplier suffered an unfortunate warehouse fire and all was lost. Not having sufficient time to make other arrangements, I had little choice but to sail empty."

"Oh, I see," Farimin muttered, looking unconvinced as he glanced around at the watching Piths above us. "A terrible tragedy indeed." I thought the dockmaster would say something about the warriors then, having studiously ignored them so far since his arrival. I was already prepared with an explanation for their presence, but the official surprised me by shrugging his pudgy shoulders as he focused back on me. "Well, even without this lost cargo, lord, I would wager your ship comes in at a very impressive two hundred tons. Would that be correct?"

I glanced at Putt, who nodded imperceptibly. "That sounds about right," I agreed, having no clue what *Sea-Wolf* weighed. It was something that I'd never given a thought to. Why would I?

"Very good then, lord," Farimin said in satisfaction. He gestured to the soldier holding the scale, having him set it on the deck. The fat man knelt on one knee with a groan, then carefully placed ten round metal discs into one of the buckets in an exaggerated manner to ensure that I saw no trickery was involved. Farimin looked up at me when he was done. "Each of these represents twenty tons, lord," he said before gesturing to the empty bucket that was now elevated as high as it could go. "If you would please place gold in there until the scales are even, then our business for today will be concluded."

I motioned to Baine, who moved to drop coins into the bucket, counting off one by one until Farimin grunted that he was satisfied. The fee was eight Jorqs, which I thought was a steep price to berth for one night, though I made no protest. The dockmaster scooped out the coins and then stood, pausing to bite down on one of them first. "No offense, lord," the fat man said apologetically as one of his soldiers collected the scale. "But we can't be too careful these days, now can we?"

"Of course not," I agreed. I held up a hand as he turned to leave. "I wonder, Dockmaster, if you can answer a question for me?"

Farimin paused, absently motioning for his men to continue off the ship without him with a flick of his fingers. "Certainly, lord, if I am able."

"I have heard some rather unsettling tales lately about ruthless pirates in the area," I said. I gestured to the closed door of the cabin. "With my wife aboard, should I be concerned, do you think?"

"Pirates?" Farimin replied, his features turning suddenly cautious.

"Yes," I said. "Word is they're called Shadow Pirates or some such ridiculous name. Have you heard of them?"

Farimin snorted. "Certainly I have, lord. But they don't actually exist. Shadow Pirates are just a silly nighttime fable used to scare the young and feeble-minded."

"You're quite sure of that?" I asked, trying my best to look concerned. "The information I have—"

"Is nothing but nonsense," Farimin assured me, cutting me off with a wave of his hand. "Trust me, lord, when I tell you that you have nothing to fear."

"Oh, well, that's certainly a relief," I replied, convinced by the way the fat man was avoiding my eyes that he knew more than he was letting on. "I'd heard the rumors, you see, and I wanted to be sure we wouldn't run afoul of them."

"No fear of that, lord," Farimin said with a chuckle. "You can't run afoul of that which does not exist."

"A fair point," I agreed with a wry grin. I clapped my hands together, then rubbed them vigorously, letting the short man know the issue was settled as far as I was concerned. "So, Dockmaster, to business, then. We could use some food, fresh water, and a hundred other items. Where would you suggest we go to purchase them?"

Farimin pointed toward a tall building with a high peak sitting back from the wharf on a hill. "That's Margrave Ingram's shop over there. You can get most of what you want there, I expect."

"Thank you," I said. "That sounds perfect."

"And where might a fellow get a drink of ale, Dockmaster?" Jebido asked.

Farimin lifted a finger and twirled it in the air, not looking back as he descended the ramp. "On every street corner in Blood Ring Isle, my good man. On every street corner."

Two hours later, after making a show of securing supplies, Baine, Jebido, and I sat in a tavern with the unenviable name of *The Drowning Man*. The building was crowded and boisterous, with sailors from every known corner of the world laughing and drinking as they told tales of their exploits on the high seas. Most, if not all I overheard was nonsense, of course, yet I listened with a keen ear anyway, hoping to pick up on any references about the Shadow Pirates.

I'd left the rest of my crew on board *Sea-Wolf* under Putt's command, since I knew letting Piths loose on an island well-known for its cheap alcohol and even cheaper whores was just asking for trouble. Luckily, Saldor had agreed with me, and he'd kept the warriors in line, despite their obvious eagerness to feel land beneath their feet once again.

"I think I'm going to stretch my legs a bit," Jebido said, giving me a knowing glance before getting up and heading away with his tankard of ale. I watched as he moved to another table across the room, where he paused to say something to the sailors there. I heard the men laugh, then smiled to myself as they made room for Jebido to sit, one man even clapping him on the back in a friendly fashion. It was almost impossible not to like Jebido.

"I still think that fat fool knew something about the pirates," Baine said from where he sat opposite me. I saw him glance over my shoulder before his expression suddenly changed in a way that I knew well. I turned, breathing noisily out of my nose when I saw the pretty barmaid that had caught my friend's attention.

"Don't you even think about it," I growled, turning back as I poked a finger at him. "We didn't come here for that."

"Yes, I know, I know. But have you ever seen such wonderful tits, Hadrack?"

"I've got more important things to keep my mind occupied," I grunted with disinterest. "Besides, tits like those can get you killed in a place like this."

"Maybe," Baine said, watching the girl wistfully as she served drinks. "But there are worse ways to go."

I just shook my head, relieved when Jebido returned to sit beside me. "I might have something," he said, leaning his head close to me so I could hear over the laughter and rumble of many voices. "Seems there's a rumor that the Shadow Pirates and Overseer might be connected somehow."

I frowned. "How?"

"Don't know," Jebido grunted. "That's all I could find out. Maybe we should pay him a little visit and ask the bastard?"

I took a deep breath, weighing my options. "Well, the Dockmaster did seem edgy when I asked him about the pirates." I glanced at Baine, who had finally given up on ogling the barmaid and was leaning forward to hear us better. "What do you think?"

"I agree with Jebido," Baine grunted. "Let's go have a talk with this Overseer and see what he knows."

"I doubt he's going to tell us anything without some kind of persuasion," Jebido warned.

"Then I guess we'll just have to give him a reason to talk," I grunted, my mind made up.

It turned out that Quilfor Wentile was a tall, rail-thin man of about fifty, with short, reddish-gray hair and a trim beard, both of which were heavily doused in oil that tickled my nose unpleasantly with its flowery scent. The Overseer wore high, pointed boots and dark breeches, a fine blue coat with a stiff collar, and a heavy gold belt around his waist. A Rock of Life hung from around his neck, suspended by a gold chain, and he wore a short sword on his right hip with a golden hilt.

"So, my dear Lord…uh…Grayerson," Wentile said as he sat down behind a massive mahogany desk after greeting me. He studied me for a moment, tapping one bejeweled finger with its carefully manicured nail on the wood in a repetitious fashion. Every one of his fingers, including the thumbs, had at least one ring, some with two or even three. "What is it exactly that I can do for you, lord?"

I glanced behind me at two stone-faced Cardian soldiers where they stood guarding the entrance to the Overseer's vast chamber, one to either side of the closed door. Both men were large and looked competent as they stared back at me through their helmets with expressionless eyes. The Cardians had insisted I give up my sword before entering, so I'd left Wolf's Head in the care of Jebido and Baine, who were waiting outside in the hallway. Clearly, physical persuasion was no longer an option for me to use on the Overseer, so I decided I'd have to get what I wanted from him with my charm—that and maybe some gold.

I let my gaze wander around the room, taking in the plush carpeting, silk draperies on the windows, and carved woodwork on the walls and ceiling. It was an impressive space, one that no doubt was meant to portray the man sitting before me as someone holding great wealth and power. That might be true enough, but it was also clear to me that the man was a pompous ass, though that didn't necessarily mean he was a stupid one. I knew I'd have to tread carefully in this room.

I leaned forward without warning, suppressing a smile when Wentile automatically flinched in his chair, reinforcing what I'd already guessed about him. Cardians were almost all cowards, and this one was no different. "I'm hoping you can give me some information," I said as I sat back in my chair.

Wentile nodded, relaxing somewhat. He clasped his hands together on top of the desk. "Such as?" he asked.

"I've heard that you might know the whereabouts of some pirates I'm looking for," I said casually.

Wentile's expression didn't change, although I thought I saw his body tense for a moment before he smiled at me. "And why would I know such a thing?" he asked politely.

I shrugged. "I was told that you know everything that goes on for miles around your island, so I just thought I'd ask."

"I see," Wentile said. "Well, I'm sorry to disappoint you, Lord Grayerson, but when it comes to these mythical Shadow Pirates that you seek, I am sadly ignorant."

"Oh, had I mentioned that was who I meant?" I asked innocently. Clearly, the Dockmaster had already informed the Overseer of our conversation.

Wentile hesitated, his face clouding briefly at his gaffe before he regained his composure and smiled. "Call it an educated guess, lord. Tall tales about these Shadow Pirates are not uncommon around these parts, nor is it unusual for travelers to require reassurances from me that these foul creatures do not exist."

"Ah," I said with a nod, knowing by Wentile's hard eyes that I would get nothing more from this man, not even with the promise of gold. My gut told me something was wrong here, and I felt a sudden, almost overwhelming need to get away from this room. I stood abruptly, again causing Wentile to shrink back, while I heard one of the guards mutter an oath behind me. I didn't bother to look over my shoulder as I offered the seated Cardian a slight bow. "Then please forgive the intrusion, Overseer. I should have known better than to trouble you with such a trivial matter."

"Of course," Wentile said graciously, waving a hand as the rings there glittered and winked at me like tiny stars. He stared up at me, and our eyes locked while a silent message passed between us. I could see amusement playing about his thin lips. "If there is anything else that I can do for you, Lord...uh...Grayerson," Wentile said after a moment. "Then please do not hesitate to ask."

"Thank you," I replied, nodding before breaking eye contact.

I turned and walked across the carpeted floor, feeling the Overseer's gaze boring into my back like twin red-hot pokers as one of the Cardian guards moved to open the door for me.

"Well?" Jebido asked once I'd stepped out into the corridor and the door had closed firmly behind me.

I let out a sigh of relief, having felt certain that I wouldn't even get this far. Several Cardian soldiers watched us from the far end of the passageway, though they made no threatening moves. I took Wolf's Head from Baine and slid the weapon into its sheath, glad to have the familiar weight on my hip again. I wished now that I'd brought my father's axe with me as well, but hadn't believed it would be needed. After seeing the look on Quilfor Wentile's face as I'd left, I knew now that I'd been wrong about that.

"The bastard knows who I am," I grunted in a low voice. "And they're coming for us."

Chapter 5: Escape From Blood Ring Isle

Night had fallen by the time Jebido, Baine, and I made it outside, with a three-quarter moon giving off faint light through a thin covering of clouds. I could see dense fog patches creeping along the narrow dirt road below the house, thinking that they looked like hungry ghouls searching for blood. I had a sudden premonition of disaster, wondering if perhaps the sinister fog was an omen of things to come. I dearly hoped I was wrong as Jebido and Baine followed me down the wide stairs of the Overseer's sprawling home and then along the cobblestone pathway to the street. We paused there as a group of perhaps ten mounted men appeared to the east, riding slowly toward us in a dark line down the middle of the deserted road. I groaned low in my chest, knowing my gut feeling had been correct—they were there for us.

"Damn," Jebido muttered from my right side.

Baine stood to my left, saying nothing, although a knife had suddenly appeared in his hand as if conjured there. We turned to face the riders just I saw more movement out of the corner of my eye in the deep shadows across the street, followed by the heavy clump of boots. I groaned as men on foot trotted out from between two darkened buildings that rose to either side of a wider road leading away to the north—a road that we needed to take. One of the men carried a flaming torch, and I could see the unmistakable wink of naked blades and the shine from conical helmets in the firelight.

"Well, I knew this trip was going to get messy sooner or later," Jebido said with a sigh as he drew his sword with a ring of steel.

I hesitated and looked around, searching for inspiration. Our only recourse seemed to be to turn west and run that way, but I knew if we did that, it would take us further away from *Sea-Wolf*, which I guessed was the point. With our right flank cut off by the horsemen, and the way forward to the ship blocked, it was either that or retreat back into the Overseer's house. Going back inside was a tempting thought, since I knew if I could get my hands on that worm, Wentile, I could use him to negotiate our safe passage back to the ship. All it would take was the sharp point of one of Baine's knives against the Overseer's skinny neck to ensure that happened.

But, even as the idea crossed my mind, I discarded it. Wentile had known who I was before I'd even arrived here, and he'd been prepared for me. It's doubtful that a coward such as he would take a chance with the Wolf of Corwick under his roof unless he'd felt supremely confident that he was safe. Which probably meant his house was filled with soldiers. I guessed the only reason he'd allowed us to leave at all was to avoid making a mess of the place. It just seemed the kind of thing that a man like him would do, especially considering what he knew waited for us outside.

"We can't go back into the Overseer's house, Hadrack," Jebido said, having the same thoughts as me. "I'm betting the place is packed with those Cardian bastards just itching to skewer us. We'll get boxed in."

"I agree," I replied, thinking we probably had only moments left before armed men burst out the door. The wind suddenly picked up then, sending the fog hovering along the street into swirling tendrils of madness that twisted and danced around us like wraiths. Good, I thought as I drew Wolf's Head, knowing it would help. Perhaps my gut instinct had been wrong and The Mother was watching over us this night after all.

The mounted men came to an abrupt halt fifty yards away with a creak of leather and jingle of bits, staying well clear. Their job, I knew, would be to chase down any survivors if one or more of us somehow managed to get away from the Cardians on foot.

Those soldiers were cautiously edging out onto the street now, where they began to spread out, with the one holding the torch staying at the back. I counted fifteen men, noticing that they were careful to leave a generous gap open along our western flank, clearly hoping that we would be foolish enough to take it.

"I imagine there's a nasty surprise waiting for us down there," I grunted, motioning with my head to the empty street on our left.

"I expect so," Jebido agreed, sounding calm and relaxed, though I did see him glance more than once behind us at the house. So far, all was quiet in there. Would it last, or was Wentile arrogant enough to think that those men inside weren't needed?

"Then I guess there's only one thing for us to do," I muttered, my voice filled with grim purpose.

Jebido sighed. "I was afraid you were going to say that, Hadrack."

I glanced up. A thick cloud bank was drifting toward the moon, only moments away from extinguishing its white glow. I looked at Baine, wishing he'd brought his bow with him before I nodded. My friend nodded back wordlessly, his face a grim mask of death as he drew a second knife before gliding with practiced ease three paces to my left. I knew there was no need to say anything to my companions about my plans, for we three had done this kind of thing many times before.

"Who are you?" I demanded in a belligerent tone. I stepped forward, waving my sword, wanting the Cardians' attention to be focused on me. A moment later, the moon slid behind the cloud. I sensed Baine slip silently away into the fog, almost invisible in his black clothing. I was careful not to glance his way. It would take my friend a minute or two to find an alley between the buildings lining the street and get behind our adversaries. I needed to buy him some time to do that. "How dare you accost me on the street like this!" I shouted in outrage. "I'll have your heads for your arrogance!"

"You'll have nothing but cold steel and a painful death unless you drop your weapons," a man called out. He stepped forward, his face cast in shadow beneath his helmet as he gestured with his blade toward me. I saw with satisfaction that he carried no shield, praying that none of his companions did either. "Do it now, Wolf," the Cardian said. "Do it, and maybe you'll live to see another sunrise."

"Wolf?" I said, doing my best to sound confused. "What the blazes are you talking about? My name is Lord Grayerson, you fool. You're making a huge mistake."

"No, you are Lord Hadrack of Ganderland," the man spat back at me, taking another step. "A murderer and a coward who is about to crawl on his knees to me like a beaten dog and beg for mercy."

I could hear the Cardians behind him laughing now, their courage and confidence stoked by what they mistakenly thought was our fear, that and their leader's blustery words along with their superior numbers. We'd soon see about that, I thought as I glanced sideways at Jebido. "Leave the one with the big mouth to me," I whispered. "He's mine."

"Gladly," Jebido grunted. He looked east down the street. "The riders are going to be a problem, Hadrack."

"One thing at a time," I said, glaring ahead at the Cardians on foot. "We'll deal with these turd-suckers first. Once we're in amongst them, I'm betting those riders will wait to see what happens rather than take the chance of running down their own men." I took a moment to smile, grateful none of the Cardians on horseback had lances with them. If they'd had, then I knew our chances of getting out of this alive would have been almost non-existent. "Besides," I added. "We're going to need rides to get back to the ship as quick as possible, now aren't we?"

Jebido grimaced. "You're assuming those bastards care what happens to the others, Hadrack."

I didn't reply, knowing my friend had a valid point.

"Well, what's it to be?" the Cardian with the big mouth demanded as he took another aggressive step forward. The moon slid back out from the cloud bank just then, revealing a short yet stocky man in dark armor wearing a cape that billowed behind him like a living thing as fog swirled around his lower legs and waist. He was wearing a conical helmet like the others, though his was adorned with a white plume at the crest that seemed to glow in the moonlight. I thought it looked ridiculous. "Are you ready to surrender to me like the coward you are?" the man sneered when I said nothing. "We've already captured your ship, Wolf." He paused dramatically then. "And your wife. So throw down your weapons now. There's nowhere for you to go."

I glanced at Jebido, who shook his head, clearing not buying what our Cardian friend was trying to sell. I didn't buy it either. I had thirty-three men in my crew, twenty-one of them seasoned Pith warriors, not to mention Putt, Niko, and Tyris. I knew it would take a lot more men than Wentile probably had at his disposal to overcome them without a major fight on his hands.

I cleared my throat. "And if we don't?"

"Then your bitch dies, Wolf," the man sneered. "After my men and I use her like a whore first, of course."

I growled low in my chest, fighting the urge to throw myself at the bastard and tear his heart out. None of the Cardians seemed aware that Baine wasn't with us anymore, but I knew that wouldn't last much longer. I tightened my grip on Wolf's Head. I was looking forward to silencing Big Mouth for good, but I needed to wait until just the right moment before I made a move. That moment came seconds later when a sudden, high-pitched scream sounded from the man holding the torch, which went out moments later. I bared my teeth in a wolfish grin as the soldiers—including Big Mouth—turned in surprise to look behind them. But it was already too late. Baine was among them now, alone in the darkness with his speed and knives. These stinking Cardians had no idea what they were in for.

"Kill them!" I roared, raising Wolf's Head and charging forward. "Kill the bastards!"

I was across the street in four long strides with murder in my heart, while Big Mouth stood frozen in confusion as more screams of agony sounded around him. He twisted one way, then the other, trying to see what was happening before finally becoming aware that I was almost on top of him. The Cardian's eyes went round with fear as I swung Wolf's Head, his jaw dropping open even as he lifted his sword in a reflex motion.

"Never speak ill about my wife, you Cardian scum," I growled as I batted the man's weak parry aside effortlessly.

I slammed my elbow into Big Mouth's face, crushing his nose as blood splattered. The soldier fell back two steps from the force of the blow, stunned and shaking his head. I swept low with Wolf's Head, not giving him time to recover as I cut deep into his right leg just above the top of his absurdly-pointed boot. The Cardian screamed and collapsed to one knee, his sword arm tangled up in his red cape as he tried to lift the weapon above his head. I smiled mirthlessly down at him, letting the man recognize his death before I ran my sword deep into his open mouth and out the back of his head, silencing him for good.

I looked up as I withdrew Wolf's Head from the Cardian, barely noticing as my blade made a wet sucking sound before popping free. Enemy soldiers were shouting and screaming all around me, milling about in confusion as the fog and dim moonlight worked in tandem to stoke the panic that Baine had started. Jebido stood to my right, grunting with determined effort as he held off two Cardians. I moved to help him, only to have a dark form appear in front of me out of the fog, his blade already whistling in an arc for my head. I dropped to my knees without thinking, feeling the whoosh of cold steel sizzling over me. I stabbed Wolf's Head forward like a spear, gratified to hear the man bellow in surprise, followed by a whimper as he fell with a clatter of armor.

I stood then and glanced again toward Jebido, who'd dispatched one of his opponents and had the second one backpedaling in terror as he hammered away at him with his sword, cursing with fury. I smiled. Jebido might be getting old and may have slowed in recent years, but he was still more than a match for any of these filthy Cardians.

"Hadrack!" I heard Baine shout.

I saw the shadowy outline of his slim body kneeling by a dead Cardian at the point where the two streets met. He pointed east even as I heard the rumble of hooves. I cursed, knowing the horsemen were coming. It seemed Jebido had been right after all.

I hurried forward, pausing to kick a Cardian in the stomach when I came across him crouched in the dirt on his hands and knees, struggling to rise. The man cried out and collapsed onto his back, lifting his hands defensively as he started to beg for mercy. But I had none to spare for the likes of him. I saw one of Baine's many knives buried to the hilt in his upper thigh, so I stooped and tore it from his flesh in a single motion while the Cardian howled in agony.

"Be quiet," I grunted, slashing the man's throat open with the knife as steaming blood sprayed over me in a fine mist.

I wiped my eyes free of the mess, then glanced up in alarm as a figure appeared above me with a drawn sword, only to have the man groan and then sag as a thrown knife appeared in his back. He collapsed on top of me, and it took a moment of struggling to shove his dead weight to the side.

"Are you hurt, Hadrack?" Baine asked, worry in his voice as he appeared from the gloom and helped me to my feet.

I just shook my head and handed him the bloody knife I held as shouts arose from the mounted Cardians, who had now joined the melee. A gigantic horse suddenly exploded out from a fog bank like some kind of mystical creature, bearing down on us. I cried out a warning even as I pushed Baine aside, diving in the opposite direction just as the beast swept past us, dragging white tendrils in its wake. I landed hard on my stomach, then rolled, coming up on the balls of my feet to see a second mounted Cardian heading directly for me. The man leaned forward over his horse's head with his sword pointed down like a lance as a wide grin broke out across his heavily-bearded face.

That face turned to terror, though, when Baine suddenly appeared, latching onto the soldier's cape as he dragged himself nimbly onto the horse's back behind him. I'd always despised capes, finding them nothing but a hindrance in a battle, as this Cardian was about to learn. The soldier cried out, his horse veering away from me while he desperately tried to turn in the saddle and swipe at his attacker. My friend easily dodged the clumsy swing, then dragged the soldier's head back with one strong arm and cut his exposed throat effortlessly before tossing the body aside. I looked around warily but couldn't tell where our first attacker had gone.

Baine reined in the horse and swung it around, then raced back to me before jumping to the ground. "Do what you do best, Hadrack," he grunted, thrusting the reins in my hand. "I'll take care of that other bastard." Then he was gone, disappearing back into the fog like a phantom.

I growled low in my chest, swinging up onto the horse's back as I felt the killing blood surging along my limbs. My new ride wasn't Angry, of course, who I'd left back with the Peshwin, but he was a sturdy white stallion with plenty of energy just the same, which would do just fine for what I intended. I kicked him into a gallop just as a Cardian soldier appeared on foot in front of me, crouched low as he tried to peer through the shifting fog. I had a brief glimpse of a young face with a wispy beard and wide, frightened eyes before Wolf's Head rose and fell and the man spun away, his face now a crimson mess of gore and blood.

I kept moving, aiming for three mounted Cardians bunched together in obvious confusion in the middle of the road just as the wind suddenly gusted, hiding them from my view when a massive blanket of fog rolled over them. I caught a quick glimpse of Jebido to my left as he cut down his opponent before the mist enveloped him as well. Then total darkness fell when another cloud slipped across the face of the moon. I grimaced, almost blind now and forced to work on memory as I held Wolf's Head down low by my horse's flank, picturing where each of the three riders had been as I urged my mount forward more cautiously.

Moments later, the stallion's right shoulder bumped heavily into another horse. I tasted instant blood in my mouth, having bitten down on my tongue from the impact as the animal I'd run into snorted and shook its head while the man riding it started to curse. I slashed outward with a flick of my wrist at the sound, gratified to hear a bloodcurdling shriek rise from the cursing man, followed by a thud as he fell to the ground. I reached out, fumbling in the darkness until I felt the rump of my victim's horse, which shied away from me. I spoke softly to the animal, trying to calm it as I urged my mount forward until I had the frightened horse's reins held firmly in my hand.

"Calfort, is that you?" I heard a voice hiss from somewhere off to my left.

"Yes," I whispered back as I searched the fog for any signs of the man. I could see nothing at all. "I just killed one of the Gander bastards," I added, hoping to keep him talking.

"Which one?"

"The old one, it looks like."

"Thank the gods," the man said. "I think we're the only ones left, Calfort. I heard the others riding away a moment ago."

"Damn cowards," I said with a snort, keeping my voice low. "There's only the two of them now."

"Yeah, but one of them is the Wolf," I heard the man mutter fearfully. "Stay where you are, Calfort. I'll come to you."

I waited, giving the reins of the extra horse I held a tug when it started to shy away. I heard the telltale clump of hooves in front of me, then the unmistakable smell of human sweat on the wind as the barely discernible forms of a horse and rider appeared.

"Calfort?"

"Here," I hissed, ready with my sword as the man guided his mount closer to mine.

The Cardian stopped beside me, his lower leg touching mine. I heard his saddle creak as he leaned closer. "What do you think we should do?" he whispered. I could smell stale beer and garlic on his breath.

"I'm going back to my ship," I growled, stabbing upward with Wolf's Head. I heard the man gasp, then a familiar gurgle as my blade tore open his windpipe. I steadied the Cardian by the shoulder as I pulled Wolf's Head free. "But you, my friend, are on your way to see The Father," I added as I let the rider drop limply to the ground.

I paused then to listen, but all was quiet. The dead Cardian had claimed his companions had run, but I wasn't convinced of that yet. I listened a moment longer, then whistled twice, imitating a black-capped chickadee. I heard an answering jug-jug-jug of a nightingale off to my right seconds later, then the harsh cruck-cruck of a raven from ahead—all distinctive calls that Jebido, Baine, and I had been using for years. I waited where I was until my two friends joined me, while above, the moon's faint glow appeared once again, struggling to break through the heavy mist.

Jebido was leading a black mare, I saw, and his right cheek looked dark with blood, whether his own or someone else's, I didn't know. "Well?" I asked.

"They're all either dead or still running," Jebido grunted with contempt. He rubbed at his cheek, pausing to glance down at his hand in surprise before wiping it on his trousers. "The way to the ship seems clear, Hadrack. For now, anyway."

"Then let's get moving before it becomes unclear," I said grimly as I handed the reins of my extra horse to Baine.

I knew we'd been lucky so far. We'd caught the Cardians by surprise, but there was still more work to be done before this night was through—undoubtedly the bloody, messy kind, as Jebido liked to say.

My friends mounted quickly, and we began picking our way around the dead bodies, pausing at the head of the northern street so Baine could retrieve two of his knives. I turned to glance back at the Overseer's towering house while I waited, watching as the fog drifted lazily along the steps leading up to it. I could see the silhouette of a man backed by lantern light peering down at the street from one of the top-floor windows. I snorted with contempt, hoping the Overseer could see me and would realize that his plan had failed. I knew if Wentile wasn't such a coward that the three of us would probably be dead by now. All he'd had to do was send the men inside his house out to attack our rear. But, being the kind of weak-kneed man that he was, the Overseer clearly hadn't wanted to risk losing his protection. It was a mistake that I promised myself I would make him come to regret.

Baine finally remounted and we trotted away, but not before I shot the house one last, appraising glance. They say there is no fury like that of a woman scorned, and I've lived long enough to know the truth of that. But the wrath of a wolf is not something easily dismissed, either, which I vowed Quilfor Wentile would come to learn—if not on this night, then one in the very near future.

We were only a few blocks away from the harbor when the first shouts and sounds of battle reached our ears, echoing over the buildings lining the street. I felt my heart lurch, thinking of Shana. I hunched low over the stallion's back, urging him into a gallop as his hooves pounded along the dirt road, sending small clouds of dust up in our wake.

Baine was riding a brown gelding with four white socks, but he was lagging behind with every stride, now almost four lengths back. Jebido's black mare was just as quick as my mount, though, and we raced forward together neck and neck. I glanced sideways at my friend, whose face was set in a grim line of determination. He must have sensed my gaze on him, for he turned for just a moment, the worry evident in his eyes mirroring what I felt. I tried not to think about Shana being in danger then, putting my head down and concentrating on my riding instead. I knew my men would protect my wife with their lives. I just hoped that protection would be enough until we got there. After that, I pitied any fool that got in our way.

We finally reached a crossroads and swerved left, hurtling past a tavern, where curious patrons wondering what was going on had spilled out from the interior and were milling about in the street. I shouted at them to get out of the way, narrowly missing a portly fellow in a blood-stained apron, who just managed to spin aside at the last moment before I swept past him. I heard the man curse at me, then felt a well-aimed metal tankard bounce off my shoulder. I barely acknowledged it as warm beer splashed down my back.

After another minute of hard riding, we came to a long dirt ramp that led down to the wharf where *Sea-Wolf* lay moored. I yanked up hard on the white stallion at the ramp's crest as Jebido came to a shuddering halt beside me. My horse was blowing wind, his great sides heaving, as was Jebido's mare, whose glossy black coat was alight in a sheen of sweat. Baine joined us a moment later, his eyes dark and murderous as we stared down at *Sea-Wolf* in silence.

"Well, that's going to be something of a problem," Jebido finally muttered.

The partial cloud cover obstructing the moon all night had finally blown away now, lighting the bay stretched out beneath us in an eerie white glow. Fog drifted sluggishly along the water to the shore, reflecting the moonlight, though it had thinned enough to reveal a dark mass of Cardian soldiers swarming along the pier beneath the hull of my ship. I noted with approval that Putt had had the foresight to withdraw the ramp, although he had not cut the mooring lines yet. I assumed he was waiting in the hopes that we would show ourselves. His hopes were about to be realized.

Saldor's archers were shooting down into the mass of Cardians from both the fore and aftercastles with deadly accuracy. But, even beneath that withering barrage, the Cardians seemed determined to get aboard. Those soldiers weren't displaying the usual cowardice that I normally associated with them—which, quite frankly, I thought was a damn shame. It seemed whoever was in command of these men had a tight hold on them.

I saw a group of five Cardian archers with their great longbows standing two hundred yards back from the pier on my left. They were lined up in formation in front of a three-story warehouse that stood on a slight rise and were shooting across at the ship. The position they'd chosen was a good one, I noted sourly, affording good sightlines while keeping out of range of the Piths' smaller bows. Tyris' longbow was the exception, and I saw several Cardian archers lying unmoving on the ground, guessing that he had brought them down. But, the blond archer had his hands full now dealing with the attackers trying to board *Sea-Wolf*, so he was no longer shooting that way.

The enemy soldiers were tossing ropes with grappling hooks across the short span of water separating the wharf and the giant vessel, latching onto the embattled ship's railings. The moment they had a firm grip, the Cardians would jump into the bay and then begin hauling themselves upward hand over hand. Saldor, Putt, Niko, and several other Pith warriors were hacking with swords, axes, and war-hammers at any man who managed to reach the gunwale, but there were too many. I had a sudden vision of Gasterny when it had fallen to Pernissy Raybold's forces years ago and I cursed. Unless we did something soon, it was only a matter of time, just like at Gasterny, before my men were overwhelmed and the ship was taken.

"Hadrack!" Baine called in alarm. He pointed out into the bay, where I could see two darkened longboats knifing through the water toward *Sea-Wolf's* unprotected rear as the fog parted before them. The ships were crammed with armored Cardians, and as yet, none of my men had seen them approaching. We had to act now before it was too late.

"Baine, Jebido," I snapped, pointing below to a narrow road that followed the wharf to our right. I could see all manner of buildings lined up fifty yards or more back from that road. "We need a distraction. Start firing those warehouses down there, as many as you can. Fire the wharf, too, while you're at it. They can either fight us or watch their precious island burn to the ground. That should give those Cardian bastards something to think about."

"What are you going to do?" Baine asked.

"I'm going to warn Putt about those ships and then deal with those turd-sucking archers," I growled.

"Be careful," Jebido said before he and Baine raced away.

I waited until they'd reached the road and had turned southward, then I was off, hurtling the white stallion down the ramp at a dead run. I turned north at the bottom, following the road as it curved along the dock. My ears were filled with the sounds of the stallion's hooves pounding a beat against the dirt and the cries of battle in front of me. None of the enemy had seen me yet, though I didn't know how long that would last. I paused behind the massed Cardians, pulling the stallion's head back sharply. The white horse reared back on his hind legs, his heavily shod front hooves pawing at the air as I swung Wolf's Head over my head.

"Putt!" I cried, noticing the red-bearded man on the main deck. He was bent over, hacking down at a rope as a Cardian below him desperately tried to pull himself out of the water. Putt glanced up at me, his expression turning from ferocious concentration to relief when he saw who it was. The stallion dropped to four legs beneath me as I pointed urgently with my sword. "To the rear! Enemy to your rear!"

Putt hesitated for a moment, and then he glanced over his shoulder. I saw his body stiffen when he saw the approaching longboats before he turned back and raised his sword to me in understanding. He took one more swipe at the rope below him, severing it as the Cardian cried out, then stood and began shouting to the archers on the fore and aftercastles. I breathed a sigh of relief as the Piths moved quickly to deal with the new threat. I'd done what I could, and now it was time to take care of those Cardian longbowmen.

Two soldiers who'd been hanging back from the assault on the ship had heard my cries, and they were now edging toward me, although neither man looked enthused with the idea. I kicked the stallion directly toward them, spinning one soldier around even as I lashed out with Wolf's Head at the other, cutting him down. More of the Cardian bastards were turning their heads to look back at me now, and some started to shout and point as I galloped along their rear. But despite that, no more came after me. I guessed they believed a single rider wasn't much of a threat, which suited me just fine.

I reached the narrow dirt road that led up to the warehouse where the enemy archers were stationed and swung onto it at full gallop. I felt an arrow hiss past my left shoulder moments later, followed by a second shaft whistling over my head as the Cardians saw me coming. I pressed my face into the stallion's neck, making myself as small a target as possible while the horse labored up the incline and more arrows flitted around us on all sides. I felt a sudden, sharp pain in my right arm where a barbed point had torn open my tunic and then kept going, relieved that it hadn't been worse. I chanced a look ahead then, guessing I was less than fifty yards away from the compact group of archers aiming down at me. I grinned when I saw two of them turn and flee into the warehouse as I came on. Trust Cardians to run away when things get a little tough.

That grin quickly faded from my lips when I felt my horse stumble as an arrow smacked solidly into its chest. My ride grunted and immediately slowed, wavering to the right even as a second arrow appeared, lodging halfway to the feathers in its neck. The gallant stallion let out a heart-wrenching scream, still trying to forge ahead gamely before it faltered and began to fall. I flung myself from the dying animal's back, landing hard on my shoulder and rolling several times. Then I was on my feet and running, now less than ten yards away from the Cardians.

I bellowed, ignoring one final, hastily shot arrow that sizzled past my right ear before the remaining archers panicked and finally broke. But they'd waited too long to run, for now I was in amongst them. I swung Wolf's Head at the closest man, slashing open his chest as blood exploded outward. Then I reversed my grip and whirled with a vicious backhand, tearing a great gash in another archer's throat that nearly severed his head from his shoulders. The man gurgled, collapsing like a ragdoll as I stalked toward the last Cardian, who had tossed aside his bow and run to the warehouse door, sobbing as he pounded on it. Not surprisingly, no one came to his aid. I snorted, guessing his companions were hiding somewhere inside like the frightened rabbits that they were. I stalked toward the sobbing archer, pausing three feet away as he finally turned and drew a rusty knife.

The Cardian held the blade out toward me with a shaking hand. "Stay back!" he pleaded. The archer was young, I saw, no more than seventeen at most, with narrow eyes and ruddy skin marred by pockmarks all across his cheeks. "Please, just stay back! I don't want to die!"

I sighed. The boy wasn't a threat anymore, I knew. But he'd helped to kill a damn fine horse, which was something that couldn't be easily forgiven. "You shouldn't have shot my horse," I growled, putting the tip of Wolf's Head to the youth's chest. I leaned forward, letting him see my resolve. "He was worth more than a hundred of you." Then I shoved hard, feeling Wolf's Head puncture the youth's chest until it crunched out his back, the point stopped only by the heavy oak door behind him.

The archer looked down in shock at the cold steel impaling him, then he lifted his head, staring at me with bulging eyes filled with disbelief and horror. He opened his mouth to say something, though all that came out was a stream of dark blood that ran down his leather jerkin before he sagged and died. I yanked my sword free, letting the Cardian drop to the ground as I glanced at the bloodstained door. I was debating whether or not to kick it in and finish the job just as the sounds of hooves clattering up the road came from behind me, settling the issue for me.

I turned, watching as Jebido and Baine approached, each of them covered in dark soot. Below, things had changed dramatically in only a few short minutes. The Cardians around the ship had cleared out now as huge plumes of billowing smoke rose a quarter-mile away, with wind-fueled flames licking hungrily along the peaks of several sprawling warehouses. Those flames were sending thousands of sparks inland, where they were landing on vulnerable thatch and wooden roofs. I saw the pier in front of those warehouses was also aflame, with many of the small fishing craft and larger vessels burning.

My friends had accomplished more than I could have hoped for, drawing the Cardian soldiers who'd been attacking *Sea-Wolf* away in a bid to try and contain the fires. Even the soldiers in the longboats had veered back to shore to help, leaving the battle and my ship forgotten—at least for the moment.

Jebido stopped his mare ten feet from me and leaned forward in the saddle. I saw the gleam of his teeth appear through the thick soot covering his beard and skin. "Your wife asked me to tell you to stop fooling around, Hadrack, and get back to the ship." He chuckled. "Apparently, she's not overly fond of this island anymore and would like to leave."

I took a deep breath, then let it out as I sheathed Wolf's Head. "So would I, my friend. So would I."

Ten minutes later, *Sea-Wolf* was slicing uncontested through the waters of the bay, heading east toward the narrow inlet and freedom. The wind wasn't in our favor, though, still blowing inland, so Saldor's Piths were working the oars, their great muscles powering us forward. Shana stood next to me on the aftercastle, unwilling to leave my side. I turned to look back at the orange glow that lit up the basin of the bay. More than half the wharf was ablaze now, with many warehouses nothing but raging infernos as hungry orange and red flames stretched to the sky. I could see small pockets of fire burning all across the town of Blood Ring Isle, even back in the hills where the richer merchants and officials lived.

Nothing is more terrifying to a settlement than fire, be it on the mainland or an island like this one. Given the right conditions, with most buildings made from vulnerable wood, fire can spread out of control in minutes, as evidenced by what we were seeing this night. I smiled, imagining the look on the Overseer's face as he stared out his window and watched his town burn. I fixed my gaze where I thought the bastard's house lay. All was in darkness there still, I saw with disappointment. I prayed to The Mother, asking her to intervene and ensure the flames reached his precious house and burned it to the ground.

"What are you smiling at?" Shana asked me, cutting into my thoughts.

"Nothing, my love," I said. I felt her squeeze my shoulder once before a shout from Niko arose from the forecastle ahead.

We were about to enter the inlet I saw. My smile quickly faded as the great cliffs rose to either side of us. I'd forgotten all about the island's formidable defenses in all the excitement. I glanced at Shana. "Get below," I said urgently. "Down into the hold."

"I'm not leaving you," Shana said stubbornly.

"I don't have time to argue about this," I growled. I looked up into the darkness above, having a sudden vision of a soldier pushing a stone off a ledge. I saw that rock tumbling end over end through the air in my head before striking my beloved Shana and smashing in her skull. The vision was so powerful that I almost moaned out loud in despair. "Get below, woman!" I finally snapped, almost overwhelmed with fear for her. "Or I'll drag you down there myself."

Shana glared at me for a moment, her face set in stubborn anger.

"Please," I added in a gentler voice. "I need to know you're safe."

Shana took a deep breath, then she nodded, squeezing my arm once more before climbing down the ladder to the main deck. I watched until she'd made it to the hold, breathing a sigh of relief when the hatch closed above her. My girl was as safe as she could possibly be, and all I could do now was wait and pray. I cocked my head sideways and listened, hearing nothing but the sounds of the oars splashing in the water and the grunts of effort from the Piths. I saw no movement above us as we glided along, no dark, solid objects hurtling downward. I waited, tense and holding my breath as I wrapped my hands tightly over the gunwale.

The ship was less than a hundred yards from open water and freedom, yet still, there was no motion from above. We drew closer to the mouth of the inlet with every heartbeat, though it felt to me as if we were crawling at a snail's pace. I counted seventy-five yards to go, with my fingers gripping the railing in front of me white with anxiety. Then fifty yards. Still no attack. Then twenty-five, before moments later, incredibly, *Sea-Wolf* hissed out into the open sea, intact and unharmed. The ship's huge sail caught almost immediately as the wind took hold, pushing her further out as we cut towards the west, while below me, the Piths and Ganders lifted their arms in celebration and cheered. We'd made it.

"By The Mother, lord," Putt muttered as he came to join me. "I'd not like to do that again." He removed his hat, wiping sweat from his forehead as he looked back at the rapidly receding island. The former outlaw turned to me, an expression of wonder on his bearded face. "Why do you suppose they didn't drop those rocks, my lord?" he asked. "Sinking us would have been as easy as catching a one-legged whore."

"I don't know," I said, my throat dry from tension. I shrugged. "Maybe they wanted *Sea-Wolf* for themselves and didn't want to chance wrecking her." It was the only explanation I could think of that made any sense.

Putt pursed his lips, looking thoughtful. "You're probably right about that, lord," he said. "She's a damn fine ship. Which means they'll be coming after us."

But I wasn't right, as it turned out. They hadn't wanted *Sea-Wolf* at all. They hadn't wanted me, either, for that matter. No, those bastards were after something else—something much too valuable to chance losing by sinking our ship.

And that something was the King of Ganderland's beloved cousin, Lady Shana Corwick.

Chapter 6: The Prophecy

"This is exactly why I didn't want you along," I grumbled to my wife as *Sea-Wolf* skimmed over the darkened sea. An hour had passed since we'd escaped from Blood Ring Isle, with nothing around us now but open water and black, overcast skies. I glared at Shana, wishing for the thousandth time that I'd sent her home when I'd had the chance. "You could have been hurt or killed," I added.

"But I wasn't, my lord," Shana said with infuriating calmness. "Thanks to you and your men. So, why are you so upset?" My wife's tone was composed and measured, yet I knew better. Shana was just holding back her reserves, waiting for me to say something foolish—which was only a matter of time—then I knew she'd send in her verbal cavalry to decimate me.

"This time," I grunted. "You weren't hurt or killed *this time*. But what about the next?"

We were standing together on the forecastle with her still dressed in a man's loose-fitting white tunic and dark trousers. Despite how worried I felt inside, I couldn't help but be affected by how feminine and beautiful she looked, even dressed as she was. Sometimes, it still seemed hard to believe that this incredible creature had chosen to share her life with me. Tyris was leaning on the railing as far away from us as he could get, peering out to sea as he studiously avoided looking our way.

I pointed down to the main deck, where several hanging lanterns revealed some of my men being treated for their wounds by Saldor, Niko, and a female Pith named Gislea. "We were very lucky tonight, Shana," I said grimly. "But that luck still gave us six wounded and three dead. Maybe four if Daril dies. What if that had been you? How could I have gone on after that?"

The Parnuthian sailor, Daril, had taken an arrow in the stomach, and I knew his chances of living to see tomorrow were slim. We'd also lost three of Saldor's Piths, all of them to Cardian longbows. Those dead Piths were down in the hold for now, but I knew we'd have to do something about them soon before they began to stink. The Piths still ascended their dead, despite what they'd learned from the codex, though they weren't nearly as rigid about returning them to the Ascension Grounds as they had once been. One of the Peshwin's Saldor had brought with him, named Hanon, was a Pathfinder, who had assured me that we could ascend the dead from the ship. I had no idea how that would be possible without taking a chance of setting *Sea-Wolf* ablaze. I wasn't sure I wanted to find out, either.

"My lord," Shana said. She took a deep breath, then let it out. "I understand how difficult this is for you, but yelling at me does little to help the situation."

I blinked, convinced that I'd kept my tone low and civil the entire time. "But I'm not yelling," I muttered in protest.

"Maybe not by way of volume, my lord," Shana said reproachfully. "But there's more than one way to yell at a woman."

I shook my head, as always amazed at how my wife could twist any situation her way. "What would you have me do, then?" I finally asked in exasperation, lifting my hands to my sides. "Not worry about you at all? Maybe throw you into a shield wall next time with a sword and a hearty pat on the back?"

"Well, now you're just being silly," Shana sniffed. She put her hand on my arm. "I know you worry, and I am sorry for that. Perhaps it was wrong of me to come here. But what's done is done, and squabbling about it all the time will not change that." She glanced sideways at Tyris, who was examining one of his fingernails with almost maniacal attention. "But above all else, my lord, we must show a united front to your men if we hope to succeed in our mission. Surely you know that?"

"What I know," I growled, "is that your very presence here weakens me. Every tough decision I'm going to have to make from now on will leave me worrying about how it might affect you. I can't keep doing that if we expect to find Alesia and Einrack." I hesitated then, knowing that my words—which had been spoken in the heat of the moment—were actually true. Something needed to be done about Shana, and that something was a plan that had just come to me. "So, for that reason," I added, confident now that I was making the right decision for everyone involved, "I've decided we'll sail directly to the port city of Carte in Parnuthia."

I saw Tyris look up at that in surprise as Shana's eyes narrowed. "Why, my lord?" she asked suspiciously.

"Because, from there, I can purchase passage for you on a ship back to Ganderland," I said, bracing myself for an outburst.

Shana's eyebrows rose, her mouth instantly forming into a circle of disbelief, quickly followed by her lips pressing together into a thin line of anger. A lantern tied to the stay line running from the mainmast above us to a pole on the bow slowly swung back and forth overhead, washing her rapidly clouding features in wane yellow light. "What?" Shana finally managed to gasp out. "What did you just say?"

"It's the only way," I said as I reached for her arm. "I'm sorry, but you have to go home."

Shana shrugged off my hand, shaking her head. "I will not!" she snapped.

"You will," I replied firmly. "My mind's made up and that's the end of it. I'll send Niko along to ensure you arrive safely."

"You can't do that!" Shana said, stamping one foot on the deck like a petulant child. "I won't let you!"

I sighed as Shana began to shout at me then, not really listening to her protests anymore. The cavalry was in full charge, and all I could do was let it ride over me and wait to regroup. My men below were careful not to look our way at the commotion, while the Piths showed no such reservations, watching curiously.

But even so, I didn't care what anybody on this vessel thought right now. Keeping my wife safe meant more to me than anything else at the moment—even more than my vow to Einhard. I'd allowed Shana to convince me to let her stay once already, and it had almost cost me everything. I promised myself that I wouldn't make that mistake again.

"You will do as you're told, my love," I finally said, interrupting when Shana paused to take a badly needed breath. I held up my hand before she could say anything more, meeting her obvious anger with my unbreakable resolve. "I am the Lord of Corwick, and you are my wife, which means you will obey my wishes. The matter is settled. I'll hear no more about it."

We held eyes for a long moment, neither saying anything, until finally, Shana looked down at the planks in defeat. "But you don't understand, lord," she whispered, so low that I almost missed it.

I shrugged, feeling tired and depressed now at what I'd had to do. "Perhaps not," I conceded. "Yet either way, you will be going home where it's safe. That is all the understanding I need."

Shana glanced up at me then, looking as if she wanted to say something more before she abruptly swept past me and climbed down the ladder to the main deck. I watched my wife march toward our cabin with her head lifted and her back straight. She opened the door and then paused in the entrance, glancing back as Jebido appeared from the stern and said something to her. They talked for a moment, with Jebido looking up at me once before turning back to Shana. I could only imagine what my wife was telling him.

I looked at Tyris. "You were married once, weren't you?" I asked into the uncomfortable silence.

Tyris nodded cautiously. "Yes, my lord. To a sweet young thing from Fallingbrook many years ago. Her name was Megin." The blond archer grimaced. "She died six months later from the coughing disease."

"Oh, that's right," I said, remembering him telling me that story now when we'd first met. I watched as Jebido put his hand on Shana's arm, speaking earnestly to her before she went into the cabin and shut the door. I focused back on the archer. "Did you love this girl?"

Tyris hesitated, looking thoughtful. "Love, lord? Perhaps I did. Who can say for certain? I was young, and she was young, and we greatly enjoyed each other's company. If that is love, then yes, I expect that I did."

"I see," I said. "And in the short time you had together, did Megin ever say or do things that made no worldly sense to you, Tyris?"

"Lord?"

"I mean when she got angry, did she act or say things you didn't understand sometimes?" I asked.

Tyris chuckled. "No, lord, can't say that she ever did. Whenever Megin would get mad at me, which was rare, mind you, I'd just go hunting for a day or two. By the time I got back, the lass had forgotten all about it." He shrugged. "It seemed to work for the both of us."

I sighed, leaning on the railing as I stared down at the closed cabin door. "If only it were that easy," I muttered.

"Yes, lord," Tyris replied, sounding confused. I could hardly blame him for that, for so was I.

Moments later, I saw Jebido striding across the lower deck toward us, his shoulders set in a way that I knew all too well. I groaned, watching him sourly as he reached the ladder beneath me and began to climb. Jebido's silver hair gleamed in the lantern light when he appeared moments later at the top of the ladder, pausing with most of his upper torso showing above the platform. He glanced from me to Tyris with appraising eyes before hauling himself onto the deck with a slight grunt. "Hadrack, we need to talk," he said, giving Tyris a pointed look. "Alone."

"I was just about to go check on the wounded anyway, my lord," Tyris said. He nodded to Jebido before heading down to the main deck.

"I don't want to hear it," I grunted before Jebido could say anything. I prodded a finger against his chest. "Not one word."

"Are you sure sending Lady Shana away is the right thing to do?" Jebido asked, ignoring my warning along with my finger. "Carte is a dangerous place, Hadrack."

"Not as dangerous as it is here," I muttered.

"That's not necessarily true," Jebido replied.

I waved a hand. "Niko will be with her. I'll trust in him to keep her safe."

"I trust the lad as much as you do," Jebido said. "But the journey back to Ganderland will be long and perilous. I doubt those Cardian bastards will easily forget or forgive what we did back there, Hadrack. Which means they'll be looking for us. Sending Lady Shana back with just Niko for protection is an awfully big risk to take with them out there."

"Everything I do with her here is a damn risk," I muttered. "The trick is finding the least unsavory path, which I believe I have done."

I'd tried my best to contain my anger with my wife moments ago, but I'd known Jebido since I was eight years old, and he was another matter. The non-ending worry and tension that I'd felt ever since I'd seen Shana on my ship was still coiled deep inside me, waiting to lash out at someone. The recent battle on Blood Ring Isle had helped quell that briefly, but after my conversation with Shana just now, it was back full force. Jebido coming to see me was a welcome and familiar target and one that I was glad to have at the moment.

"What does any of this have to do with you, anyway?" I growled, waving a hand. "Why don't you just mind your own damn business."

"This is my damn business," Jebido responded curtly. "What happens on this ship is everyone's business, Hadrack. So, stop being an ass and let's talk about it."

I turned away from my friend, bracing my hands on the railing and stared down at the water below me as *Sea-Wolf's* great hull knifed through the waves. "There's nothing to talk about. I've made the decision, and that's final. So, you can go back and tell my wife that her little ploy didn't work."

"What ploy?"

I snorted. "Do you think I don't know that she asked you to come up here? That maybe you could talk some sense into me and let her stay?"

"So what if she did?" Jebido grunted. He moved to stand beside me, leaning on the railing. "Having Lady Shana here is dangerous, Hadrack. I'll not deny that. But you know as well as I do that there's a reason why she came. A good one, at least from her point of view, and one that can't just be ignored."

I looked sideways at my friend, unsure about what he meant. "What reason? Helping find Alesia and Einrack, you mean? Because we both know we don't need her for that."

Jebido frowned. "Lady Shana didn't tell you about the prophecy she was given?"

I sighed then, understanding instantly now. Shana had become intrigued in recent months with an old seer living in Camwick named Otmar the All-Knowing, who read the bones of dead rats and offered gullible people obscure prophecies—for a hefty price, of course. I believed none of it, thinking Otmar would have been more aptly named the All-Conniving, but Shana was convinced everything he told her was true. I'd never understood how an obvious charlatan could fool such an intelligent woman. I had intended to run the bastard out of town at some point but had never gotten around to it. Now I dearly wished that I had.

"No, Lady Shana did not tell me about it," I said wearily. "So now you will."

Jebido pursed his lips as he thought, absently wiping sea spray from his beard that had just splashed over the both of us when *Sea-Wolf* crested a wave. I steadied myself on the platform, letting the wetness drip down my face as I waited, knowing more would be coming anyway.

"I just assumed that she'd spoken to you about this, Hadrack," Jebido finally said. He glanced back at the closed cabin door across the ship. "I'm sorry, maybe I shouldn't have said anything. Lady Shana should really tell you about it herself, not me. Forget I mentioned anything."

"It's a little late for that now," I muttered as more spray splashed upward over us. I moved back from the railing, spreading my feet on the deck as I rolled with the ship. I motioned with a hand. "Out with it, Jebido. Tell me what this prophecy said." My friend hesitated, his weathered face twisted in indecision. "Now," I finally growled in impatience.

Jebido glanced once again at the cabin, then nodded reluctantly before taking a deep breath. "The night we left Corwick with Saldor, the Lady went to Camwick and asked the seer if you would be successful in your quest."

I rolled my eyes. "Let me guess, the old bastard and his bones told her no."

Jebido shook his head. "No, he told her we would find Alesia and Einrack alive and unharmed."

I shrugged. "Then what's the problem?"

"He also told her that though the mission would be successful, you were fated to die, and the only way to keep that from happening was if Shana never left your side."

I paused then, staring at my friend in disbelief. Finally, I snorted. "You can't be serious, Jebido? She came all this way and risked her life because of some old swindler and a bunch of rat bones?"

"I'm just relaying what I know," Jebido said gravely. "It's your wife who is serious about this. So serious, in fact, that she rode after Putt, Niko, and Tyris and convinced them to take her with them to Calban, then sailed south to find you. So maybe you should give these rat bones and Lady Shana's fears a little more respect."

I sighed, my anger deflating somewhat now as I fully understood Shana's motivation for coming. I put a hand on Jebido's shoulder. "Why didn't she just tell me all this from the beginning. Why keep it from me?"

"Would you have listened to her if she had told you?" Jebido asked. "I imagine she knows what you think about that seer, yes?"

"Of course she does," I growled, removing my hand. "But I'm not wrong about him." I shook my head at what the seer had nearly cost me. "That bastard will lose his head for putting my wife in danger, mark my words," I added.

I started to make my way toward the ladder, intending to talk to Shana and deal with this nonsense. But Jebido grabbed my arm, stopping me. "Give it a little time before you go down there, Hadrack," he said. "Your wife is angry and hurt right now, and judging by the look in your eyes, you're not ready to discuss this rationally just yet."

"Rationally?" I grunted at him in amazement. "This entire thing is nothing but gibberish spouted by a greedy fool. Shana needs to accept that, and the sooner, the better."

"Perhaps," Jebido conceded, steering me away from the ladder. "But trust me, now is not the time to tell her that. Give her the night to sleep on it. Maybe things will have changed by the morning. Besides, I don't think it's a good idea if anyone else on board learns about this prophecy. At least not yet."

I allowed Jebido to guide me back to the railing, knowing that, as usual, he was right. If I went down there now it would likely lead to another argument—one which my crew didn't need to hear right now. I might not believe in some withered old rat bones, but undoubtedly some of my men would take it seriously, which could potentially lead to unrest. The Piths were very superstitious about omens and prophecies as well, so I knew keeping this quiet like Jebido had suggested was probably a good idea.

I leaned my back against the railing, staring up at the starless sky. "You know I can't think straight with her here, Jebido. She has to go home."

"I know you think that," came back the immediate reply.

"I don't think it, old friend, I know it," I said with a shake of my head. "It's like she saps my strength when I need it most, leaving me trembling like a child afraid of ghouls stalking the night."

"That's called love," Jebido said with a chuckle. "You and that girl have something very few people find in their lives, Hadrack. Don't jeopardize it now by doing or saying something that you'll regret later."

"If it means keeping Shana safe, then I'm willing to take the risk," I said stubbornly. "I need to be focused, Jebido. Can't you see that? I gave Einhard my word, and I can't...no, I won't let him down after all he did for me."

Jebido shook his head. "That's what you don't seem to understand, my boy. That lass doesn't make you weak or unfocused at all. If anything, it's the opposite. Lady Shana is the steel in your limbs that makes you who you are, Hadrack. Before her, you were just one more headstrong boy in a world filled with them." He snorted. "You could barely tell your brains from your arse half the time before you and Baine found her." Jebido pointed at me. "You changed that day, Hadrack. You changed from a boy into the man you were supposed to be, all because of her. Never forget that."

"I don't deny it," I said, knowing there was some truth to his words. I had been an angry, impatient and impulsive youth when I'd first met Shana. She had changed me; there was no question. But what Jebido just didn't seem to understand was the strength Shana gave me was easily nullified by the fear I carried that I might lose her. It was not something that I could easily overcome. She had to go home.

I thought suddenly of Tyris and his doomed marriage. Would he and Megin have been as happy as I was with Shana had the girl lived? What would Tyris' life have been like had she not died? Fate was a fickle thing, I thought gloomily, with all our lives balanced on a thread pulled by the gods for their own amusement.

I took a deep breath, needing to change the subject. "What about you?" I asked, looking at my friend appraisingly.

"What about me?" Jebido grunted.

"You don't talk much about your past," I said. "Were you ever married? Were you ever in love?" I'd asked these questions of my friend before, of course, but rarely if ever, had I received more than a vague, one or two-word answer. I hoped tonight that might change.

"This isn't about me, Hadrack," Jebido said. He looked out to sea, his face hard to read in the lantern light.

"You lost someone," I said, knowing instinctively that it was true. "Someone who meant a lot to you."

"We all lose someone eventually," Jebido replied in a low voice. "It's just a matter of time, Hadrack." He put his hands on the railing, his scarred knuckles, earned from a lifetime of battling, flexing as his fingers opened and closed on the smooth, weathered wood.

"Tell me about your family, Jebido," I prompted. "Who were they?"

"They were nobody," my friend answered moodily, staring out to sea with hooded eyes. "There's nothing to tell, so let it be."

But there was something to tell; I could sense it. I also felt that maybe Jebido was ready to talk about his life before we'd met for the first time since I'd known him. I leaned against the railing beside him, nudging his shoulder with mine. "There's always a story to tell, old friend," I said. "And I've got nowhere to be right now."

Jebido sighed. "This isn't the time for it, Hadrack."

"That's what you always say."

"And I'm always right," Jebido grunted. He looked past me, his expression turning to relief as Baine climbed up onto the platform, followed closely by Saldor.

I turned to the new arrivals, knowing that something had happened by their expressions.

"Daril died, Hadrack," Baine said bluntly. He hooked a thumb over his shoulder. "Just now. What do you want us to do with the body? Put it in the hold with the others?"

I took a deep breath, saddened by the Parnuthian's loss but hardly surprised. "No," I said. "He told me earlier that he wanted to be buried at sea if it came to it."

Baine nodded, then leaned over the railing and put two fingers in his mouth before whistling sharply. I saw Tyris look up from where he and Niko stood over the motionless body of the dead sailor. Baine pointed to the ocean, saying nothing as Tyris waved in acknowledgment before the two men began lugging the corpse to the portside railing.

"Perhaps you should say something, Hadrack," Jebido suggested. "A word or two to help him on the journey."

I shook my head. "Daril told me he's made his peace with this world and is looking forward to meeting The Mother. There's nothing I can say that will help make that happen."

I watched as Tyris and Niko reached the railing and carefully lifted Daril over it before letting the body drop. I didn't even hear the splash as I turned away, wondering how many more bodies would follow the Parnuthian before our journey was over.

"Chieftain," Saldor said. "This man, Daril, spoke of a chain of small islands less than a day away from here before he died. I would ask that we make a diversion toward them so that we might ascend our dead."

"No," I grunted. "I can't afford to waste time going there."

Saldor's face hardened. "I do not think that's a wise choice, Chieftain."

"Is that right?" I grunted, feeling sudden anger. I stepped closer to the Amenti until we were face to face. Saldor was tall, even for a Pith, but he still had to look up at me. "What you think doesn't matter to me, Saldor. I'm in charge here, and what I say goes. You'd do well to remember that."

"And you'd do well to remember who it is that you speak to," Saldor replied. His tone was calm and even, though his eyes flashed with the promise of something else if I pushed this further.

I leaned forward, our noses almost touching as I locked eyes with him. "Be careful, Saldor," I growled, dropping my hand to the hilt of my sword. "Do not tempt me, this night of all nights."

"Hadrack," Jebido said, stepping between the two of us. He pushed me back several steps. "Have you lost your mind? What's the matter with you?"

I motioned to Saldor. "That's a question for him. When I give an order, I expect it to be obeyed."

Baine had been silent and watchful until now, but he moved then, shifting to stand beside Saldor and Jebido in obvious solidarity with them. My friend crossed his arms over his chest as he stared at me. "You're being an ass, Hadrack," he said. I opened my mouth to dispute that just as Baine chopped a hand outward, stopping me. "We all understand the pressure you're under, but don't take it out on us. Saldor's request is more than reasonable, and you should grant it."

"But we don't have time for an ascension," I said, spreading my arms out. "Every day we lose means Alesia and Einrack have gotten that much further away."

"Would you rather they do it on the ship?" Baine asked. He glanced down at the closed cabin door. "Because I really don't think that's something you want your wife to witness. Do you?"

I hesitated at that. The Piths would undoubtedly want to send off their dead in the traditional fashion. There were only four female Piths among the warriors Saldor had brought, which meant they would be very busy in the rutting circles. I realized Baine was right. I couldn't expose Shana to that for any reason, but I knew the Piths would revolt if I tried to ban it from happening.

I took a deep breath, focusing on Saldor. "My apologies, brother. I lost my head just now. Please forgive me."

"Forgiven and forgotten, Chieftain," Saldor said.

I nodded, knowing that it was true. Piths settled grievances quickly—sometimes violently—but they rarely held a grudge afterward. I glanced across the ship toward the aftercastle, where I saw the dark form of Putt standing alone on the platform. I waved for him to join us.

"Yes, my lord?" Putt said when he arrived, glancing at us all with obvious curiosity.

"Daril told Saldor about a group of islands near here. Do you know of them?"

"I believe so, yes, my lord," Putt said. "They lie a day or so to the east of our position, if I'm not mistaken."

"Good," I grunted. "Then set a course for them immediately." I smiled grimly at Saldor. "We have a ceremony to perform."

"Certainly, my lord," Putt said with a slight bow.

"And what about Lady Shana?" Jebido asked.

"She still goes home," I said firmly. "That hasn't changed." I glanced around at my men, my hands on my hips. "And after that, we're going to find those damn pirates and kill them all."

My men all nodded grimly at that, though we had no idea at the time that I was wrong—we didn't find the pirates after all. No, they found us first.

Chapter 7: Ascension

The island Saldor selected for the ceremony looked almost like a saddle, with high granite cliffs on two sides and rich green grass growing wild in a deep basin in between them. Strange-looking birds with bright orange and yellow beaks, white heads and chests, and slick black feathers nested in crevices all along the faces of the cliffs. Putt told me they were called horned puffins and that the bright beaks meant that it was breeding season. I couldn't help but think that was appropriate, considering what would soon be happening on that island once the Piths arrived for the Ascension Ceremony.

There were no trees anywhere along the basin that I could see from my vantage point on *Sea-Wolf's* forecastle, though there was a small stand of tall saplings growing below the cliffs on the western shore. That was good news for the Piths, who would need poles for the bodies and brush for the ascension fires. Putt had anchored the ship two hundred yards out from the eastern point of the oddly-shaped landmass, where a gently sloping sandy beach led to a narrow gorge that gave access to the basin. I guessed that it would take the Piths twenty minutes or so to walk from the beach to the trees, maybe less, as the island was not large.

"Are you sure you won't come with us, Chieftain?" Saldor asked, not hiding a wide grin. "It might be good for you to remember what it's like to be a Pith again."

I chuckled and shook my head, knowing that the warrior was only teasing me. I'd made it clear to him during Einhard's ascension weeks ago that I wouldn't participate, and this time would be no different. "I don't think so, Saldor. Besides, somebody has to watch over your wounded." Of the five injured Piths, two felt strong enough to swim to the island for the ceremony, while the other three would have to remain on board with my crew and me.

"You Ganders are so strange," Saldor said, shaking his head in mock wonder. He glanced across the ship toward the cabin, where I'd asked Shana to remain inside with the door closed until the Piths had swum over to the island. "Bring the girl with you, Chieftain. You can rut together as husband and wife and celebrate our brothers' lives as they ascend. None will bother her or try to lie with her. You have my word on this." I just shook my head and Saldor snorted. He gestured to Baine, who stood with Gislea along the starboard railing on the main deck. The two were completely naked, as were most of the other Piths, with only a sword or axe strapped to many of the warriors' backs. "At least that little one over there still acts like a Peshwin sometimes, Chieftain."

I laughed, thinking Saldor better not call Baine that to his face. My friend had been bemoaning his small stature ever since I'd known him, even though I'd told him repeatedly that it wasn't the size of the man in the fight that mattered but the size of the fight in the man. I knew if you measured him by that, then Baine towered above us all.

Baine must have sensed my eyes on him, for he turned to look up at the forecastle, giving me a wide grin of anticipation. The lecherous bastard loved his Ascension Ceremonies. I grinned fondly back at him. Beside Baine, Gislea suddenly leaned over the railing and pointed in excitement toward several dolphins who had just surfaced and were swimming in lazy circles fifty yards to the north. The girl was slim, with taut, powerful legs and long blonde hair that almost caressed the top of the narrow cleft leading to her finely-sculpted rear end. Gislea was only sixteen, which was a little young to be on a war party of such importance. But Saldor had selected the girl for her incredible prowess with a bow, which she'd apparently put on full display during the attack on the ship. She reminded me a great deal of Ania. Baine and Gislea had become lovers in recent days, which hadn't surprised me in the least. The only surprise, I suppose, was that it had taken my friend this long.

I looked away from the couple, studying the island again as puffins dove like dark arrow shafts into the sparkling sea, only to burst out moments later with wriggling fish in their beaks. More islands filled the horizon around the ship, and I guessed that there had to be easily thirty or forty of them, with some not much bigger than *Sea-Wolf*. I looked down at the water beneath the anchored ship, which was crystal-clear with an emerald-colored tinge, allowing me to see to the rocky bottom. All manner of marine life were flitting past our hull in a dizzying array of motion, from slow-moving, majestic sea turtles to blue butterflyfish and gray and white angelfish, as well as several giant pink sea basses known as groupers. I'd even caught a brief glimpse of an eight-foot-long green moray eel slithering along the rocks of the ocean floor a few minutes ago.

Gislea squealed in delight, and I watched as one of the dolphins swam closer to *Sea-Wolf*, finally stopping less than twenty feet from her great hull. The creature rolled onto its back with its head and tail curled upwards out of the water in a comical pose, then started to make odd clicking sounds. Gislea clapped her hands together while Baine laughed, putting his arm around her slim waist.

I smiled at the girl's youthful enthusiasm, forgetting my troubles for a moment, while below me, the rest of the Piths rushed to the gunwale to watch. The dolphin must have sensed it had an audience, for it began to do flips and twirls while the Piths cheered and laughed in appreciation. The show lasted for almost ten more minutes before, finally, the playful dolphin returned to its mate and the two disappeared beneath the waves. Moments later, Piths began leaping into the water, calling to each other joyfully as they swam with powerful, measured strokes toward the island. The three dead Piths—still tightly wrapped in white sheets—were each tied to wide planks, which the Pith warriors took turns towing behind them with ropes.

Baine cupped his hands around his mouth. "See you tomorrow morning, Hadrack!" he called up to me.

I waved and my friend waved back, then he and Gislea disappeared over the side together hand in hand. I glanced sideways at Jebido as he strode up to Saldor and me with his arms crossed behind his back. "What about you?" I asked. "Planning on taking a swim?"

"Not likely," Jebido said with a snort. "I'm too damn old for that now."

"For the swim?" I asked, motioning to the island. "Or the Ascension?"

"Both," Jebido grunted.

"You're never too old for an Ascension," Saldor said.

"Spoken by someone who is still young," Jebido replied sarcastically. "Just wait until your bones constantly ache and you have to get up and piss ten times a night. Then you'll see."

"Perhaps I will," Saldor agreed with a laugh. He started climbing down the ladder. "But not today, brother. Not today."

Jebido and I watched in silence as Saldor stripped off his clothing on the main deck before he leaped onto the starboard railing, balancing there effortlessly while the ship rocked gently on the tide beneath him. The man was a natural sailor, which, as it turned out, all the Piths seemed to be. Was there nothing these people couldn't do?

Saldor turned to look up at us. "Remember, Chieftain. Death comes to us all, but a proper life must be lived first before the Master will show us the path." He turned then and sprung outward, his heavily-muscled body gleaming with youth and power as he dove, knifing down into the water with perfect form. Saldor surfaced moments later, snapping his long hair from his eyes with a flick of his head before he began to swim with easy, practiced strokes away from the ship.

I noticed many of the lead Piths had already reached the island in the distance, including Baine and Gislea. I watched as more and more warriors waded out from the surf and onto the white sand, with the corpses being carried reverently from the water onto the shore. Saldor was the last to arrive, and once he'd reached the beach, the dead—still tied to the planks—were lifted onto the shoulders of the biggest and strongest Piths before the entire procession headed up the ravine toward the basin.

"We really should consider adding a small skiff or rowboat to *Sea-Wolf*," Jebido muttered. He gestured to the climbing Piths. "It's easy for them to swim whenever they need to." He glanced at me. "Or even you and Baine and the crew, for that matter. But what about Lady Shana and me?"

"She doesn't have to worry about such things," I promised. "We'll be heading for Carte tomorrow morning, and then she'll be going home. As for you," I added, the ghost of a smile on my lips now. "I know you've put on some weight in recent months, Jebido, but I imagine you can still float well enough. If not, I suppose I could drag you along on a plank like one of those corpses."

"Very funny," Jebido grumbled. "I'm serious about this, Hadrack. We could move supplies, weapons, and men a lot easier if we had that boat. Not to mention we wouldn't need to risk getting so close to land in the future."

Despite my teasing, I knew Jebido had, as usual, a good point. "I'll keep it in mind," I said. "Maybe we can buy something when we get to Carte."

"You're still determined to go there?" Jebido asked, studying me appraisingly.

"I am," I said as I glanced up at the sun. It was already well past midday, which meant in a few more hours, darkness would fall and the ceremony would begin.

Jebido sighed. "And is the Lady still not talking to you because of it?"

I shrugged. "Just the odd word here and there right now," I admitted. "But at least the daggers aren't in her eyes anymore every time she looks at me. Shana knows I'm right about this. She's just too stubborn to admit it yet. But she will."

"Uh-huh," Jebido grunted doubtfully. He clapped me on the back. "Well, best of luck with that, Hadrack. Knowing Lady Shana as I do, I think you're going to need it. I'm going to go down to the hold and check on our fresh water supply. We'll talk later."

I stood alone on the forecastle for a long time after Jebido left, staring down into the sea at the colorful fish darting back and forth below me, lost in thought. The sun was sinking beneath the horizon to the west when I finally shook myself out of my reverie, noticing a slight chill in the air now as a cool breeze had picked up. My stomach grumbled loudly then, reminding me that I hadn't eaten anything since that morning. I climbed down to the main deck, pausing to stop and talk briefly to Niko where he sat on a casket near the hold, sharpening his sword. Then I headed for the cabin. I found Shana seated at a small desk inside the cramped space, reading a book by candlelight.

"Well, the ceremony should be starting soon," I said by way of greeting. "By this time tomorrow, we should be well on our way to Carte."

Shana glanced up at me, her expression blank before returning to her reading without saying anything.

I silently groaned, cursing myself for being a fool. My wife and I hadn't spoken in hours, yet the first thing out of my mouth was to mention Carte, which was the last place in the world I knew she wanted to go. I took a deep breath, trying to repair the damage. "Baine and Gislea seem to be having fun together. Maybe it will lead to something. He's never been the same since Flora died, and it would be good if he could settle down with someone." I waited after that in expectant silence, but was greeted by nothing other than a soft whisp as Shana turned a page. "I was going to go and get something to eat," I finally said to break the awkward stillness. "Can I get you anything, my love?"

Shana pointed with a finger to a clay bowl on the desk with several hard biscuits and the remnants of some salted pork inside. She didn't bother to look at me. I noticed a half-full mug of beer sitting by her right hand.

I sighed. "Are you ever going to talk to me again?" Shana pursed her lips, then turned another page, studiously ignoring me. I finally put my hand over the writing, which I saw was a history of the Raybold family. The book had been commissioned by Jorquin Raybold when he'd seized the throne of Ganderland, and to me, was nothing but a collection of lies and half-truths. Why Shana insisted on keeping and reading it always baffled me. "I asked you a simple question," I said, "and it's impolite of you not to answer."

Shana sat back in her chair, still not looking at me. "Yes," she simply said, staring at the wall in front of her.

"Yes?" I repeated. "Yes, you're going to talk to me again, or yes, you know you're being impolite?"

"Both," Shana replied. She undid her hair, then began to comb it out with a bone-handled brush. I hadn't failed to notice that she'd turned partially away from me, her elegant neck twisted at an angle as she worked at her silky hair with practiced strokes.

"That's it?" I asked when she said no more. "That's all you have to say?"

"What else is there?" Shana asked in an infuriatingly even tone. "Apparently, I'm just a woman whose opinion means nothing to you."

I knelt beside Shana then, putting my hands on her knee. "We must move past this, my love." My wife paused in what she was doing to look at me. I could see great suffering in her eyes, which gave me no pleasure, but nor did it weaken my resolve, either. "I know you're angry with me, and I know why, but you have to understand that the reasons behind why I've made this decision are sound."

"You ask for my understanding for the choice that you made against my will, my lord," Shana said with a hint of derision in her voice. "As though it were a simple thing hardly worth mentioning. Yet, in the same breath, you make no attempt at understanding my fears and thoughts." She waved a hand. "I suppose because I'm just a silly woman, they don't count, just like my opinions, which have clearly become inconsequential to you. That's probably why you keep me locked up in here like some kind of prisoner so that I cannot voice them."

"That's not true," I protested. I'd asked Shana to stay in the cabin because I didn't want her subjected to a bunch of rowdy, naked Piths, and for no other reason—though I didn't think now would be the time to get into that. "Have I not taken your council many times since our marriage?" I asked instead. "Even over the advice of my own men? Of course I have, Shana, for your opinions have meant a great deal to me, and they always will. Few lords, if any, show the same consideration to their wives, which is something that, if I'm not mistaken, you have constantly reminded me over the years."

"Yes, well, maybe you've become more like those other lords than you think," Shana said with a sniff. "No doubt you'll be taking a mistress or two soon as well, just as they do. I'm actually surprised you didn't go to the island with the others so you could rut freely with those young Pith women."

I sat back on my heels, stunned by the bitterness in my wife's voice. I knew she didn't actually mean what she'd just said, yet it stung just the same.

Shana must have seen the look on my face, for her features softened. She cupped my cheek gently with her hand. "Forgive me, my lord. That was a hurtful thing for me to say. No matter what our differences may be at the moment, you did not deserve that. You are a good and kind man. No one knows that better than me. I'm just angry and hurt, is all, and I am truly sorry."

"I have always been faithful to you, my love," I said, taking Shana's hand in mine. "And I always will be." I kissed her soft skin while a part of my mind reminded me about Sabina and the moment we'd shared many years ago in a cave on Mount Halas. I thrust that thought away, locking it back up in the depths where it belonged. I looked at my wife. "I do not relish sending you away, but what choice is there for me? Surely you can see it from my point of view?"

"I can," Shana said gently. She extracted her hand, letting it fall into a fist in her lap. "But I know now that Jebido told you about the seer, and what I can't get past, my lord is that despite what you've learned, you still refuse to see it from mine."

"But they're just a bunch of damn rat bones," I grunted, unable to keep the frustration from my voice. "They mean nothing."

"They mean nothing to *you*," Shana corrected. "But not to me. And what if you're wrong about them, my lord? What if you send me away, and because you do, the prediction comes true? How am I supposed to feel then, with my children now fatherless and me a widow? Is that what you want to see happen?"

"Of course not," I said with a sigh. "But that could happen anyway, rat bones or not, despite my best efforts. It could have happened at any time during the many battles I've fought in, for that matter, or even when I go hunting with Baine and Jebido. Death can find a man in any number of ways, my love, because life is always a risk. But that doesn't mean I must live every day fearing my children might become fatherless and my wife a widow. I would go mad if I had to do that, afraid of every shadow and noise in the night."

"Which is exactly my point," Shana said triumphantly. "Because you're allowing that same fear to dictate my fate when you refuse to allow it to dictate yours."

"That's different," I replied stubbornly.

"How?" Shana challenged.

I hesitated, thinking. "Because my duty is to protect you and my family to the best of my ability. Which is what I am doing by sending you home."

"And what is my duty, then?" Shana asked, her eyes aglow now with aggression. "To obey your every whim and sit by the fireside, hoping that you'll come home each night?"

I knew the answer to that question was yes—at least regarding this particular issue, anyway—but I also knew voicing it out loud right now would only make matters worse between us. Shana and I had made some progress in the last few minutes, slight as it was, and I didn't want to lose that momentum by saying anything stupid. "Your duty is to protect our family at all costs, just as mine is," I finally said, knowing it probably wasn't what she wanted to hear. "That and give me the strength I need to accomplish what must be done."

I winced then, believing that I'd still managed to say the wrong thing despite my best intentions. But Shana surprised me. Her face softened, with tears shimmering in her eyes as she got down onto her knees in front of me. She put her hands on my cheeks, her nose touching mine as she stared into my eyes. "Which is exactly what I am trying to do, love of my life. I am trying to protect my family by staying by your side and keeping you alive to return to them. But I can't do that if I am hundreds of miles away from you." I opened my mouth to speak just as Shana put a hand to my lips. "No, don't say anything, please, Hadrack. I can't fight about this anymore tonight. Please, let's just stop talking about it. All I want right now is for my husband to hold me and tell me that everything will be all right."

I put my arms around my wife then, feeling her body trembling in my grip. "Everything will be all right," I whispered dutifully into her ear. "I promise."

"Thank you," Shana whispered back. She stood slowly then, and I thought I'd lost her back to the silence. But once again, she surprised me by holding her hand out to me. "Come to bed with me, Hadrack. Come and make me forget my fears for a while."

Hours later, I awoke with a start, staring up at the slanted roof of our cabin as *Sea-Wolf* creaked and groaned beneath me, shifting on the tide. An orange glow was coming in through the single round window on the starboard wall that I'd forgotten to shutter, reflecting off the boards above me. I thought I could hear faint shouts and cries carried on the wind, guessing that's what must have awoken me. I grimaced, knowing where the sounds were coming from before I stood, naked and shivering. I moved to the window and peered out toward the island, where I could see three separate bonfires roaring in the center of the darkened basin. I also thought I saw shadowy figures moving about around them. The Ascension Ceremony was still going on, it seemed. I closed the shutter gently as Shana mumbled in her sleep before I quietly dressed and grabbed my sword, then stepped outside.

The night sky was overcast, I noted as I strapped Wolf's Head around my waist. A single lantern on the aftercastle above me cast off weak light, revealing my crew and the wounded Piths sprawled out all across the main deck, sleeping. Only Tyris was awake, standing watch in quiet solitude near the lantern. I made my way up the ladder toward the archer, nodding a greeting to him where he stood near the starboard railing with his back to the island. I could hear the cries of the rutting Piths much clearer now, with the guttural groans and moans of pleasure unnaturally amplified by the basin and water.

"I was hoping that it would end soon, lord, so that I could get some peace," Tyris said to me with a chuckle. He shrugged, reaching out to absently stroke the oiled wood of the longbow that he always kept with him where it leaned against the railing. "That was over an hour ago."

"Have you gotten any sleep tonight?" I asked.

"A little," Tyris admitted. "Not much. I was restless, so I took the watch from Niko." The blond archer glanced at me curiously, a corner of his mouth twitching upward. "What about you, lord? Did you get any?"

I grinned. The cabin beneath the aftercastle had been added by Hanley after *Sea-Wolf* had already been built. The walls were far from thick, just simple planks, and I guessed that the entire ship's complement had probably heard Shana and me making love. Not that they'd likely been shocked by it, since my men had been sharing the confines of the ship with Piths for weeks already and had probably seen and heard it all by now.

"I managed to get some," I said. "I can take the watch now if you want to try again."

"If it's all the same to you, my lord," Tyris said. "I like it up here just fine." He took in a lungful of air, then let it out as his breath steamed around him. "I find it clears my mind and relaxes me." The blond archer grimaced and hooked a thumb over his shoulder. "Well, most of the time, anyway."

I chuckled, about to respond when I heard a faint splash come from the sea to the north. Beside me, Tyris had stiffened as well, having clearly heard it, too. I moved to the portside railing, peering into the darkness, but whatever it had been wasn't repeated a second time.

"Do you see anything, lord?" Tyris whispered as he came to join me.

I shook my head, not responding as I strained my ears. Tyris and I waited for a full minute, not moving, with only the sounds of sporadic cries coming from the island behind us. Finally, I shrugged, guessing that it must have been a fish that had come to the surface to feed. I turned away, only to notice a hint of movement out of the corner of my eye. I turned back and focused on the spot, my mind finally registering what I was seeing as a long, sleek ship sitting low in the water with black sails and a black hull slipped out from the darkness below us, bearing down on *Sea-Wolf*. I knew instinctively that the attackers had to be the Shadow Pirates I'd been hunting as men in dark armor using black-painted oars began to turn the ship, revealing several archers poised on the deck aiming up at where we stood.

"Get down!" I cried out in warning. I dropped to my knees, automatically dragging Tyris along with me. A moment later, something hissed over our heads, then the sharp clang of a metal broadhead striking the boss of one of the round Pith shields hung all along the railing of the aftercastle. I rolled away to the ladder, cupping my hands to my mouth. "To arms!" I screamed. "To arms! Prepare for boarders!"

"Lord!" Tyris called. The blond archer had an arrow already nocked in his bow as he pointed behind him. "We've got a second boat coming from the south!"

Tyris stood then, drawing his bow and shooting down at the original attacking ship as arrows continued to whip past his tall frame or thud into the shields. I was gratified to hear a strangled scream rise up from the water below moments later as I hurried down the ladder, already drawing Wolf's Head. Behind me, Tyris extinguished the lantern, leaving the ship bathed in almost total darkness.

Most of my men were scrambling out of their bedding by now, reaching for their weapons as their shouts of confusion filled my ears. I felt the deck beneath my feet shudder as something collided against *Sea-Wolf's* hull, knowing what that meant. I ran to the portside railing just as a grappling hook whistled through the air before latching onto the gunwale in front of me with a solid clunk. I slashed down at the rope without thinking, severing it, but even as I did, more grappling hooks appeared all along *Sea-Wolf's* length.

"Putt!" I shouted, cutting another line as the former outlaw appeared at my side with Niko and the rest of my crewmen. I did a mental count in my head. I had five sailors, Jebido, Tyris, Putt, and Niko, to defend the ship, along with three badly injured Piths that I doubted I could count on. That was all. "Take Niko and three men with you and protect our starboard side. We've got more company coming that way. Don't let them get on board."

"I won't, my lord," Putt promised grimly.

I glanced at Jebido and the remaining two crewmembers. One of them was a short lad of around eighteen named Radolf. He held a pike in his hands as he shifted his feet back and forth on the deck nervously. The other sailor was a bald, hulking brute of a man named Walcott. I saw he clutched a sword in his massive right hand and hoped that the big man knew what to do with it.

"Nobody gets past us," I growled, ignoring an arrow that slapped into the deck near my foot.

"Yes, my lord," Walcott muttered in a deep voice. I sensed Radolf nodding beside him.

I looked up then in surprise as light suddenly filled the sky from a lantern tossed upward from the black ship. It spun end over end over our heads before shattering across *Sea-Wolf's* deck, igniting the planking. I cursed, hesitating in indecision.

"I'll deal with it, Hadrack!" Jebido shouted before he darted away just as another grappling hook took hold of the railing directly in front of me.

The hook was followed immediately by a dark figure appearing over the gunwale with a white painted face and long grey hair. I noticed the man had a curved sword clutched tightly between his teeth. The pirate saw me looming over him, and his eyes widened as I slashed at him backhanded, tearing a great gouge across his painted face. The man spat out his sword as he screamed, losing his grip before he tumbled backward out of sight. I looked down over the railing, grinning when I saw his twisted body lying on the deck of the black ship. My satisfaction was short-lived, however, for more of the white-faced bastards were climbing up the ropes beneath me.

I moved along the hull, stabbing and hacking at the attacking pirates with feverish intensity while Walcott emulated me, bellowing as he used his sword like a hammer. The big man was clearly inexperienced in wielding the weapon, but he made up for it with sheer brute strength and savagery. Behind us, Radolf was using his pike like a veteran of many battles, surprising me with his skill as he whirled and stabbed at any white face that got past our blades. But, despite our fierce determination, there were only the three of us—which meant we couldn't defend the entire length of the ship all at once.

I smashed the hilt of Wolf's Head into a pirate's face as he appeared over the railing, barely noticing when he fell. Then I groaned when I saw several dark forms jump over the gunwale along *Sea-Wolf's* bow before they dropped cat-like to the deck. I glanced behind me at Jebido, who was still trying to contain the flames, then at Walcott as his bald head gleamed in the firelight. I gestured to the railing. "Keep them back," I grunted. I turned to face the pirates who'd breached our deck. "I'll take care of those bastards over there."

"Lord!"

I glanced up at Tyris, who lifted a round shield in the air, then tossed it down to me. I caught the Pith shield one-handed, grateful to have it as I stalked toward the pirates. There were three of them now, with a fourth one hauling himself over the railing. Each man looked identical, with their black leather armor, gray hair, and white faces. It was quite unsettling, I had to admit.

"Care for some company, brother?"

I glanced to my right as one of the wounded Piths named Ekblad appeared beside me. He was bare-chested, with bandages wrapped around his midriff where a Cardian arrow had ripped into him. Ekblad carried a war-hammer in his right hand and a small battle-axe in his left.

"Glad for it, brother," I said. I saw another of the wounded Piths dragging himself up the ladder to the aftercastle with a bow and quiver of arrows across his back, while the third warrior was hopping on one leg as he tried to help Jebido douse the flames. I nodded toward our adversaries, who were spreading out on the deck as they advanced on us. "Which one do you want?"

"I'll take the ugly one with the white face," Ekblad growled.

I laughed. "So be it," I said. Then we charged.

Ekblad caught me by surprise with his speed, somehow managing to reach the first pirate two steps ahead of me despite his wound. The Pith easily deflected a sword thrust with his axe, then swung viciously with his hammer, shattering his opponent's jaw. That's all I saw before I slammed into the first pirate in front of me with my shield, pushing him back with the power of my legs. The man grunted in surprise, knocked against the railing as I twirled, sweeping Wolf's Head down and severing a second pirate's leg just below the knee. The pirate howled, dropping his weapon before falling to the deck, clutching at the spurting stump. I drew my foot back and kicked hard, crunching in his nose and shattering his jaw with my boot, then stabbed downward into his chest, silencing his cries.

The fight had barely been joined, yet two of the pirates were already down, though more were leaping over the railing by the moment. I forged onward as the man I'd pushed against the sidewall recovered his wits and lunged at me with his sword. I lifted my arms, twisting my body sideways and the blade shot past me, then I brought the reinforced steel edge of my shield down hard on the pirate's unprotected head, splitting his skull open as blood splattered. I shoved him aside, barely noticing as he flipped over the railing. I focused on a small man holding two knives in his hands. His stance and look reminded me of Baine, and I edged forward cautiously, knowing if this little pirate had half the skill that my friend did, then I needed to be careful.

The pirate smiled at me, revealing long-decayed teeth. "Come greet your death, Ganderman," he hissed. It was the first words that I'd heard spoken by any of the Shadow Pirates since the attack had begun.

I said nothing, knowing every moment lost here meant more of the enemy were getting on board. I lunged without warning with Wolf's Head, not surprised when the little man darted with blinding speed to the side, already striking like a rock snake for my eyes with his knives. It was a move I'd seen Baine do a hundred times and one that I was prepared for. I swept my shield up to protect my head, feeling two sharp raps on the wood as the pirate's blades impacted, then I dropped to my knees and shoved upward with my sword beneath my shield. Wolf's Head easily pierced the pirate's leather armor and kept going, ripping through bones and cartilage before stopping at his heart. The pirate dropped like a stone at my feet, even as I heard a shrill whistle piercing the night air over and over.

I stood at the sound, pausing in surprise when the surviving pirates began to retreat, with many of them jumping back over the railing to their ship. I moved cautiously to the gunwale and looked down, where I saw the shadowy figure of an enormous man with a flowing beard standing in the prow of the boat. His arms were crossed over his chest as he stared up at me. We held each other's gaze for a moment until finally, the oarsmen began to push the longboat away from *Sea-Wolf's* hull.

I lifted my sword to the pirate. "We'll meet again soon, you and I."

"That we will, Wolf," the man called back as the ship turned away and retreated, chased by arrows from Tyris and the wounded Pith. "That we will."

I glanced behind me after the black ship had finally disappeared back into the night from where she'd come, noting that our starboard side was clear of the enemy as well. Putt and the others were now helping Jebido put the finishing touches on extinguishing the fire on *Sea-Wolf's* deck, while behind them in the water, I could see the dark forms of Piths lit up by the bonfires on the island swimming madly toward us.

I understood now why the pirates had retreated and I grinned, though my good mood turned to sudden anger and fear a moment later when I saw Shana standing by the railing near our cabin. My wife held a sword in her hand, with the point at the throat of a pirate who was kneeling on the deck with his hands on his head. I hurried over to them, pushing aside Shana's sword. The pirate looked up at me, his mouth opening to say something. I didn't give him a chance, backhanding him across the face and sending him tumbling to the deck.

"Niko," I growled. I pointed to the prostrate pirate. "Tie this bastard up."

"Yes, my lord," Niko said as he and one of the crewmen hurried to do my bidding.

I turned on Shana, my fury turning to dread when I saw blood splattered all over her white tunic.

"It's not mine, my lord," Shana hurried to say. "So you need not worry." She brushed hair from her eyes, looking strangely content and relaxed as she pointed to a dead pirate lying nearby. "It's his blood." Shana lifted her chin proudly. "And I killed him." She motioned to the prisoner with the sword she held. "And I captured that one over there, too." One of her eyebrows rose then in a way that I knew well as she regarded me steadily. "I imagine having one of these bastards alive to question will help, no?"

I just stared at my wife in amazement, for the moment, speechless. After all, what could I say to that? She was right.

Chapter 8: Fanrissen

"You've been doing what?" I thundered at Jebido in disbelief ten minutes later.

My friend had just informed me that he'd been training Shana with a sword for over a year now, and that's why she'd been able to defend herself so admirably. It was the first I'd heard of it. We stood on the main deck, surrounded by some of the now-clothed Piths and my men as I stalked back and forth in front of Jebido. We'd thankfully suffered no casualties during the failed attack, and the rest of the Pith archers were keeping a wary eye on the sea from both the forecastle and the aftercastle. I doubted the Shadow Pirates would come back again this night, but even so, I was taking no chances.

Shana moved to stand beside Jebido and she placed her hand on his shoulder, making it clear whose side she was on while he simply waited, watching me with calm eyes. I glanced at our prisoner where he sat with his arms tied with rope around the mast and his feet jutting out on the deck. The pirate looked surprisingly relaxed, considering his current situation. I'd learned his name was Savad Fanrissen, but that was all so far. I intended to change that fact soon, but needed to vent my displeasure with Jebido first.

"I asked him to do it, my lord," Shana said as I resumed my angry pacing. "So if you need to yell at someone about this, then, by all means, yell at me."

I paused to look at her. "Why didn't you tell me what you two were doing?"

"Because I didn't want you to know," Shana simply said. "Besides, I knew you'd disapprove."

I shook my head in disgust, then moved to Jebido, where I stood towering over him. I poked a finger against his chest. "This is your fault. You should have known better. How could you betray me like this?"

"There seemed no harm to it at the time, Hadrack," Jebido said. "It began as just a way for the Lady to get exercise after little Alline could walk on her own."

"Oh, no harm to it, you say?" I grunted. "You gave my wife a false sense of confidence that could have gotten her killed just now, Jebido. She's never been in battle before, but because of you and your *training*, she took on not one but two pirates. This isn't playing with little wooden swords in the courtyard at Corwick, you know. This is real."

"I'm still here, aren't I, my lord?" Shana snapped. "So maybe give Jebido and me some credit."

I just glared at my wife as Jebido cleared his throat. "I did not know the Lady would come out from her cabin during the attack, Hadrack," he said evenly. "Nor that she would join in the defense of the ship. How could I? We had bigger problems at the time. But that said, the lass is quite accomplished. I have a great deal of faith in her abilities."

"You have faith in her abilities, do you?" I sneered sarcastically. Down deep, I knew I was on the verge of losing control, but it appeared to me as if everyone here—my wife included—seemed determined to get her killed long before we ever reached Carte.

"Yes, I do," Jebido replied. "And that with only a little over a year's worth of instruction. She's even better at this point than you were when I trained you."

I snorted. "I was just a boy then, Jebido. A slave eating slop like a hog and working twelve hours a day non-stop. It hardly bears comparison."

"Perhaps," my friend said with a shrug. "But either way, Lady Shana shows great promise with the sword."

"I don't care," I growled. I pointed at Shana. "Don't you ever let me see a weapon in your hands again."

Shana's eyes flashed. "And what if you do?"

I ignored that, turning my resentful gaze back on Jebido instead. "I expected better from you," I said bitterly.

"And I, you," Jebido replied sourly.

I hesitated, trying to contain my anger as we locked gazes. Baine must have seen something in my eyes, for he stepped between Jebido and me, pushing me back gently. "We don't have time for this petty bickering, Hadrack. What happened tonight is over, and now we need to move on from it." Baine gestured toward our prisoner. "And the best way to do that is to find out what that bastard over there knows. Not fighting among ourselves."

I took a deep breath, realizing that Baine was right. I glanced around the silent ship. Everyone on board was watching me, wearing similar expressions of disapproval on their faces, even Saldor. I've learned over the years as a commander of men that moral was imperative if you wanted to succeed. No leader, no matter how good he was, could win without the hearts, minds, and respect of those who followed him. That was something Einhard had been a master at accomplishing, and something that I'd worked hard to emulate. I knew I hadn't lost the respect of my men—yet—but I could tell that if I continued down the path I was on, I would eventually.

I felt my anger slowly dissipating, replaced with remorse for my actions. I thrust my hand out toward Jebido. "Once again, I've been a fool," I said to him. "Please, forgive me."

"You've burned hot and fast from the moment I met you, lad," Jebido said as we locked forearms. "But what makes you the man you are is that you're smart enough to see past it." He clapped me on the shoulder. "But I think if anyone deserves an apology here, it's Lady Shana, not me." He lifted a bushy silver eyebrow. "Don't you?"

I nodded and turned to my wife, taking her hands in mine. "I am sorry for my outburst, my love. It's been a trying day. When I saw you covered in blood like that, I almost lost control of my senses. Forgive me."

"It's been a trying day for all of us, my lord," Shana said, bowing her head slightly. I could tell by the twin circles of red burning high on her cheeks that my wife was not completely satisfied with my apology. But even so, it was clear she understood that there would be time later, once we were alone in the privacy of our cabin, to talk more freely about what had happened.

I kissed Shana's hand, then turned my thoughts to what came next as I glanced at Putt, where he stood next to Niko. "Have the crew throw the bodies of the dead into the sea," I ordered. I looked down at *Sea-Wolf's* blood-smeared deck. "And wash that foulness away. I don't want any trace of those murderous bastards left on my ship."

"Yes, lord," Putt said.

I turned to Jebido and Baine after that. "I think it's time for some answers from our guest," I told them.

Baine removed a knife from a sheath at his back. "Would you like me to do the honors, Hadrack?"

"No, I don't think we need to resort to that just yet," I said, loud enough for the pirate to hear me. I moved to stand over him with my hands on my hips. Some white paint had come off the prisoner's cheeks and the tip of his nose, giving him an almost comical look. But even so, I found it impossible to guess the man's age with all the gray powder in his hair and beard. Jebido and Baine followed me, with Jebido holding up a lantern so we could see. Fanrissen just blinked up at us in the harsh light, saying nothing, so I crouched down until I was at eye level with him. "Do I need to poke some holes in you before you'll talk to me?" I asked him in a threatening voice.

The pirate stared at me steadily as if weighing my resolve, then glanced at Baine's knife before slowly shaking his head. The man didn't look afraid to me, more resigned than anything else. "No, lord. I'll tell you what I can."

"That's the right answer," I said approvingly. "Because I have some questions for you, Pirate, starting with how you found us so quickly."

"Lord?"

"Tonight. How did you find us? The Western Sea is a big place."

"We've had ships out searching for you ever since your escape from Blood Ring Isle, lord," Fanrissen said. "The information we had was that you were heading west to Parnuthia, so it wasn't that difficult. We caught sight of your sail this morning and followed you here." He almost smiled then. "Your ship is big and breaks the horizon easily, lord, while ours are much smaller and do not."

"Ah," I said, nodding my head in understanding. I realized the information about us heading to Parnuthia could only have come from that worm Wentile. "So, there is a connection between the Shadow Pirates and that bastard Overseer, then?" Fanrissen hesitated, looking suddenly wary. I grabbed his right ankle without warning, twisting it savagely until he cried out. "Now, you listen to me!" I hissed, not letting the pirate go. It felt good to unleash some of my pent-up anger on something other than my own people. "The only thing keeping you alive right now is your ability to talk. So you better keep doing just that, or I promise you a long, horrible death this night, the likes of which you can't even imagine. Do you understand me?"

"Yes, lord," Fanrissen managed to gasp. "I understand."

I released him then and the pirate sagged back against the mast, sucking in gulps of air. I could tell he was afraid now—who wouldn't be in his place?—but he was doing his best to retain his composure. I was greatly impressed. "I'm glad we understand each other," I said. "Now, how are the Shadow Pirates and Overseer connected?"

Fanrissen hesitated again and I casually dropped my hand back to his ankle. "Captain Bear is his younger brother, lord," the pirate hurried to say.

"Captain Bear?" I thought back to the big man I'd seen on the pirate ship, knowing somehow that it must have been him. "He's your leader?"

"Yes, lord. His real name is Alfonce Wentile. Everyone calls him Captain Bear, though, because of his great size."

"All right," I grunted. "And these brothers are partnered together in the slave trade, is that right?"

"Yes, lord," Fanrissen said. "That and sharing in any plunder from the ships we take."

I waved that last part away as inconsequential. I cared only about finding Alesia and Einrack. "Tell me about the slaves. Who sells them, the Shadow Pirates or the Overseer?"

"The Overseer, lord," Fanrissen answered, looking cautious now. "We deliver them to him on Blood Ring Isle for assessment."

"Are they sold there as well?" I asked, feeling growing excitement that Alesia and Einrack might still be back on Blood Ring Isle. I vowed if they were, then the island would receive a second visit from me. And this time, I'd make sure to raze the entire place to the ground before cutting out the Overseer's heart. Fanrissen hesitated as a trickle of drool slipped out from one corner of his mouth and ran down into his powdered beard. "Well?" I prodded.

"No, lord," Fanrissen said. "They're shipped somewhere else for sale."

"I see," I said. "How long do new slaves stay on the Isle before they're moved?"

Fanrissen shrugged. "A week, usually, lord. No more than that."

"Damn," I grunted, sharing a disappointed look with Jebido before turning back to the pirate. "Where are they shipped?"

Fanrissen shifted his eyes away from me. "That I cannot tell you, lord."

I growled low in my chest and leaned forward, placing my hand deliberately on the pirate's ankle again. "You might wish to reconsider your position, my friend. If you don't answer me right now, I promise I'll break it this time, and then I'll start to work on the other one."

Fanrissen's face was filled with apprehension, but he surprised me by shaking his head emphatically from side to side. "Do what you must, lord, for I dare not answer. Ask me anything else but that, and I'll gladly tell you what you want to know."

"All I want to know is where the slaves are kept," I said. "And believe me, Pirate, you won't enjoy what I'm going to do to you if you don't give me what I want."

"I cannot tell you, lord," Fanrissen said firmly.

I frowned, perplexed by the man's behavior. "Why not?"

"Because that bastard will find out," the pirate replied. "And when he does, he will kill my wife and child." Fanrissen took a deep breath. "I've seen him do it before, lord. I can't take that chance. So, do what you must with me, but I will not tell you the location."

I sat back on my haunches. "You're talking about this Captain Bear? That's who you're afraid of?"

Fanrissen nodded slowly. "Yes, lord. I'm sorry. If it were just me to worry about, I would tell you."

Baine stepped forward then with hard, dark eyes, his knife poised to strike. I held up a hand, stopping him as I stayed focused on the pirate. "What if I guarantee no harm will come to your family, and when I find this Captain Bear, that I'll kill him?"

The pirate examined me with experienced eyes. "You clearly are a formidable warrior, lord. But not even you can kill a man like that. He's unbeatable."

I chuckled at that while my men and the Piths all laughed. All men were beatable—the only trick was finding out how.

"Do you know who it is you're talking to?" Jebido asked with a snort. "This is the Wolf of Corwick, fool."

"Yes, I know who he is," Fanrissen replied in an even tone. He turned his gaze on me. "I have heard the stories about you, lord. But it won't matter how good you are. Captain Bear is better."

"Chieftain," Saldor grunted, stepping forward. "Give this man to me and my brothers and sisters. Do that, and I promise you'll have what you seek soon enough."

I hesitated, tempted as I studied Fanrissen. The pirate was scared, but not for his own safety. That was clear. I could sense an aura of determination about him. A steel-like resolve that I suspected would be tough to break through, even for Piths. And as much as I needed information from this man, I couldn't help but admire the dedication he was showing to his family. Would I have acted any different if I were in his place and my wife and child were threatened?

I glanced at Baine, coming to a decision. "Cut him free."

My friend gaped at me. "What?"

"You heard me," I grunted as I stood. I gestured down to the pirate. "Cut him free."

Baine hesitated a moment longer, then he shrugged and did as I asked. Once the pirate's bonds were cut away, I helped the man to his feet as he stared at me in confusion. "Would you care for some beer?" I asked pleasantly.

Fanrissen blinked in surprise, and then he bobbed his head. "Yes, lord. Very much."

I nodded to Niko, who frowned, but went to get the beer anyway. I waited in silence until he'd returned and the pirate had drunk his fill.

"Now," I said, taking the wooden mug from him. "I understand and respect your devotion to your family, for I have a wife and children of my own." I sighed. "But, having said that, I also have a sworn duty to a friend who died while trying to save *his* family." I paused, studying the pirate to see what effect my words were having. Fanrissen wouldn't meet my eyes, though I could tell he was listening intently. "Most of that family were murdered by you people, and his wife and eldest son were taken as slaves. That's why we're here, to get them back."

Fanrissen looked up at me then, regret and sorrow evident on his face. He opened his mouth to say something, then he closed it, his expression hardening. I knew I'd lost him.

I shook my head at the needless waste. "Which means, Pirate, that you and I have a big problem. Because I have to know what you know, and trust me, I'll do whatever it takes to get that information from you."

Fanrissen absently wiped foam from the beer off his beard with the back of his hand as he looked back down at the deck. I noticed that his hand was steady, which impressed me even more. "I am truly sorry, lord, that I cannot help you. I do not believe that I am a bad man, though I confess I have done bad things in my life." He looked around at my crew and the silent Piths. "But who among us has not? I was young and headstrong when I joined these pirates, and not a day has gone by since that I wish that I hadn't."

"Why not leave, then, if you are so unhappy with them?" I asked.

"No one leaves Captain Bear, lord," Fanrissen said. "Not alive, anyway."

I took a deep breath as I thought. My gut told me Fanrissen was exactly what he claimed to be—a good man in a bad situation. But even so, I had made a promise to Einhard on his deathbed, and that promise could not be broken. It seemed that we'd come to an impasse, the pirate and me. One that I knew I could not allow to continue any longer.

"I don't want to kill you," I finally said, meaning it. I shook my head regretfully. "I don't want to torture you, either. But unless you tell me what I want to know right now, you'll leave me no choice in the matter."

"I understand, lord," the pirate replied calmly. He squared his shoulders as he locked eyes with me. "I am ready. But I promise you I will not talk, regardless of what you do to me."

"I pray for both of us that you're wrong about that," I said grimly as I turned to Niko. "Get me a rope. A long one."

"Yes, lord."

I waited, catching Shana's eye for a moment, gratified when she gave me a nod of encouragement. What was about to happen wouldn't be pleasant, but all on board knew how imperative the pirate's information was for us, including my wife. I briefly considered sending her back to our cabin until it was over, then decided against it. Shana was a part of this expedition, too—at least for now—which was something that I needed to remember. Even the mighty oak needs to bend in the wind sometimes to keep from breaking, and my letting her remain was a perfect example of that.

"You sure you don't want me to motivate him?" Baine asked as he came to stand beside me. He glared at the pirate, who stared back at him with an almost disinterested expression.

I shook my head. "No. Something tells me a blade, no matter how expertly wielded, won't help persuade this one to talk."

Niko returned moments later with a length of coiled rope. "Tie his feet," I ordered. "Make sure it's good and tight." Niko did as I asked, double-knotting just in case as I turned to face Fanrissen again. "Tell me where Captain Bear is, Pirate, and you have my word that I'll let you live."

"Yes, but by living, I'll be condemning my wife and daughter to death," the pirate replied. "So, respectfully, lord, it's an easy choice for me to make."

"You damn fool," I grunted, shaking my head. "Just remember, this is your fault, not mine."

I took the free end of the rope from Niko and wrapped it twice around my left wrist as the pirate watched me with a blank face. Then I grabbed the man by the front of his leather armor and dragged him unresisting to the gunwale, where I held him halfway over the railing so that he was staring down at the dark water below.

"This is your last chance," I growled. "Tell me!"

I waited, letting what was about to happen sink in, but Fanrissen stayed limp in my arms and never said a word. Finally, losing patience, I cursed and flipped the man over the side. The pirate remained silent as he fell, splashing moments later into the water. Jebido brought his lantern closer and he held it over the side as I looked down at the man while he forced his way to the surface. When he started treading water, I began to haul upwards on the rope, using the railing for leverage until Fanrissen was suspended upside-down. Then I lowered him again until his head and shoulders were beneath the waves. The pirate was not tall, but he was thick in the body and weighed a considerable amount. But I was a strong man and wanted to send a clear message to him, so I worked alone despite offers of help.

    I waited and watched as Fanrissen thrashed his arms wildly, banging and thudding against *Sea-Wolf's* hull before finally he contorted his body, lifting his head out of the water and gasping for needed air. I let him have some, and then I lowered him again until he was down to his waist in the surf. I counted to five, then dragged him back up until his hair grazed the water as he spluttered and spat out seawater.

    "I can do this all night!" I shouted down to the pirate before I lowered him back into the water again. I repeated the process ten more times before my arms finally began to tire. The Piths and my men had all run to the railing to watch the moment the pirate had entered the water, and I glanced at Saldor, who stood nearby. "Help me pull him up," I grunted.

    The Amenti chieftain and I hauled Fanrissen to the railing and dragged his saturated body back over it, where he fell on his stomach to the deck in a soggy mess, coughing and gagging.

    I dropped to my knees and grabbed the pirate's wet hair, dragging his head up so he could see me. The paint was all gone now, as was the powder, revealing what might have been a handsome face if not for his distorted features and bulging eyes. "Tell me," I grunted. "Tell me where the slaves are sold and this ends."

    "Never, lord," Fanrissen spat out.

I cursed, ignoring the man's cry as I pulled him to his feet by his hair, then flung him over the side once again.

"That's one tough bastard, Hadrack," Jebido grunted, peering downward as the pirate plunged into the water for a second time. "It's a damn shame, really."

I said nothing, waiting until Fanrissen had resurfaced before Saldor and I suspended him upside-down once again with his upper body submerged in water. Around us, the Piths and my men were in a festive mood, betting now on how long it would take for the pirate to either die or give in. I noticed Shana among them, her face set in a grim mask as she stared down at the struggling man, but at least she wasn't laying bets.

"All right," I growled at Saldor after five minutes of raising and lowering the pirate. "Let's bring him back up again."

This time when the pirate landed on the floor, he lay unmoving, and I thought for a moment that we'd killed him. But Fanrissen suddenly gasped, bucking on the decking as seawater exploded from his mouth before he turned on his side. He retched loudly, the sound hoarse and rattling as he heaved up more water from his lungs. No one moved to help him, all of us watching dispassionately as the horrible noises continued for several long minutes.

Finally, I lowered myself to my knees beside the pirate when he was done. "It doesn't have to go this way for you," I said, trying to sound reasonable. "Just tell me what I want to know. I give you my word as the Lord of Corwick, witnessed by all here that no harm will come to your family if you do."

"I...I can't take the chance, lord," the pirate whispered. He pushed himself up until he was half-sitting, staring at me stubbornly as he wiped the wetness from his eyes. "I wish I could believe you. I truly do, lord. But I know what Captain Bear is capable of. You don't."

"How will he even know you told us?" I asked in frustration. "The man no doubt believes you're dead. Don't you realize you're throwing your life away for nothing?"

"He'll know, lord," Fanrissen rasped. "He always does. So you might as well just throw me back in the water and get the damn thing over with."

I sighed wearily, about to comply when Shana appeared by my side. She knelt on the deck beside me, placing her hand on my arm. "Lord, there has to be another way."

"Another way?" I said bitterly. I gestured to the drenched pirate. "This damn fool is determined to die."

"Only because—" Fanrissen started to say.

"Yes, I know your reason for not talking, Pirate," I said, cutting him off. "And I'll grant you that it's a good one. But so is mine for being here, which takes precedence over yours." I gestured to Baine, waving him over as I focused back on Fanrissen. "I need you to talk. But unfortunately, it appears my way isn't working, so it's time for a new approach. Maybe the taste of my friend's steel will get your tongue wagging after all. We'll soon see."

"Wait, my lord," Shana said urgently, lifting a hand to stop Baine. "Let me talk to him first."

"What good will that do?" I asked as Fanrissen hacked up a glob of wet green bile beside me. "You've seen how determined this man is. What can words do now that the ocean could not?"

"I don't know," Shana said. "But I want to try. All Baine is going to do is make matters worse."

I sighed, glancing up at Saldor, who shook his head. I shifted my gaze to Jebido. "What do you think?"

Jebido shrugged. "What's another few minutes, Hadrack? If the Lady can't get him to talk, then I say we let Baine have a go at him. And if that doesn't work, then there's always the Piths to fall back on. Sooner or later, he's going to break."

"Or die on us," I grumbled.

"Yes, well, there is that to consider," Jebido agreed. He gestured to Shana. "But words can't kill anyone the last I looked, so maybe we should give the lass a chance."

I glanced up at the slowly brightening sky, then nodded and turned to Shana. "Dawn should be here in about an hour. I'll give you until then. After that, his blood starts to flow and the screams start."

"I'll have the location by then, my lord," Shana said confidently. "You'll see."

But my wife was wrong about that. She got what we needed from the pirate well before the sun rose.

Chapter 9: Ravenhold

I rarely gave much thought to philosophy when I was a younger man. No, I was more suited to crashing into shield walls and battling with my enemies than spending time lost in deep contemplation about the world's many mysteries. That all changed as I grew steadily older, and a quill and ink became much more preferable to me than swinging a sword and shedding another man's blood. I suppose such things are far from unusual as a man's life progresses from youth to middle age and then into his twilight years.

I still recall that cool morning when Shana changed the pirate's mind and how amazed I'd been, thinking that women were fascinating, mysterious creatures compared to us. We were the ones who built things out of stone and wood with hammers and nails, utilizing our strength, sweat, blood, stubbornness, and ingenuity to raise great cities and wondrous buildings. But, for every structure that we built, there was another one torn down somewhere by violence, for we men are without question an unruly, quarrelsome lot.

I make no apologies for it, though, for I believe that is the purpose as to why we exist, always ready at a moment's notice to take up a sword to protect those we love or to fight on behalf of our king or land. The gods clearly had made us this way, and who was I to say whether they were right or wrong? Perhaps that aggression and belligerence we show as men is what makes us successful in this cruel, harsh world of ours. But then again, maybe that's why the world is so cruel and harsh to begin with, too.

I remember thinking that women like my wife were as different from men as a thorn bush was to a lily flower or a daisy. For the most part, females are gentler, softer, and more compassionate than males—well, except for Piths, I suppose, for even flowers can have thorns sometimes. When something stands in the way of a man, his first instinct is to bash it aside using brute force, where women like my wife must take a different path around it, leaving violence as a last, unsavory resort. Sometimes the male approach seems the only way—at least it did to me back then—simply because it often works if you are determined enough, strong enough, and ruthless enough. But sometimes, like with the pirate, Fanrissen, that approach leads you nowhere, and a different way is the only chance at success.

"So," I said to Fanrissen that cool morning. He, Shana, Baine, and Jebido, along with Putt, Tyris, Niko, and Saldor, were all crowded together on *Sea-Wolf's* aftercastle with me. "Lady Shana informs me that you've agreed to tell us what we want to know. Is that true?"

"It is, lord," Fanrissen confirmed in an even voice.

I thought the pirate looked relaxed and calm now, despite his recent brush with death. His long hair was still partially wet but swept back from his forehead, where it hung down his back in thick strands well past his shoulder blades. I guessed that he couldn't be more than twenty-five years old. His beard was dark brown, long and pointed, and his eyes thoughtful and intelligent looking. Fanrissen's features were pleasantly handsome, with what I thought might be a trace of humor hiding in the slight creases around his eyes and mouth. I couldn't help but like the bastard.

I shifted my gaze to Shana, where she stood beside the pirate, looking quite pleased with herself. I could hardly begrudge her for that. "Tell me then," I said to Fanrissen eagerly.

The pirate glanced sideways at my wife, who nodded encouragement. "I offer you my sword and my loyalty, lord," he said formerly. "All I ask in return is a pledge from you first before speaking of what I know."

"A pledge?" I said warily, caught off-guard. "I thought you were ready to talk to me?"

"I am, lord. But only if you agree to what I want."

"And if I refuse?'

Fanrissen's lips twitched. "Then I expect I'll be swimming with the fishes shortly once again, lord."

"Very well," I grunted, amused but unwilling to show it. "What is it you ask of me?"

"Your solemn vow, lord, that regardless of what happens when we get to our destination, your first task will be to locate my wife and daughter and ensure that they are safe. And, once you've done what you came here to do, you will take them back with you and make a place for them within your castle in Ganderland. Offer my family a good and full life, lord, and I swear that I will follow you to the ends of this world and beyond for as long as I am able."

I hesitated. The pirate's request was no small thing, for as anyone who knew me could attest, I took vows like this very seriously. The problem I faced, though, was as obvious to me as a single black cow grazing in a flock of white sheep. If I gave Fanrissen what he wanted, then there was a good chance that promise might conflict at some point with my vow to Einhard. I had no idea what I would do then if it did. I glanced at Shana as I mulled things over. My wife had clearly orchestrated this, and I wondered if she'd thought it through first and had realized where it could potentially lead.

"It's the only way, my lord," Shana said softly, looking suddenly apprehensive as she sensed my reservations.

"This could become a problem later," I muttered. "For all of us."

"I think it's a chance that we need to take, Hadrack," Jebido said as the rest of my men, along with Saldor, all nodded. "He's already proven that torture won't make him talk."

"Yes, he has at that," I agreed as I studied the pirate. "And what of you?" I asked him as I absently stroked my beard. "What assurances do you ask for yourself?"

"None, lord," Fanrissen stated with a shake of his head. "I do not expect to live that long."

"You think I will kill you?" I grunted in surprise.

The pirate shook his head. "No, lord. But I think Captain Bear will. I believe the gods will make certain of it." He shrugged. "But if that is my fate, then so be it. As long as I go to meet The Father knowing that my family is safe, then I will greet death with no regrets."

"What makes you think I won't go back on my vow and just toss you overboard once I have what I want from you?"

Fanrissen slowly smiled. "Honor, lord," he said. "Something that Lady Shana assures me you possess in abundance."

I pursed my lips. The bastard was right, of course, and we both knew it. Once I gave my word on something, I would rather die than go back on it. "I imagine I have you to thank for this?" I finally said, turning to Shana.

"It was the only solution I saw available to us, my lord," my wife replied. "I am sorry, but it was necessary."

I nodded, taking a deep breath before finally I offered Fanrissen my hand. Shana was right. It was the only solution. "You have my pledge," I told the pirate. "Everything you asked for will be done." We briefly locked forearms before I stepped back and crossed my arms over my chest. "Now, where are the slaves sold?"

"A place called Ravenhold, lord," Fanrissen replied immediately.

I looked at Putt, who shrugged. "And where is that, exactly?" I asked.

"Five hundred miles due south of here, lord," Fanrissen answered. "It's an island citadel thirty miles off the southern coast of Swailand."

I frowned at that. I had a vague notion of where Swailand was, since Aenor, a woman who had briefly been my lover before my marriage to Shana, had come from there. I also knew that the city of Carte, where I'd intended to put Shana on a boat for home, was an equal distance or more away to the northwest from *Sea-Wolf's* current position. I caught a momentary gleam in my wife's eyes before she looked down at the deck, and I did my best to ignore it as I debated what to do.

"How long are slaves kept in this place before they're sold," Jebido asked into the silence.

"Not long," Fanrissen answered. "Market Day is held on the last day of each month."

"And are all the slaves sold every month?" Baine wanted to know.

"Usually, but not always," Fanrissen admitted.

"So, whichever ones are not sold on Market Day, they remain on the island until the following month?" my friend asked.

"That's correct," the pirate agreed. He glanced at Saldor. "But if it's Pith slaves you hope to find at Ravenhold, then I fear you will be greatly disappointed."

I thrust all thoughts of Shana and Carte from my mind as I focused on the present. I would deal with that problem later. "Why?" I grunted.

"Because Piths are highly sought after, lord. I have never seen one passed over until the following Market Day."

"There was an attack on a Pith fortress about a month ago?" I said as I processed what the pirate was saying. "Are you aware of it?"

"Yes, lord."

"And were you there?" I asked him, my words low and unfriendly now.

Fanrissen shook his head. "No, lord, I wasn't. I was on garrison duty in Ravenhold when that particular raid happened. Each of us rotates from the walls to the ships every two weeks."

"I see," I said, relieved. I hadn't wanted to think this man might have had anything to do with the slaughtering of Einhard's family. "Did Captain Bear lead the attack on the Piths?"

"Yes, lord," the pirate said before he hesitated. "He said that it was easy."

Saldor growled at that and stepped forward. "Easy, you say? I'll teach you easy, dog!"

I put a hand on the Pith's arm, stopping him. "What's done is done, brother. It's what we do now in revenge of Einhard that matters." I gestured to Fanrissen. "And this man is the point of the blade that we'll use to tear these bastards apart." Saldor stepped back, glaring at Fanrissen with little love in his eyes as I focused on the pirate again. "Why go all the way to the land of the Piths for slaves? Surely there are closer prey?"

"And why take mainly children?" Baine added.

Fanrissen glanced at Baine before answering me. "The Overseer has customers from all across the world, lord, even Ganderland." I pursed my lips at that. King Tyden had outlawed slavery in Ganderland several years ago, so hearing it still existed was something of a surprise to me. I motioned for the pirate to continue. "Children are highly prized for any number of jobs," Fanrissen added. "From mining coal in Cardia where the tunnels are narrow, to collecting salt in the Friesian desert, not to mention domestic duty in the great cities of Parnuthia and Cardia. Children are also easier to train than older slaves, who can be troublesome, and you get many more years of service from them. It's all about productivity and cost-efficiency, lord."

"But why Piths?" I asked. "And why now? My understanding is that the Shadow Pirates only started to raid their lands recently."

"That's true, lord," Fanrissen said. "Most of the slaves traditionally came from Swailand until now. But the quality of the supply there has dwindled in recent years, while at the same time demand has steadily been increasing."

"Which means the pirates needed to go further out," I grunted in disgust.

"Yes," Fanrissen said. "It wasn't safe anymore to raid Ganderland's coasts or Parnuthia's, either, for that matter. Both kingdoms have grown in strength, and the brothers feared that if the raids became too much of a nuisance to them, something would be done about it."

"So, that's why you turned your eyes to the land of the Piths," Saldor grunted, his nostrils flaring with suppressed anger.

"Yes," Fanrissen agreed. "One of Captain Bear's ships attacked a Pith encampment last year for the first time, and they were amazed by the children they took. Both the boys and the girls were much healthier and stronger than Swails, Parnuthians, or even Ganders of a similar age. Once these children were put up for auction, the price quickly tripled for them."

"Which no doubt made that greedy Overseer bastard very happy," I growled. "And that's why raids against the Piths have increased."

"True, lord," Fanrissen said regretfully.

I nodded as I began to pace back and forth. If only we'd been quicker, I thought in frustration. The last day of the month had been the previous week, which undoubtedly meant Alesia and Einrack had been sold by now and were already well on their way to their new destination. I paused as a realization struck me. It was entirely possible that the boy and his mother had been sold to separate owners, which meant things had just gotten that much more difficult for us.

"So, if the woman and the boy we seek are already gone," I said. "How do we find them? Do we go back to Blood Ring Isle and drag the information out of the Overseer?"

"I wouldn't recommend you try that, lord," Fanrissen said. "Hundreds of slaves are sold each month at Ravenhold, and it's doubtful that he would know anything about individual ones."

"But you said he's the one that sells the slaves," Jebido interrupted with a frown.

"By proxy only," the pirate explained. "The Overseer rarely makes the long journey to Ravenhold anymore. He has several agents who go back and forth now and take care of that task for him."

"Would he have a record of the sales, perhaps?" Shana asked.

Fanrissen shrugged. "I imagine it's possible, Lady. But getting to the Overseer would be very difficult, if not impossible, after the recent events involving you people." He glanced at me. "But either way, lord, my family are at Ravenhold, not Blood Ring Isle. So that is where we must go next."

I nodded, not surprised by Fanrissen's answer. His focus was clearly on his family and nothing else, as mine would be were I in his position. Besides, the pirate was right about going to Ravenhold, anyway. While I would dearly love the chance to carve up the Overseer, I doubted somehow that he'd let *Sea-Wolf* slip through the Isle's defenses a second time. I figured there must be some records kept at Ravenhold regarding each slave and who had bought them, so we would have to start there.

I glanced at Shana, knowing she was about to get the one thing she coveted the most—staying by my side. I now had two vows to fulfill, both of which led me to the south and away from Parnuthia. Taking the time to sail to Carte now just wasn't feasible, and I could tell by my wife's expression that she was well aware of that fact. All I could do now was pray to the gods that I wouldn't come to regret my decision later.

But unfortunately, the gods were busy and they weren't paying any attention to me.

I sat by a small fire, warming my hands as a half-moon and hundreds of twinkling stars looked down at me with equal disinterest from a dark, cloudless sky. Jebido lay beside me on the grass-covered hillock where we'd made camp the night before. He had a cloak lined with wolf's fur rolled up into a ball under his head, and his arms were crossed over his chest. My friend's eyes were closed, but I knew that he wasn't asleep—nor were the other four men lying around the fire with us, either. Each man was dressed in full armor and clutched a weapon close to hand beneath their bedding. I could hear the endless chirping of thousands of crickets in the fields around us while the deep bass of a lamenting bullfrog hidden somewhere in the sprawling, shadowy stand of trees nearby rose behind me. The frog wasn't the only thing hidden within those trees this night.

"Don't look directly into the flames, lad," Jebido grunted a moment later, not opening his eyes. "You won't be able to see in the dark when they come."

I just shook my head and said nothing, not needing to be told something so obvious. I think Jebido sometimes forgot that I wasn't a child with snot running down my nose anymore, but a grown man and a veteran of many battles. I looked east to the shoreline fifty yards below me as the tide hissed across the wet sand and loose shale before finally losing momentum and receding, only to repeat the process moments later in an endless cycle. I could see no sign of a ship anywhere, just white-tipped crests kissed by moonlight breaking against a rocky outcrop two hundred yards out in the water to my left.

I sighed as I looked down at my hands. It had been four days since the attack on *Sea-Wolf*, and despite my expectations and willingness to fight, Captain Bear and his Shadow Pirates had not returned to try again. I knew time was running out for Alesia and Einrack, so I'd come up with a plan that I hoped would give me a way into Ravenhold that no one would be expecting.

"What's the name of this place again, Pirate?" I whispered after a time.

"Anapos, lord," Fanrissen muttered from where he lay on his side facing me.

"Anapos," I repeated. The island was shaped like a bell, with a dense forest growing at the head that was slowly creeping northward toward the fatter body dominated by rocky hills and open fields. A small, inactive volcano rose in the center of the landmass, and I glanced behind me at its peak as the moonlight reflected off the circular rim. I turned away after a moment and sighed again as I looked once more at the ground. "And you're sure they'll come?"

"Oh, they will come, lord," Fanrissen answered. "Have no fear about that."

"That's what you said last night," Jebido grunted.

"Maybe they haven't gotten the message yet," I heard Niko suggest from the other side of the fire.

"It's possible," Fanrissen replied. "But trust me, they patrol all along the coast here at night, so we just need to be patient. They will come."

"Well, it better be soon," I grumbled, resentful that we had already lost two full days.

I threw a couple of pieces of driftwood on the flames, sending bright sparks snapping upward in an orange trail into the night sky. We were less than two miles off the northeastern tip of Swailand where it bordered a small kingdom known as Marcuria, which still left us a long way from our destination. But that couldn't be helped. *Sea-Wolf* was well-known to the pirates, and I knew there would be no chance of us getting her anywhere close to Ravenhold without being seen. Because of that fact, I'd hatched a plan with Fanrissen to capture one of the Shadow Pirate's black ships and try to sneak in instead.

"This Marcurian village you spoke of," I said to the pirate. "How long have they been working for Captain Bear?"

"Probably at least five years now," Fanrissen replied. He shrugged. "They didn't have much choice, really. It was either that or get slaughtered."

I nodded in understanding. That, unfortunately, was the way of our world in many places—comply or die. The village was called Tacot, a small fishing community that identified vessels traveling along the coast that might be rich with plunder and slaves and then relayed that information to the Shadow Pirates. Fanrissen had said that the pirates had the same deal with many of the villages all along Marcuria's and Swailand's coasts and that one of their ships was constantly traveling from one place to another.

We'd managed to get close to the shore near Tacot before dawn had broken yesterday without being seen, and I'd sent Baine, Putt, and Saldor overboard to steal one of the fishing boats there. Fanrissen insisted that a Shadow Pirate would contact them once they were out to sea using an agreed-upon signal—a single lantern hanging from the top of the fishing boat's mast at night. When the Shadow Pirates arrived, Baine was to tell them about a great cog shipwrecked near Anapos Island. He would also inform them that only a few men had survived the wreck and were now trapped on the island. *Sea-Wolf* wasn't wrecked, of course, but instead was anchored in a small cove at the top of the island's bell, where I prayed she wouldn't be seen.

I figured it was as good a plan as any, with a better than fair chance at success—assuming the pirates ever came, of course. I just needed to take Fanrissen's advice and remain patient until they did. An hour later, that advice and patience paid off. One moment I was staring out at an empty sea, and the next, I saw a sleek, dark form appear out of the gloom, heading directly for the beach below where we'd camped.

I prodded Jebido with my boot. "They're here," I whispered in relief.

"About damn time," Jebido grunted back.

I could sense my men tensing beneath their bedding, but none of them moved. I slowly stood and stretched, careful to keep my back to the water. "Remember," I said in a low voice. "Stay quiet until I say so."

I glanced toward the silent trees, then did a soft bird-whistle, signaling to the Piths waiting there that the pirates were coming. Then I stooped and threw some more wood on the fire, thinking that the more light my archers had, the better. I slowly moved to stand some distance away from the others, where I pretended to be taking a piss on a bush. I heard the muffled sounds of the approaching ship's oars that Fanrissen had told me were wrapped in cloth, then an unmistakable screeching noise as the boat's keel made landfall. I remained where I was, staring up at the night sky as if lost in thought, while the pirates ran stealthily up the beach behind me, with only the muted crunch of the shale beneath their boots giving them away.

Finally, when they reached the base of the hill, one of the pirates cried out, followed by the rest of them. It was intended to confuse and demoralize sleeping men, I knew, but we had a surprise in store for the bastards instead. I turned and drew my sword, though I made no move to attack. I counted at least twelve white-faced and grey-powdered men charging up the hill toward my camp just as several of them veered toward me.

I waited, letting them come until the first of the pirates reached the crest, then I shouted, "Now!"

Pith warriors immediately stepped out from the trees with their bows thrumming, sending at least four of the surprised pirates twisting and writhing to the ground. Several of them rolled back down the hill, tripping up those coming from behind. That's all I saw before my attackers were on me. The first man to reach me was short and built like a bull, and he bellowed like one too as he swung at me with his curved sword. I dodged to my left and spun in a tight circle, already swinging two-handed. My blade caught the pirate beneath his left armpit, cutting deep into bone and cartilage as he cried out and fell. I tore Wolf's Head from his flesh just in time to deflect the second pirate's attack. This man was of medium height, with strange eyes that seemed to glow in the firelight as they bulged out of their sockets around the white paint. I could see out of my peripheral vision that my men around the fire were now on their feet, engaging with the remaining pirates, while the Piths from the trees raced forward with swords and war-hammers. It would be over in moments.

I glanced toward the water, feeling alarm shoot through me when I saw two pirates who'd stayed behind with the ship trying to push it back off the shore in panic. I growled, knowing that all my careful planning would be for nothing if they succeeded. I focused back on my opponent, who was slashing his curved sword in front of him in wild arcs as he advanced. I snorted with contempt. If the pirate was trying to intimidate me, he was wasting his time, as all the fool had managed to do so far was cut through empty air and use up valuable energy.

I waited, letting the pirate come to me, then flicked my wrist when he was within reach and on one of his downstrokes, stabbing the tip of Wolf's Head into his dominant hand. The Shadow Pirate screamed and dropped his sword as if it had just come out of a red-hot forge. I grabbed the man by the front of his leather armor and flung him down the hill, then followed at a run. The pirate continued to cry out as he rolled end over end, with me charging down the hill after him. I took a quick glance toward the ship, relieved to see the two men there were having trouble as they frantically tried to push the hull off the muck and shale. I had time.

The rolling pirate finally came to rest on flat ground at the base of the hill, reaching it with me three paces behind. He lay stunned, whimpering now as I reversed Wolf's Head and stabbed downward even as I ran past him. Blood squirted and the whimpering stopped. I kept going. The two pirates working futilely to get their ship unstuck heard me coming, and they turned simultaneously. Both men drew their weapons as they automatically stepped apart, then stood crouched and ready as I approached. I nodded with approval. At least they had better form than the last fool I'd faced, not that it would do them any good.

"Wolf!"

I turned and looked back to see the Pathfinder, Hanon, waving me aside from where he stood at the crest of the hill. Pith archers were flanking him on either side with drawn bows, ready to let fly.

I turned back to the pirates and grinned. "I guess this just isn't your night."

I saluted the doomed men with my sword, then skipped to my left as dark shafts shot through the air, taking down the pirates. I closed my eyes and took out my brother's Pair Stone from where it still hung around my neck after all these years, then said a quick prayer to The Mother.

The ship was ours. Now it was on to Ravenhold.

Chapter 10: Storming the Citadel

"This damn paint is driving me out of my mind," Jebido grumbled from behind me.

"Well, stop picking at it, then," I grunted over my shoulder. "It only makes things worse when you do that."

My friend had been lamenting about the thick white paint smeared across his face for over half an hour now, and I was getting really tired of listening to his complaining. I had to admit that it did feel unpleasant against the skin, though, especially when it got wet. But at least Jebido's hair and beard were already gray and he didn't need the odd-smelling powder that the rest of us wore to look like a Shadow Pirate.

I stood in the prow of the captured longboat, one hand steadying me on a stay line as rain fell from a dark, turbulent sky above. I peered through slitted eyes at Ravenhold past the tall, carved wooden figurehead on the bow that depicted a strange creature with a wide-open snout, long teeth, and a protruding, snake-like tongue. Fanrissen had told me it was meant to represent a *Matanga*, which was a type of sea spirit that the Swails believed lived in the ocean. He said it never failed to panic the Swails whenever they saw a ship with that figurehead, which made victory over them all but assured.

We were still more than a mile away from the island, fighting through a choppy sea as the spray off the hull and the falling rain worked in tandem to soak me and my crew of twelve men. The paint on our faces seemed to be resisting the water so far, though I was worried that the powder would be gone by the time we reached our destination. All I could see of that destination was a black landmass rising from an even blacker sea, with what looked like the walls and turrets of a vast fortress on the southern cliff overlooking our approach. Torches flickered along those walls, offering small pinpoints of light against an otherwise overcast sky.

I couldn't see the moon but guessed that it had to be well past midnight by now, with the strong northwesterly wind at our backs churning up the waves as the sleek ship plowed doggedly through them. The spray from the sea continued to shoot up and over the longboat's low sides every few heartbeats with relentless repetition, leaving my men cold, wet, and miserable. Yet, even so, I couldn't help but smile, as the weather couldn't have been better for what I had in mind this night. It had also allowed me to bring *Sea-Wolf* much closer to the island than I'd anticipated. I looked behind me into the fathomless darkness but saw no sign of the bigger ship. Not that I'd expected I would. My instructions to Putt had been clear. Stay well back to give us time to breach Ravenhold's initial defenses and clear them before following.

My breath rose in a fog around me with every exhale and I shivered, fidgeting with the sleeveless, black leather armor I wore over my tunic that was several sizes too small for me. I'd taken it from the body of the biggest of the Shadow Pirates we'd killed, but even so, it was still tight in the shoulders and pinched me uncomfortably at the neck and armpits. I turned and glanced past Jebido where he huddled behind me along the gunwale, searching the dark mass of my men crouched in the belly of the ship. Except for Baine's slim outline at the tiller, I couldn't tell one from the other.

"Pirate," I finally called out.

"Lord?"

"Come here," I said, gesturing him closer, though I doubted the motion could be seen.

Fanrissen stood obediently and then staggered when the longboat crested a wave before plowing down into a trough, sending a fresh sheet of bone-chilling spray over us all once again. The pirate waited until the boat had leveled out, then he made his way to Jebido, clutching onto him as he passed before moving to my side. He wrapped his hand around the same stay line as me, using the other to support himself on the gunwale. His white-painted features were barely discernable in the darkness.

I put my lips close to Fanrissen's ear. "Tell me what to expect when we get to Ravenhold," I said.

"Again, lord?"

"Again," I grunted. The pirate had already told me the same information three times this night, but I wanted to go over it once more so that it was fresh in my mind. Besides, I figured if you looked at a plan from every angle enough times, then there was always a chance of seeing a flaw that might have been missed. "Describe the entrance to me."

"Narrow and deep, lord," Fanrissen said, sounding a little put out, I thought. Let him. I had the lives of my men to think about, not to mention my wife's. So if the pirate had to describe everything to me fifty more times until I was satisfied, then so be it. "It's wide enough for a ship as big as *Sea-Wolf* to use her oars, but just," Fanrissen continued.

"No chance that she'll run aground?" I asked.

"None, lord. Ravenhold has had ships almost as big pass through there many times before. Captain Bear had divers clear any obstacles along the floor of the channel several years ago, so there's nothing to fear."

"Fair enough," I grunted, satisfied. "How long is it?"

"Two hundred yards, near about," the pirate answered. He didn't wait for my next question, already anticipating what it would be. "The banks are steep and inaccessible to either side, lord, giving way to forested hills and then the cliff where the fortress sits a quarter mile back."

"And the defenses by the water?"

"Two narrow piers run down both sides of the channel, lord, with several shooting platforms for archers if needed."

"How are they accessed?"

"Through gates on the shore, lord."

"What's to stop an attacking force from sending men onto those piers?" I asked.

"The gates are stout, lord," Fanrissen answered. "And the alarm would have been raised long before they are breached."

"Are there guards at the gates?"

Fanrissen shrugged. I was sure I could hear his teeth chattering. "Probably not, lord. Captain Bear is normally a cautious man, but I doubt they'll be expecting any trouble on a night like this."

I nodded, silently agreeing with him. I was betting the Shadow Pirate leader wasn't even here right now, anyway, guessing that he was probably many miles to the north futilely searching for *Sea-Wolf*, believing that we were still heading for Parnuthia. The bastard was in for a surprise when he got back, I vowed. "And once we're through the channel?" I finally asked. "What next?"

"The harbor, lord. That's where we'll be expected to dock and report in."

"Will they suspect anything with us arriving this late?"

"Doubtful, lord. It's not that unusual."

"How many men will be waiting for us?"

"A small garrison of six, lord." I sensed Fanrissen smiling. "They'll be in a single guardhouse together, most likely playing dice and swapping lies. One man sits by a window watching the harbor, and the rest relax. Trust me, it's the most coveted billet on the island."

"So, they'll see us coming long before we dock, then?"

"Yes, lord. That's why sending men along the piers won't work. But in this weather, I doubt anyone will come out to greet us. They're supposed to, but I'm betting that they'll stay inside where it's dry and just let us come to them." He shrugged. "I know that's what I would do if it were me."

"I hope you're right," I muttered.

I looked past the leering *Matanga* head toward the island again as the dark mass loomed larger by the minute. Assuming the Overseer's man was there, then according to Fanrissen, we should find him at the fortress. Hopefully, that man would know something about what had happened to Alesia and Einrack. If not, then I prayed he'd at least have records somewhere showing who had bought them. As for any slaves that might have arrived since the last Market Day, they were apparently kept in a holding area outside the town that ringed the harbor. Fanrissen had warned me that they would be well-guarded, though, and I was still debating what to do about them. I wasn't willing to get into a long, drawn-out battle and possibly lose men unless I had to. I was here for Alesia, Einrack, and Fanrissen's family and nobody else, though I had to admit that leaving people behind to be sold like cattle greatly rankled me.

I planned to strike the island's defenses hard and fast while the element of surprise was still on our side. Eliminating the guards along the pier—if any—and in the garrison without allowing the alarm to be raised would be crucial to that. The problem I had was despite Fanrissen's best guess, I didn't actually know how many pirates I was dealing with. Fanrissen had told me Captain Bear had close to two-hundred pirates and mercenaries at his disposal, though many of them could be out patrolling and raiding at any given time. It was an impressive number of men and greatly worrying to me if I'd miscalculated.

Was I wrong about the pirate leader? Had he returned to Ravenhold after he'd failed to capture *Sea-Wolf*? Was I about to find myself badly outnumbered here, or had Captain Bear and his ships continued west toward Parnuthia in search of us like I dearly hoped? I wasn't sure either way now as the moment of our attack drew closer. But, as Baine expertly steered the longboat toward the entrance to the channel lit by torches sputtering in the rain, I knew we would soon find out. Behind me, Niko and a tall Pith named Assuro finished trimming the sail, and as the ship slowed and started to wallow on the tide, they joined the rest of my men at the oars and began to paddle us toward the opening.

"What's that about?" I asked the pirate when we reached the channel entrance.

I could see the twin wooden piers Fanrissen had described clearly now, for torches on long poles burned every ten feet or so down the length of the channel on both sides. Dense trees rose to either side of the shoreline, and a thick cable spanned the entrance at least a hundred feet above the waterline, tied to two towering oaks facing each other at the tops of the opposing grades. Four iron cages hung by chains from the bowed cable, and they were swinging and spinning in the wind, with a motionless body inside each one. I could see what looked like white bones in two of the cages where I guessed the corpses' flesh had been picked clean by scavengers. The other two bodies still retained their flesh, which I knew meant they were most likely still alive, though barely.

"That's what Captain Bear does to any of the men he suspects have been disloyal to him," Fanrissen said soberly as the ship's bow passed underneath the gruesome display.

I caught Baine's eye where he sat on a wooden stool at the stern, one hand on the tiller. My friend looked up at the poor bastards in the cages, his face expressionless as they passed over his head before he shrugged at me and then focused back on the waterway.

I felt Fanrissen nudge my arm. "Looks like only one guard is out tonight, lord," he muttered, gesturing toward a man walking along the weathered planks of the western pier. The guard was short and squat, wearing a dark, rain-drenched cloak with the hood up. He turned toward us, revealing a red-bearded face in the firelight. Fanrissen grimaced beside me. "I know that man well," he said as the guard watched the ship glide past him in silence.

"Is that going to be a problem?" I grunted.

"Hardly," Fanrissen said with a soft chuckle. "I never liked the bastard." He put a foot on the gunwale, then dragged himself up using the stay line. "What news, Gerey?" the pirate shouted.

"Is that you, Savad?' Gerey replied, sounding surprised. "I thought you were still out chasing the Wolf with the Captain?"

Fanrissen and I shared a relieved look. "I was," the pirate called out after a moment. "But he sent me back here with Frich and his crew."

"Why would he go and do that?" Gerey asked as he started walking quickly back along the pier, pacing us.

"How should I know?" Fanrissen retorted. He spread his arms, balancing easily on the gunwale. "I just do what I'm told. I've found you live longer that way."

Gerey laughed. "Yes, I suppose you're right about that." The Shadow Pirate halted, then gestured over his shoulder. "I just have to check on the torches, and then I'm getting out of this rain and going to Raber's for a drink. Why don't you meet me there and tell me all about it?"

Fanrissen waved. "Sure, as soon as we get settled in."

Gerey returned the wave, then headed back in the other direction while we made slow, steady progress away from him down the channel toward the cove, which I was surprised to see was smaller than I had expected. We exited the channel, with the harbor surrounded by buildings branching out to our right and left in a jagged formation before narrowing again and then leading into a wider bowl. I could see a single tall, box-like wharf along the southern shore opposite us with a black-painted vessel similar to ours docked beneath it. Smaller fishing boats were anchored in the open water, as well as a battered-looking trading cog half the size of *Sea-Wolf*.

"We go there to disembark, lord," Fanrissen said, pointing to a wooden platform floating alone in the water ten feet below the wharf. The dock above had barricades all around it, I noted with a critical eye, with only a single ramp leading down to the platform which at most was eight feet across. I could see no other access to the wharf than that. Fanrissen glanced at me. "I told you Captain Bear was a cautious man."

"So it would seem," I grunted, glad now that we hadn't tried to force our way in with just *Sea-Wolf* alone. "Where is the guardhouse?"

"On that hill over there," Fanrissen answered, using his eyes to point out a squat stone building near the shore.

I could see smoke rising from a hole in the building's thatch roof, with a bell hanging from a pole near the front door. I assumed that was to alert the town and the rest of the garrison if there was an attack. A shuttered window sat on either side of the building's front door, with the shutters on the one to my left partially open. Firelight was coming through that opening, blocked by what might be the silhouetted form of a watcher.

"All right," I grunted, tapping the pirate on the shoulder. "Go tell Baine where we need to go."

Fanrissen nodded and headed down the ship's length as I returned my eyes to the stone building. Everything remained quiet and peaceful there as we approached. I just hoped it would stay that way. Five minutes later, with the rain falling heavier now, our commandeered ship was moored securely to a piling that rose out of the water by the small platform. None of the guards had bothered to come out to talk to us, just as Fanrissen had predicted would happen.

I glanced around at my men. "Remember, no sounds," I said. I shielded my eyes from the rain, peering south, but I couldn't see Gerey anywhere along the channel now. I needed that man neutralized. "Baine," I said, focusing on my friend, thinking he was best suited for the task. "There's only the one guard along the pier. I need you to deal with him once the rest of us enter that building."

"No problem," Baine grunted. He clutched a bow in his right hand, though he'd removed the string to keep it dry. With Baine's speed and skill with a knife, I knew his bow wouldn't be needed just for one man. Afterward, though, that might be another story depending on how much resistance we found as we progressed.

"We should move, lord," Fanrissen suggested a moment later. "If we stay much longer, the guards might become suspicious."

"You take the lead up there," I said to the pirate. I nodded to Jebido. "You, Saldor, and Niko will come with us. The rest of you stay on the ship and keep an eye open. Don't come up until I call for you."

I hopped over the gunwale then, landing on the square platform that wobbled precariously on the water beneath my weight before I headed up the steep ramp. I couldn't help but admire Captain Bear's foresight as I climbed, as the platform was clearly designed to handle one man at a time safely. It gave the defenders a huge advantage against any invading force, though I imagined moving slaves, supplies, and plunder this way must be a tiresome task. I thought perhaps the pirate leader had an alternative method for that purpose.

I waited for Fanrissen and the others to join me on the wharf, then fell into step behind the pirate as he walked confidently toward the guardhouse. Fanrissen kept his head down against the rain, nodding to the man I could see clearly in the window now, then pushed open the door. The pirate stepped inside and I followed close behind, taking three steps to my right when I passed through the doorway. The building was warm inside, with a well-stoked fire burning in a central hearth surrounded by ill-fitting flagstones on the floor. An iron pot hung over the fire, and my stomach rumbled at the smells coming from inside of it.

Two men sat on benches by the fire across from each other, eating from wooden bowls, while three others knelt on the floor in the corner to my right, playing dice. The man at the window sat on a stool on the far side of the door with a steaming tin mug in his hand.

"Nasty night," Fanrissen grunted in a low voice as he stopped by the hearth. He slicked rain off his bare arms, then put his hands over the fire to warm them. Jebido, Niko, and Saldor entered the building and spread out behind the pirate. I nudged the door closed with my boot, partially shutting off the sounds of the driving rain outside. None of the guards playing dice bothered to look up, so intent were they on their game. The two men at the fire both gave us a cursory glance, then returned to their meal. None wore face paint or powder in their hair, which Fanrissen had told me was only used when out raiding or patrolling.

"Anything to report?" the man at the window asked in a bored voice as he slowly shifted on his stool to study us.

"Ah, you know how it is sometimes," Fanrissen said as he approached the seated man. He placed his hand on the pirate's shoulder and smiled.

"Savad?" the Shadow Pirate grunted in surprise, recognizing him now. "What are you doing here?"

"I've come for my wife and daughter," Fanrissen hissed as he drew a knife and stabbed it deep into the other man's ear. The guard's eyes bulged, and his mouth sagged open before a torrent of dark blood gushed out from his nose.

One of the men at the fire cried out in horror, jumping to his feet just as Saldor skewered him with his sword. Jebido grabbed the second man by the back of his tunic and dragged him off his stool to the floor while Niko moved in a blur, slashing open his neck. Everything had happened in a blink of an eye, and three of the six guards were already dead. Wolf's Head was in my hand by now, eager for blood as I rushed at the remaining three guards, who still sat on the floor staring around them in astonishment.

I saw Fanrissen yank his red-stained knife free from the seated Shadow Pirate out of the corner of my eye, then heard the thud as the body rolled off the stool to the floor. Two of the dice players had scrambled to their feet by now, clutching madly at their weapons, while the third still sat where he was in obvious shock.

That man was the first to die by my hand as I hacked down at him, nearly severing his head from his neck in a single stroke. Blood shot upward, spraying over the dead man's companions in a wide arc. I grinned as one of them staggered backward, pawing at the sticky wetness in his eyes with one hand while holding up his sword defensively with the other. I slapped aside the guard's weak block, then sliced open his stomach, allowing steaming entrails to spill out and splatter against the stone floor before he collapsed.

I turned on the third man then, the killing blood roaring in my ears, only to find that Fanrissen had already dispatched him with cold efficiency. The pirate grinned at me, his handsome face alight with battle lust before he stooped and wiped the blade of his knife clean on the dead man's tunic. I was becoming more and more grateful that I'd let the pirate live. I relaxed, grinning back. The first part of the plan had gone off without a hitch. The guardhouse was ours without anyone suffering so much as a scratch, but I knew there was still a lot of fighting left before this night was over.

"Niko," I grunted, cleaning off my own blade before I sheathed it. "Take the window. Let me know when *Sea-Wolf* arrives."

"Yes, my lord."

I turned to Saldor. "Go get the rest of our men. Have them untie the pirate ship and push it out of the way so *Sea-Wolf* can dock." I moved to the hearth after the Pith warrior had left, stooping to pick up one of the fallen bowls still half-filled with a stew-like substance. Saldor had left the door open, and I could see the rain was still coming down just as heavily as before. I sniffed the contents in the bowl, then dipped my fingers into it before putting some in my mouth. It was squirrel meat mixed with carrots and onion. It wasn't half bad.

"That went well," Jebido grunted. He straightened the bench that had tipped over before sitting down on it. "But it's going to get a lot harder from here on."

"It is," I agreed. I shrugged and set the bowl on the stones around the hearth. "But when is it ever easy?" I licked my fingers and glanced at Fanrissen. "You're certain you still want to go alone, pirate? I can send a few of my men with you if you want."

"Thank you, lord," Fanrissen said. "But my family lives some distance away and I don't want to draw any attention to myself. I can move much quicker in the dark if I'm alone."

"Understood," I replied. I motioned to the door. "Get going then, but don't take too much time. Things could go bad for us here very fast. If I have to retreat to *Sea-Wolf*, I might not be able to wait for you for very long."

"I understand, lord," Fanrissen said. He hurried to the door, stepping aside to let Baine enter before disappearing into the rain. "Any trouble?" I asked my friend.

"None," Baine replied. He shook his head like a dog, shedding water from his long hair in all directions. I could see blood sprayed across the chest of his pirate armor but didn't bother to comment. I knew it wasn't his. "Saldor has the men waiting outside, Hadrack," Baine added. "Should I bring them in out of the rain?"

"No," I grunted. "They're already as wet as they're going to get, anyway. Besides, I don't want all of us to get trapped in here if soldiers come." I glanced to the window. "Any sign of *Sea-Wolf*, Niko?" I asked.

"No, lord. Nothing yet."

"Damn," I muttered.

I started to pace. Surprise was still on our side, but the longer we waited to assault Captain Bear's stronghold, the better the chances were of discovery. I had twelve men with me—eleven now that Fanrissen was gone—but I knew I would need the rest of my force on *Sea-Wolf* if I hoped to succeed. Fanrissen had said that as many as twenty pirates patrolled the walls and interior of the fortress on any given night. Each one would have to be methodically hunted down and killed, and the stronghold secured, which would take time. I didn't want word getting out to the reinforcements at the slave holdings that we were here. Many of the locals were loyal to the pirates as well, according to Fanrissen, so I knew there was a good chance they might join in the battle if it came. I needed to make sure it didn't, which was why the more men I had at my disposal for the assault on the fort, the greater our chance at success. It was simple logic.

"Lord," Niko said, cutting into my thoughts. "The ship just entered the channel."

"Thank The Mother," I muttered in relief.

I stepped outside into the pouring rain and made my way to the wharf, where I leaned on the railing and watched *Sea-Wolf's* rapid approach along the narrow canal. The wind had picked up and was swirling and gusting now, yet even so, Putt had a partial sail up, augmented by the oars that I could see rising and falling steadily. I thought it was risky to use the sail in this weather so close to land, but Putt knew speed mattered right now, and I trusted in his seamanship to get them through.

I glanced down at the flimsy platform below me that rocked and bobbed on the growing tide as the wind stroked the water. It would take a few minutes for all my men to disembark and get ashore because of that platform, but Captain Bear's clever water defense would then be working against him once they did. I was now free to leave only a few token men to defend *Sea-Wolf* from possible attack while we were gone, since only one pirate at a time could come at her. It was a better tradeoff than I'd expected and one that I was more than willing to take.

I heard a scuffle behind me and turned. Assuro was holding a struggling boy up by the collar of his threadbare coat. The Pith warrior had a sword held threateningly in his other hand and looked like he was about to use it.

"Wait!" I called out, moving toward them. I glanced at Jebido as I passed him. "Go tell Putt to stay on board with my wife and the wounded Piths. The rest are to come ashore."

Jebido's eyebrows rose. "Even the crew?"

"Even the crew," I grunted. "We're going to need everybody."

"All right, Hadrack," Jebido said before he hurried past me and down the ramp.

I walked over to Assuro, who still held his unhappy captive in the air effortlessly while the boy twisted and kicked his feet. "Set him down," I ordered.

The tall warrior did as I asked, though he made sure to clamp a massive hand around the back of the boy's neck afterward, making him wince. "He was trying to get into the building," Assuro rumbled.

"What's your name?" I asked the boy. I could see he was visibly trembling in the big Pith's grip.

"Haf," came back the reluctant reply.

"And why were you going in there, Haf?"

"To see my Da. Mama's sick, and she said to tell Da he should come home real quick."

I pursed my lips, sharing a look with Baine, who stood leaning against the stone wall of the guardhouse out of the rain beneath the thatch roof overhang. Niko casually shut the door, cutting off any view of the bloody carnage inside.

"I'm afraid I can't let you talk to your da right now, Haf," I finally said.

I glanced behind me toward the ship as the giant sailor Walcott threw a rope ladder down to the platform before he began to descend. The big man had a sword on his hip and several shields strapped across his back. I saw he was also bringing my father's axe with him, guessing that had been Putt's idea.

"Why not?" Haf asked.

I turned back to the boy, thinking he couldn't be much older than my first-born son, Hughe. The fear had left Haf's eyes now, replaced by childish curiosity. "Because I have something more important that I need you to do right now," I said.

"You do?" the boy gasped, his eyes going round.

"Yes," I said. I laid a hand gently on his shoulder. "Something important." I nodded to Assuro, who reluctantly loosened his grip. "We need to get up to the fort, but we can't be seen going there. Can you show us the best way?"

"Why can't you be seen?" the boy asked innocently.

I put a finger to my lips. "It's a secret. Can you keep secrets?"

"I sure can," Haf said with an enthusiastic nod. "My brother killed Orlo Borl's cat last week, and I ain't told nobody." The boy's face took on a serious expression. "Well, except for Hooper, I mean." He shrugged his thin shoulders. "But Hooper's just a goat and can't talk, so I don't think he counts."

"No, I don't think he does either," I said, suppressing a smile. "So, can you help us, Haf?"

"I guess," the boy said. His eyes suddenly took on a hint of caution. "But Fungus said if he saw me in the fort again without a good reason, he'd give my ass a thrashing."

I frowned. "Fungus? Do you mean Captain Bear?"

"Naw, the other one that smells like fish and yells at everyone. He's not very nice."

I paused for a moment. Was the boy talking about the Overseer's man? "Is Fungus the one who sells the slaves?" I asked.

"That's him," Haf answered. "His real name is Fungee Filace." The boy put a hand to his mouth and giggled. "But everyone calls him Fungus Face when he's not around."

I couldn't help but smile, feeling relief as I rifled Haf's hair. "Tell you what. You get us up there so I can talk to this Fungee, and I'll give you a nice shiny gold coin or two. I'll also make sure he doesn't lay a hand on you. Is it a deal?"

The boy thought about that for a moment, then he nodded and stuck out his hand. "It's a deal."

I locked forearms with the lad, careful not to crush his thin bones as we shook. The boy's eyes were shining with excitement, his mission to fetch his father now forgotten, at least for the moment. Eventually, Haf would learn the man was dead, but there was little that I could do about it now. Unfortunately, there were always unintentional victims when men took up swords, and although I couldn't bring Haf's father back, I could at least give him and his family enough gold to help blunt the loss. It wasn't much and certainly wouldn't have done much for me at his age, but it was better than nothing.

Twenty minutes later, wearing my own armor again and a Pith shield on my arm, my men and I followed Haf as he led us down a narrow street lit only by occasional candlelight filtering through shuttered windows. The houses here were built close together, with most being nothing more than simple mud shacks. A dog appeared from an alley, growling at us, but it quickly fled when Walcott advanced on it, wielding my father's axe. I'd allowed the big sailor to keep the weapon for the time being, thinking it was better suited for him than a sword for what was coming.

Haf finally stopped when the street ended at a dense copse of tall ash and pine trees. He pointed to the south. "There's a trail through here that some of the women in town use to get up to the fort."

I knelt beside the boy so that we were almost at eye level. "Does it lead to the front gates?"

"No," Haf said. "To a well outside one of the walls. There's a doorway close by, though, that goes inside."

"Is the door left unlocked?"

The boy shook his head. "No, but the guards open it when the women knock. They always let them in, too." He shrugged. "I don't know why; they just do. I tried it once and got a boot in the rump for my trouble."

I heard some of the men behind me snickering and making jokes, but Haf seemed oblivious to their meaning.

"All right, lad," I said. I stood. "Lead on."

Less than fifteen minutes later, my men and I were huddled within the trees, staring out at an open area of sparse grass dominated by granite slabs that overlooked the sea. The rain had stopped now, though the wind coming off the water was much stronger here than it had been down below. The towering walls of the fortress rose to our right, with a cobbled walkway leading away from a closed, solid oak door toward a circular stone well. Two metal braziers with their flames whipped by the wind burned near the well. A wooden gable roof protected the well's opening, with a rope winch for lowering and raising buckets dissecting the two posts holding up the roof.

I shook my head as I studied the area, the soldier in me recognizing a serious flaw in the fort's defenses. If that well out there was the occupant's only source of water, then even if it was piped into the fort somehow, all it would take was an attacker throwing a rotting corpse down the hole, leaving the people inside cut off from fresh water.

"How many guards are at the door?" I asked Haf.

"Two, I think," the boy answered. The gleam of excitement was gone from his face now, replaced by puzzlement. "But I told you, they won't let you in. Only girls are allowed."

"Good thing I brought some of those with me, then," I said with a wink.

I glanced at Gislea and another Pith female named Finja, who were both crouched down beside me on my left. The women were young and pretty, which I expected would dissuade any doubts that the guards at the door might have about the unexpected visit. Ania used to tell me years ago that a man's lust could be used against him, and this was going to be a perfect example of that. The pirates on the other side of that door were going to be dead very soon because of lust, yet I lost little time worrying about it. These men had murdered and enslaved people I cared about, and there would be no mercy offered for any of them from me.

"Do you know where Fungee is staying?" I asked Haf, not really expecting an answer.

Haf pointed to a round tower that joined the south and west walls. "My mother does his laundry sometimes. His chambers are on the upper floor there."

I laughed in unexpected delight, thinking that The Mother must have sent this boy to me on purpose. I rifled his hair a second time. "Good work, lad," I said. "You just earned yourself another coin."

I had all the information I needed now, but there was still the problem of what to do with the boy. I couldn't let Haf go and take the chance he might tell someone about us. But I couldn't bring myself to harm him, either. I glanced behind me, searching my men until I saw Hanon the Pathfinder kneeling amongst his brothers. The priest was as good a fighter as any of the Piths, though he was mostly used in battle as a last resort, since he was here mainly for spiritual reasons. Leaving Hanon with Haf would not only solve my problem of what to do with the boy, but the decision would probably sit well with the other Piths, too. I dearly hated the idea of losing a man right now just before the attack, but saw no other recourse, so I crooked a finger at the Pathfinder.

"Wolf?" the priest said as Gislea made room for him and he crouched down beside me.

"This is Haf," I said, gesturing to the boy. "I want you to stay here with him until the job is done." Hanon glanced at Haf, his face expressionless. "No harm is to come to him," I added. "If it does, I'll hold you directly responsible."

"I understand, Wolf. The child will be as safe with me as if he were my own offspring."

"Good," I grunted, satisfied.

I focused back on the fortress. I'd seen no signs of guards walking the battlements, but knew they had to be up there somewhere. I guessed that they'd probably taken shelter from the rain earlier, though now that it had stopped, they might return at any moment. We needed to move.

I waited until Hanon drew Haf away, and once the boy was out of sight, I nudged Gislea's arm. "Go," I whispered. "Make it quick and quiet."

"I'm always quick and quiet when I kill, Wolf," Gislea said with a flash of white teeth. "It's only when I make love that things get noisy and drawn out."

I chuckled, watching as the two women slipped out from the trees and darted across the clearing. I held my breath, expecting a cry of discovery at any moment, but the night remained silent. The Piths reached the door, where they immediately dropped their weapons and armor to either side of it, then stripped down to their waists. Finja turned to face the trees and she shook her large breasts at us, which gleamed almost orange in the firelight. The two Pith women giggled while the men hidden among the foliage muttered in appreciation. I could only shake my head, though it was done with a smile on my face. Even in the direst of circumstances, Piths could be like children sometimes.

I felt Baine slide in beside me. "That Finja sure has a nice pair of—"

"Don't start," I cut in. "You're just as bad as they are."

"I was going to say ears," Baine replied with a chuckle.

"Uh-huh," I grunted.

Gislea lifted a fist to the door and I tensed, the smile gone from my face now, replaced by deadly intensity as I waited in anticipation. The Pith rapped three times sharply, with the sound echoing loudly across the clearing. I heard a muffled voice come from behind the oak door, followed by Gislea saying something in a soft tone. Moments later, the door opened with a creak, enveloping the walkway and two bare-chested women in a yellow glow of warm light.

"Mother's tit!" I heard the man standing in the doorway exclaim as he stared in astonishment at the Piths.

"Compliments of Captain Bear," Finja said as she wiggled her breasts again. "May we please come in?"

"By The Father's balls, yes," the guard gushed. He stepped back out of the light, allowing the women inside.

I waited until the door closed again behind them. "All right," I called out in a low voice. "Let's move."

My men and I ran across the clearing in a tight group, then spread out to either side of the entranceway. Less than a minute later, the door creaked open again, revealing Gislea wiping fresh blood from her face and naked chest with a man's torn tunic.

"Any problems?" I asked.

"Couldn't have been easier," the girl said with a shrug. "There were only two of them."

I nodded, stepping past her into a modest-sized room. A wide archway stood opposite me, with a second, smaller doorway to my left. The pirate who'd answered the door lay dead to my right with his throat cut and a shocked expression on his face. A second man lay splayed over a desk, his chest torn open by multiple stab wounds. Finja was busily searching his clothing for silver.

"Get dressed," I grunted at the women as my men filed into the building. I crossed to the smaller doorway and glanced inside to see that it was just a small storage room filled with water caskets. There was only one entrance. I moved to the archway next and looked out into the corridor that I saw ran left to right. There was no one around. Fanrissen had given us a rundown of the fort's layout, and I guessed the corridor must lead to the courtyard outside and the main gate. "Niko," I said, pointing down the passage to my right. "Take three men and secure the gate. No one gets in, and no one gets out."

"Yes, my lord," Niko said. He selected Walcott and another crewman, plus one of the Piths, then headed with them at a trot down the corridor.

"The rest of you break up into teams of four," I ordered. "Sweep this place clean of pirates, but don't kill anyone else unless they raise a hand against you." I glared at the Piths. "Remember, no raping, or you answer to me. That's not what we came here for." I let that thought sink in for a moment. "Baine, Jebido, you're with me," I added as I headed left down the corridor. "Let's go have a talk with Fungus Face."

The screams of panic and fear started less than five minutes later, and I paused on the flight of steps leading to the tower where I believed Fungee might be, listening. Most of the cries were feminine, I realized after a moment, feeling my face hardening.

"I'm sure it's not that, Hadrack," Jebido said from behind me, anticipating my thoughts. "The Piths heard you and will obey."

"They had better," I growled.

We started up again, climbing another flight of stairs to a landing, where I found two women huddled together on the floor, sobbing. The women screamed when they saw us, crying out in terror and clutching at one another.

"Sorry for the inconvenience, ladies," I said as I walked past them with barely a glance. "Just stay where you are and you won't be harmed."

The women stopped crying, staring after us in befuddlement as we climbed the next flight of stairs. I heard them scurry away the moment we were out of sight, and I shrugged. There was nowhere for them to go. We reached another landing, then another set of stairs, until finally, we stood in a long corridor on the top floor. A closed door led off to my immediate right, with another one ten feet further to my left and a final one at the far end of the passage. I motioned for Jebido to go right, and Baine left while I headed for the last door.

I shifted my shield on my arm when I reached the end of the hallway, my gut telling me Fungee was on the other side of the doorway. I took a deep breath, then reared back and kicked the door open. I rushed into the room, my sword raised, then paused in surprise at the sight that greeted me. I was staring at the back and very shapely rear end of a naked woman, who was crouched down on the floor straddling a man's body. The woman held a knife in her right hand, and it rose and fell over and over again, sending trails of red blood spraying across the room as she plunged the blade into the prone man's chest. The woman seemed completely oblivious of me and the shattered door as she continued to stab frantically.

"Well," I finally said as I slowly lowered my sword. "This is rather unexpected."

The naked woman turned in surprise at the sound of my voice, the fierce expression on her face switching to shocked disbelief when she saw me.

It was Alesia, Queen of the Piths.

Chapter 11: Alesia

"Hadrack?" Alesia gasped. She stood in one smooth motion, stepping away from the corpse with the still-dripping knife in her hand. I saw her forehead, cheeks, chest, stomach, and even her thighs were splattered with blood, but she appeared to be unharmed. "Is that really you standing there?" Alesia asked, sounding as if she didn't quite believe it.

"It's me," I said, offering her a relieved grin. I still couldn't quite believe that I'd actually found her, either. I sheathed Wolf's Head. "Are you all right?"

"I am now," Alesia replied, giving the corpse a contemptuous glance.

The dead man was thin and looked like he would have been tall when alive, with fine, delicate facial bones and white skin virtually untouched by the sun. He was dressed in a long-sleeved brown cotton tunic with laces at the neck and a black leather belt with a gold buckle encircled his waist. The tunic would normally have reached his knees, but was now hitched up, revealing what little was left of his manhood hanging in torn, bloody strips. Worn leather sandals clung to the dead man's feet, and I noticed that the big toe on his right foot was missing, though the wound had clearly healed long ago.

I gestured toward the body. "I'm guessing this would be Fungee Filace?"

"It was," Alesia confirmed in a satisfied voice. She wiped blood from her brow with the back of her hand, then spat on the dead man. "I've been waiting a long time for the opportunity to kill this turd-sucking scum, Hadrack." She glanced at me. "I guess I have you to thank for that."

"What happened?" I asked.

Alesia shrugged. "We heard screams and sounds of fighting coming from outside and he went to investigate. The coward came back blubbering like a child that we were under attack. I told him that I was good with a sword and could protect him, all he had to do was untie me." Alesia grinned savagely. "The fool should have known better, but fear makes men like him stupid and careless."

I nodded and let my gaze roam around the large room. Thick carpets with intricate gold and red patterns covered the floor beneath my feet, with lush tapestries softening the roughness of the cold granite walls. Candles flickered all around the space on tall poles of gilded bronze, lighting the interior. A bed sat at the opposite end of the room on a wooden platform, with a thin, almost see-thru white canopy draped over it like a veil. The side curtains were drawn back and held by blue sashes, revealing thin ropes tied to each of the four carved mahogany posts. I glanced at Alesia's wrists and ankles, all of which had bands of angry red and purple flesh surrounding them. I felt anger and disgust hardening my features, knowing with certainty what had been going on in this room.

Alesia saw my expression and she put a hand on my arm. "What's done is done, brother. The dog paid for his lust, and he will go to the next world without that which made him a man. It is enough."

"He may have paid," I growled. "But there's more of the bastards out there. They'll all pay for what they did before this is over."

"That they will," Alesia agreed in a gruff voice.

She absently rubbed at a patch of blood that had thickened across her left nipple and I tried not to stare. The Piths were probably the least self-conscious people in the world, and Alesia seemed completely oblivious to the fact that she was still naked. Unfortunately, I was not quite so oblivious. The Pith queen had given birth to six children since we'd first met, and though she was a little heavier than I remembered, she was still breathtakingly beautiful. I tried not to think about the one and only time we'd rutted during an Ascension Ceremony many years ago. I had been young and foolish then, as had she, and it had almost gotten Baine, Jebido, and me killed.

"What about Einrack?" I asked, turning my focus back to the present. "Is he here too?"

Alesia grimaced. "No, he's been sold. He's gone, Hadrack."

"Do you know where?" I asked. Alesia just shook her head. I took a deep breath, disappointed. "We'll get him back," I promised. "You have my word."

Alesia lifted her chin, her face set with resolve. "Yes, we will." She hesitated then, her eyes filling with something that I couldn't quite read. "And what news of my husband? Does he live, Hadrack? Is he here with you?" Alesia's tone told me what her eyes had not, and I knew that she'd already guessed the truth and was preparing herself for it. I said nothing until Alesia nodded sadly in understanding. "And what of my children, then?" she finally asked. "Did any of them survive the flames?"

I lowered my gaze. "I am truly sorry, sister."

Alesia's only reaction was to blow air out of her nostrils slowly. Finally, she dropped the knife to the carpeted floor and moved to a small table where a bronze basin half-filled with water sat. Alesia splashed some water on her face, neck, and chest and then began to rub at the blood with methodical concentration.

"After Einrack and I were taken to the Black Ship and we started to sail away," Alesia said, not looking at me while she cleaned herself, "I saw Einhard run into the burning hall where the rest of my children were hiding." Her voice was flat and emotionless as she picked up a cloth and began to dry her body. "The building collapsed a few moments later. A part of me had hoped ever since then that maybe he got out, but—" Alesia hesitated there, and I thought that she might cry then, but she just shrugged off the tears and continued, "Anyway, I can't say that I'm surprised he's dead, Hadrack. Einhard and my children are with the Master now, and someday, perhaps soon, I will join them." She looked at me then, her expression turning fierce and determined. "But not before those who did this are all dead."

"Einhard did manage to get out," I said. I lifted my hands at the sudden look of hope on Alesia's face. "He died much later from his burns." I thought about moving to take Alesia in my arms and holding her then, but something told me that now wasn't the right time for it. "Einhard sent Saldor to bring me back from Corwick," I added. "He said he had no intention of dying until I got there." I shook my head and smiled sadly. "You know what a stubborn bastard he was."

"My husband made you promise to find Einrack and me, didn't he?" Alesia asked in a soft voice, the pain of loss evident now on her face. "And he refused to die until he received that pledge from you."

"Yes," I said. "That and to avenge him and his murdered family."

"Another vow of blood for the Wolf to carry on his mighty shoulders," Alesia whispered, sounding tired now. She threw the red-smeared cloth aside as she walked over to me and put a hand to my scarred cheek. "You have already carried so much in your life, Hadrack. I am sorry to involve you in this."

"Don't be," I replied. I squeezed her hand with mine. "You and Einhard are family to me, Alesia. My brother and my sister. I would have done it whether he asked me to or not."

"Thank you, brother and dear friend," Alesia said before kissing me on the cheek. "Both Einhard and I knew from the moment we met you that you were destined for greatness. You have not disappointed."

Alesia leaned into me then and I put my arms around her, feeling her body shake as she finally let loose and cried. We stood that way for some time, grieving together for Einhard and her family, before finally, footsteps sounded from behind me. I glanced over my shoulder at Baine and Jebido, who had paused in the doorway in surprise. I knew they couldn't see Alesia's face pressed to my chest, and I could only imagine what they must be thinking seeing me embracing a naked woman like this.

"It's all right," I said to my friends. "It's Alesia."

"By The Mother," Jebido gasped. He strode forward as Alesia and I broke apart, then put his arms around her. "I'm so glad you're safe. We were all so afraid for you."

"Good old Jebido," Alesia said, hugging him back warmly. "It's been so long since I've seen you. I'm glad to see you looking so well." She glanced past Jebido to Baine, who still stood in the doorway. "And Baine, too. You're older now but just as handsome as ever, I see." She chuckled, a flash of the carefree Alesia that I'd known when we first met returning for a moment. "I had always hoped to lie with you in the Rutting Circles someday and find out what all the fuss was about, but the chance never arose."

Baine looked down in embarrassment, fidgeting with his bow. I couldn't help but smile at his expression, as I hadn't seen my friend looking so awkward since we were boys.

"What about Einrack?" Jebido asked eagerly as he took a step back from Alesia. "Is he here?"

"Gone," I said regretfully.

Alesia turned away then and began undoing the belt around the corpse's waist. "Help me, Hadrack," she grunted.

Together, we stripped the body of its tunic, leaving Fungee lying naked on the carpet. I thought he looked like a gelded, giant white slug as Alesia drew the tunic over herself, then cinched the belt around her waist. She crouched and picked up the fallen knife, then slashed at the blood-stained cloth that hung well past her knees, freeing up her legs.

Alesia nodded in satisfaction when she was done. "Shall we get going, Hadrack?" Her tone was all business now, the practical and tough woman who had led a nation for many years returning.

"Where?" I asked, knowing by the determined look in her eyes that wherever she expected to go, it wasn't off the island.

"There's a compound on the other side of the town where they keep the slaves," Alesia said. "We need to go there right now."

"I'm not sure that's a good idea, Alesia," I said. "I heard that place is well-guarded. I only have one ship, and I didn't bring enough men with me to take on the entire island."

"But you did bring Piths on this ship, yes?" Alesia asked.

"I did," I admitted. "Both Peshwin and Amenti. Saldor leads them."

Alesia smiled in satisfaction. "Then, however many of my brothers and sisters there are, it will be enough. There's a man I must speak with, Hadrack, and he's at that compound. There is no choice."

"He knows where Einrack was taken," I guessed, understanding now.

"Yes. He's the only one other than Fungee who does." Alesia looked slightly embarrassed as she glanced at the mutilated corpse. "I should have asked the bastard first before I killed him, but I got carried away once the blood started to flow."

I hesitated as I mulled it over. I glanced at Baine, who just shrugged, looking indifferent to the idea either way, then Jebido, who simply nodded. "All right," I said, knowing there was little choice. "But first, we make sure the fortress has been cleared of pirates before we find this man. I don't want any of the bastards cutting us off from behind."

"That part's easy," Alesia said with a cold smile. "The last time I looked, Hadrack, there's only one way to get rats out of a building." She turned and took a candle off one of the poles, then walked over to the closest hanging tapestry and lit the corner. The rich cloth smoked for a moment, then burst into flames. The moment it was burning well, Alesia moved to the next one and went to work on it.

I turned to Jebido and Baine as thick black smoke began to fill the room. "Go get our people out. Have them meet us at the front gates."

"What about the pirates?" Baine asked.

"Wait for them there," I growled. "If any make it that far, kill the bastards. Just make sure you let everybody else through. Our quarrel isn't with them unless they try something."

I waited after Baine and Jebido had left as Alesia went through the room, lighting each of the tapestries. The flames had already reached the high ceiling in places where they curled and rolled against the stone like living creatures, searching for more fuel to feed upon. Alesia seemed oblivious to the growing heat and smoke as she worked, lighting anything that would burn.

I coughed as black smoke swirled around me, cursing when I lost sight of Alesia in the thick haze. Alarmed, I cupped my hands around my mouth. "Alesia! That's enough! We have to go! Alesia!" I saw her reappear a moment later when the smoke shifted, standing in front of the bed and staring at it as if in a trance. "Alesia!" I shouted again, preparing to dash forward and draw her away. "Alesia, we have to go now!"

The Queen of the Piths finally heard me and she turned to glance back. She waved in acknowledgment, then threw the candle on the bed. Alesia watched until the bedding caught fire and the flames started creeping up the curtains. Then satisfied, she turned and ran back to me through the smoke.

"Are you all right?" I asked when she reached me. Alesia's face was streaked with soot, and I could see an angry red burn across her left cheek. I put an arm around her shoulders and hustled her from the room.

"I've never been better, Hadrack," Alesia said, her eyes glowing. "Never been better."

Twenty minutes later, I led my men away from the main gates of the fortress that was now a raging inferno. Parts of the eastern side of the building had collapsed moments ago, shaking the ground like an earthquake and sending up a cloud of dust into the sky to rival the sparks, flames, and smoke. The bodies of six dead Shadow Pirates lay twisted on the road outside the gates, having been the only ones to make it out alive—not that it had done them much good in the end. We'd allowed the servants—both men and women—and the children inside the fort to go free, and they now streamed down the road ahead of us in a panicked group. None had seemed a threat to me, though later, I knew I might come to regret my decision if the townspeople decided to turn on us.

"They'll raise the alarm, you know," Jebido grunted, gesturing ahead. He was already breathing heavily as he trotted along the downward-sloped road beside me.

I glanced over my shoulder. Hungry flames rose a hundred feet above the burning tower where Fungee Filace had died, lighting up the sky for miles as if it were daytime. I thought it ironic that the tower looked like a giant version of the candle Alesia had used to start the blaze. "I don't think it matters," I said to my friend. "The only people who haven't seen that fire by now are either dead or blind."

Neither of us said anything after that, conserving our energy as we ran, with only the sounds of our weapons and armor clanking in our ears. Baine and Tyris flanked us with their bows ready, while behind me, the Piths continued to whoop and laugh with joy as they paced their queen, who ran among them like a conquering hero. The Peshwin and Amenti had reacted with ecstasy when I'd first appeared at the gates with Alesia, and they still hadn't quite gotten over the fact that she was safe and leading them once more.

We'd only lost one man during the attack, an Amenti who had surprised a cook in his kitchen brandishing a cleaver. The cook had been killed, but not before he'd slashed open the Amenti's neck in an unexpected and unprovoked attack. Hamon the Pathfinder was carrying the dead warrior on his shoulders, and I'd told him to return to *Sea-Wolf* with his burden and inform Putt what was happening while the rest of us forged ahead. Surprisingly,

Haf had chosen to stay with us—perhaps overcome by the excitement—and he tagged along behind my force, doing his best to keep pace with us. I didn't give the boy much thought, though, other than to hope that he'd be smart enough to stay out of the way once the fighting began.

We finally reached level ground, where I could see by the combined light from the fire and the moon overhead that the road split in two fifty feet in front of me. The fleeing children and servants had turned right, following the pathway around a jumble of rocks and bushes that led toward the village and the cove. The second road continued straight as an arrow toward a long, steep grade that cut through a stand of trees a mile away. I knew that was the direction we needed to go to reach the slave compound.

I led my force onward, trotting at a fast pace until we arrived at the base of the grade, where I signaled a halt to take a brief rest before the climb. I wondered what had become of Fanrissen as I sucked in great gulps of air. Had he found his wife and child and was even now waiting anxiously for us on *Sea-Wolf*? I'd made a vow to get his family away from Ravenhold safely, and I intended to keep that vow. But first, I needed to learn where Einrack had gone, so the pirate would just have to wait.

"Hadrack," Baine called out in warning, cutting into my thoughts. He gestured above, where a group of horsemen had just appeared at the crest of the grade. The riders paused there for a moment, looking down at us before they wheeled their mounts around and galloped back the way they'd come.

"Well, they know where we're heading now," Jebido gasped. He leaned over with his hands on his knees as he fought to regain his wind.

"Yes," I agreed, feeling a sudden uneasiness come over me. The way the horsemen had moved had seemed planned to me, almost like they'd wanted to be seen before racing away. I studied the dark trees to either side of the road above us, then glanced at

Baine and Tyris. "You two go scout ahead. Make sure there isn't a nasty surprise waiting for us somewhere up there."

Baine and the tall blond archer headed away while I glanced at Alesia as she and Saldor joined me. "Any idea what kind of resistance there'll be when we arrive at this compound?" I asked her.

"Perhaps thirty or forty fighters," Alesia said. I noticed neither she nor Saldor were breathing heavily from the run while I was still trying to catch my breath. "Maybe more. They have a garrison there inside the walls."

"Can they defend those walls?" Jebido asked.

Alesia shook her head. "Not really, no. There are no ramparts to speak of. Just pointed barbs on the top."

I saw my friend grin at that. "Well, that makes things a little easier."

I nodded in agreement. "This man you seek," I said to Alesia. "Is he one of the pirates? Do we have to be careful who we kill?"

"No," Alesia said. "He's a slave."

"A slave?" I repeated in surprise.

"His name is Dagric. He's a harmless old man who's been at the compound for years."

"And this slave knows where Einrack was taken?" Jebido asked in disbelief. "How?"

Alesia shrugged. "The pirates consider him the slaves' unofficial leader, and they use him to issue orders to the others."

"That doesn't answer the question," Jebido grunted.

"I don't know how he knows these things," Alesia replied with a sigh. "I've just heard that nothing happens in the compound or on the island without his knowledge."

Jebido looked at me doubtfully, then he shook his head and walked away.

"I hope you know what you're doing, Alesia," I said. "We're taking a big risk going this far inland. If you're wrong—"

"Trust me," Alesia cut in. "I'm not wrong. Dagric will know."

We waited at the base of the slope for almost ten minutes before Baine and Tyris finally returned to report that the trees were clear of the enemy. I decided there was no need to run now and wear out my men, since the Shadow Pirates knew we were coming and would be prepared for us long before we arrived anyway. We trudged up the long grade and through the trees at a much slower pace, with Baine, Tyris, and Gislea fifty yards ahead of my main force, while the rest of the archers remained in the rear. I still wasn't convinced there wouldn't be some form of an attack along our route. The terrain was marked by dark, forested hills and rock-strewn plains as we progressed, offering numerous places for an ambush. The fire from the fortress was still a bright beacon on the horizon to our rear, though the weak moonlight was mainly all we had left now to help light our path.

We finally reached a small jumble of darkened houses built around a tavern, all of which looked abandoned. There were no signs of human movement anywhere that I could see, with only a single white cat cleaning itself with fastidious intensity on the tavern's wooden doorstep. Where were the inhabitants?

"It's too damn quiet," Jebido grunted from beside me.

I nodded my agreement, not saying anything as I shifted my grip on Wolf's Head. The cat paused in its task to watch us approach with eyes that glowed in the moonlight, then it finally turned and slunk away into the night. A stone bridge rose fifty feet from the last of the buildings, spanning a fast-flowing stream that broke the stillness of the night with its energetic gurgling as we crossed over it. A stable and several more houses stood on the other side of the bridge, and this time I thought I saw furtive movement behind an ill-fitting shutter on one of the buildings. I pointed to my eyes with two fingers, then the house as Jebido nodded his understanding. I held up my hand to halt my men, then made my way to the rickety door of the rough wattle and daub dwelling while Jebido stood to one side of it with his sword ready. I raised a boot to kick in the weathered door made from uneven planks.

"Wait!"

I hesitated and looked back to see Haf running anxiously toward me.

"Don't do it! Please! This is my home!"

Haf ran up to us, his little chest heaving with exertion as he hammered on the door. "Aldwel? It's me, Haf. Open up."

The door creaked open a crack after a short pause. "Haf?" a young voice said in confusion. "Is that really you? What are you doing out here with *them*?"

"Aldwel's my brother," Haf explained as he looked up at me. He turned back. "It's all right. They won't hurt you. How is Mama?"

"About the same," Aldwel said, a shake to his voice now. "I couldn't get her out of bed." The door opened wider, revealing a boy that I'd guess was a year or so older than Haf.

"Where is everyone else?" Haf asked.

"They've retreated to the slave compound," his brother answered. He lifted his chin in a show of defiance as he glared up at me. "That's where they plan to kill these heathens."

"Then I guess we'd better not keep them waiting," I growled down at the boy. Aldwel shrank back from me; his moment of defiance quickly cowed as I put a hand on Haf's thin shoulder. "Stay here where you'll be safe. I'll return once the job is done and give you that gold I promised you." I pushed the boy into the house before he could argue, then closed the door firmly. "None of you come out until I say it's safe," I added.

I headed back to the road then and gestured for the youth, Radolf, to join me.

"Yes, lord?" he said.

I motioned to the stables and the abandoned houses across the bridge. "Search the buildings. I'll need blankets, as many as you can get. Catch up to us when you find them."

"Of course, lord," Radolf said before running toward the stables.

"Blankets?" Jebido asked, looking sideways at me as I signaled for my men to keep moving.

"For the spikes on the walls," I explained.

Jebido nodded in understanding, and five minutes later, we crested a small knoll to see a group of tall buildings rising in the distance that were completely enclosed by ten-foot-high walls. I could hear a dog barking from inside the enclosure, which was brightly lit by torches on the walls. Metal spikes about three inches long jutted upward from the top of those walls every few inches, just as Alesia had described, though I was pleased to see that the main gates were made of wrought iron bars and not solid wood. That meant any defenders who tried to protect those gates would be easy targets for my archers. There were spikes above the gates as well, and it was clear to me that the place had been designed to keep the slaves inside, not an attacking force out, which would now work in our favor.

"Is that the only way in?" I asked Alesia.

"There's another gate on the northern wall," Alesia replied. She crouched down and used her fingers to draw a rectangle in the loose dirt of the road. "This is the main gate facing us," Alesia said, marking a spot along the southern line. She made a similar mark on the opposite line. "This is the smaller one to the north."

"Is it designed the same as this one?" I asked.

Alesia shook her head. "No, it's made of wood and reinforced steel. But both gates are chained and padlocked from the inside, so we won't be able to break through without some kind of ram." I frowned at that as she made depressions all along the eastern wall. "The guards' and servants' quarters are located here." Alesia made more depressions along the northern and southern walls. "And this is where the slaves are penned."

"How close are the buildings to the walls?" I asked.

Alesia pursed her lips as she thought. "Maybe ten feet or so. Why?"

"Can we get men over those walls without them being seen?"

"Doubtful," Alesia said frankly.

"I'm sure they'll be watching for that, Hadrack," Jebido warned.

"Unless the watchers are pulled away first," I mused as I studied the compound critically. "What's that tall building to the west?" I asked.

Alesia curled her lip. "That's where potential bidders view the slaves. I was supposed to be sold there along with Einrack and the others, but Fungee decided to keep me for himself."

"All right," I grunted, coming to a decision. I glanced at Assuro, who, other than me, was the tallest man with us. "Think you can pull yourself up and look over the wall without being seen? I need to know what they're doing in there."

"Child's play, Wolf," Assuro rumbled.

The big Pith headed away while I focused on the others. "I imagine the pirates are expecting us to come at them from the southern gate, which means most of their numbers will probably be massed there." I smiled. "So, let's not disappoint the bastards. Some of us will climb over the gate while Baine, Gislea, and Tyris shoot through the bars and drive the defenders back. That should make the pirates believe it's a full-scale attack, which should draw whoever is watching the other walls away." I glanced around at my men as I drew two lines to the east and west on Alesia's rough sketch. "I want the rest of you to split up and go here and here. Get over those walls and hit them from both sides." I looked up. "Any questions?"

"What about the townspeople?" Baine asked. "That boy back there said they were going to fight us, too."

I grimaced. "I hope that's not the case, but if they try, then we'll have no choice but to treat them the same as the pirates." I stood up then as Assuro rejoined us.

"I counted at least thirty men waiting in the middle of the courtyard, Wolf. All with shields, strange helmets, and armor."

"Any archers?" Baine asked.

The big Pith shook his head. "Not that I saw."

"They'll have more men than just that," Jebido said with conviction.

"Every man and woman here is worth at least three of them," I grunted with a shrug. "Either way, we need to get over those walls."

I waited for Radolf to return, pleased when he arrived with a bundle of thick horse blankets in his arms. I selected Saldor, Assuro, Niko, Radolf, and the huge, bald-headed Walcott to join me in the attack on the gates. The rest were broken up into two groups, one led by Alesia, the other Jebido. Alesia and Jebido would initially make it look like they were part of the attack, then break off with their blankets and lead their forces east and west along the walls, hidden from view. I knew if I were the pirates inside that compound, I'd be sure to have eyes focused on us right now from some of the taller buildings. I needed those eyes to be fooled into thinking that it was a full-frontal attack only and abandon their posts to join in the defense. I knew there was still a chance the pirates might have archers stationed in the buildings or on the roofs that Assuro might have missed seeing. If there were, then I would have to depend on the skill of my archers to eliminate them.

I drew Wolf's Head. "Are we ready?" I shouted as I clanged the metal blade against my shield.

"Ready!" my men roared with enthusiasm.

I glanced toward the compound, where I knew the pirates could hear us. There was nothing but silence coming from inside now, and even the dog had stopped barking as if sensing something momentous was about to happen.

I raised my sword and pointed toward the gate. "Then let's kill them all! Tear the bastards' hearts out and make them bleed!"

I started to run forward along the road, while behind me, both Piths and Ganders cheered, making as much noise as possible. I grinned, knowing the pirates on the other side of the wall would be gripping their swords tighter when they heard that savage roar, with their throats going dry and their bowels softening. These were Piths they were about to face, after all.

I reached the gate and peered through the bars, getting my first glimpse of the compound's interior. The pirates had formed a shield wall of ten men two sword-lengths back from the chained gate, with more men bunched behind them on the far side of the compound. The enemy wore odd, conical-shaped helmets with a curved visor, and I saw in surprise that the ones guarding the gate carried spears, all of which were leveled our way. Assuro had made no mention of spears. I sensed, rather than saw, an iron-tipped point coming for my face, and I twisted aside as it stabbed through the bars, just missing me before being retracted.

"Stay back!" I shouted, waving off Radolf as he hurried forward with several blankets.

I pressed my body against the safety of the cold stone of the wall as several thrown spears whizzed through the bars to land in the road. One of them narrowly missed Radolf's foot. The youth tucked the blankets under his arm, then picked the spear up and flung it back over the barrier. We shared a grin as shouts of fear and alarm arose from inside.

"Archers!" I cried. I pointed to the gate. "Push those bastards back so we can get over!"

Baine, Tyris, and the Piths—including Alesia—immediately stepped forward and loosed a barrage of dark shafts through the bars. I took a quick look to see what effect the arrows had. Three pirates were down, with two of them wounded and the third lying still. The remaining seven were backing away uncertainly, while from behind them, I could hear harsh commands for them to stand their ground. I grinned. We'd soon see about that.

"Again!" I shouted. "Hit the bastards again!"

Another hail of arrows whipped through the bars, striking shields, helmets, and armor. Two more men fell, one with a bolt buried in his right eye. The rest turned and fled.

"Alesia!" I called out again. I pointed up and over the gates. "Give the cowards something to think about as they run."

Alesia grinned. "Archers!" she cried. "Nock! Draw! Loose!"

A host of arrows screamed up almost straight into the air, then finally lost momentum and fell back into the compound while a second flight was already on the way to join them. I heard the clanging and meaty thunk, thunk, thunk as the first volley of iron-tipped points struck shields, helmets, and the ground, gratified when a startled scream sounded from inside the compound. I peered through the bars again to see the spear-wielding pirates had rejoined the main group, all of whom were now crouched down with their shields over their heads. There were no signs of enemy archers anywhere that I could see.

"Perfect," I grunted. I looked behind me. "Alesia, send another volley!" I motioned my meager attacking force closer as more arrows bombarded the compound. I took a blanket from Radolf. "We go up and over now," I growled. "Hard and fast. Don't stop no matter what happens."

I slung my shield over my back, then the blanket over my shoulder before I leaped as high as possible, grabbing hold of the iron bars. I began hauling myself upward using sheer brute strength alone. Niko joined me, matching my pace as we climbed rapidly foot by foot, with Radolf, Walcott, and Saldor not far behind. The rest of my force clambered around the gates below us, shouting encouragement and waving weapons as they pushed and shook the bars. There was no chance of breaking those gates open, of course, but I imagine we must have looked terrifying from the pirates' point of view.

I reached the top of the gate, hanging by one hand as I flung the blanket over the barbs blocking our way, then I cursed. The spikes were made of iron and filed to a razor sharpness, and they cut through the wool cloth effortlessly. It wasn't going to work without a lot more blankets than what we currently had. I hung where I was, caught in indecision.

"Chieftain!"

I looked down at Saldor, who was reaching up to me with a war-hammer in his hand.

"Break them off," he grunted.

I nodded, still hanging on by my left hand as I reached down and took the war-hammer with my right. I could feel my left shoulder protesting from the strain, but ignored it as I swung at the spikes above my head. The first one bent slightly from the awkward blow, with a chunk of metal flying off, but it held stubbornly. I cursed in frustration and hit it again, relieved this time when the entire thing snapped at the base and caromed away. I glanced at the pirates, who I saw were regrouping now, then banged away at a second spike until it broke apart. I needed at least two more before I figured it would be safe to pass through. A thrown spear cracked into the wall four feet to my left just then, sending up a shower of stone chunks. I grimaced as I saw several more pirates running forward, preparing to throw.

"Baine," I growled, glancing below. "Keep those bastards off of us!"

Baine merely nodded, his eyes dark and murderous as he, Tyris, and Gislea began shooting arrows at the advancing pirates. Jebido and Alesia had taken their forces and left the moment I'd thrown the blanket over the fence, and I prayed that they'd come to the same conclusion about what to do as Saldor had. If not, then my frontal attack was going to be pretty lonely.

Two of the spearmen were down, but the third one had enough time to fling his missile at us before an arrow struck his chest and he collapsed. That spear whistled through the air, heading directly for me before it dipped and caught Radolf in the stomach where he clung to the bars below me. The boy gasped in surprise, his eyes going round before his hands weakened and he dropped to the ground. Tyris immediately fell to his knees beside the boy and rolled him over, then looked up at me and shook his head.

I turned away, feeding on my anger at Radolf's loss. I roared, snapping my body upward even as I swung sideways with all my strength. The war-hammer smashed through one, then a second, then a third metal spike, clearing the way. I looked down at Saldor, baring my teeth in a wolfish grimace of rage as I dropped his war-hammer to him. Then I dragged myself up onto the top of the fence, where I balanced there, glaring down at the pirates.

"I am the Wolf of Corwick!" I thundered as I drew Wolf's Head and shook it over my head. "And your lives belong to me now, you turd-suckers!"

Then I jumped to the ground, the killing blood roaring in my ears as I landed on the balls of my feet and rolled forward in the dirt. I came up snarling, ignoring the friendly arrows coming from behind as they flitted past me on both sides, doing a good job of keeping the pirates huddled defensively behind their shields. I smiled, knowing I should wait for the others to join me before I attacked, but the battle rage had its grip on me now, and all thoughts of anything but killing were gone from my mind.

It was foolish and stupid of me, I know, but I was young and in the prime of my life, and, quite frankly, I just didn't care. The pirates who stood cowering across the compound from me had hurt and killed people that I loved, and now it was time for me to return the favor. I roared a challenge, then charged toward my foes with nothing but the promise of death and destruction burning in my eyes. Every man inside this compound would pay with their lives, I vowed. Every last one of them!

Chapter 12: Captain Bear

Bodies lay everywhere in the compound. Most of the dead were Shadow Pirates, with some townspeople lying among them who had foolishly tried to fight us. The bulk of the villagers, though, had wisely stayed hidden within the buildings along the perimeter, where I hoped they'd be smart enough to remain until we left. I wiped blood from my face, the unnatural quiet seeming strange to me now after the harsh cries and sounds of battle that had filled my ears for almost an hour. A dog with curly black fur and white around its jaws and eyes lay on its side close by, fighting to breathe as it looked up at me. The injured animal whined and attempted to stand, but only its front legs were working, and after a brief struggle, it gave up and collapsed in a heap. Blood matted the beast's fur down the length of its spine, and I could see white on the rump where a fragmented hipbone stuck out. The dog had made the mistake of launching itself at Walcott, who'd crushed its back with my father's axe.

I was about to put the animal out of its misery when Baine appeared and mercifully cut its throat, silencing the whimpers. He nodded to me, his face expressionless as he walked away. I closed my eyes, weary of the death and destruction now as I lifted my face to the night sky. I took a deep breath, enjoying the cool breeze drying the sweat and blood on my face. I stood that way for long minutes, ignoring the sounds of excitement as the Piths started to search the dead for valuables. Occasionally, I'd hear a desperate plea from a wounded pirate found alive as he begged for his life, but the words always fell on deaf ears. I'd promised no mercy for any of these bastards, and I'd meant it.

I sensed, rather than heard, someone approach me and I cracked open my eyes.

"You should have waited for us, Chieftain," Saldor grunted with disapproval. His right arm was streaked with blood, and a long gash was weeping redness from his forehead. I could see large clumps of hair and viscera sticking to the head of the war-hammer that the Pith held in his right hand.

I chuckled. "You're getting slow, Saldor," I said. "If I'd waited for you to get over that fence, the pirates would have died from old age."

Saldor grinned and shook his head in mock wonder. "Are you certain your father wasn't a Pith and not a Gander?"

I laughed at that and shrugged. "Maybe he was, brother, maybe he was at that."

Saldor wiped the head of the war-hammer off on his trousers. "The attack went well with only the one dead, Chieftain," he said, referring to Radolf. "There are some wounded, of course, but nothing too serious."

"That's good news," I grunted, relieved. "Each man I lost now was one more I couldn't replace on a quest that I knew was far from finished.

Saldor looked past me before he motioned to the south with his weapon. "It would appear that the Queen has found the man we came here for, Chieftain."

I turned to look across the compound, where Alesia stood in front of a group of squat stone buildings. An old man was with her, talking animatedly, while startled-looking slaves slowly emerged from the dark interiors behind them. The slaves began to cluster together near the buildings, clinging to each other in uncertainty as Tyris, Niko, and Jebido escorted more of them outside. Most of the slaves were women and children, with their tense, frightened faces lit up by the torches on the walls. I had absolutely no idea what I was going to do about them. There had to be close to seventy, maybe more, which surprised me. I knew there wouldn't be enough room on *Sea-Wolf* to get them all off the island, but I also knew I couldn't abandon them here for Captain Bear to vent his wrath on when he returned.

"Tell your men they've only got a few more minutes to search the bodies," I grunted to Saldor. "I want to get back to the ship as fast as possible."

"Yes, Chieftain," Saldor said. "I will tell them."

I made my way to the nearest corpse, where I carefully cleaned the blood, entrails, and fragments of bone off Wolf's Head on the dead man's clothing. Gislea and Finja were kneeling by the body of a pirate missing most of his face not far away, arguing over who should get the silver ring that they'd found. They finally decided on an archery competition to settle it, which quickly caught the interest of the other Piths. Assuro and another warrior named Jorian dragged a one-legged corpse against a building across the compound and propped him up there. The targets were to be his eyes, nose, and mouth, they announced, and whoever missed first lost.

I stood as the bets started to flow, shaking my head as I sheathed my sword and walked over to Alesia. I knew there would be no leaving now until the issue was resolved and a winner declared, but that might take a while with those two women. My money would be on Gislea, were I in a betting mood, but Finja was older and more experienced and was an expert with the bow, so you never knew.

"This is Dagric," Alesia said when I reached her, indicating her older companion. "You are going to want to hear what he has to say, Hadrack."

I studied Dagric curiously. He was short and stocky, with a rounded belly, a fringe of dirty gray hair encircling a bald scalp, and a bulbous nose covered with angry red sores. He wore a simple, knee-length white tunic and leather sandals, as did all the slaves.

"Tell Lord Hadrack what you told me," Alesia instructed the old man.

Dagric was studying me just as intently as I had him. I could tell he didn't trust me, which was mutual because I didn't trust him, either.

"I understand you're trying to find out where the slave, Einrack, was taken, lord," Dagric said. His voice was soft and filled with obvious compassion, surprising me. I nodded, feeling my distrust fading slightly. Dagric sighed. "He was a good lad, that one. Smart, but maybe a little too headstrong." He indicated Alesia. "When they took his mother away, it was all I could do to keep him from attacking the guards and getting himself killed."

I nodded, not the least bit surprised. Einrack had inherited his father's charm and intelligence, but with it had come a wild recklessness and stubborn tenacity to do what he wanted. The boy would make a fearsome warrior one day, I was certain, assuming he lived to see manhood, of course.

"Where was Einrack taken?" I growled.

"Cardia," Dagric answered.

I pursed my lips in distaste. Oh, how I hated Cardians. "Do you know who bought him?" I grunted.

Dagric shook his head. "No, lord, sadly I don't. But only three Cardians come to Ravenhold to purchase slaves, so I imagine it would have to have been one of them."

"Who are they?"

"A woman named Falix Deneux," the old man said. "There's also Lord Fauchet and Lord Boudin, though he comes rarely."

"Lord Boudin?" I muttered in surprise.

Lord Boudin had aligned himself with Pernissy Raybold in an attempt to overthrow King Tyden and take the throne of Ganderland many years ago, which I'd stopped. He'd also been behind a clever plot to try and have me killed. I'd eventually tricked the bastard into surrendering to me at the Battle of Silver Valley, even though he'd had an overwhelmingly superior force to mine. Since then, he'd returned to Cardia and I'd heard nothing more about him, though I doubt he'd ever forgiven me for making a fool of him. I'd hoped the man had died by now, preferably in a long and painful way.

"You know this Cardian?" Alesia asked.

"Unfortunately, I do," I replied. "I should have killed the turd-sucker years ago."

Alesia nodded, her face set with determination. "Well, brother, it looks like you might still get that chance."

"Yes, it does," I agreed. I turned and looked behind me as cheers rang out. Gislea had just won the contest. I focused back on Dagric. "Do you know where in Cardia we can find them?"

"No, lord, I'm sorry, but I don't," Dagric replied. "I did overhear the woman mentioning something about Bahyrst once." The old man must have seen the look of confusion on my face, for he added, "It's a Cardian city along the southeastern coast, lord."

"Very well," I said, nodding. I knew next to nothing about Cardia, which had suited me just fine so far in my life. Unfortunately, that was now going to have to change. I glanced at Alesia. "We need to get going. The sooner, the better."

"I agree," she said. Alesia turned and put her thumb and forefinger in her mouth, emitting an ear-splitting whistle. The compound fell silent as all eyes turned to us. "Listen up. We're heading back. Grab your weapons and prepare to move out." Alesia glanced at me. "What do you want to do about the slaves?"

"They come with us," I said firmly. "I'm not leaving them."

Alesia nodded, not looking surprised by my decision as she turned to the old man. "Dagric, the slaves listen to you. Make sure they stay close and do as they're told."

"But where will we go?" Dagric asked, looking a little frightened now, I thought. "Captain Bear will return soon, and I shudder to imagine his fury when he sees what you've done."

Alesia turned to me with a question on her face. I focused on the slaves. Most of them looked foreign to me, with odd clothes and hairstyles. I didn't see any Piths among them, so I guessed this group was most likely composed of Swails and possibly Parnuthians.

"We'll transport them to the coast of Swailand," I said, coming to a decision. "They're on their own after that."

I knew there wasn't enough room for all of the slaves on *Sea-Wolf* combined with my men, but there were two pirate ships in the cove, not to mention the small cog that I'd seen anchored there. I would need experienced sailors if I wanted this to work, though, which was something, unfortunately, that I couldn't spare from *Sea-Wolf*.

"And anybody else who wants to leave, too," I added. Hopefully, some of the townspeople would take the opportunity to get away from Ravenhold like Fanrissen's family had and would know how to sail. If not, then I'd have to find men who did—even if they came with us at the point of a sword.

We started out ten minutes later, with half my force at the head of the long column of slaves and the other half behind. I was fairly certain we'd broken whatever resistance still remained on the island with our actions at the compound. But I saw no reason to take unnecessary risks if I was wrong and there were more pirates around. We reached Haf's home, where I could see faint candlelight coming from inside the building and movement again at the broken shutter.

"Keep them moving," I said to Jebido. I gestured to the house. "I'll be right back."

"Want me to go with you?" Jebido asked.

I just shook my head as I walked away. I stopped at the door of the silent building. "Open up," I said. "It's Lord Hadrack. You're safe now."

The door creaked open, revealing Haf. His older brother, Aldwel, stood behind him, holding a sputtering candle of sheep's fat in both his hands.

"Is it really over?" Haf asked.

"It is," I grunted.

"Is that him, Haf?" a female voice croaked from deeper within the single room.

I glanced past the boys, where I saw a woman lying on the floor on a bed of straw with several blankets pulled up to her chin. Her hair was long, black, and stringy, and her face in the candlelight gleamed with sweat.

"Yes, Mama," Haf said as he turned to look back.

The woman struggled to get her arm out from beneath the blankets, and she crooked a finger at me when she finally succeeded. "Come to me, lord," she croaked. I hesitated, and she moaned in such a pitiful way that I knew I couldn't say no. "Please, great lord," she begged. "I'm soon to be gone from this world. Please, take a moment to speak with an old woman before the journey begins."

I reluctantly stepped inside the small room as the boys backed away from me, both of them looking equal parts confused and scared. I crossed to the woman, my boots scraping loudly on the hard dirt floor before I stopped above the bed, staring down at her. I waited, saying nothing.

"Haf promised me that you would return here and bring gold with you, lord," the sickly mother finally said. She flicked her eyes to her son, her expression softening. "I didn't believe him, and I am sorry for that."

"I am a man of my word," I said.

"That's what I'm dearly counting on, lord," the woman replied in a whisper. "But I don't want your money." She paused then to cough, the sounds grating and prolonged. I could hear the last of my force marching past the open door behind me and I tried not to show my irritation. Aldwel dropped to his knees beside the bed, using a filth-encrusted cloth to dab at his mother's mouth and chin. The woman gently pushed his hand away after a moment, her eyes alight with determination. "I need you to take my sons away with you, lord," she rasped. "I will not see another sunrise in this world, and I can't bear the thought of them being left alone in this dreadful place."

"No, Mama!" both boys said in alarm at the same time.

"Da will be back soon, Mama," Haf insisted, looking anxious now. "He will know what to do."

The boy's mother looked at me, and we shared a silent message. I could tell she saw the truth in my eyes. She turned away, focusing on her sons as her features hardened. "Your father is dead," she said bluntly. "And thank The Mother for that, for he was an evil, drunken, good-for-nothing bastard."

Aldwel started to cry then, while Haf stood rooted to the spot, though I could tell he was also on the verge of tears.

The boys' mother looked back up at me. "If they stay here, great lord, then Captain Bear will twist them into something horrible like he did with my husband. They will fight, murder, steal, and rape, all for that animal. That cannot be allowed to happen." She pointed a withered finger at me. "Only you can prevent that, great lord. So, I beg you with my dying breath, take them away from this place. Take their oath of service and let them become good men."

There were tears in the woman's eyes now, and I shifted my feet uncomfortably. I'd never been able to deal with feminine tears.

"I can't do that," I finally said. "There will be fighting where I'm going. It's too dangerous for them."

"More dangerous than here, lord?" the woman asked. She snorted and weakly shook her head. "I think not."

I fished in my clothing and drew out three Jorqs. "I am sorry," I said, unable to meet the mother's eyes as I turned away from her. I placed the coins in Haf's small hands, closing his fingers around them. "Use these wisely," I told the boy. He stared up at me, his young face twisted with dismay and confusion as I turned away and headed for the open door.

"Bastard!" I heard the woman hiss. "You have condemned my sons to evil. Shame on you!"

I hesitated in the doorway, my resolve wavering before I took a deep breath and walked outside. You can't save them all, I told myself over and over again as I walked alone along the deserted road, heading for the stone bridge. I already had Fanrissen's wife and child that I'd sworn to look after, not to mention ensuring my wife remained safe. I couldn't possibly take on responsibility for two young boys as well. Not with what I still needed to do. I reached the bridge and started to cross, feeling guilt pulling at my insides with every step. I paused in the middle to look back as the stream gurgled pleasantly beneath me, oblivious to the plights and follies of men.

I saw a dark shadow dart across the road near the stables, and I dropped my hand to the hilt of my sword. "I see you there. So unless you want my blade tickling your innards, state your intentions."

"Lord Hadrack? It's me, Haf."

I relaxed, waiting as the boy hurried toward me. Haf stopped and offered his cupped hands to me.

"What's this?" I grunted.

"Mama says it should be enough to pay my way." The boy opened his hands, revealing the three gold coins that I'd just given him gleaming in the moonlight along with several smaller copper and silver coins.

I rolled my eyes. The woman might be dying, but she was tenacious. I'd give her that. "And what about your brother?"

Haf lowered his hands, his face twisted with despair. "Mama said that he must stay here with her. She said the gods meant for you and me to meet for a reason and that if she can only save one of us, then it must be me."

I sighed, pinching the bridge of my nose with my thumb and forefinger. Was it a coincidence that I'd thought those very same thoughts about the gods hours earlier? Had the boy been sent to me by them, just as his mother claimed? And if so, would I suffer their wrath if I rejected him a second time?

"And what do you want, Haf?" I finally asked, feeling my resistance crumbling as the boy stared up at me breathlessly. "What do you want to do?"

Haf blinked at my words, looking startled. "Why, I don't know, lord. Whatever you tell me to, I guess."

"Do you want to stay here?"

Haf looked back toward his home, then he shook his head reluctantly. "Mama said I can't."

I sighed again, then put my hand across the boy's bony shoulders as I led him away from his family. "Then I guess we'll just have to see what the gods have in store for us both, eh, Haf?"

I didn't know it then, of course, but Haf would one day grow up to become a great man who would do much to reshape our world. But that was many years down the road from now and an entirely different tale from this one.

Two hours later, with the sun rising in the east and the Piths and my crew working the oars, *Sea-Wolf* cut through the choppy waters of the cove, heading for the channel that led away from Ravenhold. I'd placed the bulk of the slaves on the smaller cog that we'd seized from a fat, sobbing Parnuthian trader, and I watched as it sailed well ahead of us into the channel, commanded by Niko. A small flotilla of different-sized fishing craft and the sleek pirate ship that we'd used to enter Ravenhold followed the cog, filled with the rest of the slaves and some villagers who'd chosen to flee the island.

I'd also planned to use the second pirate ship, but it was now burning briskly where it still sat moored to the wharf, lit on fire by Captain Bear's supporters among the townspeople. Luckily, *Sea-Wolf* had managed to escape a similar fate, though my archers had been forced to repel a determined effort to get to us first before we'd managed to slip away. I was still surprised by how many residents of the island had been eager to leave with us, though the much larger amount who'd chosen to stay had been infuriated by the perceived betrayal and had tried to stop them.

The fortress above me still burned briskly, joined now by growing pockets of flames from the town itself, looking much like Blood Ring Isle had when we'd left there days ago. The fact that the fire in the village hadn't been started by us this time did little to make me feel better as I watched the raging flames from the aftercastle. Those innocents who'd chosen to stay behind and take their chances with Captain Bear and his supporters were probably regretting that decision now, I guessed, as they watched their homes and businesses burn to the ground. The fools who'd lit the pirate ship ablaze hadn't thought far enough ahead, and the flames had quickly consumed the wharf along with the boat. Now, that fire was well on its way to being out of control, jumping from rooftop to rooftop fueled by a persistent wind, with only the remnants of the wetness from the rain hours ago helping to slow its progress. Judging by what I was seeing, I doubted anything would be left standing by the time the flames had finished with the town.

"It's not your fault, lord," Fanrissen said from beside me, correctly reading the look on my face. He shrugged. "The people enabled Captain Bear for years, so perhaps this is the gods' way of punishing them for it."

"Perhaps," I said, not convinced. "But not everyone here was evil, pirate. You of all people should know that."

I thought of Aldwel and his mother. What would become of the boy now? I knew the house where he lived was too far inland to be threatened by the flames, but fire wasn't the only danger Aldwel would soon be dealing with if his mother died. I sighed, regretting now that I hadn't brought him along with me as well. Every action has a cost attached to it, I thought moodily, and I wondered what that cost would be for leaving Aldwel behind. It was a question that I wouldn't find out the answer to until many years later, and when I did, it would not be pleasant.

I finally shrugged away that which I could not change, and instead, I turned my eyes away from the flames to the main deck. I could see Fanrissen's wife, Nota, and their daughter, Amalone, sitting on benches and talking with Shana near our cabin. The two women seemed to be getting along well, which didn't surprise me since everyone who met my wife quickly came to love her.

"Did you have any trouble getting them here?" I asked the pirate, motioning to his family.

Fanrissen leaned on the railing, his face unreadable. "Nothing that I couldn't handle, lord."

I nodded, having expected that answer. The pirate struck me as a most capable man. "I'm planning on leading the slaves and villagers to the coast of Swailand," I said. "They'll be on their own from there. Do you know of a suitable place their ships can make landfall?"

Fanrissen hesitated, then he glanced at Putt, who stood with us. "May I speak freely, lord?" the pirate asked.

"I would expect no less of you," I replied.

Fanrissen took in a deep breath. "If you leave them unprotected in Swailand, lord, then I fear it won't be long before these people are enslaved once again."

I frowned. "Why? Won't Captain Bear have bigger problems to deal with than them right now?"

"Most likely, lord," the pirate said. "But there are other slave dealers around who prey along the coast. Many of them have even fewer scruples than Captain Bear."

"Aren't most of the slaves Swails?" I asked. "Can they not just go back to their homes?"

"Not without food, water, and protection, lord," the pirate said. "Keep in mind most are women and children, and without our swords as a deterrent, how will they defend themselves?"

I grimaced at that. What had I gotten myself into? "Do you have a better idea, Pirate?" I asked.

"Possibly, lord," Fanrissen said. "I suggest we take them to Gatharam, which is a small Parnuthian port on the kingdom's southern tip. There's a Holy House there well known for taking in any who needs help. It's the best chance for them to survive."

I glanced at Putt. "That would mean heading north again, lord," the former outlaw said, his face expressionless.

"And Cardia is where?"

"Further south, lord," Putt answered. "We need to sail around Swailand's outer-most southern tip, then west toward the Gulf of Shells."

"And I imagine bringing everyone with us to Cardia would be a mistake," I said to Fanrissen.

The pirate pursed his lips. "I understand you've met Cardians before, lord. So I expect I don't need to answer that question."

"No," I said thoughtfully. "No, you don't. How long would it take to get to Gatharam?" I asked.

"Four, maybe five days, lord," the pirate answered immediately.

I winced, trying to imagine herding my ragged group of vessels along the coast for that long. Even a minor storm, which Fanrissen had told me was quite common at this time of year, could sink half the boats.

"Should you choose to go north, lord," Putt said. "We'll have to ration what food and water we have. But even then, it's likely with this many people that we'll run out long before we reach Gatharam."

"Is there somewhere along the way where we can stop for provisions?" I asked Fanrissen.

The pirate shook his head. "Unfortunately, no, lord. There are small villages here and there, but the Swails have no cities or ports to speak of and the coastline is mostly wild and inaccessible. The only sizable Swail town I've ever heard talk of is Zirazin, but it's located somewhere in central Swailand."

I nodded in understanding, then leaned against the railing and stared down at the swirling water. We were still fifty yards from entering the channel, and I knew the smartest choice to make would be to ignore Fanrissen's warnings and follow the plan. But doing that probably meant putting many of the people who were now looking to me for protection in harm's way. What was the point of saving them here, I thought, only to throw them back into the same cauldron of burning water somewhere else?

"Wolf!"

I looked up at the cry of alarm coming from the forecastle. It was Finja, who was pointing urgently ahead. Niko had just steered his cog out of the channel entrance, but even as her sails were starting to unfurl in the open, I could see three dark shapes sliding across the waves toward her like pouncing wolves, moving to intercept. They were Shadow Pirates.

I cursed as I watched the black ships tack hard into the wind, with one sweeping expertly across the small cog's bow while the other two moved into position along her sides just as they had done with us days before. Niko tried his best to evade the ship in front but only partially succeeded, and the two hulls collided, sounding like a clap of thunder in the distance. Had Niko been going any faster, I guessed the bigger boat would have crushed the sleeker pirate ship beneath her, but as it was, all the collision did was perhaps rattle the teeth of the pirates a little. That collision, though, managed to slow the cog to a crawl, allowing the other two ships to slide in beside her and throw grappling hooks across to her railings.

I glared at Putt. "Get us over there, now!" I roared.

The former outlaw began shouting orders to unfurl the sail while I raced to the ladder and joined the Piths and my men on the oars.

"Wolf!" Finja called again moments later. "They're boarding the ship!"

I glanced at the Pathfinder, Hanan, who stood beside me as we worked.

"Go!" he hissed between his teeth as he stroked the oar. "You're not needed here. I can do the work of two men!"

I raced across the main deck and clambered up to the forecastle, watching in impotent anger as black-armored pirates began swarming over the cog's sides. Moments later, I heard the first screams coming from the terrified women and children. I cursed, urging the great ship beneath me to greater speed. The flotilla of fishing craft in the channel ahead of us began to desperately turn left and right, trying to go back and avoid the attacking pirates. But all they managed to do was become entangled in the narrow space, with some of them colliding so hard that they capsized. Men, women, and children went spilling into the water, crying out in fear, while the captured pirate ship commanded by Dagric—who'd turned out to be an experienced sailor—began to slow to help them. While I applauded the man's instincts, I knew we'd have no chance of saving the trading cog if he didn't get out of the way.

"Dagric!" I shouted, cupping my hands around my mouth. "Dagric!" I saw the old man look back as we bore down on the channel. I waved my arms frantically. "Leave them! Get out of the way!"

The old slave paused on the deck to stare at me, and then I saw him look ahead toward the embattled trading cog. His sail rose moments later, with the oars once again powering the longboat forward. Villagers and slaves inside the ship reached down to help any of the swimmers they could as they passed, but Dagric fully understood the bigger danger now and he kept his boat moving regardless. I breathed a sigh of relief. That relief quickly dissipated, though, replaced by renewed fear as I looked once more to Niko's cog, which had come to an almost standstill. Pirates were throwing burning lanterns onto the trading ship's deck now, and already the forecastle was smoking, and flames were rippling up her sail. I could see other pirates on board moving about, herding the cowering slaves together on the main deck, but surprisingly, they were not hurting them.

"Wolf," I heard Finja say in warning. She pointed. "Look there, at the back."

I gripped the railing in front of me, leaning forward with a growl of rage arising deep in my chest when I saw Niko on the aftercastle desperately fighting off three attackers. One of them was monstrous, and I knew it could only be Captain Bear. Niko spun left and lunged, skewering one of the pirates, then he rolled as Captain Bear swung his sword and missed. Niko came up on the balls of his feet, crouched and ready while the two pirates split apart, one to either side of him. I saw Captain Bear motion the other man away, leaving himself alone to face Niko.

"Finja!" I snapped. "Can you hit that big bastard from here?"

"It's much too far, Wolf," the Pith said regretfully. "Maybe in another minute at this speed."

I turned and looked down to the main deck. "Tyris!" I shouted. "I need you!"

The tall blond archer left his post at the oars and raced to the ladder with his longbow over his shoulder.

"No!" I heard Shana gasp in horror. I'd been unaware that she'd joined us on the forecastle.

I turned back just as *Sea-Wolf* finally entered the channel, feeling dismay tear through my body. Captain Bear held Niko by the neck with one hand, his sword in the other. Niko's weapon was gone, and he began to pummel the big pirate with his fists, though the blows seemed to have no effect.

"Lord!" Tyris shouted in warning. I drew Shana out of the way as the blond archer reached the railing, already nocking an arrow to his bow. He grunted with effort, pulling the string to his chin, then aimed even as Captain Bear lifted Niko off his feet and drew back his sword.

I clutched at my Pair Stone, praying to the gods as Tyris let fly. The arrow hissed through the air straight and true. I held my breath as I watched it, then groaned when the shaft wavered as the wind caught hold of it, losing momentum before slapping into the hull of the trading cog just above the waterline. Captain Bear must have sensed our eyes on him, or perhaps he'd heard the arrow strike, for he looked our way for a moment before he plunged his sword into Niko's side.

I heard the youth's cry of anguish echoing across the water, unaware that I'd drawn my own sword and was screaming in agony along with him. Tyris drew another arrow with cold precision and shot, but the ship was a long way away, and again the unpredictable winds further out from the channel sent the shaft off course. I finally went silent as Captain Bear rammed his sword into Niko a second time, then a third before he dropped him contemptuously to the deck. Our eyes met across the distance, and though his face was just a blur to me, I could have sworn the big bastard smiled.

"I'm going to kill you for that," I promised, whispering the words as *Sea-Wolf* swept forward. "I swear this by the gods. I'm going to kill you."

Chapter 13: Battle at Sea

Sea-Wolf slid along the channel, propelled forward by intermittent, swirling winds rippling her giant sail, our rapidly sweeping oars, and my crew's desire for revenge. The sleeker, smaller pirate ship commanded by Dagric cut steadily through the water ahead of us, while the trading cog continued to burn as it drifted rudderless out on the open sea. *Sea-Wolf* was still more than a hundred and fifty yards away from the entrance, frustratingly trapped within the confines of the narrow channel. For the moment, we could do nothing to help the terrified slaves on the cog, but soon, the gods willing, I hoped that would change.

Thick black smoke trailed upwards in a fine plume from the trader as bright sunlight broke through the trees to the east, where a cheerful orange sun slowly rose, belying the tragedy unfolding beneath it. The beleaguered cog's sail was now nothing but a charred ruin while hungry flames licked all along the mast, spars, and rigging. The aftercastle was also burning briskly, though I could no longer see Captain Bear standing there nor the ship that had initially collided with the cog. I prayed that the bastard hadn't turned tail and run like he had before, for I dearly wanted his blood.

I had my archers ready with arrows nocked along the forecastle but kept them in check despite being almost in range, afraid to accidentally hit some of the slaves herded into a tight group on the main deck. Unfortunately, waiting proved to have been a pointless caution as angry curses and mutterings suddenly arose from my men. The Shadow Pirates had just begun hacking down the innocent women and children without warning, leaving twisted and bloody bodies writhing on the deck in a mindless slaughter.

I stared in speechless outrage for a moment, then glanced at Alesia. "Do it!" I growled.

"Archers!" the Pith Queen shouted. "Draw! Loose!"

I knew the effective shooting range for my archers was within forty to sixty yards, with pin-point accuracy dropping off after that, even for Piths, especially from an unstable platform. But now that it was clear to me that the pirates had no intentions of letting any of the slaves live anyway, their only hope lay with my archers' skill—that and the mercy of the gods. I watched as a horde of dark arrows screamed into the air, arcing over Dagric's black ship ahead of us before raining down on the cog and two pirate ships that clung to her hull like giant leeches.

Several black-clad men immediately spun and fell from the barrage, and I groaned when a bawling girlchild on the main deck missing half an arm and covered in blood was also struck and silenced. I closed my eyes and prayed to The Mother to take care of her even as I felt a cold, steely resolve come over me. These men would pay for what they had done this day. They would pay in blood for Niko, and they would pay for that little girl and all the other innocent lives they'd just taken for no reason.

I opened my eyes and looked at Alesia. "Do it again," I grunted, trying to block out the screams of the dying slaves. "And keep doing it until all of those white-faced bastards are dead."

"Nock! Draw! Loose!" Alesia cried.

More arrows hissed away, with several additional pirates dropping beneath them before I heard the sounds of a familiar whistle carrying over the water. I put one hand on the railing, squeezing it anxiously as the pirates began scrambling to their ships while the Piths, Baine, and Tyris sent host after host of deadly barbs their way. I saw a pirate on the cog's starboard side, one foot on the railing as he prepared to jump down to his ship. He hesitated to look at us for a moment, which cost him his life as an arrow pierced his neck, sending him spinning to the deck. Another pirate screamed as a shaft transfixed his leg, but he still managed to drag himself forward and flip over the side to safety.

The moment the pirates were all back on board their own vessels, they frantically began cutting the lines securing their ships to the doomed cog. Some of the black-clad men took up oars, pushing the two ships away simultaneously from the burning trader before heading further south around the edge of the island while my archers peppered them with arrows. Men were dropping inside the black ships here and there, but not nearly enough for my liking. Some of the enemy had taken up bows and were shooting back at us, though not one shaft came close enough to make anyone even flinch. Both pirate ships finally slid out of view around the island's sloping wall of rock, dirt, and trees, and my archers slowly lowered their bows, taking precious moments to catch their breath. We all knew that wouldn't last long.

"Those poor bastards are going to get cut to pieces," Finja said, motioning ahead.

She was talking about Dagric and his passengers, of course. The old slave had to know what their fate would be once his boat reached the open water. But to his credit, Dagric had not only kept the vessel on course down the channel, but he had rallied the villagers and slaves into some semblance of defense as well. Women and children now manned the oars while the men stood guard over them to either side, clutching whatever they could find to use as a weapon. They were doomed to fail, of course, but I couldn't help but admire their resolve.

"No," Jebido grunted in disagreement from beside me. "They won't bother with them."

"Why not?" Finja asked.

"Because they mean nothing," my friend said. "They're not the threat. We are. They'll wait for us to appear before attacking again."

"Then why did they go after Niko like that?" Baine asked. "Why not let them pass, too?"

Jebido grimaced. "Because I'm guessing they made a mistake," he said. "The sun was just rising, and when they saw a cog appear, they attacked, mistakenly thinking it was *Sea-Wolf*."

Baine nodded his head in understanding just as Dagric reached the end of the waterway and slid through into the open. The wily old slave automatically cut the ship sharply to his right, then to his left, anticipating an attack—which did not come, just as Jebido had foretold it wouldn't. We were now less than forty yards from the entrance and closing fast, with the wind blowing stronger and steadier at our backs and filling the sail. If only that wind had chosen to arrive a little earlier, I thought bitterly.

"Shana," I said, focusing on my wife. "Take Fanrissen's wife and daughter and Haf down to the hold."

"But—" Shana began.

"Now is not the time," I growled. "They need to be protected. I can't spare anyone else."

Shana nodded in understanding. She rubbed my arm, then hurried down the ladder to the main deck, where half my force still labored at the oars. The need for speed was gone now, and all that was left for the crew of *Sea-Wolf* was to offer death and bloodshed to our enemies.

"To arms!" I shouted down to them. "Prepare for boarders!" My men hastily began to withdraw the oars. I turned to Alesia. "Put half your archers on the aftercastle," I said. "They're going to hit us from both sides just like they did with Niko, so be ready."

Alesia gave me a determined nod, her pretty features filled with deadly promise. "We'll teach these pirate dogs a lesson here today, brother."

"Yes, we will," I growled with resolve.

I dearly hoped Captain Bear would be foolish enough to use his earlier tactic and try to block our way with his ship. If he did, I thought with a grim smile, then the bastard was in for a surprise when he saw Hanley's steel-reinforced ram bearing down on him. I still held Wolf's Head in my hand, and I slowly returned the weapon to its sheath. I reached behind me afterward and drew my father's axe, holding it in both my hands as I stood on the deck. I breathed in and out slowly, steadying myself with my feet spread wide as I waited, my mind filled with images of what I planned to do to the pirate leader.

We were now thirty yards from the entrance, and I stared as if in a trance at the expanse of the open sea ahead of us. I could see nothing but shimmering green water and a bright blue sky stained with orange, pink, and red streaks. No one talked, with only the sounds of the ship creaking, the snap of the sail, and the clink of weapons as my forces prepared themselves. We all knew what was coming, but this time the Shadow Pirates wouldn't find a ship filled with helpless women and children but one teeming with battle-hardened warriors with a deep grudge to bear.

We reached the channel entrance and I looked up at the metal cages swinging above my head. A man was staring down at me from within one of them, his emancipated face looking like a withered skull. Our eyes met for the briefest of moments, and I saw a message of defiance and hope burning there mixed with a fierce need for retribution. I nodded to the man, letting him know that I understood and would do that which he could not. Then we hissed through the water into the open and he was left behind, with everyone tensing for the expected attack. But that attack didn't come. The Shadow Pirates were gone.

I cursed, flexing my fingers on the carved shaft of my father's axe. I'd had that shaft repaired years ago after Pernissy Raybold had broken it during the Battle of Silver Valley, and it was now impossible to tell that it had once been shattered. Dagric's captured boat was tacking into the wind and coming about, and I could hear cheers coming from the slaves and villagers inside. I moved so I could see Putt where he stood on the aftercastle and motioned for him to trim the sail before returning to my original position. I shielded my eyes, searching the horizon for any signs of the pirates.

"There!" Baine finally said, pointing northwest.

I could see the clear outlines of a black sail and hull on the horizon. I turned. "Putt!" I shouted.

"Lord?" came back the reply.

"Take us northwest, and hurry!"

"Yes, lord!"

"Lord, if I may?" Fanrissen said urgently as he came to join me. I just stared at the retreating ship and nodded, thinking it could only be Captain Bear out there. "Chasing after him is exactly what they want you to do, lord," Fanrissen continued.

I frowned and turned to face the pirate. "Explain," I grunted.

"It's a common tactic he uses against the Afrenians, lord," Fanrissen answered.

I furrowed my brow. "Afrenians?" I said. "What does a kingdom a thousand miles to the east of us have to do with anything?"

"They're traders, lord, with big fat ships filled with valuable goods," Fanrissen explained. "Captain Bear has been targeting them for some time, but rich lords get upset when their ships disappear without a trace. So, in the past year, they've begun sending escorts along to keep them safe."

"Ah," I said, beginning to understand now. "So he pretends to attack, then breaks it off and flees."

"Yes, lord," the pirate agreed. "The escort chases after them, leaving the trader alone and vulnerable. It's then attacked and overwhelmed by others while Captain Bear leads the escort into an ambush." Fanrissen shrugged. "He's done it many times, lord, and I expect he's doing it here again with you."

I took a deep breath, thinking.

"That's why the bastard had the women and children killed," Jebido growled from beside me. My friend's face was red with indignant anger.

"Yes," Fanrissen agreed. He turned to me. "He knew it would most likely infuriate you, lord. He wants you to follow."

I glanced at Baine. "Go tell Putt to slow us down but not to drop anchor until I decide what to do."

Baine nodded and went to do my bidding. I looked to the east, where Dagric slowly guided his ship alongside the burning cog with an expert hand. Once they were close enough, several men used grappling hooks to pull them against the hull, while others climbed aboard the ship, desperately searching for survivors. Moments later, I heard a shout of discovery and saw the men carrying a woman's blackened body to the railing, where they gently lowered her to eager hands waiting below. After that, the villagers returned to their search but quickly gave it up when the flames took hold of the entire lower deck and forced them back.

I watched anxiously as the heroic villagers made a hasty retreat, only satisfied when they were safe back on Dagric's ship. "What's Captain Bear got waiting for us out there?" I finally grunted, turning to Fanrissen as Dagric sailed his boat toward us.

"I don't know for certain, lord," the pirate replied. "But whatever it is, I guarantee you that it's going to be more than we can handle. The man rarely strikes unless the odds are in his favor."

"Then why did he attack us at all?" Jebido asked. "Or rather, why did he attack the other cog just now? He knows how well-armed we are."

"I imagine he was counting on surprise," Fanrissen answered, though he looked suddenly uncomfortable and wouldn't meet Jebido's eyes. I wondered why.

"Well, the surprise was on him," I growled, my mind turning to more important things. "Tell me about the other two ships," I said. "Where did they go?"

"I'd guess they cut around the eastern side of the island to the north, lord," Fanrissen answered. "That's where they'll wait."

"For what?" Baine asked.

"Until they see our sail and are sure we've taken the bait," Fanrissen answered. "Then they'll follow us, with the intent to attack from the rear while we're dealing with Captain Bear and whatever he has waiting for us."

I shared a look with Jebido and we both grinned at the same time. "Then I suggest we pay those pirates a visit right now," I said.

"A damn fine idea," Jebido growled.

I looked at Fanrissen. "Will they be anchored, do you think?"

"Most likely, lord," Fanrissen said. "There's a small inlet along the northwestern coast where the water is calm and the fish are always biting. It's a perfect spot to wait to see what we do. My guess is they'll be there."

"Can they see us right now from there?"

"No, lord," Fanrissen said. "There are too many trees."

"Good," I grunted. "Then this is what we're going to do."

Half an hour later, *Sea-Wolf* was slogging through choppy seas along the island's eastern coast as a steady headwind pushed against her bow and slowed our progress. Putt had most of our men on the oars with our sail reefed, but the moment we broke around the island's northern tip, I knew we'd be able to unfurl it again and use the crosswinds to pick up speed when we turned west. Fanrissen had said the pirate ships might be anchored within an inlet on the northwestern corner of the island, but if they weren't and were instead waiting somewhere offshore, then I planned on ramming right through them—but for that, I would need speed.

Black smoke still rose into the pale sky from the destroyed fortress on the clifftop to the south, though we were sailing too close to the shore to see the flames or buildings. More smoke rose from further inland, rising in great plumes from at least fifteen different locations where I guessed the harbor and village lay. I wondered what had become of Aldwel, while beside me, Haf stood on his toes so he could look down into the frothing water beneath us being deflected by our hull. Despite living on an island all his life, this was the boy's first time on a large ship.

I could see Ravenhold's tree-covered shoreline curving dramatically away to the west, less than a mile ahead. "We're getting close," I said. "You'll have to get back below soon."

"I know," Haf replied, not looking at me.

"You are to call me, my lord," I grunted with disapproval. I'd brought the boy up from the hold to formally take his oath of service, but it seemed that he still didn't fully understand the implications of what that had meant.

Haf looked up then, his face filled with dismay. "Forgive me, my lord. I won't forget again."

"See that you don't," I said gruffly. Haf had to learn proper etiquette if he was to serve me, and this seemed as good a time as any for him to start.

Haf returned his eyes to the water, and after a moment, he asked in a faint voice, "Do you think that my mother is dead, my lord?"

I sighed and put my hand on his thin shoulder. "I don't know, lad," I said. "I hope not."

"And my brother?"

"I'm sure he'll be just fine," I lied, squeezing the boy reassuringly as sea spray shot upwards around us.

Fanrissen came to join me then, and I motioned to Haf. "Get below with the others now," I ordered. "And don't come back up until you're told."

"Yes, my lord," Haf said.

I watched the boy climb nimbly down the forecastle ladder, then head toward the hold where Shana was helping those who could not fight down the steep stairs. We'd sunk the pirates' captured longboat and had brought Dagric and his people on board *Sea-Wolf*. Conditions would be cramped and uncomfortable below deck, but there'd been no choice in my view, since I refused to leave them alone and at the mercy of the Shadow Pirates.

After assisting a female slave, my wife straightened, pausing to pull several long strands of black hair away from her eyes while the wind swept around her, rifling her clothing. Our gazes met and held across the distance, and I mouthed the words, *I love you*, smiling when she responded the same way. We maintained our connection for a moment longer before she finally broke eye contact to help a wounded villager make his way downward.

Fanrissen remained silent beside me, though I could tell by his posture and how he kept shifting his feet on the deck that something was troubling him.

I focused on my companion. "What is it, Pirate?" I grunted. "What's got you looking like you just found a turd in your favorite broth?"

Fanrissen pursed his lips, looking uncomfortable and, I thought surprisingly, somewhat apprehensive. "There is something that I haven't told you, lord." He lowered his eyes. "I should have mentioned it right from the beginning, but I didn't because I wasn't certain." I saw the pirate glance down toward the hold where his wife and daughter were returning to its suffocating depths, helped by Shana and Haf. "But after what happened during the attack, I believe I am now."

Something about the pirate's serious manner sent a cold shiver up and down my spine. I waited, leaning against the railing as Jebido and Baine joined us, having overheard the pirate's words.

"What's this, then?" Jebido asked aggressively. "Have you been lying to us about something, you bastard?"

I raised a hand. "Let him speak, Jebido," I said. "The man has earned the right."

Fanrissen took a deep breath. "Before we attacked your ship, lord, there were rumors that a substantial bounty had been offered to Captain Bear if he could capture a person of great importance alive. The rumor was that bounty was being offered up by Cardians."

"Do you have the names of these Cardians?" I asked, though I was pretty certain I knew who one of them was.

"No, lord."

Baine spat with distaste. "You're talking about Hadrack, is that right?" he demanded. "He's the one the Cardians want to capture alive."

Fanrissen glanced at me and I could see the apprehension in his eyes growing. I'd known the man long enough to know he had no concerns for himself, so whatever was frightening him could only have to do with his family. The pirate shook his head. "That's what I thought, too. But now I don't think that at all."

"Tell me," I said as I felt uneasiness tickling my spine like skeletal fingers of ice once again.

"I now believe, lord," Fanrissen said reluctantly. "That the bounty is actually for the capture of Lady Shana."

"What?" Jebido thundered in disbelief. He shook his head. "That's impossible."

I waited, saying nothing as a sort of unnatural calm came over me. There would be time for anger and regrets later, I knew, but for now, I just wanted to understand what Fanrissen was saying so that I could best decide what to do.

"Why do you think it's her they want, Pirate?" I finally asked. I saw Shana entering the hold out of the corner of my eye, then the hatch close behind her, but I remained wholly focused on Fanrissen.

"Because of what Captain Bear did earlier with those slaves, lord," the pirate said. "I know the man well. The moment he realized that it wasn't *Sea-Wolf* he was attacking, his normal course of action would have been just to kill everyone outright and then retreat. But he didn't do that, at least, not right away. Instead, he gathered them all together, particularly the women."

"Why?" I asked.

"My guess is he wanted to be sure Lady Shana wasn't among them."

I took a deep breath while I thought. What Fanrissen was saying did make a certain kind of sense. But why would Cardians try to take my wife? Did they hope to gain some sort of advantage over me? I shook my head at that thought. I knew I was hated intensely in the kingdom of Cardia, so why not just kill me and be done with it?

"Why didn't you say anything about this sooner?" Jebido demanded. He stepped in front of the pirate, glaring into his face.

"Because he was holding that information back," I answered for Fanrissen. "Isn't that right?" I asked the pirate. "You wanted some leverage over me if something went wrong with our agreement. Information that might buy you and your family their lives. Is that what you were thinking?" I could tell my guess was right by the look on the pirate's face and the fact that he chose not to deny any of it.

"I am sorry, lord," Fanrissen said. "I certainly understand if you kill me for not telling you sooner. When I chose not to say anything, I wasn't aware yet about what type of man you were, and, as you say, I wanted to have something to bargain with. I hope you can forgive what I have done, but if not, then I beg you to at least honor your vow to my family once I am dead. They are innocent in this and should not have to pay the price for my stupidity."

I crossed my arms over my chest as I studied the pirate with cold eyes. "Is there anything else that you haven't told me?" I asked.

Fanrissen shook his head emphatically. "No, lord. I swear to you that there isn't."

"Very well," I grunted, coming to a decision. I pointed a finger at him. "This is your only chance, Pirate. If something like this happens again, I will not only take your head but will consider our agreement void and will leave your wife and child to the fates. Do you understand me?"

Fanrissen lowered his eyes. "I do, lord. You will never find cause to do that, I swear."

I took a deep breath and turned away, staring once more toward our rapidly approaching destination. "See that I don't," I growled. I glanced sideways at him. "Now go take up your station with Putt, and do me proud. We'll talk more about this once we've killed these bastards."

"Yes, lord," the pirate said, looking relieved. He bowed slightly, then headed down to the main deck.

"Do you think we can trust him?" Jebido asked me after Fanrissen was gone.

I shrugged. "I think we have to, at least for now. My bigger concern is why Cardians would be trying to get their hands on Shana."

"I think you already answered that question a moment ago, Hadrack," Baine said. "And it's called leverage."

"Over me, you mean?" I asked with a snort. I shook my head. "I already thought of that. Why would they bother? It makes more sense for them just to kill me."

"I don't think this is about you, Hadrack," Baine said. "I doubt any Cardian would shed a tear if you were dead, but you know as well as I do that everyone in Ganderland loves the Lamb, including the king. Cardians are always meddling in our affairs, so imagine what concessions they could gain from King Tyden if they held her hostage."

"Not to mention the ransom they could command for her safe return," Jebido added, looking thoughtful.

I cursed, physically restraining myself from grinding my teeth at the thought of Shana in the clutches of filthy Cardians. If only I'd sent her home long ago, I thought with bitterness as I grasped the railing and stared ahead. Always it came back to that, my failure to make the right decision when it mattered. We were less than fifty yards away from the island's curve, and I knew I needed to push all thoughts of Shana and the Cardians from my mind right now. Once we'd crushed the pirates, there would be time later to decide how to react to this new information.

"You might be right," I finally said to Baine. "And I swear to The Mother that I'll get to the bottom of it and make whoever is behind this *bounty* pay." I pointed ahead. "But right now, we have other things to contend with."

Jebido and Baine fell silent beside me as my men labored at the oars while *Sea-Wolf* swept past a small peninsula shaped like a teardrop that was covered by dense pine and fir trees. There was nothing but open sea after that, for we'd finally reached the island's windward side. I heard Putt's orders to unfurl the sail even as the giant ship turned westward. The sail dropped, luffing in the wind before the great spar turned and the strong gusts that had been in our face all this time began to fill it. Below, my men retracted the oars, then took up their weapons and waited.

"By The Mother," Jebido said from beside me, his eyes gleaming as he stared ahead. "Now, that's a pretty sight if ever I've seen one."

I growled deep in my chest in agreement as the crosswinds took hold of the ship and she leaped forward like a hound on the trail of a wounded fox. The Cardian longboats were both lying anchored together a hundred yards off Ravenhold's northern shore at the mouth of the inlet, rocking on the tide while men lounged inside. I could see several pirates peering northwest intently, where I could just make out Captain Bear's dark sail against the blue sky as he circled, trying to draw us away. I laughed. We had the bastards!

Sea-Wolf was still at least five hundred yards away but was bearing down on the two oblivious longboats with breathtaking speed. The wind was howling in my ears, my hair and beard whipping about me as the ship pounded through the surf, sending spray up in all directions. I heard a sudden shout of alarm echo out over the water from the pirates' ships when we were finally spotted, then frantic movements inside. But the delay had been costly for our quarry, as we'd already closed to within half the distance.

I grinned and drew Wolf's Head, holding the railing with one hand while I pointed my sword at the enemy. "Ram the bastards!" I roared. "Send them to the bottom of the sea!"

I could see the sails on the pirate ships dropping even as their anchor lines were hurriedly cut. Some of the pirates had dashed to take up the oars, but the ships were facing into the wind—something Putt called *in irons*—and they were moving sluggishly as they tried to come about. I howled with delight as Putt changed course slightly to intercept the first pirate ship, which had been slower to react at getting their oars working. We swept forward, with my entire crew howling with bloodlust as we drew to within seventy-five yards, then fifty yards, then ten yards. We loomed over the first black ship like an unstoppable juggernaut of vengeance, our giant hull casting the longboat into deep shadow. I could see individual, white-painted faces looking up at us now from the deck of the boat, their features twisted in panic and terror. I laughed down at them in delight, knowing that they were doomed.

"Hold on!" I screamed in exhilaration to my men as I clutched the railing tighter, anticipating the collision.

Sea-Wolf barrelled forward, her great ram impacting the much smaller vessel just below amidships as pirates shouted in alarm and dove overboard. I felt the ship beneath my feet shudder while my ears were filled with the crunch and screech of splintering wood. We kept going, barely losing any momentum as the steel-covered ram cut the pirate ship in half like a hot blade slicing through a block of lard. Wreckage flew into the air in all directions, with the slower pirates who'd not had time to jump overboard screaming as they tumbled into the churning sea.

"Take that, you bastards!" Baine shouted as *Sea-Wolf* hissed past the sinking, shattered longboat moments later. He stood on the railing holding a stay line, his long black hair streaming behind him as he shook his bow down at the pirates struggling in the water. "Don't worry. We'll come back for any of you that manage to live once we deal with your brothers!"

My friend laughed, his face alight with excitement, while ahead, the second pirate ship had managed to turn about and was now running across the wind just as we were. The longboat was only thirty yards ahead of us, but they were smaller and lighter than us and were slowly pulling away despite our bigger sail. I couldn't allow that to happen.

"Baine," I said, yanking at my friend's boot to get his attention. He looked down. I pointed. "Think you can hit that bastard?"

I was referring to the pirate on the rudder, who stood at the stern looking back fearfully at us as he steered the black ship.

Baine grinned and nodded, then jumped down to the decking. I had other archers on the platform with us and they began laying bets as Baine nocked an arrow, then drew it back. He paused that way for a moment, the ship beneath him rolling on the waves as he aimed. Baine's body was just as straight as the arrow in his bow, his shoulders taught and his face etched with fierce concentration. I held my breath as Baine released, then watched the arrow streak away. It thudded moments later into the longboat's carved, forked animal tail at the stern, only a foot to the right of where the pirate stood half-crouched with his back and shoulders exposed above the railing. If the man noticed he'd been shot at, he gave no sign of it, as his attention was focused squarely ahead of him now.

Baine grunted something under his breath, and then he drew again. A second arrow hissed through the air, and this time it caught the pirate in the left shoulder, spinning him around before he dropped out of sight. My men all cheered, shaking their bows and swords as the longboat instantly began to flounder without a steady hand to guide her. Another pirate raced to the stern to take the rudder, but the damage had already been done. We'd closed the gap now and were running neck and neck with the longboat on our starboard side.

"Archers!" Alesia cried.

Piths rushed to the railing and began shooting down at the pirates, who could do little but try to hide behind shields or duck along the ship's walls. Several tried to shoot back, but they were quickly silenced. I saw the man who'd taken up the tiller slump as first one, then a second shaft struck his chest. He fell over the wooden rudder and hung there, the weight of his body pushing it hard to starboard. The black ship immediately cut toward us, colliding with our hull and scraping along it with a screech.

I felt the killing blood roaring in my ears, the need to vent my rage unstoppable now. I leaped onto the railing, then out into empty air, landing on the pirate ship's deck near the bow. I stood, snarling while a pirate cowered from the Pith arrows four paces away from me, the shield he held over his head riddled with three or four dark shafts. The man finally saw me as I rushed forward and he shouted something unintelligible. Perhaps he was surrendering to me or pleading for his life; I didn't know for certain. But either way, I just didn't care. I rammed my boot against the man's shield, sending him crashing back against the ship's hull, where his powdered head collided with a meaty thunk against the hard wood. The pirate cried out and I slashed downward when his shield involuntarily lowered, tearing open his face from his forehead down to his bearded jaw. The man spasmed, his eyes bulging as blood sprayed before he dropped his shield and fell writhing to the deck.

I heard a sudden thud behind me and whirled, then grinned at Saldor, who carried a war-hammer in either hand.

The Pith grinned back. "I can't let you have all the fun, brother."

I laughed as several more Piths landed on the deck. Saldor howled at the sky, then rushed toward a knot of Shadow Pirates who had rallied themselves in the center of the ship beneath an overhung white canvas. It was a savvy move by the pirates, for my archers couldn't target them as easily there. Not that it would do the bastards any good in the end. I charged after Saldor, my sword singing sweet death to any of the enemy who dared stand against me. Bolts were slapping into the deck and hull or cutting into vulnerable pirate flesh all along the length of the ship. Ahead of me, Saldor roared, flinging himself at the pirates beneath the canvas. I saw one of the black-clad men spin away from the Pith's attack, his face a twisted mess of blood and torn flesh.

A pirate broke away from the group to face me, and I smiled with contempt as he awkwardly lunged for my belly with his sword. I easily blocked it, slapping his weapon aside, then ducked and spun with Wolf's Head cutting through the air like a scythe. The metal blade caught the pirate low in the thigh, ripping deep into flesh, muscle, and bone. The pirate cried out, his attack forgotten as he dropped his sword. I yanked Wolf's Head free with a savage tug, then grabbed the man by the front of his leather armor and flung him with all my strength toward the railing. The pirate screamed, flipping over the side into the narrow gap that had opened between *Sea-Wolf* and the longboat before I heard a satisfying crunch as the two hulls came crashing together once again.

I paused then, taking a moment to catch my breath while I watched the Piths work on the last of the pirates. Saldor was leading them, his face bathed in a sheet of blood, his white teeth grinning from within all the gore as he smashed his war-hammers one after another down into an unmoving pirate's unrecognizable face. Beside him, Hanon the Pathfinder sat straddling a pirate, his great hands encircled around the man's throat as he choked the life out of him. The Pathfinder was chanting words that I couldn't understand, not that it really mattered, I suppose. I was surprised to see Gislea among the Piths as well, using a bloody knife as she hacked and stabbed at a stunned-looking pirate.

I saw movement to my right from behind several water barrels lashed to the sidewall. I moved around the obstructions to find a pirate pressed into them as far as he could go. The man was visibly shaking, his trousers wet from pissing himself. He looked up at me and hurriedly tossed the curved sword he held to the deck.

"Please don't kill me," the pirate said with a whine.

I grinned down at him. "But why not?" I asked before I tore open his throat.

Behind me, the Piths and my crew atop *Sea-Wolf* began cheering. The pirates were all dead and their ship was ours.

Chapter 14: The Lion's Mouth

One week later, *Sea-Wolf* lay anchored off the southern tip of Swailand near the mouth of a massive river delta as the morning sun's red curve broke over the horizon to the east. The river was called the Fivefingers, and I studied the slow-moving brownish water that spilled out from it into the Western Sea, thinking that the heavy build-up of sand, silt, clay, and gravel at the waterway's entrance did indeed look like five outstretched fingers. We'd seen no sign of Captain Bear and whatever still remained of his Shadow Pirates since leaving Ravenhold behind. And though I'd vowed to kill the bastard, I was satisfied enough with how things had played out that I'd chosen not to go after him. The man's power had been shattered, with most of his force killed and his base destroyed. It was enough, at least for now. Someday, maybe soon—the gods' willing—I'd get the opportunity to cross swords with Captain Bear. But until that day came, I was content to turn my focus away from him and toward finding Einrack.

I looked up at the sky above *Sea-Wolf* filled with teeming birds of all kinds, though none could compare to the giant, majestic albatross with its great wingspan that glided high over the ship as if curious about what we might be. Thousands of gray gulls with black wingtips circled in a ceaseless display of energy below the albatross, their harsh cries echoing across the water. I could also see fork-tailed terns swooping in among the gulls before diving into the sea, only to return moments later with wiggling fish in their beaks. A flight of dark birds called shearwaters glided past *Sea-Wolf* along the surf with blazing speed, their wingtips grazing the surface and sending up spray as they fed on surface fish, plankton, and squid.

"May I join you, lord?"

I turned and nodded permission to Dagric where he stood waiting on the ladder leading to the forecastle, looking unsure of himself. The old slave pulled himself up, his breath clearly visible in the chill morning air. He came to stand beside me, saying nothing as he stared at the coast with obvious longing in his eyes. I had come up here to be alone with my thoughts but truthfully didn't mind the intrusion, for, over the past week, I'd come to enjoy the older man's company and surprising wit. I wondered now how I could have ever mistrusted him.

"I imagine you're looking forward to being home soon," I said.

Dagric was a Swail and had been chieftain of a village called Evrar, which lay several days journey down the Fivefingers River from our current position. The Shadow Pirates had raided there more than ten years ago, back before Captain Bear had become their leader, Dagric had said. They'd taken him prisoner along with many others, and he'd spent all his days since at Ravenhold, for the pirates had quickly seen his value as a go-between with the other slaves. Besides, Dagric had added with a faint laugh, he'd been old even then, and few buyers had shown much interest in him. He'd always wondered why the pirates had bothered to take him at all.

"Yes, lord," Dagric said. "Assuming my village is still there."

"As chief, I imagine you lived in an *aestrand*, yes?" I said. The *aestrand* was a tall house on legs that overlooked the village center.

The old slave looked surprised. "You know of *aestrands*, lord?"

"A little," I admitted. "I knew a Swail years ago, a girl named Aenor. She's the one who told me about them. She's dead now."

"Ah, I see," Dagric said with a sad nod. "This girl meant much to you, I gather?"

"Yes," I said. I felt a sudden tightness in my chest as I pictured Aenor the last time I'd seen her alive. She'd died trying to help Shana escape from Calban Castle—murdered by Lord Demay. I had loved Aenor. Not in the way that I did my wife now, of course, nor even how I had felt about the beautiful Pith warrior, Ania. No, my feelings for Aenor had been more about friendship, companionship, and respect than true love. But even so, I truly missed her to this day.

"She was a slave in Ganderland, lord?" Dagric asked, cutting into my thoughts.

"She was," I agreed with a sigh. "Taken when she was just a child."

The old man didn't look surprised. "So many of my people have been taken that way, lord. Ripped from their homes and their mother's breasts to feed the greed of other kingdoms. It is to weep for."

I said nothing and just nodded, for in truth, what could I say to this man to ease his pain? Words were easy, but they would not bring back all the men, women, and children that the Shadow Pirates and others had been stealing from this land for countless years.

Dagric sighed. "Forgive me, lord. I'm normally not such a sentimental old fool. It's a wasted emotion most of the time." He swept a hand toward the wild, inhospitable-looking shoreline filled with trees and dark rocks. "It's just that I never expected to see Swailand again." He glanced at me. "I have you to thank for that, lord."

I waved in dismissal. "I only wish that I could have brought more of you home than this." Dagric clutched at the railing with his wrinkled and age-spotted hands and stared west, both of us content now not to speak. He eventually closed his eyes, breathing in and out deeply as the sun continued to rise and a light breeze rifled his gray hair. "This village of yours," I said after a time. "Will there be horses there that we can purchase?"

"There can be no life without horses, lord," Dagric said, keeping his eyes closed. "Being half Pith, I am told, I expect you must know this."

"Will there be enough for my needs, though?"

"More than enough, lord. If the village still stands, then all that you require will be waiting for you there."

"And you are certain the river is deep enough for *Sea-Wolf* to pass along its length?"

"Without question, lord." Dagric opened his eyes and swept a hand toward the river mouth. I could see tall, strange-looking birds with long legs and elegant necks waddling awkwardly along the muddy bars that partially blocked the entrance. Dagric had called them sand cranes. "The Fivefingers is the mightiest of all our kingdom's great rivers," the old slave said. "Your ship, impressive as it is, will be but a minnow swimming upstream and will be barely noticed. This I assure you."

"That's good," I grunted. "What about this Cardian city, Bahyrst? How far away is it from your village?"

Dagric shrugged. "Perhaps ten days by horseback as the crow flies, lord." He chuckled sarcastically. "But you're not a crow, now are you, lord? So I expect it will take much longer."

"No, I'm not," I agreed, undaunted. I grinned. "I'm a wolf."

Dagric laughed admiringly. "That you are, lord. And a most fearsome one at that."

The delay was regrettable, but I knew that if I tried to sail *Sea-Wolf* anywhere near Cardian territory, it wouldn't be long before I was spotted and my enemies heard of it. That was something that I could not risk. I planned to leave the great cog anchored in the river near Dagric's village, then make the journey on horseback with a select chosen group across a natural land bridge that Dagric had told me connected the two landmasses to the northwest. It would take much time to get there, I knew, but there seemed no other way to accomplish what I needed to do without being detected.

"The sun is high enough to enter the river now, lord," Putt said as he joined us on the forecastle. He looked up at the sky, his nostrils flaring as he sniffed the air. "We've got a good tailwind building too, so if you agree, I suggest we get moving."

"Very good, Putt," I grunted. "See to it."

"Yes, lord," Putt said. He glanced sideways at Dagric. "May I borrow your companion, lord? I don't know these waters the way he does."

"I haven't been here in many years," the old slave said. "The Fivefingers has most likely changed some since then."

Putt shrugged. "Perhaps, but I've never been here at all, which makes you an expert compared to me."

"Go with Putt, Dagric," I said. "Offer him any assistance you can."

The old man bowed. "Of course, lord."

I stood alone for a time after the two men left, enjoying the chill of the morning, though already I could feel the heat from the sun building as it rose, a harbinger of things to come. The last three days had been scorching hot, even with the cooler prevailing winds at sea, and it seemed this day would be no different.

Sea-Wolf creaked and shuddered beneath me as her anchor rose before the Piths and my crew began rowing us toward the jutting banks of the fingers. I could hear Putt shouting orders down to Baine, who, despite his horrific experience on *Sea-Dragon's* rudder years ago, was still the best pilot we had and seemed to enjoy it. The aftercastle overhung the steerage on the main deck, and Putt was forced to constantly lean over and look down to relay his orders to Baine. It was, I thought, an awkward way to guide the boat at the best of times. I vowed once we returned to Ganderland that I'd set Hanley to figuring out a better system. For now, though, it would have to do.

Sea-Wolf slowly nudged her way into the river's mouth, gliding carefully between the second and third fingers as the oars rose and fell with a steady rhythm. My biggest fear was getting hung up on a hidden shoal, but so far we'd encountered no obstacles, though Putt had sent Walcott with his experienced eyes to help me watch out for them. Hundreds of sand cranes lined the bars to either side of *Sea-Wolf*, showing no interest in the passing ship as they busily dug and poked in the mud with their hooked bills, searching for everything from plant tubers and roots to insects, crayfish, snakes, and frogs. I could see a vast marshland to the north of the river where more cranes flew above the wetlands, looking ungainly yet somehow regal with their great wings, arrow-like necks, and long legs trailing behind them.

The heady scent of mud filled my nostrils as we cautiously progressed further into the maw of the giant river, mixed with the sweet, almost sickly aroma of the dancing riverweed that lined the coast and the edges of the fingers like long hairs. Ten minutes later, we finally passed the last evidence of the bars jutting up from the murky brown water and Putt ordered the sail to be lowered halfway, his voice sounding relieved even from where I stood. The canvas quickly took the wind while the crew retracted the oars and *Sea-Wolf* surged forward. We were on our way, and as I stared ahead, I could only wonder what the next few days and weeks would hold for my little company.

On the morning of the second day of our journey up the river, *Sea-Wolf* passed around a bend in the waterway, revealing thousands of small and large stones lying jumbled along the swoop of the western bank as if they'd been scattered there by a bored giant. We'd been traveling through heavily forested areas during the trip so far, but now those trees had miraculously thinned out without warning, revealing open fields and rocky hills to the west. This, I knew, was the place where we would anchor the ship and go on foot to Dagric's village. Putt would stay behind on *Sea-Wolf* with Hanon the Pathfinder and the four surviving original members of the ship's crew. Several of the wounded warriors who couldn't walk would also remain, as well as Haf and Fanrissen's wife and daughter. The rest, including my wife and the remaining slaves and villagers we'd brought with us, would be making the trek overland to the Swail village, where Dagric assured me they would be well received.

I was eager to be off after we'd anchored, but it was almost midday by the time my company was finally fully disembarked from the big cog and ready to go. Dagric and I led the procession northward over the hills, where the old slave had told me his village was located several hours away. We had twelve Swail women with us and eight children, as well as ten villagers who'd come along simply because they had nowhere else to go. Only one of the slaves had been lost during the sea journey; a young Swail named Elsri, who'd died on the night we'd reached Swailand's coast. She had been the girl the brave villagers had rescued from the burning trading cog at Ravenhold, though few of us had expected her to last as long as she had, considering her terrible wounds.

Dagric had begged us to keep Elsri's body back from the sea so that he could bury her in the soils of her homeland, so we had stopped not long after entering the Fivefingers to do just that. It was the least that I could do for her bravery, I'd thought at the time, though I'd regretted it afterward, for the Swail funeral ceremony had turned out to be a long and cumbersome affair filled with odd phrases and songs in a language that none of us could understand. The Piths had initially attended but had quickly returned to the ship, shaking their heads in disappointment. I think the warriors had been hoping for something similar to their own ceremonies of death, since I'd been clear that not one Swail slave was to be touched in a sexual way while onboard ship. That decree had not gone over well with the Piths, as most of the Swail women were young and attractive, yet it had been obeyed as far as I knew.

I heard laughter rising from behind me and glanced over my shoulder to see Alesia and Shana deep in conversation together within the group of Swail slaves. Gislea and Finja walked to either side of the women, giggling. My wife and the Pith Queen had never been all that close over the years that they'd known each other. Perhaps they had sensed in each other a rival, I wasn't sure, but I had never been curious or foolish enough to ask. However, something had changed since we'd left Ravenhold, and the two were now fast friends and almost inseparable.

It had been Alesia who'd convinced me to let Shana come with us to the village, as I'd originally planned on leaving her behind with Putt. I was sure the two women were plotting something together right now, but regardless of how hard they pleaded with me later, I had no intentions of letting my wife accompany me to Cardia. There was a bounty on her head there, and until I'd dealt with those behind it, I was convinced there was no safer place for her to be than hidden deep within the heart of Swailand. Unfortunately, that conviction would soon be proved wrong in a most tragic way.

"Thirteen days," I grumbled. I glanced at Jebido, who sat beside me astride a four-year-old brown mare with soft, doe-like eyes. "Thirteen damn days to get here."

Jebido stroked his beard, looking tired and dirty, while the white stallion I rode stamped its right hoof as if eager to be off. The rest of my band, consisting of Baine, Alesia, Saldor, Fanrissen, and Dagric, all looked no different than my friend did. Nor, I suppose, did I, for that matter, for we'd taken little time to rest on our journey. I studied the well-traveled road that cut through the middle of a wide stretch of rocky land ahead of us, buttressed by deep water to either side. I could see heavy wagons going back and forth along the road's length, and I guessed those heading toward us were empty, judging by the ease with which the horses or oxen drew them along. According to Dagric, the wagons heading away were filled with iron ore, copper, silver, gold, and lead mined from the hills that lay miles away to the north. The old slave had told me the resources of Swailand were slowly being stolen one wagon at a time by the Cardians, day in and day out, year after year.

Small craft sat out on the water to either side of the roadway, with fishermen casting nets to pluck the abundant mullet, herring, and mackerel that I could see teeming in vast schools along the surface. We were still officially on Swail land where we sat our horses, and I could see a coastline more than a mile away to the west where the road met an open plain surrounded by forested land. A small hillfort sat back from the shoreline on a knoll, which Dagric had informed me was an outpost called Ironhold that guarded Cardia's outer frontier.

"It couldn't be helped, Hadrack," Jebido finally said with a weary shrug. "You knew getting here wouldn't be easy and would take time."

"I did," I muttered grudgingly. Dagric sat to my left on a spotted gelding, and I glanced at him as I motioned toward a waystation behind us where we'd just bought some supplies from a Cardian trader. "How come you allow Cardians to trade on your land?" I asked the old man.

Dagric snorted. "How are we to stop them, lord? Their army is immense." He paused as a wagon creaked past us, kicking up volumes of dust as it headed northward on its way to take out one more sliver of lifeblood from the land of the Swails. The old man's eyes were filled with bitterness as he watched the wagon clatter away. "These people have no souls, lord. They are like locusts, stripping everything in their path before moving on. They take whatever they want from us and laugh at our weakness."

"Then why do you keep rolling over and presenting your ass to them?" Baine asked from behind us. I hadn't failed to hear a note of derision in his voice. "Fight the bastards."

Dagric glanced at my friend, a trace of annoyance on his weathered face now. "Do you think that we haven't tried, youngster? Of course we have. We have fought, and we have sometimes beaten them, too. But not for long, for always there are more Cardians to replace those we kill. If we cut down a hundred, two hundred take their place. If we kill those two hundred, then four hundred come. It is endless. Victory over these creatures is nothing but a temporary illusion, with the reality of cold steel and death always waiting at the end." Dagric clucked his tongue sadly.

"It is better, we have learned, to let the Cardians mine our metals in peace than to try to stop them and die. I had hoped during my time as a slave that things might have changed in my homeland, but alas, that is clearly not the case."

I knew there was nothing that I could say to Dagric that could help the Swails. The gods had given these people a raw deal, with both Cardians and slavers preying upon them at the same time. But as much as I sympathized with the plight of the Swails, I had a job to do. I was here to find Einrack, nothing more, and that task would now begin in earnest once we finally set foot in Cardia. I kicked my horse forward, motioning the others to follow as we fell in behind a wagon pulled by several oxen and covered by thick canvas sheets. Two men sat in front of the wagon, and though the driver looked back to give me an appraising, unfriendly glance at first, he quickly seemed to lose interest in us.

I was glad of that fact, for the last thing I wanted right now was for my little band to be noticed. That's why I'd brought such a small force with me and had left the rest behind in the village of Evrar, which thankfully had not only been standing when we'd arrived, but thriving. The village's chieftain, Olffur, had been just as generous to us as Dagric had promised, and he'd mentioned that one of the previously conquered provinces in Cardia far to the west had rebelled against Cardia's Emperor, Matheo Cheval. Olffur had said the battle for control of the region had been going on for more than a year now and that mercenaries from all across the known world were flocking there to fight—which was why I planned on my band posing as some of them.

Most of us could pass as Afrenian mercenaries, though Saldor and Alesia were another story, as they were obviously Piths. Saldor had graciously shorn his long blond locks and was now dressed in Cardian armor with a helmet that he constantly complained itched him without let up. While Alesia, who would certainly have stood out with her shaven head on one side in the common female Pith manner, had simply shaved the rest of her head to match. I confess that I still hadn't quite gotten used to the look, though strangely, I found, if anything, Alesia's gleaming bald pate added even more to her feminine appeal somehow.

The driver ahead turned again to look at us, this time with greater interest. I saw him lean over to say something to his companion before they glanced back furtively at us.

"Stay here," I grunted to the others. I kicked the white stallion into a trot, guiding him alongside the head of the wagon. "Greetings," I said to the driver in a pleasant voice. The man looked me up and down sourly and nodded but said nothing. He was perhaps middle-aged but solidly built, with thick forearms and biceps. I guessed he would have been formidable once, though now the great circle of flesh bulging at his waist told me the march of time was quickly winning the battle and turning him soft. "I understand your emperor is offering gold for men who can fight?"

I saw the driver's demeanor thaw slightly. "You're mercenaries?" he asked.

"We are," I agreed with a grin. "From Afrenia."

The driver frowned. "What were you doing in Swailand, then? There's no fighting back there, you daft fool." He chuckled, nudging his companion with his elbow. "You'll only find meek little mice with no teeth in Swailand, along with maybe the odd rat or two. Those people are no threat to anyone, which means there's no money to be made for the likes of you."

"But the cunny can be mighty fine," the other man added as he leaned forward to look at me. "That is as long as you don't mind the smell much."

The two men laughed at that, and I paused the stallion to let a wagon coming in the opposite direction go by, then trotted back to the driver. "I had a disagreement with the captain of the ship we booked passage on," I said. "It became in our best interests to disembark early."

"Oh," the driver said, looking interested. "What was the disagreement about?"

I winked at him. "Why cunny, of course. Isn't that always the way?" I gestured to Baine, who simply stared back at us, looking fierce and deadly. "My companion mistakenly thought the captain's daughter was just a simple whore. Once the unfortunate error was discovered, too late, of course, things quickly got out of hand. So, rather than slaughter the entire ship's crew and other passengers, we agreed that it would be best for all concerned if we leave." I motioned to Alesia, who looked breathtakingly beautiful in the sunlight despite her armor and bald head. "But not before the daughter decided to join with us and seek her fortune with a sword."

The two Cardians studied Alesia in wonder, then they laughed, relaxing completely. The driver's companion even turned and gave Baine a hearty wave of approval. My friend just glowered back at him, and the man quickly turned around again with his grin dissolving.

"So, you're offering your swords to the Emperor to fight the Walerians in the west, then?" the stocky driver asked.

I shrugged. "We're mercenaries, friend. Our services always go to the highest bidder." I motioned toward Ironhold rising in the distance. "Is there a man over there who we should deal with?"

The driver stuck out his lower lip as he thought. "There's Captain Timas Nadieux, I suppose. He's in charge of the outpost, though I don't know if he has the authority to negotiate something like that. You might be better off going to Bahyrst and talking to the provincial regent there. I know he has the power to approve applications like yours."

"And this man's name?" I asked.

"Albor Boudin," the driver replied.

I tried not to show my surprise. "Do you mean Lord Boudin?"

The driver shook his head. "No, I believe that's his brother."

"Isn't Lord Boudin one of the Seven Rings?" the other man asked.

"Seven Rings?" I said.

The driver looked at me pityingly. "I sometimes forget how ill-informed Afrenians are." I growled low in my chest and dropped my hand to Wolf's Head, and the man quickly lifted a hand. "I was just joking, friend. No need for that."

I guided my horse aside to let another wagon pass, then slid in beside the driver once again. "What are the Seven Rings?" I asked.

"The Emperor's council," the driver explained. "Seven men, each with a ring representing the kingdoms that have fallen to the empire. Lord Boudin holds one of the rings. His brother, Regent Boudin, does not." The driver winked. "Though if the rumors about a coming offensive are true, then perhaps there will be another ring or two sitting around the council table soon."

"What offensive?"

The driver shrugged. "Don't know. Ganderland, maybe, or perhaps Parnuthia. Who can say for certain?"

I pursed my lips at that, then nodded. "Thank you for the information. I think my companions and I will meet with this regent you spoke of and see what he can offer us."

"A good choice," the driver said. "I wish you luck on the battlefield, mercenary."

I tipped my helmet to the men, then dropped back to join the others before I told them what I'd learned. I didn't think we had anything to fear from the two men now since I was sure they'd bought my story completely. But even if they still had some suspicions, I had no intention of stopping in Ironhold anyway after what I'd just learned. No, we were heading directly to Bahyrst, where I hoped to kill two birds with one stone. There was a good chance that the Cardian woman, Falix Deneux, had bought Einrack. But if she hadn't, that left only Lord Fauchet or Lord Boudin as the buyer—and Lord Boudin's brother was the provincial regent based in Bahyrst. Was it a coincidence, or were the gods still on my side? I'd soon find out.

Two days later, I studied Bahyrst with a critical eye. The town was situated at the end of a sweeping peninsula that jutted out into the Western Sea like a bent fish hook. Green-covered mountains rose above the city to the north and the west, with an estuary filled with brackish water running along the base of the western mountain, separating the peninsula from the mainland. The town was heavily fortified, with high walls and turrets, which I saw were flying the Cardian royal banner from tall poles. I planned on going into the city alone, a decision that was not sitting well with Jebido.

"Have you ever heard the story about the man who stuck his head inside the mouth of a lion?" Jebido asked me as I urged my horse down a steep slope leading to the town.

I rolled my eyes when we reached level ground. "No," I said. "But something tells me that I'm about to."

"Seems there was this fellow," Jebido continued, ignoring me. "He was always taking risks. You know, doing things that those of us with, shall we say, saner faculties would never even consider."

"You must be talking about yourself, then," Baine grunted from behind us. "Because you're as crazy as they come."

"Ha!" Jebido grunted over his shoulder sarcastically. "Aren't you the clever one." He turned back to me. "Anyway, one day he came to this town, oh, let's call it Bahyrst just for fun."

"Yes, why don't we," I grunted, barely listening.

"So, this man goes into the town, and he sees this strange old fellow standing alone in the market holding a tiny little gold chain attached to a pet lion."

"What was the lion's name?" Saldor asked in a serious voice.

Jebido's bushy eyebrows rose in surprise and he turned to look back. "What does the name matter?"

The Pith warrior shrugged. "Don't know. I was just curious, is all."

"Humph," Jebido grunted, clearly thrown off by the question. "Anyway, the old fellow with the lion—"

"Fang," Baine cut in.

"Eh?" Jebido said.

"The lion," Baine replied with a straight face. "Let's call it Fang."

Jebido pursed his lips. "Anyway," he said, dragging out the word. "The old fellow holding the lion's chain—"

"Fang's chain," Baine insisted.

Jebido groaned low in his chest, and I could see two spots of red starting high on his cheeks. I couldn't help but smile. "Fine, the old fellow holding Fang's chain asked this man if he would mind watching his pet while he went to take a piss."

"Why not just piss right there?" Alesia asked, joining in the fun. "Was he afraid someone would see his wrinkled snake? I'm sure the lion already pissed on the ground anyway, so who would care?"

"You mean Fang already pissed on the ground," Baine corrected.

"Yes, of course," Alesia said to him, unable to suppress a giggle. "Fang."

I could hear Jebido's teeth grinding in frustration beside me. "Do you people want to hear the story or not?" he asked in a huff.

"No!" Alesia, Baine and I all said together.

Jebido grunted something under his breath, his eyes flashing with deep anger. I knew my friend well, and it was rare for him to display such emotion. I looked behind me at the others, who I could tell were not yet ready to stop their teasing. I made a gesture with my hand, letting them know that it was enough. I guided my stallion closer to Jebido, who studiously ignored me, his face set in an obvious pout.

"So, what happened?" I asked. Jebido didn't answer and I sighed, then used my foot to nudge his leg. "What happened with the lion?"

"Fang," Baine said from behind me.

I turned and glared at him, then focused back on Jebido. "Finish the story. I want to hear it."

I could see Jebido's expression thawing. He cleared his throat. "Well," he said. "The old fellow went away to take his piss, and the man just stood there, holding the lion's...er...holding Fang's chain. Eventually, this little boy walks up to him and offers the man a gold coin."

"What for?" I asked, feigning interest.

"He wanted the man to put his head in Fang's mouth. Now, the man thought the idea was crazy at first, of course, but a crowd had gathered by that time, and they all insisted that's what the old fellow and Fang did every day to earn money. The lion was as tame as a castle cat, they claimed. Well, the man hadn't eaten in days and he was starving, so it seemed an easy way to make some money."

I could tell the others were listening intently to Jebido's story now; their interest peaked. I had to admit mine was too. Jebido must have sensed he had an attentive audience all of a sudden, for he became more animated.

"So, the man makes a great show of things, pretending to be afraid as he approaches Fang, who just stares at him with these big gentle eyes. The man pries open Fang's jaws and stares at the huge teeth inside, each one the size of a short sword and razor-sharp. He starts to get cold feet, but the crowd is urging him on by then, with others pledging more coins. So, unable to resist the thought of so much money, the man finally shrugs and sticks his head in the lion's mouth."

Jebido paused there, saying nothing, and finally, Baine snorted. "Well, what happened next?"

Jebido looked back at him. "What do you think happened? Fang bit his head off, of course."

"But why?" Baine asked in surprise.

"Because that's what he was trained to do. Fang was the emperor's prized executioner, you see, and he was on his way to the palace to entertain the emperor's guests."

I rolled my eyes as my little band fell silent. "So, what's the point of the story, Jebido?" I finally asked.

"The point, my friend, is that people can't be trusted. The lion did exactly what it was supposed to do because that's what animals always do. They are predictable. Animals do not try to trick you, and they do not lie to you. They have forgotten all about yesterday, and they don't care about tomorrow. They only live for today." He motioned to the city as we approached. "But the creatures walking around on two legs in there are different. They are cunning, treacherous, untrustworthy, and greedy, and because of that, they will say anything to get you to put your head in the jaws of that lion." I opened my mouth to say something, but Jebido held up a hand. "But, if that man's friends had been with him, Hadrack, watching his back, he would never have thrown his life away like that."

I sighed. "That was a long way to go just to make your point," I said. I halted the stallion a hundred yards from the city gates, with the others circling me.

"Yes, it was," Jebido agreed. He lifted an eyebrow. "So, are you going to stick your head in the lion's mouth without us like a fool or let us watch your back?"

I glanced at my companions one by one. "Well, I guess after that story, I have no choice now." I swung the stallion toward the city. "Come on," I said. "Let's go find Einrack—together."

Chapter 15: Bahyrst

Bahyrst was a depressing, filthy place. The streets were lined with refuse and dung from both animals and humans, with the rotting corpses of dead rats and other things that I chose not to examine too closely lying everywhere, giving off suffocating fumes. We made our way down the central street covered with chipped and broken cobblestones, where hawkers in small stalls covered by canvas awnings on either side of the road competed with each other to gain the attention of the passersby. I saw both men and women selling everything from trinkets to wine and beer, fish, poultry, leather, salt, and pork. One old man with a long beard even had a boy standing on a stool, shouting that he'd sell his grandson for as little as two gold coins or a mule.

I shook my head, as always disgusted by Cardians, though in truth, I knew many of the cities and towns of Ganderland were not much better. I continued onward, leading my little band past a small platform where an enormously fat man sat cross-legged playing an oddly flared flute while a sleek black rock snake lay coiled menacingly at his feet. The snake was well within striking distance of the fat man, though surprisingly, it showed no inclination to attack him, nor the amazed crowd watching from a safe distance. I had to admit I was hugely impressed by the feat as we trotted past, for people usually headed the other way fast whenever they saw one of the deadly snakes. At least the sane ones did, anyway.

A dead goat lay in the middle of a cross street when we reached it, the beast's eyes forever staring at nothing while several scrawny hounds with matted fur tore at its belly with savage desperation. A cloud of buzzing flies rose and fell from the carcass with each rip of flesh, snarl, or growl coming from the starving dogs, though the people on the streets seemed neither surprised nor interested in what was happening. There was no sign of the goat's owner, which surprised me, for the animal still held value for its meat. I halted the white stallion and glanced at Jebido, who grimaced and shrugged. Children seemed to be everywhere among the filth, their grime-covered faces looking almost as black as I'd heard the men from the island kingdom of Pelnisia were said to be.

"What now?" Jebido asked me.

"I'm thinking we find ourselves a tavern," I replied. "One where we can get some decent food and maybe find out more about this Falix Deneux woman."

Several grizzled soldiers in red capes appeared along the dirt path beside the roadway on foot, and I watched them warily out of the corner of my eye. But thankfully, they showed no interest in us, as they were deeply engaged in a heated conversation. I waited until the soldiers had disappeared down a side street, then guided the white stallion toward a skinny man walking toward me down the road with an air of importance about him. Other travelers in front of our procession were being careful to avoid him, though I had no such reservations. The man seemed oblivious to my approach; his concentration fixated on a parchment he held in his hands. He only looked up when I stopped my horse in front of him, casting his body in shadow as I blocked his path.

The man blinked at me in surprise, then his thin face, which was covered by a bushy mustache and wispy beard, turned mean. "Out of my way, you careless oaf!" he snapped. He tapped a pendant depicting a golden shield with two crossed swords on it pinned to the lapel of his tight red coat. "Can't you see I'm engaged in city business here?"

"Sorry for the intrusion, friend," I replied down to him, trying to remain polite. Inside, I was itching to ram my horse's chest into him. Why did all Cardians have to be so unpleasant? "We're looking for a nice place to get a drink and some good food nearby. I was wondering if you could recommend one?"

"And I'm looking for a whore without the clap and a pair of tits that don't hang down to her knees," the man retorted sourly.

"But this is Bahyrst, so it looks like we're both out of luck, eh?" The skinny man waved his hand dismissively. "Now, move that beast out of my way before I send for the city constable."

I sighed. So much for politeness. I slipped aside the black cloak that I'd donned that morning, showing the hilt of Wolf's Head. "Are you sure you want to do that? I simply asked you a friendly question, and it's rude not to answer it."

The man looked at me warily for a moment before his natural demeanor took over. "I'm on official business for the regent, you stupid, hairy ass! I'm a very important man, and I don't have time to answer silly questions from obvious riffraff like you. So, you'd best do as I say, or I'll have you thrown in irons this minute."

"The regent, you say?" I responded, perking up.

I glanced at Jebido and grinned at our good fortune, then slowly dismounted. I handed the stallion's reins to my friend while the rest of my company waited patiently behind us. I moved closer until I towered over the other man, one hand on my sword.

"You stay back!" the skinny man whined, his bluster gone now as he saw just how big and menacing I was. He stumbled away from me several paces, then squealed in alarm when he slipped on some horse dung and fell hard on his rump. I just shook my head in mock sympathy while my companions snickered. "Now look what you've done, you giant imbecile!" the man cried in dismay.

I sighed, then approached and took hold of his tunic and hauled him to his feet. If the man hadn't mentioned that he worked for the regent I would have left him where he was. But something told me this meeting had been orchestrated by the gods, which meant I needed to see where it led.

I smoothed my features, trying not to let my dislike for the skinny Cardian show. "Perhaps we've gotten off on the wrong foot, you and me," I said, smiling at him in what I hoped would be a disarming way. "My name is Korid Engmar from Afrenia. My associates and I are here to offer our services to your great emperor in his noble fight against the traitors out west. A nice captain in Ironhold told me that I should speak with Regent Boudin about possible employment."

"Oh," the skinny man said, looking slightly mollified. "You're Afrenians. I might have guessed." He brushed at his clothing, grimacing at the shit stuck to his fingers, then groaned when he noticed a streak of brown smeared across the back of the parchment he still held. He wiped his hand on his trousers, then stupidly offered that hand to me moments later. "I'm Renol Deparde, assistant to the assistant of the regent's assistant."

I blinked, then shook my head as I tried to grasp exactly what that was supposed to mean. Something told me that whatever Renol's actual job was, judging by the lack of intelligence in his eyes and his puffed-up importance, it was probably nothing more than a glorified errand boy. I glanced down at the shit-covered hand Renol still held out to me, making no move to accept it.

"Does that mean you have the regent's ear, then?" I asked.

"Of course I do," Renol said, looking insulted as he retracted his proffered hand. I wasn't sure whether he was angry about my refusing to shake it or what I'd just said. "We're great friends, he and I," the man added as if it were obvious.

I guessed that Renol was lying to me about how close he and the regent were, and I wondered if I'd been wrong about the gods and he really wasn't worth the effort. The assistant to the assistant's assistant grimaced as he held the fouled parchment up by one corner. He clucked his tongue and tried wiping it clean on the ground, but that only made things worse. I sighed as the man looked around helplessly, seemingly at a loss about what to do.

I motioned to a horse trough sitting alongside a building nearby. "You could try using some water," I suggested.

"Of course," Renol said, looking relieved. "How stupid of me."

Indeed, I thought as I waited impatiently for the man to return. Renol's hand was cleaner when he rejoined me, and the leather parchment he held was damp but mostly free from the worst of the shit. "I would like to meet with the regent," I said. "Right now."

Renol held the parchment up, waving it in the air so the late afternoon sun and wind could dry it. "Now?" he asked. "Surely you must be joking? The regent is a busy man."

"Do I look like the kind of man who makes jokes?" I growled.

Renol shook his head as he took in my armor and weapons beneath my cloak. None of us carried any shields, though, having stashed them several miles to the north. I didn't want anyone noticing that they were obviously Pith. "No, no, you don't," Renol said. "But just the same, Regent Boudin is meeting with the head of the Traders' Guild for the rest of the day. Perhaps, if you—"

I put my hand on Renol's shoulder and squeezed until he hissed in pain. I'd had enough of this pompous fool. "I think the regent and I should talk right now. What do you think?"

"I think," the assistant managed to gasp out as I applied more pressure. "That your suggestion is a splendid idea." He looked past me down the street. "But first, I must deliver this message."

"Where?" I grunted.

"Just a few blocks away at the surveyor's office." I saw his eyes turn sly. "You can wait for me here if you like. I promise I won't be but a moment."

"Fair enough," I replied. I gestured to Baine. "But my companion will go with you."

"Why that's very kind of you," Renol said, looking disappointed. I knew by his expression that he'd had no intention of returning to help us. "But it's really not necessary."

"Of course it is," I said. I squeezed the man's shoulder again. "I wouldn't want you to get lost on the way back or hurt somehow. This is a rough town, after all, and you never know when something bad might happen to you. So, what do you say?"

Renol groaned from the pressure, and finally, he nodded in acceptance. I let him go, pretending not to notice when the skinny man gave me a look of loathing. I knew exactly how he felt.

"Well, you'd best be off," I growled. "Time is wasting."

"Yes, you're right," Renol said weakly. He nodded to me. "I'll be right back."

"I know," I grunted.

Renol opened his mouth to say something more, then thought better of it. He lowered his head in defeat and headed up the street, looking back several times while Baine followed sedately behind on his horse.

"So, are we going to see this regent with swords in our hands, then?" Jebido asked as I retrieved my horse from him. "Is that your plan?"

I swung up into the saddle. "No. What makes you think that?"

Jebido shook his head. "You're a smart man most of the time, Hadrack. But there are times when a little less aggression and a little more diplomacy are called for. This is one of them. You can catch more flies with honey than you can with vinegar, you know."

"I'm not going to hurt the regent," I grunted. "I'm just going to ask him some questions."

"Uh-huh," Jebido said doubtfully. "He's Lord Boudin's brother, after all, and we both know how you feel about that man."

"I won't hurt him," I insisted stubbornly, though inside, I too had my doubts. "I just want to find out what he might know about all of this."

Jebido lifted his hands from his sides in frustration. "And just how do you expect to learn anything useful from him? He's not about to volunteer any information willingly, you know. Not to mention if he figures out who you are, then our mission is in serious jeopardy. There aren't that many men as big as you are walking around with a scarred face and a wolf sword, Hadrack."

"He won't figure it out."

"That's what you said about the Overseer. How did that end up?"

I sighed, knowing my friend had a fair point. I glanced at the others as they moved their horses closer. "What do you four think?"

"I say we twist the bastard's neck until he tells us everything he knows about Einrack and the bounty on your wife, Chieftain," Saldor growled.

Now it was Jebido's turn to sigh. "And then what, Saldor?"

The Pith shrugged. "Then we kill him. Dead men can't talk last time I looked."

Jebido shook his head. "You can't just murder a Cardian provincial regent and expect there won't be a reaction, Saldor. They'll close the gates and turn the city upside down looking for us."

"Not if we get out before they discover him," Saldor replied.

"You're assuming the regent even knows what's going on," Jebido shot back. "What if he doesn't? What if we torture the poor bastard and learn nothing? We can't leave him alive after that, but if we kill him, we'll have the entire city up in arms and still be no closer to finding Einrack."

"Jebido is right," Alesia said. "As much as I want to put a blade to the dog's throat and make him tell me where my son is, we have no way of knowing if he even knows or not. It's too big a risk to go in there roaring like a lion."

I glanced at Fanrissen, glad Baine wasn't here with us. I was certain my friend would have corrected Alesia and said, Fang. "What do you say, Pirate?"

Fanrissen shrugged. "I agree with Alesia, lord. I don't know him, but Regent Boudin has a reputation for being a smart, hard man who rules this province with an iron fist. Your going in there right now might not be the wisest choice. Perhaps we should poke around the city first and see what we can learn?"

I nodded. "And you?" I asked, turning to Dagric.

"I'm just an old man, lord," the Swail said, his expression blank.

"Does that make your opinion somehow less relevant?" I asked.

Dagric's eyes sparkled and his lips twitched in amusement. "No, lord. Some would say more so."

"As would I," I agreed. "So then, what do you say?"

"May I speak honestly, lord?"

"Please do."

Dagric nodded. "I do not know you that well, lord," he said, carefully choosing his words. "But my impression is that you sometimes lead with a closed fist when an open hand might be more appropriate." I saw Jebido grin out of the corner of my eye, but didn't give him the satisfaction of looking at him.

"True," I said instead. "But not always." I paused as I thought about Shana back at the Swail village. I knew we wouldn't be standing here today if not for the different approach she'd used when I'd first met Fanrissen. Was this the same thing? Something told me that it was. "All right," I said, coming to a decision. "We won't go in like a lion." I grinned. "We'll go in like a lamb instead."

Jebido pursed his lips. "How?"

Fifteen minutes later, Renol returned with Baine still following him. But this time, I was seated on my horse with a sour expression on my face while Jebido had dismounted to meet the assistant.

"Ah," Jebido said when he saw the Cardian in his tight red coat approaching. "There you are." He offered his hand, shaking the other man's warmly. Renol looked up at me in confusion, then at Jebido. "I want to ask for your forgiveness, sir," Jebido said. He gestured to me. "That hulking fool is my son, and I should never have allowed him to bully you that way. You are truly an important man and I am ashamed of how he acted toward you."

"Well, that's...uh...well," Renol said, clearly startled.

"My name is Aremm Engmar, and these are my men." He paused to smile, nodding graciously to Alesia. "And lady, of course." Jebido drew Renol aside while Baine guided his horse beside me, looking confused as he tried to get my attention. I ignored him. "I understand how busy you and the regent must be, and I again apologize for my son's belligerent attitude. He was dropped on his head as a young lad, you see, and sadly it has addled his wits. The only thing he's good for now is violence, it seems."

"Yes, I can see that," Renol replied, giving me a disapproving look.

"I wonder, sir," Jebido continued, "if perhaps I could meet with the regent alone to offer our services?"

"Well," Renol said, looking unsure of himself. "You have to understand that Regent Boudin is a very busy man and that he might not have the time to talk."

"Oh, I understand perfectly," Jebido replied, nodding his head enthusiastically. "I'm sure he's busy, as no doubt you are since you are obviously a highly regarded and important man in this great city's administration. But, since we're friends now, you and me, perhaps you could use your influence to let me speak with the regent? Even if it's just for a few minutes?"

Renol glanced at me, the look of pleasure from Jebido's words quickly sliding away, replaced by dislike. "You won't bring that beast with you?" he asked.

"Of course not," Jebido snorted. "My son likes only three things, I'm afraid. Bad beer, unscrupulous whores, and fighting. All of which, I'd wager he can find at some seedy tavern somewhere while we men of, shall we say, a more advanced intellect can enjoy each other's company. Now, what do you say?"

Renol grinned, giving me a look of triumph. For a moment, I thought he was even going to stick his tongue out at me before he turned away and took Jebido's arm in his. "So be it, friend," the assistant said, leading Jebido away.

"We should have just killed the bastard," Saldor growled under his breath as we watched the two walk away.

I hauled on the stallion's reins, turning him down the cross street. "The night is still young, brother," I said. "The night is still young."

The first tavern we came across was called *The Leaky Roof*, which seemed appropriate, judging by the water stains on the plastered ceiling and painted crossbeams. The floor was a mixture of brick and flagstones, which surprised me. I'd expected dirt. The ceiling was low, only a few inches above my head, and I had to duck each time I passed beneath one of the beams. We took a table near the back of the square room while the few sleepy patrons inside examined us with wary, unfriendly eyes.

A thin barmaid with a beak of a nose, a cleft chin, and dull, listless eyes hinting at low intelligence came to our table and recited the tavern's few options for food and drink in a bored voice. I ordered beer for everyone along with some pottage served in trenchers and some egg custard tarts. The barmaid made a point to mention the house special several times, which was roasted pork flavored with exotic spices, vinegar, and verjuice. But I politely declined each time. I knew the meat in taverns like this was often heavily spiced to hide the fact that it had gone bad, and something told me that this was the case here. The last thing I needed was my men throwing up and shitting themselves if we had to fight our way out of Bahyrst.

The beer and food arrived in short order, and I paid for the fare with several Pith silver fingers, not wanting to bring attention to us by paying with Jorqs. The woman studied the silver suspiciously; the first time I'd actually seen any emotion other than dull-witted boredom and hopelessness cross her features.

"I'm not sure we can take these," the barmaid finally said. "We usually only accept gold." She glanced behind her toward a grey-haired man standing behind a bar made from several crates covered with rough planks. I assumed he was the owner. Alesia and the others had already begun to eat by now, and the woman clearly couldn't decide what to do about the payment.

"It's a little late for that now," I said with a shrug. "Besides, that's all we have. We're Afrenian mercenaries and that was how we were paid for our last job." The barmaid looked confused, shifting from one foot to another as she tried to process what I'd said. I bit into a piping hot tart and sighed, savoring the taste, for it was surprisingly good. After being out on the road for almost two weeks, hot food seemed like a forgotten luxury. "Is that the owner over there?" I asked around the tart as I motioned toward the man at the bar.

"Yes."

"I'm sure everything is fine, but if you're worried, why don't you just go ask him if the silver is all right?"

The barmaid's features brightened. "Why yes, I think that's a good idea. I'll do that."

"Not too smart, that one," Alesia said as she watched the woman head toward the bar. "Uglier than a hog's arse, too."

I chuckled, agreeing with her as the barmaid spoke with the owner, who came over to our table a few moments later. "Good day," he said pleasantly. "I'm the tavern keeper, Demee."

I nodded to him as I drained the last of my beer. "Is there something wrong with the payment?"

Demee looked down at the silver fingers he held in his hand. "On no, most certainly not. It's quite appropriate, actually."

"That's good the hear," I said, wondering why the man had come over then.

"I understand you're mercenaries from Afrenia?"

I burped loudly, then sat back on the rough bench and stared at the tavern owner. "That's right. Why?"

"I'm Afrenian myself, though I haven't been back in almost twenty years." Demee gestured to an open spot on the bench opposite me. "May I sit?" I shrugged, waiting as the man settled himself beside Saldor. The Pith seemed oblivious as he crammed the last of his dripping trencher into his mouth. Demee set the two silver fingers on the rough wood of the table, then slid them toward me dramatically. I just stared at him with a question on my face. "I have a rather, shall we say, unfortunate problem," the tavern keeper said. "And I wonder if you might consider using your particular skills to help?" He gestured to the silver. "In exchange for these and the food you've eaten, of course."

"Ah," I said, understanding now. I leaned forward. "And what might that problem be?"

Demee sighed. "*The Angry Frog*," he said. I frowned, waiting. "It's the tavern down the street." Demee motioned around him. "Hardly anyone comes here anymore because of them."

"Maybe you need to serve better food," Saldor grunted as he picked at his teeth.

"There's nothing wrong with my food," Demee retorted. "No, the problem is *The Angry Frog* is operated by Cantin Poloeu." He paused there as if expecting me to react. "Poloeu is Regent Boudin's brother-in-law," he added when I didn't say anything. "You've heard of him, I imagine?"

"I have," I agreed.

"Well, Poloeu wants my place," Demee said. "He's been buying up half the taverns in the city, all for next to nothing while the regent pretends not to notice. I refused to sell for any price, and ever since, Poloeu has been sending men in here to threaten my customers and me. Just last week, they killed a man right where you're sitting for no good reason." Demee shook his head as he looked around at the sparse customers. "I'm barely surviving day to day. Another week of this and I'll be destitute."

"So, why not fight back?" Baine asked. "Kill this Poloeu bastard and be done with it."

"I wish I could," Demee said. "I have more than enough evidence about what he's been doing. But as long as Regent Boudin is in power and backing him, it's useless. All I would get for my troubles is a stretched neck."

"Same could be said for us, I imagine," I said. "So why would we want to risk what you won't?"

"I can pay you more in gold if you want," Demee suggested hopefully. "It might take a little while, though." He rubbed at his thick grey hair when I didn't show any interest. "I'm sorry. It's just that I don't know where else to turn. I heard that you were from Afrenia, and I guess I thought because we're fellow countrymen—" The tavern keeper trailed off, looking miserable.

I pushed the two silver fingers back to him. "I'm sorry, too, friend. I wish we could help you, but we've got our own problems."

I looked up just then as Jebido entered the building. My friend paused to glance around the dim room, and I saw the relief on his face when he noticed us. "There you are," Jebido said as he hurried over. "We have to go...now!"

"What's happened?" I asked, alarmed by the look on Jebido's face.

"My talk with the regent kind of took a turn for the worst," Jebido said, not meeting my eyes.

I scowled. "How?"

Jebido looked embarrassed. "You know that thing I warned you not to do if you met him?"

I could feel my jaw drop open. "You didn't?"

"Well, the bastard has a big mouth and he made me kill him!"

I glanced sharply at Demee, whose eyes widened.

"Damn," Jebido whispered, looking crestfallen, having clearly not noticed the tavern owner sitting there. "I've gone and stepped in it again, haven't I?" He gestured to Demee. "Who is this?"

"A friend," I grunted.

"I don't understand," Demee said. "Is this man saying Regent Boudin is dead?"

I could see sudden hope growing in the tavern keeper's eyes. "Looks that way," I replied. I stood, motioning for the others to do likewise. I picked up the fingers from the table. "It appears we've earned these after all," I added. "Which means the rest is up to you." I turned to Jebido. "Did you learn anything about Einrack?"

"No," Jebido replied. "But I found out who put a bounty on Lady Shana."

"Who?" I growled.

Jebido took a deep breath. "You're not going to like this, Hadrack, but it was Matheo Cheval."

"The Emperor?" I said in disbelief. Jebido simply nodded as I let that sink in. "What about Falix Deneux?" I finally asked.

Jebido looked embarrassed again. "The regent kind of died before I could ask him about her. I'm sorry."

"Kind of?" I grunted in disbelief. Jebido continued to look miserable, but he said nothing in his defense.

"You're looking for Lady Deneux?" Demee asked me.

"You know her?"

"Of course," Demee replied. "She's the wife of the head of the Traders' Guild, Lord Deneux. They have a large holding outside the city in the mountains."

"Are there guards?"

Demee nodded. "Some, I believe. Not many."

I grinned then. "I'll make you a deal, my friend. You show us where this holding is, and we'll take care of Cantin Poloeu and *The Angry Frog* for you. What do you say?"

Demee stood, his face set in determination as he thrust out his hand. "I say you've got yourself a deal!"

Night had fallen by the time Demee led us on horseback away from Bahyrst. We traveled at a trot in a tight group along a dirt road that wound its way upward into the mountains to the west of the city. We'd dealt with the tavern keeper's problem just as promised, and *The Angry Frog* was now nothing but a smoking ruin, with its owner, Cantin Poloeu, no longer counted among the living. I felt no regrets for what we'd done to him, for Demee had told me more about the man's activities and it was clear that his death would be mourned by no one and cheered by many. I couldn't say how the city's inhabitants would react to the regent's death, though, which surprisingly seemed not to have been discovered yet. It was a fact that I was eternally grateful for as we progressed up the mountain. I prayed that our good fortune would continue.

We passed through a small village of thatch houses almost an hour after leaving Bahyrst behind, still with no pursuit in sight. I was beginning to think that our actions there had gone unnoticed. There was no one about in the village other than a man relieving himself against the side of one of the buildings. He watched us trot by in wary silence as we followed the road upward until the man and the group of thatch houses were finally lost from view. Demee led us ever upward for another hour until we eventually reached level ground, where we halted our horses a quarter-mile away from a fair-sized holding situated in a deep valley. The holding was surrounded by high walls and protected by a formidable gate.

"This is where I leave you," Demee said to me.

I held out my hand. "It's been a pleasure. I hope your business flourishes now."

"So do I, Lord Hadrack," Demee said as we locked forearms. I hesitated, and he chuckled. "Fear not, lord. I will tell no one that you were here. I promise your secret is safe with me."

"I appreciate that," I said, knowing the man spoke true.

Demee nodded and swung his horse around. "You never know," he added. "Maybe if things go well and I make enough money, I'll travel to Ganderland and start a tavern there. I could use a change of scenery from Cardia."

"Our kingdom would be lucky to have you," I said, meaning it. "Just make sure the meat is always fresh if you do."

Demee laughed and waved, then headed back down the road.

"How do you want to handle this, Hadrack?" Jebido asked after the tavern keeper was gone.

I pointed to the west, where some overgrown hedges inside the compound partially obscured the view from the main house. "We'll go over the wall there. Quick and quiet."

"What about the guards?" Baine asked.

I grimaced. I didn't know if Falix Deneux had Einrack or not, but the fact that she'd been buying slaves in Ravenhold was enough for me. I had no sympathy for her or anyone who worked for her. "We kill them if they get in our way," I grunted.

Saldor and I lifted Baine over the wall, and he secured a rope to the trunk of one of the hedges, then threw it back to us. After that, it was a simple matter to gain access to the interior of the holding. I crouched down on the grass in the shadows of the hedges and studied the three-story stone house that sat back from a diamond-shaped courtyard. Stone steps led up to a pair of carved wooden doors, with a metal brazier burning brightly to either side. A small fountain sat in the courtyard's center, lit by flickering torches, with several outbuildings sitting further back to the east of the house. Two men were standing together in front of what looked like a stable. Both wore shiny metal helmets and leather armor and carried weapons and shields. I grimaced, wishing now that we had ours, but I hadn't wanted to take the time to get them before heading up the mountain.

"Baine," I grunted, motioning to the men with my head.

My friend nodded, then silently slipped away into the darkness. I waited, watching the house intently, but I saw no signs of movement coming from there.

"By the gods, he's quick," I heard Fanrissen mutter not long after Baine had left.

I glanced back to the two guards, but they were both gone now, though I could see a metal helmet lying on the ground, still wobbling as it reflected the firelight.

"All right," I said, satisfied that Baine would deal with any other guards around the buildings. "Alesia and I will go into the house. The rest of you guard the perimeter." I looked specifically at Saldor. "Only kill them if they're armed or resist, brother. Remember, there's bound to be innocent women and children about."

"Of course, Chieftain," Saldor grunted, sounding offended. "I do not war on children."

"Then let's go," I said.

I drew my sword as I stood, then ran across the courtyard toward the house, heading for the stairs with Alesia while Saldor, Fanrissen, Jebido, and Dagric spread out across the grounds. I reached the doors without hearing any cries of discovery and threw them open, only to find an empty, marbled entrance hall lit by flickering lanterns hanging off metal brackets set in the walls. A white statue of a naked woman on her knees stood in the center of the hall, her hands clasped together with manacles as her misery-filled eyes stared upward at the curved ceiling high above. A set of wide stairs rose to my right from where I could hear music drifting down from the next floor. I took the steps two at a time, with Alesia right behind me. The music was much louder at the top, coming from an open archway at the end of a long corridor. The walls to either side of me were plastered and painted a light red, with small alcoves set every three feet where the sculpted marble heads of men and women sat. I found it strangely unsettling as I passed beneath their disapproving gazes.

I reached the archway and glanced back at Alesia, who nodded to me, her face set, then I stepped through. A white wall stood facing me six feet away, with another sculpted head of a scowling, bearded figure glaring at me from a recessed alcove. I turned left down the corridor, following the music until I entered a tiled room where a gleaming tub of gilded bronze filled with water sat in the center. A naked woman lay in the tub while a small group of boys and girls dressed in brown tunics encircled her, playing stringed instruments. The woman's eyes were closed, and her head was resting on a silk pillow while a boy massaged oils into her shoulders and neck.

    That boy was Einrack.

Chapter 16: Lady Deneux

Einrack paused in his work, and his eyes widened at our sudden appearance. "Mother?" he gasped in surprise.

Einhard's son had been nothing but a jumble of arms and legs the last time I'd seen him several years ago. But the boy was twelve now and he had grown a great deal since then, with the hint of the powerful man he would one day become already showing in the breadth of his shoulders and muscles in his arms. His long hair was the color of harvested wheat and tied down his back with string, and his eyes were the same mesmerizing green as his father's had been. Einrack looked like a smaller version of Einhard, and I felt a sudden pang of loss as I stared at the boy who reminded me so much of my friend.

Einrack rushed toward his mother with his arms outstretched while the other slaves abruptly stopped playing their instruments, looking unsure of what was happening. The woman in the tub—who I assumed was Falix Deneux—opened her eyes almost lazily, although she didn't react to our presence and instead continued to lie where she was, looking at ease. The boy threw his arms around Alesia, laughing with joy while I studied the Cardian woman with wary interest. She ignored me and just watched the reunion between mother and son with a detached smile on her face. The fact that she was naked and vulnerable seemed not to bother her at all, and I wondered if perhaps she was intoxicated, which might explain her puzzling lack of alarm at our appearance.

"You found me," Einrack said in wonder when he broke the embrace. "You actually found me. I thought I'd never see you again."

"I promised you I would when they took you away," Alesia replied. "And I meant it." She motioned to me. "But it wouldn't have been possible without Hadrack's help."

There were no tears in Alesia's eyes, nor in the boy's either, for they were Piths and rarely showed such things. But even so, I could sense the immense love and affection the two felt for each other. I couldn't help but smile as I watched mother and son together, though it was tinged with sadness as I thought of Einhard and his other children who were no longer with us.

Einrack turned to me and he nodded in greeting. "It's good to see you again, Wolf."

"And you," I replied. "We've come a long way to find you."

"Thank you for taking care of my mother."

I grinned. "Who's been taking care of who?"

Einrack chuckled knowingly. "What about the Shadow Pirates?"

"Most are dead," I replied. "The rest soon will be if I have my way."

"Ravenhold?"

"In flames the last time I saw it."

"That's good," Einrack said with a satisfied smile. "That's very good." He turned back to his mother. "And what of my father?"

"With the Master now, my son," Alesia replied.

Einrack blinked at the news, but he showed no reaction other than that. "My brothers and sisters?" he asked after a moment.

"They have taken the path as well and are by your father's side where he can watch over them."

Einrack closed his eyes, the first signs of inner torment showing on his young face now. Finally, his features smoothed and he nodded in acceptance. The boy's calmness and maturity for his age was remarkable. I was greatly impressed.

"Well, this has certainly been a touching reunion," Falix Deneux muttered in an almost bored-sounding voice. She stretched and yawned, then stood in one smooth motion, sending water splashing onto the tiled floor. "But as entertaining as this has been, I'm starting to get cold."

I guessed the Cardian woman was at least thirty years old, maybe more. But her body was surprisingly firm, with heavy breasts and slim legs leading to the mound of her sex, which I was startled to see was completely hairless. I had never seen a mature woman bared in that particular way before, and despite the situation we found ourselves in, I had to admit that I found it quite intriguing.

Falix Deneux stood in water that rose just past her knees with her hands on her hips, unashamed as she stared boldly at me. I could tell by the smirk on her lips that she hadn't failed to see where my eyes had been drawn. "So, I'm guessing you would be the famous Wolf of Corwick that Einrack has been telling me about." She sniffed, looking me up and down. "I actually thought you'd be more frightening than this."

"Be careful what you wish for, woman," I growled as Wolf's Head swished in my hand.

Falix laughed, looking unconcerned as she lifted one finely-sculpted leg onto the rim of the tub before she bent and slowly slicked water off her skin with her hands. She stared at me the entire time, then finally lowered her foot onto the tiled floor and accepted a large cloth from one of the slaves.

"Einrack, dear, do introduce me to your mother, won't you?" the Cardian woman ordered as she stepped completely out of the tub and began to dab at her damp breasts with the cloth.

The boy stared at Falix Deneux with obvious infatuation and I silently groaned inside, starting to get an inclination as to why this woman felt so safe in our presence. Einrack gestured to his mother. "Lady, this is Alesia, Queen of the Piths. Mother, this is Lady Falix Deneux."

Lady Deneux snapped her fingers and another slave brought her a dressing gown, helping her to put it on. She gave me a mocking look before tying the sash and hiding her nakedness from view.

"Your son told me how beautiful you were," Falix said, turning her gaze to Alesia. "But truly, his description did not do you justice. The bald head is something of an acquired taste, I suppose, yet it does have a certain charm. Sadly, I was not able to bid on you in Ravenhold, as you'd already been pulled off the market by that worm, Fungee Filace, by the time I arrived. The lecherous bastard selfishly decided to keep you for himself." Falix studied Alesia with bold eyes. "A shame, really, as I would have enjoyed breaking you. I usually prefer my slaves to be younger, but I think you would have made an interesting addition to my little group." She lifted an eyebrow. "By the way, did you kill Fungee?"

"Not right away," Alesia replied. Her eyes glinted with a promise of violence that I knew all too well. "I cut his cock and shriveled sack off and fed them to him first," Alesia added. "Then I killed him."

Lady Deneux clapped her hands together, showing no signs of revulsion or horror at the news about Fungee Filace's unpleasant demise. In fact, judging by the odd glow I saw in her eyes, I guessed the woman was excited about his torture and death. "How fitting," Lady Deneux cooed. "I never liked that man."

I found the woman's obvious lack of fear for her safety strange and guessed that she still didn't realize just who it was that she was dealing with in Alesia, nor that her death was only a few heartbeats away. I had no intention of intervening when that death came, either, knowing it was more than justified. I watched dispassionately as Alesia handed her bow to her son with an air of determination about her. Here we go, I thought.

"You don't have a cock or a sack," Alesia said to the Cardian woman as she drew a knife. "But that won't stop me from finding parts to cut off you just the same."

"No, Mother!" Einrack shouted when Alesia began to stalk toward Lady Deneux. He flung himself in front of her, protecting the woman from his mother's vengeance. "I won't let you do it."

"Get out of my way, boy," Alesia grunted.

There was still no sign of fear on Falix's face, and I saw her smile as she gently put a hand on the back of Einrack's neck before running a finger up and down his skin in an intimate way. The boy's handsome features softened for a moment at the touch, then hardened again with determination as he faced down his mother. I grimaced, my suspicions confirmed. The young fool was in love with her.

"It's not her fault," Einrack said, putting his large hands on Alesia's shoulders to hold her back. "She's been nothing but kind to me."

"Oh, I bet she has," Alesia growled.

"I mean it, Mother," Einrack said. His green eyes flashed in a way that I remembered all too well from his father. "I won't let you hurt her, so don't test me."

"You would dare to speak to your queen that way?" Alesia snapped in anger.

"Not with any joy, Mother," Einrack said. "But I promised Lady Deneux that I would protect her, and I stand by my word."

"Protect her?" Alesia said with a snort. "From what? Me?"

"If need be," Einrack responded. The boy's face was set in a hard, stubborn mask, and I knew there would be no dissuading him.

"What has this witch done to you?" Alesia demanded.

"I told you, she's been good to me."

"Offering herself up like a bitch in heat does not make her good," Alesia retorted. She glared at the Cardian woman. "It just makes her a filthy whore who takes advantage of children."

Lady Deneux chuckled. "Your son is no child, Alesia, believe me. My well-satisfied loins can attest to that."

Alesia's eyes flashed with rage and she started forward again, but Einrack was big and strong and he held her back.

"Oh," Lady Deneux said. "Perhaps this might be a good time to mention that my husband is due home at any time now."

"Then I guess you'll be widowed when he arrives," I grunted.

"Perhaps," Lady Deneux said with a shrug. "But do bear in mind he is an important man and rarely travels without an armed escort." She smiled mockingly. "The mountains around here are just filled with the worst kind of people, you see."

I snorted. "You're lying."

The words had barely escaped my lips before I heard running footsteps from the hallway behind me. I turned, bracing myself for an attack, but it was Baine who appeared around the inner wall. I frowned, for the tavern keeper, Demee, was with him as well. Both men looked anxious.

"Hadrack, we've got trouble," Baine said.

"Told you so," Lady Deneux said with a chuckle. She turned, snapping a finger at one of the slaves, who produced a basket filled with plump dates. She selected one and bit into it.

"What kind of trouble?" I grunted, trying to ignore the woman's smug look.

"Riders, lord," Demee said. The tavern keeper was out of breath, and he hesitated as he drew in a gulp of air. "I was halfway back to the city when I saw them. I recognized the constable among them and rode back to warn you. They're probably only ten or fifteen minutes behind me."

"How many?"

"Perhaps as much as twenty, lord."

"How did they know we were here?" I asked. "No one saw us." I paused then, thinking about the villager that I'd seen outside his house on the way up the mountain. Could it have been him?

"I don't know, lord," Demee said. "But I suggest you don't wait around to find out."

I glanced at Alesia, who was still glaring past her son at Lady Deneux. "We have to go," I said.

Alesia pointed her knife at the Cardian woman. "I'm not leaving here with that bitch still breathing," she responded hotly.

I saw Einrack's eyes narrow and his body tense. I shook my head, knowing the boy would rather die than let anything happen to Lady Deneux. His devotion was clearly misguided, yet I could tell by his expression that nothing his mother or I could say right now would get that fact through his head. Einrack was young, naïve, and obviously in love—all things that usually added up to nothing but trouble.

I put my hand on Alesia's wrist, forcing her knife down. "Look at your son, Alesia. Really look at him. He's not a boy anymore but a man, and he's completely bewitched right now. That woman's life isn't worth what will happen next if you press him on this. So, let's just go. Take your son and go. The gods will deal with the bitch in their own way, whether it be today or years from now." Alesia hesitated, and I added, "Please. I promised Einhard that I would get you both home safe, and I didn't come all this way to fail now because of some arrogant Cardian whore."

Alesia bit down on her lower lip, her entire body shaking with anger as she thought about my words. I glanced at Lady Deneux, whose smug confidence had faltered somewhat, replaced by apprehension and maybe just an inkling of fear. Good, I thought, the bitch should be afraid.

Finally, Alesia came to a decision and she slammed her knife back in its sheath with a frustrated snort. "Out," she snarled at her son, shoving him toward the entrance hall. "Now!"

The boy opened his mouth to say something, and I knew by the stubborn look on his face that whatever he uttered next wasn't going to be good. I put a hand on his shoulder and squeezed, just as I had done with Renol. Einrack was already more muscular than the skinny Cardian, but I was a big man and very strong.

Einrack hissed in pain. "Do not force me to carry you, boy," I growled in his ear. "There are others outside and they will forever remember it if you do. The choice is yours, walk out of here like a man or be carried like a child."

"But—" Einrack said as he twisted to stare longingly at Lady Deneux.

I could see the gleam of love and adoration in his eyes and I squeezed harder until there was nothing left but pain, then I pushed him toward his mother. "Get Einrack out of here," I grunted. "I'll be right behind you."

Alesia and I shared a look for a moment and then she nodded. I turned my baleful gaze on Lady Deneux, who stood protected behind her slaves, each of whom had the same stubborn expressions on their faces that Einrack had just had. Several of the children had picked up whatever they could find for weapons, with one boy even brandishing a lute by the neck. I shook my head at the display, for they had to know that they would be no match for me. It seemed that the witch's evil hooks ran deep in these deluded children.

"Don't hurt her, Wolf!" Einrack cried as Alesia hustled him away. "I beg of you! Let her be!"

I turned to watch them follow after Baine and Demee. "I won't hurt her," I assured the boy. "You have my word, brother." The boy sagged in relief, and I waited until he and his mother were gone before turning to face Lady Deneux.

"So?" she said, one hand on the shoulder of the young girl in front of her. I was pleased to hear a slight shake in Lady Deneux's voice now as she watched me warily. "What's it to be, Lord Hadrack? Will you go back on your word to Einrack and murder an innocent woman in cold blood?"

"Innocent?" I scoffed. I shook my head as I took a threatening step forward. The children all tensed, watching me with frightened yet determined eyes. "You are many things, but innocent is not among them," I added in a harsh voice.

Lady Deneux licked her lips, looking unsure of herself now at my tone. "I heard a song about you once, Lord Hadrack," she said. "The verses described you as an honorable man who refuses to make war on women." She raised an eyebrow. "Were those words true, or were they just something the bards made up, paid for by your gold to portray you in a more flattering light?" I hesitated at the woman's words and she chuckled, the fear in her eyes slowly receding, replaced by growing confidence at my continued silence. I could feel my anger deflating, turning into an almost detached coldness. "That's what I thought," Lady Deneux finally said in satisfaction when I still didn't respond. "Then the songs are true. I knew your honor would not allow you to hurt me."

I took a deep breath and sighed, then spread my arms to my sides as I looked down at the tiled floor. There was nothing that needed to be said now. A rivulet of water from the tub was trickling past my boots, and I was careful to step over it as I darted forward three steps without warning. I effortlessly swept the girl standing in front of the Cardian woman out of my way with my left arm, then stabbed outward with Wolf's Head. My blade sliced into Lady Deneux's stomach with little resistance, hitting several inches above her shaved sex before angling upward. I felt the point cut easily through bone and cartilage before it burst out of her back while sticky warm blood sprayed across my hand. Lady Deneux gasped in shock, her eyes round and horrified. The boy with the lute was the first to recover from his surprise and he screamed, then began to smash the instrument across my shoulders over and over. The lute finally shattered after the third or fourth blow, but I felt nothing at all as I stared into Lady Deneux's pain-filled, terrified eyes.

"Consider this a message from Einhard, Sword of the Queen," I hissed as I viciously twisted the sword in the woman's guts. "This is for what you did to his son and every other son and daughter you've corrupted with your vile touch. Dwell on that as you burn at The Father's feet for all eternity, you loathsome bitch."

I withdrew my blade inch by inch as I turned it back and forth, letting Lady Deneux suffer the agony of cold steel inside her for as long as possible while she whimpered and begged me not to let her die. Gone now was the arrogance and smugness that I'd witnessed earlier, replaced by horror and terror. Yet I felt no pity for her at all. I finally withdrew Wolf's Head from the woman's flesh and stepped back quickly as her intestines spilled out onto the smeared tiles with a sucking sound, instantly filling the room with the foul stench of blood and death. Falix Deneux moaned and I watched dispassionately as she slowly folded to her knees, clutching at the hideous gash in her abdomen while the children surrounded her, weeping as they tried and failed to keep her on her feet.

"But...you're not supposed to—" Lady Deneux managed to say in disbelief before her eyes rolled up into her skull and she pitched forward onto the tiles, where she lay unmoving in a puddle of blood and viscera.

I took a deep breath, staring down at the dead woman while the horrified children dropped to their knees around her, heedless of the blood and gore. The improvised weapons of the slaves, along with my presence, were forgotten now as they moaned and sobbed in obvious grief. Seeing that grief gave me no pleasure and I sighed, weary now as I sheathed Wolf's Head. The witch's power over the slaves was broken with her death, but I guessed it would take some time for these children to realize it, if they ever did at all.

I carefully rubbed the woman's blood off my hand on my trousers as the wailing of the children intensified. I'd lied to Einrack about my intentions earlier, for I'd known all along that I intended to kill Falix Deneux. I felt sudden guilt and doubt wash over me about what I'd done, knowing that the boy would never forgive me for my actions this night. But then, an image of me holding Einhard's ravaged hand arose and I felt all my doubts and guilt slip away. I'd sworn to my friend that I'd kill anyone involved who'd taken his wife and child, and that promise superseded whatever I'd told Einrack. Falix Deneux had been just as complicit in what had happened as Captain Bear was, maybe more so in some ways, and so she'd paid the price, as would the pirate leader, his brother the Overseer, and any others who'd had a hand in the attack on the stronghold. As for Einrack, I thought with a grimace as I strode from the room without a backward glance. I would just have to make certain he never learned about what I'd done.

Outside, I found my men already mounted and waiting for me in the courtyard near the fountain. The front gates were open now, though I could see no signs of riders approaching along the darkened road. I knew that probably wouldn't last for much longer. Someone had found Einrack a horse, and I could feel his eyes on me from where he sat in the saddle as I leaped onto my white stallion's back. I was thankful for the dancing shadows cast by the torches flickering around the fountain, which were helping to hide the dark stain of blood on my trousers.

"Tell me you didn't hurt her, Wolf," Einrack pleaded.

I trotted past him without meeting his eyes. "I never laid a finger on her," I grunted, which was true to some degree.

I sensed rather than saw the boy's relief, and as I passed his mother, our eyes met. I could see a question on Alesia's face and I nodded to her imperceptibly, letting her know it was done. Alesia didn't react other than a slight tightening around her mouth, but I knew she understood and was now satisfied that justice had been served.

"Demee," I said to the tavern keeper. "Where do we go?"

"There's a path about a half-mile back down the road that leads further up into the mountains, lord," the man replied. "If we can reach it before they get there, we should be able to lose them in the hills."

"Then what are we waiting for?" I grunted. "You lead."

We left the holding behind, heading east at full gallop, still with no sign of those hunting us. Demee led my small band along the narrow road faintly lit by a pale moon, with only the thunder of our horses' hooves, the steady creak of leather, and the jingle of bits filling my ears. I was worried and on edge, expecting to see a mass of dark riders appear on the road at any moment, cutting us off. Even though our pursuers were only filthy Cardians, there were just nine of us, and if our guide was right about how many men were coming, the enemy would outnumber my men by more than two to one.

Normally those odds wouldn't bother me when dealing with Cardians, but two of my force were old, while another was just a boy. I knew Dagric would do the best he could, as would the tavern keeper, but neither were experienced fighting men and would most likely just get in the way. Saldor had given Einrack one of his war-hammers, and though the boy was young, he'd been training with weapons almost from the moment he could walk. I was confident that Einrack would handle himself well enough if needed, but I didn't want to have to test that theory and be proved wrong.

"How much further?" I called to Demee.

"Almost there, lord," the tavern keeper shouted back. He pointed ahead. "Just past that bend ahead."

We reached the bend moments later and swept around it, then came to a shuddering halt in the middle of the road. I heard Demee hiss in dismay, though no one else said anything while we watched bitterly as a tight group of riders moved toward us at a gallop. Our pursuers were only moments away from reaching the entrance to a faint trail that I could see cutting away to our left through a gap in a wall of darkened trees. I cursed as shouts of discovery arose. We'd been seen. The terrain to either side of the road was sloped and rocky, with dense dried brambles and thick bushes blocking our path. I knew sending the horses up those slopes to cut across to the trail would be dangerous and foolhardy, with no guarantees that we would make it. That left me only one of two choices; flee back the way we'd come and try to make a stand at the holding, or charge ahead and take our chances by surprising the enemy. I chose the latter.

"Saldor, Jebido, Pirate, you're with me," I said. "Alesia, Baine, support us with your bows. Einrack, hold back with Demee and Dagric until we engage, then you move fast for the trail and head up the mountain. We'll follow once we deal with these turd-suckers."

"But I can fight, Wolf!" Einrack protested.

I glanced at him. "I know that, brother. But I need someone I can trust to keep Dagric and Demee safe. Will you do that for me?"

I saw Einrack's shoulders straighten. "Yes, brother, I understand."

"Good," I grunted. "Are we ready?" I saw heads nodding around me, the faces all looking grim in the moonlight. "All right then," I growled. "Let's move."

I drew Wolf's Head, then kicked my heels into my horse's flanks. The stallion burst forward, driving straight toward the heart of the approaching enemy. Jebido rode to my right with his body pressed close to his horse and his sword held at his side at an angle. Saldor was on my left; his mouth stretched in a wolfish grin as he twirled his war-hammer expertly in his hand. Fanrissen rode next to the Pith, while Alesia and Baine flanked us to either side, holding back several horse lengths. I knew shooting a bow from a galloping horse was no easy feat, for I'd tried it several times in the past with less than flattering results. You needed a steady hand and nerves of steel—both of which I possessed—along with superb horsemanship—which, unfortunately, I did not. Luckily, I knew Alesia and Baine had all those qualities in abundance, for I would need their incredible skills to be at their sharpest if we hoped to triumph.

The two groups of horses were less than seventy yards apart, with the gap between us closing fast. I calculated that our forces would meet right at the entrance to the trail, which should still allow Einrack and the others enough time to slip away unnoticed during the coming melee. I heard the hum of a bowstring from behind me and grinned when moments later, a cry arose from ahead as a man twisted and fell off his horse. I aimed the stallion directly at the lead rider, who was shouting encouragement to his companions while waving a sword over his head.

Another bow thrummed to my left, and the man closest to the leader cried out, clutching at his shoulder. The man's horse suddenly swerved sideways, colliding with the lead rider's mount.

Saldor howled with delight as the front legs of the two beasts became entangled and they went tumbling to the ground, while behind them, other riders desperately swerved to avoid the falling animals. One horse tried to leap over the obstacles in its path but didn't make it. I heard a sickening crack as the horse's foreleg snapped, followed by a squeal of pain as it collapsed nose-first in the dirt, sending its rider spilling forward onto the road. Then we were among them.

"Kill them!" I roared.

I swung sideways with Wolf's Head across my body as I approached a shadowy form, gratified when my blade bit deep into the man's left arm. He screamed as our horses streaked past each other, but I had no time to see what he would do next, as suddenly I had two more riders attacking to either side of me. More of the Cardians were milling about in front of me, turning to form a wall that blocked my forward momentum. The stallion slowed almost to a stop just as I felt the air hiss near my left ear as a blade narrowly missed me even as I parried a blow from the rider to my right. I struck back, just grazing his leg before the Cardian grunted and kicked his horse away out of my reach. The second rider had backed off as well after his initial attempt, and I snorted with contempt. The stupidity and cowardice of Cardians never ceased to amaze me. The man had had his chance moments ago when my attention was elsewhere and he'd failed to take it. I vowed I wouldn't allow him a second one.

I could hear the sounds of metal blades colliding all around me, and I caught a glimpse of Fanrissen hacking away at one of the Cardians to my left. Jebido was off to my right, fighting hard to get to me, but there was no sign of Saldor. That's all I had time to notice before the Cardians shared some unheard signal and spurred their horses toward me once again. I immediately hauled hard to the right on the stallion's reins and whistled shrilly as I slapped his rump with Wolf's Head. Startled, the horse leaped toward the man coming at me, colliding moments later with his mount.

The Cardian shouted a curse as his helmet went flying off his head from the impact, though the bastard still had the presence of mind to swing his weapon at my head. I ducked low as cold steel sizzled past me, then jabbed upward, catching him in the armpit with the deadly point. The rider howled and toppled from the saddle while I turned my focus to the man on my left, who was bearing down on me with his sword raised. I swung around to meet him, but the oncoming rider suddenly threw up his arms and dropped his sword as an arrow slammed into his chest, sending him somersaulting back over his saddle.

"Come on!" I screamed at the mass of Cardians ahead, many of whom seemed reluctant to enter the fray. "Come and meet your fate, you gutless bastards!"

I surged forward, my sword singing a tune of death as first one, then a second rider reacted to my taunts and moved to intercept me, only to drop as my blade cut them down. I could hear Saldor bellowing close by, and moments later, I saw the Pith just as he launched himself from his horse's back at two mounted Cardians pressed tightly together. All three men tumbled to the ground in a jumble of arms and legs while the terrified horses they'd been riding raced away. One of the enemy remained where he'd fallen, his neck broken, while the second screamed in terror as Saldor sprung onto his chest. I saw the Pith's war-hammer rise and I grinned as it fell with a meaty thud and the man's screams abruptly ended.

I heard a huge Cardian curse at his hesitant companions from the line in front of me, then he broke away and raced forward, his bearded face twisted in hatred as he twirled a giant mace in his hand. I waited, holding the stallion in check with my left flank facing the man, giving him the advantage, since I didn't have a shield. I saw the Cardian's eyes light up at my perceived vulnerability, and I waited until he was almost on top of me before I yanked hard on my horse's reins, spinning the stallion around so that my sword arm was now facing him. Einhard had taught me the maneuver years ago, and I'd only ever tried it while riding Angry. But the white stallion I rode was game and well-trained, and it succeeded better than I could have hoped for, as now the big Cardian suddenly faced my weapon head-on. The man's triumphant eyes turned to shock as I slashed upward, cutting the top of the mace he held off at the neck guard, sending the head spinning away.

The Cardian just stared at his ruined weapon with a stupid expression on his face, and I laughed as I skewered him in the neck. I watched dispassionately as the man slid off his horse and landed with a thud in the churned-up dirt of the road. Another rider approached me, though he did so warily, his body language telling me that he was clearly afraid. Around us, more of the enemy continued to scream and die as Fanrissen, Jebido, and Saldor tore into them with the kind of skill and savagery that I guessed these city Cardians had rarely seen before. An arrow from Alesia's bow suddenly glanced off the approaching rider's helmet and he sagged in the saddle, stunned. I roared, sending the stallion hurtling forward, eager to add another victim to the growing count on my blade. The Cardian quickly regained his senses, though, and seeing me charging toward him, he desperately swung his mount around and tore away, staring back at me over his shoulder in terror.

I slowed my horse, breathing heavily now as I watched the terrified man drive his mount through the Cardian lines and then flee down the road. I chuckled and shook my head as, one by one, the others lost their nerve and will to fight and followed after him until only a few too slow to realize what was happening remained. Fanrissen cut one of them down with a vicious slash of his sword, while the others fell to Baine's and Alesia's arrows. We'd won the battle and killed almost half the enemy without sustaining any losses of our own. But as I watched the survivors fleeing, something told me that the Cardians weren't done with us yet. No, they would regroup and come back, this time with a lot more men. They wouldn't make the same mistake again, I was certain of it.

And I was right.

Chapter 17: The Bridge of Betrayal

    We rode through the mountains for the rest of that night, led by Demee, who turned out to be an excellent woodsman and guide despite his occupation and advanced age. The night was cool, with a crisp wind whistling through the trees that tugged at my cloak as I guided my mount after Demee's shadowy form along a faint, mostly overgrown trail that was at times no wider than the combined span of my hands. The tavern keeper had told me shepherds from the village drove sheep along the route during the fall, heading for an enclosed valley further up the mountain to the north. There, the animals would spend the long, cold winter months snowed in and reasonably safe from wolves and other predators before finally returning after the spring thaw. Other than that single purpose, though, the trail was rarely used except for maybe the occasional hunter and whatever forest creatures might be living nearby.

    The valley we sought was remote and difficult to access, Demee assured me. But it also housed a small lake fed by sparkling mountain streams and almost sixty acres of lush grasses for the horses to graze. We could also expect to find several buildings where the shepherds sheltered, whiling away the long winter months by playing dice. Demee had been quick to point out that there would be little in the way of supplies to be found inside those buildings, though, which was disappointing news since we were running uncomfortably low on food supplies. I'd intended to rectify that fact once we reached Bahyrst, but unfortunately, circumstances and Jebido's uncharacteristic actions had made that impossible.

I glanced up at the impenetrable night sky above but could see nothing through the cloud cover, not even the faintest twinkling of a star. I guessed it to be around two o'clock in the morning, but I couldn't be certain without the moon for guidance—which had now sunk behind the crest of a second mountain to the west with only a faint glow revealing its presence. An owl hooted somewhere off to my left, though it wasn't one of the rare golden-masked variety that always meant the gods were watching. Even so, I hoped the bird's presence could be taken as an omen of good things to come. There had been no signs of pursuit from the Cardians so far, but I feared that would quickly change once the sun rose.

I planned to rest in the valley for the remainder of the night while the horses ate and drank their fill. We would then set out again at first light through a narrow pass in the mountains that Demee had told me led northeastward. The moment we were finally clear of the hill country, I would lead my small force back to Swailand and *Sea-Wolf* before returning Alesia, Einrack, and the rest of the Piths to their homeland. After that, I planned to pick up Angry and the rest of our horses and sail back to Calban, where Shana, Haf, and Fanrissen's wife and daughter would be safe. Then, once I'd resupplied the ship and recruited more men, I would return to Blood Ring Isle and finish what I'd started there.

I knew what I'd decided to do would take time to accomplish, perhaps several months or more. But my vow to Einhard demanded that every last man and woman involved in his death pay the price for what they'd done. Getting Einrack and Alesia back safely had been a part of that vow, but only a part, and once they were home where they belonged and my wife was safe, I would then be free to finish the job. I knew Shana would not be pleased with my decision when she learned of it, but sometimes a man's honor and word came before all else, regardless of the cost. This was one of those times. All I could hope for was that she would understand, though a part of me had serious doubts about that ever actually happening.

"We're getting close, lord," Demee called over his shoulder, cutting into my thoughts. He paused his horse beside a giant hickory tree that overhung the trail. His mount, like him, was not young, and it was blowing hard, its rounded sides heaving. "Maybe a mile or so," the tavern keeper added. "But I suggest we walk the horses now. The trail ahead gets pretty rocky and unstable for a while."

"All right," I agreed. I dismounted, motioning for the others to do the same.

Demee led us single file along sloping ground riddled with loose shale, clumps of dried clay, and small stones. The tavern keeper had been right to have us dismount, for the horses struggled across the uneven terrain, with even my sturdy stallion laboring. It got to the point that I had to haul on my horse's reins and drag him upwards in places, as did many of my company with their own mounts. Finally, after more than an hour of climbing, slipping, and sliding, we reached a rocky plateau where Demee indicated that we could remount.

We arrived at the entrance to a narrow ravine not long after, guarded by a stand of twisted, ancient yew trees. Inside, the sloping walls of the canyon were comprised of solid granite that towered over our heads, with the odd stubborn, shadowy bush somehow having squeezed its way through the cracks in the walls. The ravine eventually began to angle upward, and after ten more minutes of riding, Demee finally paused his horse along the crest of a second plateau, though this one was much roomier and wider than the first. The wind was stronger here, toying with my beard and hair as I moved my horse beside our guide. I immediately sensed that nothing other than open land lay below us in the darkness.

"This is it, lord," Demee confirmed. "The valley is shaped like a snake, with the lake at the tail." He gestured below toward a faint trail that disappeared quickly into the gloom. "Down there is the head."

"And the pass you spoke of to get out?" I asked.

"Near the tail, lord, around the north side of the lake."

I nodded, thinking that perhaps I could just see the first faint signs of dawn beginning in the sky to the east. It appeared we wouldn't have that much time to rest and recoup after all.

"Good," I grunted. "You have my gratitude, my friend. Most men would have just kept riding earlier and left our fates to the gods. I will not forget what you did for us."

"I am old and have been around Cardians for far too long, lord," Demee said. "But even so, I still remember what it means to have honor." He offered his hand to me. "Unfortunately, I must leave you here, lord, for your way through these mountains is long and arduous, and I still have my business to run back in the city."

I took the man's hand and shook it warmly. "I understand, Demee. Thank you." After we'd shaken, I reached into my clothing and drew out a bag of gold. "This is for you," I said.

"No, lord," Demee protested, looking surprised. "I did not help you in the hopes of receiving money."

"I know that," I said with a smile. "Which is why you must take it."

The tavern owner slowly reached for the bag, his hand shaking as he closed his fingers around the leather. "I don't know what to say, lord."

I waved his words away. "There is no need." I shifted my weight in the saddle as I pointed to the bag. "There's enough there for you to fix up your tavern and give it a worthier name, or better yet, leave this vile place and come to Ganderland. We have a thriving town close to Corwick Castle where I'm sure a man of your skills could set up a profitable business."

"I might just do that, lord," Demee said wistfully. He hefted the bag as the coins tinkled musically, then lifted it to me in salute. "I wish you luck, lord. Just remember to stay in the pass and keep going northeast. You should make it out of the mountains in two days or so."

Demee turned away then, saying farewell to the others before trotting back the way we'd come. I watched him go until he was out of sight, then I guided the stallion downward into the valley. Fifteen minutes later, my company approached the shores of the small lake Demee had told us about where it lay nestled peacefully at the end of the valley. The stallion and other horses had all perked up at the smell of water, and they trotted forward eagerly as we drew closer, but I held them back while I studied the area warily. Demee had promised no one would be here, but I'd become a more cautious man as I'd aged—at least I liked to think so—and I saw no reason to take chances. I could see the dark outlines of two outbuildings standing a hundred yards back from the lake's calm waters, built near the sloping valley wall. There were no horses outside, nor did the buildings look like they were being lived in. I glanced to the east, where I could now see a distinct pink glow breaking the darkness.

"All right," I said, finally satisfied as I dismounted. "Let's get these horses watered and picketed. Judging by that sky, we won't have that long to rest."

Two hours later, having eaten a small portion of what little supplies we had left in our packs, we were on the move again. The narrow pass Demee had told me about was just that, narrow and treacherous, and once again, we were forced to dismount and lead the horses over the uneven terrain. The day had begun with welcome sunshine, but after an hour of navigating the pass, thick clouds had slowly rolled in from the west, accompanied by increasing winds.

It began to drizzle sporadically by midday, until eventually, the rain turned into a continuous downpour that quickly soaked my men and me to the skin, leaving us cold, shivering, and miserable. The skies had turned dark and menacing, almost returning to night, with thunder rolling over the hills constantly, paired with bright flashes of lightning that lit the sky to the west. The downpour had transformed the already unstable ground into a quagmire of muck and puddles that gave off a not unpleasant earthy scent, filling my nostrils. It was the only positive thing I had to focus on, and I clung to it like a lifeline.

I plodded onward, leaning into the wind that fought my progress with every step, my head lowered against the rain that pelted my helmet and shoulders. Walking had become an adventure now, with the wind working in tandem with the slippery, sucking mud pulling at my boots, trying to either sap my strength or make me fall. Behind me, the white stallion followed faithfully and without protest, seemingly unaffected by the rain, though the beast would roll its eyes nervously every time the thunder rumbled. The sounds of the storm seemed amplified even more by the rock walls to either side of me while the wind continued to funnel through the pass with a fury that only appeared to be increasing.

"It's all right, boy," I said soothingly, pausing to stroke the stallion's muzzle after a particularly loud boom had just shaken the ground and rattled my teeth.

Jebido was in the middle of the line, and moments later, he cupped his hands to his mouth and shouted over the wind, "Hadrack!" I looked up as my friend pointed behind him, where I could see Saldor and Fanrissen had abandoned their horses and were running back the way we'd come. "It's Dagric!"

I cursed under my breath, then motioned for Alesia to take the stallion's reins before I made my way back carefully along the path past the line of horses. I groaned when I saw Dagric lying in the muck, with his mount standing off to one side. The animal's left flank was streaked with blood and mud, and Saldor and Fanrissen were kneeling by Dagric, who was moaning in pain as he clutched at his right leg. I could see white bone jutting out from his shin.

"What happened?" I asked the old Swail, though by now I'd already guessed.

"My horse got spooked by the thunder," Dagric said through clenched teeth. "It reared back and slipped. I tried to get out of the way, but..." The old man shrugged, wincing when he moved his leg.

"We need to set this," I said as wind-driven rain swept into my face. Above, lightning flashed, followed moments later by a crack of thunder that set my teeth on edge. I'd been hoping that the storm would move away soon or weaken, but it seemed, if anything, that it was getting closer and stronger.

"If you'll allow me, lord," Fanrissen said, almost having to shout above the shrieking wind. "I've done this before. But I'm going to need something to splint his leg with."

I nodded, tapping him on the shoulder before I stood and slogged back through the mud to the others. There were no trees to speak of in the pass, just featureless rock walls, stone, and muck. That was it. I knew I'd have to improvise.

"Baine," I said to my friend. "We need rope and some of your arrows."

"How bad is he?" Baine asked as he unraveled a length of rope from his saddle.

"Bad," I grunted. "His leg is broken."

Baine grimaced but said nothing as he handed me the rope and a sheath of arrows. I hurried back to Dagric, then watched with my arms folded over my chest as Fanrissen expertly cut the rope into even sections. He then cut off the heads and feathers from six arrows, careful to keep them free of mud.

"Now, the hard part," the pirate said to me. He glanced at Dagric, whose face was as white as fallen snow. "This will hurt, my friend," Fanrissen said to the Swail. "Forgive me."

Dagric waved a hand dismissively, though I could see the apprehension in his eyes. "I've suffered worse, youngster. Do what needs to be done."

Fanrissen nodded, then he glanced at Saldor. "Hold him tightly."

The Pith moved to take a firm grip on Dagric's shoulders while Fanrissen took hold of his right foot. Then the pirate pulled hard without warning. The old Swail howled, his arms fluttering out to his sides like frightened birds as the stark white bone of his broken shin slid back into the blood-stained flesh around it. But even as the bone in Dagric's leg disappeared back where it belonged, dark blood welled up in alarming amounts to replace it.

"Good," Fanrissen muttered, looking unfazed. "Very good." He glanced up at me. "I need some cloth to stop the bleeding before we go further, lord. I should have thought of that before I began."

I hurried to cut a section off the hem of my cloak with Wolf's Head and then handed it to him. Fanrissen tied the cloth tightly around the wound while Dagric's eyes fluttered and he moaned. Then the pirate used the arrow shafts as splints, tying three of them tightly to either side of the old man's leg with rope. The work was crude, but considering our current situation, it was the best that could be done for the Swail.

"Just give me a moment to catch my breath, lord," Dagric gasped after Fanrissen finally nodded to me that he was finished. "I'll be ready to go again in no time at all."

I frowned. "Are you sure you can ride?"

"Just watch me, lord," Dagric growled in determination.

I shook my head, admiring the man's bravery and fortitude. "All right," I grunted. "We rest here for ten minutes, then we start out again."

Dagric insisted he was ready to go long before the ten minutes were up, and with Saldor's help, we lifted the old man into the saddle. Dagric hissed with pain, but other than that, he made no complaints as he settled into place. I returned to the front of the procession and accepted the stallion's reins from Alesia before setting out again. The storm continued to rage around us, with the wind buffeting my small company relentlessly. I glanced back once through the driving rain to see Dagric hunched over on his horse while Saldor led it and his own mount onward. I remembered my own time riding with a broken leg during the Battle of Silver Valley, and while I didn't envy the old Swail, I certainly could understand the terrible agony he was going through right now.

In the end, it took us two and a half days to finally make it through the mountains. Dagric's lower leg had swollen greatly during that time, and though he'd remained mostly cheerful and positive the entire way, it had become clear to me very quickly that if the Swail didn't get some help soon, he wouldn't make it. Fanrissen had repeatedly changed the old man's bandages, with the pirate hovering over him like a fussy mother hen day and night. But even with Fanrissen's constant attention, an infection had managed to set in by the morning of the second day. Dagric was barely lucid by that time, and we'd been forced to tie him to his horse to keep him in the saddle. Had the Swail been a younger man, I was sure he would have weathered the storm fairly easily, but his age was now the primary factor working against him.

"He's not going to make it," Jebido said pessimistically from where he rode beside me. Once again, my friend had anticipated my thoughts.

We'd just entered a sprawling woodland dominated by elegant elm and tall ash trees, which told me we were almost out of the mountains. Demee had described this area to me, explaining that once we exited these woods, we needed to ride north until we came to a river called the Dogtrot. From there, we'd have to travel west along the waterway's length until we reached a bridge that would allow us access to Cardia's northern province known as the Parnaval Expanse. After that, it would be a straight ride east until we reached Ironhold and the land bridge that separated Cardia from Swailand.

"He'll make it," I growled stubbornly, belying my own doubts.

"That Swail is a tough old bastard," Baine added from behind me. He glanced back at the old man, who was swaying in the saddle with Fanrissen riding to one side of him and Einrack on the other. "I wouldn't bet against him."

Both Saldor and Alesia perked up at Baine's words. "You laying odds?" Saldor asked with sudden interest.

Baine snorted and shook his head. "No. What's the matter with you? Dagric is a friend."

Saldor shrugged. "Yes, but his life or death is now in the Master's hands. Betting on whether or not he decides to take the old man is perfectly acceptable and does not reflect my opinion of Dagric, which, as you know, is favorable."

"Maybe betting on his life is acceptable to you," Baine grumbled. "But it's not to me."

I looked back at Saldor. "I'll take that bet," I grunted. "Three fingers he lives, and another three that he uses that leg once it's healed to kick your backside."

Saldor grinned. "Done, Chieftain. It's always a pleasure taking your silver."

"And you?" I asked, fixing my gaze on Alesia. Her head had a fine fuzz growing on it as the hair had started to come back, giving her an almost boyish look.

"Three fingers against him living," Alesia said, her face serious. "But if he does live and tries to kick my backside, he'll have bigger problems to deal with than just a broken leg."

I laughed as I turned around again. The conversation had lifted my spirits for some reason, even though the basis of it had been somewhat morbid. I knew both Alesia and Saldor would be more than happy to lose the bet if it meant the Swail lived. But at the end of the day, the Piths were practical people, and they, like me, understood that we still had a long way to travel. Dagric's chances were slim at his age, even if we found a healer in time by some miracle, which I knew we wouldn't. But even so, I refused to give up on the man. Hopefully, we would get lucky in the next day or two and come across some goldenseal along the way, or if not that, then maybe a village where we could purchase what we needed.

Unfortunately, we found neither but instead found something far, far worse.

We finally reached the Dogtrot River just as dusk was settling over the land, and satisfied with our progress that day, I decided to make camp along the river's southern bank in a stand of tall cottonwoods. The Dogtrot was much calmer than the White Rock was back home in Ganderland, but it was infinitely wider, with a span that I guessed must be near a mile or more, even at the narrowest point that I could see. The terrain around the river was mostly open meadows, with only an occasional woodland thrown in as if by accident. I could hear the pleasant songs of skylarks as they flew overhead while sparrows, bobolinks, and pipits flitted and darted busily through the long grasses and wildflowers, searching for grasshoppers, caterpillars, beetles, and other insects. I'd even caught a glimpse of a green woodpecker on our way to the river, recognizing its distinctive red cap and green feathers as it pecked at the top of an anthill that rose almost as high as my stallion's belly.

It was our third day since we'd rescued Einrack and fought off the Cardian force near Falix Deneux's holding, yet still, there had been no signs of anyone following our backtrail. I was actually starting to gain some hope that I'd been wrong and the bastards had lost interest in us after the beating that they'd taken at our hands.

"How soon until we reach the bridge?" Alesia asked me after we'd seen to Dagric's comfort as best we could and rubbed down and cared for our horses.

I'd allowed Einrack to make us a small fire, which he'd been careful to surround with river rocks to hide the flames from prying eyes as much as possible. Baine had sighted a fox earlier in the day, and moving with lightning speed, he'd snatched his bow from his shoulder and caught the animal in mid-leap just before it would have darted away. That fox now hung over the weak flames on a spit, impaled from mouth to arse with its snout set in a permanent snarl and its luxurious coat skinned away. Einrack knelt by the fire near his mother, carefully turning the spit while occasionally pouring water on the carcass as it cooked.

I could smell the roasting meat and my stomach growled, eager for hot food after eating cold rations for so long. The hunting must not have been good in these parts lately, I guessed, since the fox was lean and clearly half-starved. There wouldn't be a lot of meat to go around when all was said and done, but even a few hot bites would do wonders for our morale.

"Demee said it should take us half a day or so once we reached the river," I finally answered, remembering Alesia had just asked me a question.

I glanced sideways at Fanrissen, where he sat with Dagric some distance away from the fire. The pirate had the old man's head propped up on his knees and was trying to coax some water into his mouth from a skin. The Swail was lucid half the time now, though his infection was regrettably no better. I nodded to Baine and Jebido as they came to join Alesia, Einrack, and me around the fire. Saldor had gone down to the river, hoping to skewer a fish or two.

"Ironhold is about three days ride once we cross the bridge into the Parnaval Expanse," I added. "If The Mother and The Father are merciful, then maybe Dagric can hold out long enough for us to reach it."

"Your faith in your gods is misguided, brother," Alesia grunted. She looked behind her at Dagric and Fanrissen. "Besides, the old man will be dead by morning." She shrugged. "And your purse will be six fingers lighter. This is the way of things."

"Maybe, maybe not," I grunted. "But don't be so quick to scoff at my gods, sister, for they are your gods now, too."

Alesia grimaced. "A few Pathfinders may think as you do, brother, but not many among the tribes agree with them, including me."

"It's more than just a few Pathfinders," I replied wearily. "And you know that. I don't think you're being truthful about the tribes, either."

"What does it matter what Pathfinders think, anyway?" Einrack demanded, surprising me by joining in on the conversation. The boy's expression was combative, and I saw a sparkle of challenge rise in his eyes that had nothing to do with the flames separating us. "The Master is the one and true God, and the rest is just noise with no meaning or substance. To speak in any other way is nothing but an insult to him. I recommend you dwell on that, Wolf."

I pursed my lips, impressed by the boy's conviction, though less so by his lack of respect toward me. "And I recommend you remember who you speak to," I said softly.

Einrack turned the spit aggressively, looking as though my words had swept through the space between his ears without stopping long enough to be acknowledged. "You have my respect, always, brother," Einrack said. His upper lip curled. "But your made-up gods do not."

I looked past him and met Alesia's eyes, wondering if she'd been holding back the revelations in the codex from her son all this time. Alesia just smiled and shrugged, though I could tell that she was secretly pleased by her son's stance.

"The Mother and Father are no more made-up than the Master is," I said. "This has been proven."

Einrack snorted. "By who, brother? A book of chicken scratches written by beer-addled priests?"

Despite the conversation, I couldn't help but smile at the boy's words. Clearly, I'd been wrong about what Einrack knew about the codex, since he'd just described that troublesome tome in the exact same way Einhard had done on more than one occasion. Even the boy's contemptuous tone had sounded much like I remembered his father's had. It seemed for just a moment that with the shadows dancing across the boy's face from the flames that it was Einhard squatting opposite me, with us arguing over the gods and life just as we had done many times in the past. I had to remind myself that it wasn't my friend, much as I wished it were.

"That book of chicken scratches, as you call it," I said, working now to keep my voice even. "Is what helped stop a war and bring enlightenment to your people. The Master and the First Pair deserve equal reverence from you and everyone else."

"Nonsense," Einrack exclaimed heatedly. "Tell me, brother, do the gods you worship with such blind devotion not kneel at the Master's feet and pay homage to him just as we do? Are they not, in truth, according to your silly book, his children, and thus beholden to him and his power?" I hesitated at that, and the boy grinned, looking pleased with himself. "That's what I thought. Your Gander gods are nothing but smoke and wind, and all they and your book of chicken scratches do is muddle the truth that we Piths have known since the beginning of time. That truth is the Master rules this world and all that walks upon it. Why waste words talking of inferior gods, whether they exist or not? The Master is the ultimate god, and that is all that matters in the end."

I could sense Fanrissen listening from his place away from the fire, and I glanced his way, recognizing the look of confusion on his face. The pirate and Dagric were the only ones here who didn't know the truth. Perhaps I would tell them both someday when the opportunity arose, but this wasn't the time.

I pointed to the fox, which was smoking now and blackened. "Best pay attention to your task, boy," I said gruffly. "Let those better suited to higher thoughts do the thinking."

I saw Einrack's features tighten, but he wisely kept his mouth shut and started dousing the meat while turning the spit once more. I just shook my head, imagining the thousand arguments I would have with this boy over the coming years. A part of me was actually looking forward to it. I shifted my gaze to Jebido, who rolled his eyes at me. I grinned. Youth was something that was wasted on the young, my friend had told me once. But I wasn't so sure about that. The beauty of youth was that hopes and dreams seemed limitless at that age, and for every young fool out there dreaming of riches, fame, and conquest, there was a wiser man waiting on the other side of life when reality arrived. The only trick was getting that young fool to live long enough to someday become that older, wiser man.

The next morning, we awoke to find that Alesia's prediction had sadly come true. Dagric had died at some point during the night. We buried the Swail by the Dogtrot river in the cool shade of the cottonwoods, where he could watch the waters roll by for all eternity. Then we set out westward. My heart was heavy after the old man's loss, but my purse was also lighter by six fingers, just as Alesia had predicted. Neither Saldor nor Alesia had shown much joy in their victory, though, and we were a somber, silent group that finally arrived at the river crossing well past midday. I reined in my horse on a knoll overlooking a sturdy stone bridge that spanned a narrow part of the river no more than sixty yards across. I felt a thud hit me in the gut as I stared downward in disbelief.

"That bastard!" Jebido finally spat out from beside me.

I said nothing as I watched a dozen mounted men trot across the bridge toward us. The riders were Cardians, and Demee, the tavern keeper, was leading them.

Chapter 18: Not Everything Is What It Seems

My first instinct was to draw my sword and charge down the hill and cut Demee's treacherous head from his neck. But then the older, wiser man in me took a second look, and I realized that something about what I was seeing wasn't quite right. Demee was indeed at the head of the line of Cardians, but he was sitting oddly in the saddle, and when he saw us cresting the skyline, he began to shake his head emphatically back and forth. A large man sat his horse beside the tavern keeper, his face hidden by a gleaming helmet. That man put his hand on Demee's shoulder and his antics immediately stopped. Several Cardian longboats lay moored along the northern bank of the river to the right of the bridge, and I could see signs of a rough campsite nearby, though there were no tents and no one else in sight. I guessed these men hadn't been here for long, judging by the looks of things.

"The dog betrayed us," Saldor growled, still under the impression that Demee had sold us out. He twirled his war-hammer aggressively in his hand, his handsome features twisted in fury.

"No," I responded with a shake of my head. "He didn't. Look at Demee's feet. They're tied under the belly of his horse. His hands are tied, too. I'm guessing the Cardians captured him on his way back to Bahyrst, then sailed here to cut us off."

Jebido shaded his eyes and squinted. "Does his face look bloodied to you?"

"Yes, it does," Baine said. "They must have tortured the poor bastard to find out where we were going."

I nodded in agreement, having already come to that conclusion. The Cardian procession was flying a red and black banner with a coiled dragon on it as they clattered across the bridge that I guessed was perhaps at most twelve feet wide. I knew they'd seen us by now, but except for a few taunting shouts, the Cardians maintained their steady pace, looking relaxed and almost disinterested in us. I wondered why. We were outnumbered once again, but not by much, and certainly not by the amount that I had been expecting. My men and I had already defeated a force larger than this, so why would whoever was leading these soldiers take the chance that we might be able to do it again? But, even as I asked myself that question, I knew in my gut what the answer was. The man in charge down there knew something that I didn't, which meant that he wasn't taking a chance at all from his viewpoint. Demee and the temptingly small force of Cardians on the bridge were bait, I realized—but if that was the case, where were the jaws of the trap?

"Something seem wrong about this to you?" I muttered to Jebido.

"Damn right it does," my friend grunted. "Those ships can carry a lot more men and horses than just these few."

I studied the empty, open field around us, cut by the winding dirt road we'd been traveling. A forest rose at least a mile to the west, with a drought-ravaged flood plain lying to the east dominated by drifting, dried-out tumbleweeds that eventually merged with more woodlands several miles away. A line of long-abandoned carts stood along the side of the road behind me, wrapped in the embrace of possessive weeds. The wooden wheels on most of the carts had long since collapsed from the ravages of time, with the beds, benches, and sidewalls all covered in a thick layer of brown and yellow moss. I couldn't fathom why the carts had been left there, though it hardly mattered since no threats were hiding behind or inside them. I glanced across the river to the north, but there was nothing to see other than open fields, with a sparse stand of trees two hundred yards back from the water that would struggle to hide anything bigger than a squirrel.

"These bastards aren't the only ones here, Hadrack," Jebido added, cutting into my thoughts. "I can feel it."

"I know," I said. "Me too. Looks like they're just begging for us to attack."

"Then maybe we should give them what they want," Alesia growled as she fingered her bow.

I hesitated. The Cardian procession was more than halfway across the bridge now, but they'd slowed to a walk, giving me time to think. I looked around warily once more, but there really was nowhere close for an ambushing party to hide that I could see. The two longboats had been pulled high up on the far bank's slope, giving me a good view inside them. There was no one there either, which meant the only options for concealment were the trees to the west or somewhere out on the plains east of us. Either way, I knew we would have plenty of time to smash through these few soldiers and rescue Demee before anyone could get close. But unless the Cardian leader was a complete and utter fool—which was possible, although unlikely—he had to know that, too. It didn't make sense.

"Brother," Einrack said. He pointed downward. "Look to the bridge."

I did so, studying every stone but saw nothing unusual. I frowned. "What about it?"

"The shore," Einrack said. "There's thick grass and weeds growing all along the riverbank except on both sides of the bridge. I see only mud there." He looked at me pointedly. "A trail of mud going up and down made by many feet, perhaps, brother?"

It took me a moment to understand what Einrack was saying, then I nodded. More Cardians were lying in wait beneath the bridge. Maybe on the opposite side of the river, too, I thought, just in case we managed to punch through. "Clever," I grunted. "Very clever." I glanced at Einrack. "Well done, brother. Well done." The boy straightened in his saddle with pride at my praise. I could hardly begrudge him that, for he might have just saved all our lives.

"What do you want to do?" Jebido asked me.

I didn't respond, watching instead as the Cardians reached the head of the bridge. They guided their horses off the weathered stone onto the shore, then spread out in a double line across the dusty road, waiting. I now knew their plan, but that didn't mean there weren't more men hidden somewhere else other than beneath the bridge as I'd first thought. If we retreated, those men would run us down. But if we attacked, they would most likely hit us from behind, cutting off any chance of escape. It was a fine trap, I thought grimly. But it had a flaw. And that flaw was these Cardian fools still didn't seem to understand just who it was they were dealing with. I intended to refresh their memories.

"I've never tried this before," I finally said. "But I'm thinking we show these bastards what a flee and strike looks like."

Alesia pursed her lips. "We might lose people doing that, brother," she warned.

"We might lose people no matter what we do," I responded. "Either way, we need to get across that bridge."

"What's a flee and strike, lord?" Fanrissen asked.

"It's a Pith maneuver they use when dealing with a larger opponent," Baine answered for me. "The idea is that we ride towards the enemy in a charge, then, once we get close, we break off and scatter in all directions. They'll naturally give chase and split up, reducing their force. We then lead them away on a merry run, and once the smaller groups are out of sight of each other, we turn and start picking them off one by one."

Saldor frowned. "Seven warriors is not enough for this to work, Chieftain," he said bluntly. "Flee and strike takes practice and is meant to be done in teams of three or more with archers. Not alone with only two bows between us."

"I know," I agreed. "But it's our only chance." I looked west to the line of trees. My gut told me that's where the Cardian leader was holding his reserve force, so that's where I intended to go to draw them out. "If we can deal with whatever the Cardians have waiting for us out there first," I said. "Then we can return here without worrying about an attack from that direction." I looked at Jebido. "If it was you, how many men would you station under that bridge?"

Jebido studied the river crossing thoughtfully. "Maybe ten or so," he finally said. "Just enough to hem us in before the mounted reserve force arrives."

I grinned. "But they're going to be on foot, aren't they?"

"Yes, they will," Jebido growled. He smiled. "Which makes them easy prey."

"Exactly," I agreed. "So, as long as we deal with their reserves first, then we should be able to handle the rest of these bastards at our leisure."

I watched as the man sitting next to Demee handed the reins of the captive's horse to one of his men, then kicked his mount forward twenty yards down the road. He paused there, crossing one leg nonchalantly over his saddle as he stared up at us.

"Lord Hadrack," the man finally called out when we didn't react to his presence. "I know you are busy conspiring with your men, but might I interrupt and have a word with you before you decide on a course of action?"

I glanced at Jebido, who shrugged. "Wait here," I grunted to the others. I guided the stallion down the hill, stopping him well away from the waiting Cardian.

"Ah, you're a cautious man, I see," the man said with a chuckle. He dropped his foot back into the stirrup, then moved closer before halting ten feet from me. The Cardian removed his helmet and balanced it on his saddle, revealing a thirtyish, handsome face with closely-cropped black hair and a trim beard. "My name is Lord Deneux," the man said. He smiled, but there was no humor in it. "I believe you murdered my wife several days ago, Lord Hadrack."

I lowered my hand to my sword hilt, preparing myself. "I believe I did," I agreed, holding his gaze. "The stupid bitch got what she deserved, too."

Lord Deneux chuckled at my taunt, looking unfazed, which disappointed me. I had been hoping he'd do something foolish. "Yes, well, the savage beast lives closer to the surface with some men than others, it seems."

"Not just men," I retorted. "But women, too. But at least now that your wife is dead, there's one less ugly beast to worry about."

The skin around Lord Deneux's mouth tightened at that, but it was his only reaction. The man's control was impressive, I had to admit. "Unfortunately," the Cardian lord said, "it appears that we have something of a problem, you and me."

I shrugged. "One that can be settled right here and now over swords, if you like. Just the two of us."

"Oh, I'm not so foolish as to contemplate that," Lord Deneux replied. He shook his head, some of the tightness leaving his face now. "No, your fearsome reputation precedes you, Lord Hadrack. While quite noble and romantic sounding, crossing swords with you in retribution for my wife's death will do me little good if I'm dead." The Cardian chuckled. "Though I suppose the bards' songs about the battle would be something to enjoy." He shook his head. "No, you see, Lord Hadrack, the dilemma I currently face is that I have been instructed to let you pass unharmed."

I blinked in surprise. "By who?"

Lord Deneux pursed his lips. "The Seven Rings," he said with obvious distaste.

"Why?"

"My understanding is that they have their own plans for you, which do not include revenge over a murdered wife."

I thought about that for a moment. "Then I guess you'll just have to stew over it while you and your rabble get out of my way."

Lord Deneux held up a hand. "Not so fast, Lord Hadrack. While I imagine my attitude regarding my wife's death must seem rather callous and cold to you, the truth is I had immense affection for her and mourn her loss more than it might appear. And while it's true that a wife can be replaced by a man in my position just as easily as a horse or a hog, someone with Lady Deneux's, shall we say, special charms, unfortunately, cannot."

"Am I supposed to care?" I said with disinterest. "Your wife was an evil bitch, and she's burning at The Father's feet as we speak." I looked down my nose at the man. "As for you, Lord Deneux, I know exactly who and what you are."

"Oh?" Lord Deneux said curiously. "And what might that be, Lord Hadrack?"

"A puffed-up, preening, boot-licking dog who owes his life to men much stronger and more powerful than he is." I waved a hand in impatience when Lord Deneux didn't react to my harsh words, tired of trying to goad the man into action. I was eager for a fight, but by the looks of Lord Deneux, it was clear he could sit here all day trading insults with me. I didn't have that kind of time. "Enough of this talk," I grunted gruffly. "If you're too much of a coward to fight me like a man, then step aside like the obedient little cur that you are and get out of my way."

"Yes, well," Lord Deneux said with infuriating calmness. "I believe you misunderstand my intentions, Lord Hadrack. For you see, even a boot-licking dog, as you say, has teeth." He smiled to prove it. I had to concede that he had very good teeth. "I think you'll find to your displeasure that this dog's are sharper than most."

"Words are easy," I growled. "Actions are what count."

"Very true," Lord Deneux agreed. "That is why, despite my orders to the contrary, I have no intention of letting you go. No, in fact, once my men have defeated your little band of heathens and you are on your knees in front of me, I will make you pay dearly for what you did to my wife." He hesitated, studying me with interest.

"Unless you'd care to save us all the trouble and surrender to me right now?" I glared back at Lord Deneux, not bothering to answer until he finally shrugged and put his helmet back on. "Well, I can't say that I'm surprised by your decision. A cornered beast always goes down snarling, after all." The Cardian swung his horse around, then paused to look back at me. "Just remember, Lord Hadrack, that your payment will be a long and painful process once I have you at my mercy. Dwell on that."

"I guess we'll find out how this all goes soon enough," I growled. I pointed at him. "Fair warning, though. I'll be coming for you first."

Lord Deneux inclined his head smugly. "I would expect no less of you."

The Cardian lord headed back toward the bridge without another word. I watched him go in silence, and when he reached his lines, he paused to speak with the man holding Demee's horse while the tavern keeper met my eyes. I saw one of his bound hands was heavily bandaged but his arms were free, which gave me an idea. I nodded to the older man, then slowly drew my sword, gesturing behind me with my head as I pretended to slap the stallion's flank with the weapon. The tavern keeper understood immediately what I was trying to say, and he suddenly slammed his horse's side with his bound fists, crying out in pain as the animal darted forward.

The Cardian soldier holding the reins of Demee's horse shouted in surprise, desperately trying to grab the flapping strips of leather that had torn from his fingers, but he was too late. I urged the stallion into a run down the road, heading for the fleeing tavern keeper, while behind him, a mounted Cardian began to give chase. I saw others start to follow as well, but they stopped abruptly at a shouted command from Lord Deneux. That was a shame, I thought with disappointment. I'd been hoping to draw them all away from the bridge, where we could slaughter them before the hidden soldiers beneath it could do anything to stop us.

"Keep going!" I shouted at Demee moments later as my mount shot past him.

The old man's face was a map of pain, with so many cuts and bruises that they all seemed to blend together in a brutal tapestry of swollen blues, yellows, and reds. The tavern keeper had clearly not given us up easily if those bruises were any indication. I growled with anger as I focused my attention squarely on the approaching Cardian, who was leaning low over his horse's neck, his sword pointed forward. We met moments later with a clash of steel that rang out across the meadow, with neither of us doing damage to the other as we hurtled past each other. I swung the stallion around on the dirt road, sending up a cloud of dust and a spray of small rocks. My opponent did the same, though he held his horse in check, declining to charge again.

I could see the soldier flexing his sword arm with discomfort, though he tried hard not to show it. There was great power in my arm from years of battle and endless practice—power that after our initial test, I knew the other man could not match. I grinned and twirled Wolf's Head as the stallion beneath me pawed at the dirt with a front hoof, eager to go again. He was a game one, that horse, reminding me a great deal of the mount I'd ridden at Blood Ring Isle.

I held the stallion back as he chomped at the bit while I took a quick glance behind me. Lord Deneux's men were watching the battle intently, but the Cardian lord had complete control over them and none had ventured away from the front of the bridge. I looked to my own small force. Demee had reached the knoll's crest by now, and Einrack was busy cutting his bonds. Baine was already halfway down the hill with an arrow nocked to his bow. I knew what he intended to do and I held up a hand, stopping him. This bastard was mine.

"Cardian!" I shouted. "Do you want to die on the back of a horse or with your feet on the ground? I leave the choice to you."

"We'll see who dies, Gander dog," the Cardian spat back. He twirled his sword expertly as I had mine. "But I want to look into your eyes and listen to you whimper like a girl when I gut you."

The choice made, the Cardian swung a leg over his horse, then dropped nimbly to the road. I smiled and did the same. I always preferred to do my fighting with two feet on solid ground, anyway. I swatted the stallion's flank with the flat of my blade, sending him trotting back toward the hill where I knew he'd be safe with Baine. The Cardian's horse was a fine-looking brown mare, and she slowly wandered off the road, then began to nibble at the sparse grass a hundred feet away, unconcerned by the war-like antics of men.

I strode toward the Cardian, studying him. The man was average in height, but he had thick shoulders and a powerful neck. His face beneath his helmet was bearded, with a long nose marred by a purple scar running down the bridge and piercing blue eyes filled with determination and confidence. No coward this one, I realized as we began to circle each other.

"Are you married," I asked my opponent in a friendly voice.

The Cardian hesitated in mid-step, glaring at me warily. "Yes. Why?"

"Children? A son, perhaps?"

"Two boys," he grunted, resuming his circling.

"Ah, that's good," I replied. "I'm glad to hear you have an heir. At least your bloodline will continue after I kill you."

The Cardian snorted. "I thought we were here to fight, not chatter like old women."

I chuckled, not reacting when the Cardian feinted toward me other than to slap his probing blade aside with Wolf's Head. My opponent had moved incredibly fast without warning, but I'd countered him with even greater speed. He backed off grudgingly, muttering to himself. I noticed that some of his determination and confidence had receded just a little now.

"You could always go back," I said sympathetically. I lifted Wolf's Head and offered up the tip of my blade. The Cardian obliged and matched his sword against mine, both of us testing the other man's strength as the sound of steel grating against steel rang out.

"Go back?"

"Yes," I said as we circled in the dirt. I nodded my head toward the bridge and the others watching there. "To them. You might even live if you do, though I wouldn't lay odds on that happening."

"Now, how would that look if I turned tail and ran?" the Cardian grunted dismissively.

"It would look like you're a smart man who knows when he's overmatched."

"Says you."

I'd been holding back while we jousted, and I suddenly twisted my wrists and pressed down on his blade, using more strength in my arms, though not all yet. It was a clear message, and the Cardian's eyes widened in surprise as I easily forced his weapon toward the ground. "Last chance," I growled, holding his gaze. This was the first time I'd come across a Cardian who wasn't thoroughly unpleasant and a coward, and I was suddenly reluctant to kill him. It seemed there might be hope for the race yet. "Get on your horse and ride out of here."

"I can't," the man gasped as he fought to keep his sword up. "There is my honor to think of."

I sighed, understanding now. "You're not from Cardia, are you?"

My opponent shook his head. "No, I was born in Parnuthia."

"That's what I thought," I grunted. "A shame." Then I killed him.

I could hear howls of anger coming from the enemy side as their man fell, but like true Cardians, they blustered and cursed me, but in the end, they did nothing. I placed the fallen Parnuthian's sword on his bloodied chest, then crossed his arms over it in a sign of respect. Then I collected the dead man's mare and headed back up the hill. I didn't bother looking behind me at the bridge, letting them see the contempt I felt for them in my turned back. Demee had dismounted and was sitting on the grass with his head down, and he stood as I approached, looking apprehensive. I put my arms around the man to alleviate his fears and gave him a gentle embrace, afraid to cause him any more pain than he was clearly already in.

"I am so sorry, lord," the tavern keeper mumbled. He was trembling, and there were tears in his eyes when we broke apart. I glanced down in concern at the bandage on Demee's right hand that I noticed was covered in fresh blood. "They cut off my thumb and little finger, lord," he explained. "I didn't want to tell them anything. I promised myself I wouldn't, but the pain—" The tavern keeper trailed off, looking miserable.

I put my hand on his shoulder and squeezed. "You have nothing to be sorry for, my friend. I know you did all that you could and more. I don't blame you for any of this."

Demee just nodded, not looking all that convinced by my words. I motioned to the mare, which I knew would be a much better ride than his weary old nag. "Let me help you up. I'm afraid we're not out of this mess just yet, so you'll need to ride some more."

"Yes, lord," Demee said. His swollen and battered face turned hard with determination. "I can still fight with my left hand, lord. Just give me a weapon."

"That's the spirit," I grunted. I stooped and cupped my hands together in a basket, enabling him to put his foot inside, then lifted the old man up effortlessly. I waited until he'd settled himself into the mare's saddle while I held her bridle and kept her quiet. "Demee," I said as a sudden thought struck me. "Where does this river go?"

"Go, lord?"

"Yes, does the Dogtrot flow all the way to the Western Sea?"

Demee frowned as he thought. "I believe so, lord, by way of the Gulf of Shells, if I'm not mistaken."

I patted his leg in satisfaction, my hunch confirmed. "Good enough. Thank you." I turned then and retrieved my horse from Baine and swung into the saddle.

"So, are we still going with the flee and strike plan?" Jebido asked me after I'd guided the stallion beside him once more.

I shook my head. "No, I think I have a better idea." I motioned to Baine and then Alesia. "You two look bored. Why don't you go down to the bridge and say hello to our friends?"

Alesia's face broke out into a wide grin while Baine's eyes narrowed and darkened in anticipation. "What are you up to, Hadrack?" my friend asked.

"That big fellow I was just talking to was none other than Lord Deneux," I said. "And he's got himself something of a problem now. He desperately wants us to chase him over that bridge, but he doesn't know that we're aware of his little surprise beneath it yet. My guess is he won't risk revealing that bit of information, either. Not until we've committed ourselves, anyway."

"Which means he won't attack Alesia and Baine and take a chance of losing his advantage," Jebido said in understanding. "He'll have no other choice but to retreat across the bridge."

"Exactly," I agreed. "But I'm betting Lord Deneux will be reluctant to leave the other side undefended because he knows if we manage to get across before his trap springs, then he could lose us."

"So he'll have to stay close enough to make sure that doesn't happen," Alesia said eagerly. "Leaving his men well within the range of our arrows."

"That's right," I replied. I smiled as I looked around at the others. "Something of a dilemma for him, wouldn't you say? He'll have to make a decision sooner or later or chance losing all his men."

"The bastard could still have soldiers hidden on the far side of that bridge," Jebido warned. "I know I would if I was him. He might just surprise you and try his own flee and strike, hoping we'll fall for it. Then all he'd have to do is double back while his soldiers block the bridge. We could still get boxed in here, Hadrack."

"Yes," I agreed. "He might try that. But even if he does, we'd still be closer to the right side of the river." I grinned. "Life is about taking chances, eh?"

"What do we do if you're wrong and they charge us instead?" Alesia asked.

I chuckled. "I doubt they will, sister. Lord Deneux might feint an attack to run you off, but I'm betting that's all. He doesn't have archers of his own, which means he's caught in this trap of his own making as much, if not more than we are. We have the advantage here, and I plan to use it."

"And if you're wrong and he does attack them?" Jebido asked.

I shrugged. "If Lord Deneux is foolish to do that, then we'll make short work of them once they've strayed too far from the bridge. Either way, the bastards are going to lose some men."

Baine smiled. "It all sounds like good fun, Hadrack. I can't wait."

"Then get to it," I grunted. "Make us proud. I want to see a bunch of empty Cardian saddles."

Baine and Alesia nodded with determination before guiding their horses down the hill. I turned to Fanrissen. "Pirate, did you notice those old carts we passed on the road earlier?"

"Yes, lord. What was left of them, anyway."

"Take Demee and Einrack and bring me the best two. Drag the damn things here in the dirt if you have to."

Fanrissen pressed his lips together before he nodded assent. "Yes, lord."

"Oh, and Pirate," I called out as the three began to head back down the road the way we'd come. "Fill them with as much dry brush as you can find, first."

Fanrissen hesitated, looking as if he wanted to ask why. "Of course, lord," he replied after a moment.

"What are the carts for?" Jebido asked after the three had ridden away.

I turned back to watch Baine and Alesia. They'd reached the base of the hill now, where they paused, talking together. Both had their bows casually strung across their shoulders, though none of the Cardians seemed alarmed by their presence. I knew that would quickly change.

"Just a little something to slow down Lord Deneux's reserves and those bastards under the bridge," I grunted.

Alesia and Baine suddenly charged forward down the road, whipping their bows off their shoulders and nocking arrows in a blur of motion. The Cardians hesitated for the briefest of moments, unsure of what to do, which was their undoing. Both Alesia and Baine let loose simultaneously, and the dark shafts screamed through the air even as the two nocked more arrows and shot a second volley. A man in the front line screamed moments later, clutching at a shaft in his side, while another simply sagged and fell from the saddle with an arrow in his neck. I heard Lord Deneux screaming at his men to retreat, and they wheeled their horses around and pounded across the bridge, though not before a third man flung up his hands as an arrow took him between the shoulder blades.

"Beautiful," Saldor said, shaking his head in admiration.

Baine and Alesia reached the head of the bridge and they paused their horses there, shooting across the length at the Cardians who'd made it to the other side. Lord Deneux sat his horse farther back from the others, and though I couldn't see his face from this far away, I knew he was glaring at me in anger and frustration.

"Now what, you bastard?" I grunted. "Your perfect plan has just fallen apart, so what are you going to do?" I turned and looked behind me as Fanrissen, Demee, and Einrack returned, dragging two carts overflowing with tumbleweeds down the road by ropes attached to their horses' saddles.

"Pirate," I said, nodding to Fanrissen. "Start a fire. We're going to need torches."

Fanrissen's face lit up in understanding. "Certainly, lord," he said with a big grin.

The pirate dropped to the ground, then rummaged around in his saddlebag for char cloth and flint before grabbing some brush from one of the carts and piling it on the ground. I turned back to the bridge, where Baine and Alesia were circling at its head, sending arrow after arrow toward the milling Cardians on the far bank. They hadn't managed to hit anyone else since the initial attack, but I wasn't all that concerned about it. The two had already taken down three men, and with the Parnuthian that I'd reluctantly had to kill earlier, Lord Deneux was now reduced to eight riders. I grinned, liking our odds. Now, I just needed the bastard to decide not to call for his reserves just yet and instead pretend to flee. If he did that, then we had him and I could implement the second part of my plan.

"Are you going to tell me what you're up to?" Jebido asked. "Or am I supposed to guess?"

I glanced to the west, but there were still no signs of Lord Deneux's men that I was sure were waiting in the trees there. I wasn't all that surprised. Those soldiers would have been instructed to remain hidden until they heard a clear signal—most likely a horn—before attacking, which I knew the Cardian leader would be reluctant to do until my entire force was committed to the bridge. I intended to give him exactly what he wanted, as long as he gave me what I wanted first.

"Hadrack?" Jebido prodded.

"Demee told me this river runs to the Gulf of Shells," I said. I pointed across the water toward the Cardian longboats. "All we need is a few minutes to get everyone aboard one of those, then we can sail all the way back to Swailand." I grinned at my friend. "It couldn't be any easier."

"They'll come after us," Jebido warned.

I shrugged. "Let them."

"Chieftain," Saldor said. He pointed. "The dogs are running."

And so they were. Lord Deneux had finally had enough of Baine's and Alesia's arrows, and he'd made the decision to retreat, though I knew he wouldn't go very far. That suited me just fine.

"All right," I snapped. "We have to be fast. Pirate, you and Einrack follow us with the carts. As soon as we're all across the bridge, block it and set fire to the brush." I motioned to Demee. "We're going to punch a hole through their defenses when they appear. Once it's safe, I want you to take a torch and set that first ship along the shore ablaze. Understand?"

"Yes, lord," the tavern keeper nodded, looking surprisingly calm.

"Just the first one," I stressed. "We'll need the second ship to get us out of here."

"I failed you once, lord," Demee said. "I promise you I won't do so again."

"Good man," I grunted. I glanced around at my small force. "Now, let's go teach these Cardian bastards a lesson they won't soon forget!"

I drew Wolf's Head, then kicked the stallion into motion, shouting with the others at the top of my lungs. We swept down the hill at full speed, aiming for the bridge and making as much noise as possible. I wanted Lord Deneux to hear us and think the trap he'd so carefully laid and which had seemed doomed to failure moments ago was suddenly saved. False hope can make even the most cautious of men make mistakes. We slowed as we approached the bridge with Baine and Alesia joining us, still with no signs of Lord Deneux's men concealed only a few feet away. I wondered when he'd blow the horn as my stallion stepped onto the bridge.

Would the Cardian leader wait until we were halfway across or call for the signal much sooner?

I didn't have long to find out, for just as Einrack and Fanrissen crossed onto the bridge behind me, I heard the blaring sounds of a horn coming from across the river.

"Quick now!" I grunted, motioning for everyone to dismount. We ran back, working to wedge the two carts across the bridge even as I heard the sounds of men in armor cursing as they clambered up the muddy shore beneath us. "Light them," I ordered Fanrissen when the carts were in position.

The pirate did as instructed, and within seconds the dried weeds caught fire, sending up white smoke while the flames licked hungrily at the tumbleweeds and then began to work at the rotted boards. I glanced west, where I could just make out the faint wink of armor as riders broke out from the forest. So far, everything was going according to plan.

"They're coming!" I shouted, running back to my horse. "Let's go!" I leaped into the saddle just as more men appeared on foot on the far side of the bridge, blocking our path, also as expected. I was relieved to see that none had spears, though most were carrying heavy shields. That, I knew, was going to be a problem. "Baine, Alesia," I said, pointing ahead. "See what you can do about those bastards."

A man suddenly came hurtling over the carts, cutting through the smoke and flames with his sword held in both his hands above his head. He swung at Einrack while still in mid-air, but the boy moved with blazing speed, avoiding the blow by rolling along the ground. The Cardian landed hard on the stone, where he paused for a heartbeat, crouched and growling before he started to stand up. Then his face exploded in a mass of gore and blood as Saldor's war-hammer caught him from the side.

"Go, Chieftain," the Pith warrior grunted. "I'll be right behind you."

I nodded, then kicked my horse into a gallop. The Cardians had tried to form a shield wall across the end of the bridge, but it was poorly executed, with several glaring gaps in the line. I shook my head at the incredible ineptness of these people. Both Baine and Alesia could hit a Jorq at forty paces nine times out of ten, and they'd already taken advantage of the enemy's lack of discipline, cutting down two of their number, resulting in an even bigger hole in the wall now. I bent low over the stallion's neck, aiming directly for it. My mount surged forward eagerly, barring its teeth on the bit as we swept past Baine and Alesia at full gallop.

"Die, Cardian dogs!" I shouted just before I hit the line.

The stallion's left shoulder impacted the Cardian shield to my left, sending the man huddling behind it spinning away effortlessly. I swung Wolf's Head to my right, feeling the vibration in my arm as hard steel met solid shield. The man staggered beneath the blow as I swept past him but did not fall. It hardly mattered, though, because now I was through their lines. A shield wall is an intimidating sight and can be hugely effective when implemented correctly—right up until the moment that it's breached. After that, unless the men are led by a competent commander who thinks quickly on his feet, then the battle usually becomes a free-for-all mass of confusion and slaughter. Luckily for us, the Cardians did not have such a commander.

I swung the white stallion hard around and came charging back, hitting the disorganized Cardian wall from behind while Fanrissen, Jebido, and Einrack assaulted it from the front. Baine and Alesia continued to shoot at the slightest hint of flesh, and within moments, the enemy's will wavered and then broke completely beneath the pressure. The surviving Cardians began to shuck their heavy shields and weapons as they turned and ran away in terror, with some even jumping off the bridge into the water below to escape our fury.

"Let them go," I grunted as Baine and Alesia began to target the running men. "They don't matter." I pointed to Demee, who held a burning torch and looked stunned by the speed and savagery of what had just happened. "Go now, Demee, and hurry."

The tavern keeper swallowed hard, then galloped away without a word, turning east along the shoreline as he headed for the beached longboats. I glanced back the way we'd come to see that the carts were still burning furiously, creating an impenetrable barrier, though I knew it wouldn't last much longer. I noticed several more bodies lay near the flames as Saldor rode his horse at a trot down the bridge's length toward us.

"We don't have much time, Hadrack," Jebido growled.

"Lord," Fanrissen called out. He pointed to the northwest, where riders had just appeared. Lord Deneux had returned, though he held his men back out of range of our arrows.

"You two make sure those bastards stay exactly where they are," I grunted to Alesia and Baine. "The rest of you come with me."

I led my men to the second longboat, and together we struggled to push it off the shore before finally, it slipped into the water. Demee had set the second ship on fire by now, and it was slowly starting to take, but for good measure, Saldor used his war-hammer to bash in the hull. I could hear Lord Deneux's men cursing us as they watched helplessly, but they made no move to do anything about it. Having already been acquainted with the incredible prowess of Baine and Alesia, I couldn't say that I blamed them.

"What do we do about the horses?" Jebido asked once the longboat was ready to sail.

I grimaced as I glanced to the bridge, where the barrier was now nothing but smoking ruins with only the occasional flick of flames. Soldiers on foot were already streaming around the charred obstructions, while others worked to make more room for the mounted men to pass. I counted at least twenty Cardians on horseback waiting to get through and knew that our time had run out.

"We leave them behind," I grunted, though I was saddened to have to part with the stallion.

Less than a minute later, I had everyone in the boat. We used the oars to maneuver into the center of the river, then lowered the sail as a strong wind filled the cloth. Cardians watched us bitterly from all along the bridge and the shore, with many yelling insults and curses at us.

A lone rider suddenly broke away from the others to follow us along the grassy shoreline, pacing the ship. "We will meet again, Lord Hadrack!" Lord Deneux called out. "Mark my words! We will meet again!"

I cupped my hands around my mouth as the ship began to pick up speed, leaving the horseman behind. "I'm sure your wife is lonely without you, lord!" I shouted back. "When next we meet, I'll be sure to send you to her! You have the word of the Wolf of Corwick on that!"

I heard Lord Deneux curse as he halted his horse, and I gave the bastard one last triumphant wave before I turned my back to him and sat. I glanced at Einrack where he stood along the starboard side, but thankfully the boy didn't seem to have understood what my taunt had meant about Lord Deneux's wife. I'd almost given it away there. I tilted my head to the sky and closed my eyes, enjoying the sun and wind on my face. I smiled. It had turned out to be a glorious day.

Chapter 19: Cryptic Message

Jebido was wrong. The Cardians didn't come after us at all. In fact, we were mostly ignored by those few people we came across while we traveled down the waters of the Dogtrot. Two Cardian longboats filled with soldiers in red capes had appeared on the second day of our journey, and though we'd anticipated a bloody battle, they just passed us by with barely a second glance, heading in the opposite direction. I had to admit that I was just as surprised and mystified as everyone else had been, but then I remembered what Lord Deneux had said about the Seven Rings. Those men had other plans for me, the Cardian lord had insisted, which most likely explained why we were being left to our own devices. I decided to keep that information to myself for the time being, though, while I tried to figure out what those plans might entail.

It took us four days to reach the Gulf of Shells, and those four days were spent relaxing and swapping jokes and tall tales while we lounged away the time, enjoying plenty of warm ale and food. The Cardians had graciously left behind a fully-stocked ship that would easily last my small band the entire trip and beyond, and we were making full and grateful use of it. My men were content and happy for the first time in a long while, confident in the knowledge that our long odyssey was almost at an end. I didn't have the heart to tell them otherwise. I knew there would be time for that later, once Alesia and Einrack were returned home and Shana was back in Calban. But for now, I just let them enjoy themselves. They'd damned well earned it.

The Gulf of Shells turned out to be a large body of water that connected the Western Sea to the Straight of Forgotten Wishes that separated Cardia from Swailand. A sprawling port city known as Acospool was located on the northwestern shore of the gulf, with Swailand nothing but a barely-seen landmass hovering on the horizon sixty miles across the water to the southeast. We would have had to travel north along the gulf and through the straight to reach the land bridge and Ironhold, but I'd decided to keep going east and sail around Swailand's southern tip instead. It made more sense just to head back to the Fivefingers River and retrace the path we'd taken earlier with *Sea-Wolf*, saving us both time and the expense of buying horses.

I studied Acospool with curiosity as we sailed past the city, with the Cardian longboat beneath me shuddering and rocking as the sleek vessel cut through the rough, wind-swept waves on our way deeper into the gulf. I was greatly impressed by the majestic white walls of the city and the golden-domed towers and buildings that rose above them with their rooftops gleaming in the sunlight like miniature suns. Hundreds of fishing vessels were out on the water around the port, looking like energetic water bugs as they skimmed the calmer surface near the shoreline.

I could also see half a dozen larger trading ships running off the coast and a network of flat barges transporting goods from Acospool to a smaller town to the north called Flafstead. Demee had told me the goods would then be loaded onto wagons where they would travel overland along a trading route known as the Emerald Passage, heading west to the larger inland cities that were the heart of Cardia's power. The Empire was strong and getting stronger by the day, the tavern keeper had informed me, while smaller, weaker kingdoms around it watched with growing trepidation and fear that the lumbering beast might strike them at any moment. Their concerns were well justified, in my opinion.

"May I sit with you a while, brother?" Einrack asked, cutting into my thoughts an hour after we'd left the white walls of the city behind.

I was taking my turn on the tiller, enjoying the sights and warm breeze on my skin as we sailed along the wild coastline of Swailand. "Of course," I said. I motioned to a bench built against the hull beside me. I glanced sideways at the boy while he sat, amazed, as always, by how much he resembled Einhard.

"Demee's wounds are healing nicely," Einrack announced. "He won't be able to hold a mug or sword in that hand anymore, but at least there are no signs of infection. Mother believes he'll be able to keep the other fingers because of it."

"That's good news," I grunted. "Demee is a good man who got caught in a bad situation."

Einrack nodded at my words, looking distracted. I could tell there was more on his mind than just Demee's health. "Mother tells me we'll be going home once we return to *Sea-Wolf*."

"Yes, that's true," I agreed.

The boy focused his piercing green eyes on me. "And what will you do afterward, brother?"

I shrugged, pausing to watch as a great white pelican with its oversized beak flapped lazily past us overhead. Several smaller birds were following it suspiciously, but the pelican seemed oblivious. "I'll be returning to Calban," I answered.

"And then?" the boy prodded.

"And then we'll just have to see," I said evasively.

Einrack grinned. "I knew it." He sat back on the bench and spread his arms to either side of him along the gunwale, then tapped his fingers on the wooden railing. "You're going after the bastards, aren't you?"

"What makes you think that?"

"My father told me many stories about you, Wolf," Einrack said. "And in every one of them, you don't stop until those who've wronged the people you care about are dead."

"Your father tended to embellish things a great deal," I grunted, not allowing myself to be drawn in by Einrack's charm. I'd spent half my life trying to avoid the very same thing with Einhard—usually with little success. I winked at the boy. "He drank a lot, you know."

Einrack laughed pleasantly, and I could tell he was enjoying being with me as much as I was with him. "Father swore that everything he told me about you was true," the boy said. "Every last word."

"Yes, well," I replied. "I wouldn't put much stock in that if I were you. The truth is, if you took all those stories and cut them in half, then you might be a little closer to what really happened. Maybe."

"You killed the nine," Einrack said matter-of-factly, looking impressed. "Just like you swore to your murdered family you would."

"Yes, I did," I agreed.

"Tell me about it."

I sighed. I'd been in a good mood when Einrack sat down, and I wasn't eager to ruin it by raising the ghosts of the past and the dark emotions they always evoked in me just to satisfy the boy's curiosity. "There's nothing to tell," I grunted. "I made a vow of vengeance, and it was satisfied. End of story."

"Did you really break a man's back with your bare hands?" Einrack asked me as if I hadn't just responded.

I rolled my eyes. "What does it matter?"

"It matters because I've listened along with my brothers and sisters to my father's tales about you all my life. You always seemed larger than life to us, and at times what Father claimed you'd done seemed impossible for any man to achieve." The boy shook his head, his expression filled with wonder. "But after what I've seen these last few days, I know now that there is nothing that you cannot do."

I snorted, unable to contain a laugh at the suddenly childish look of worship on Einrack's face. I had to keep reminding myself that he was only twelve, for most of the time he seemed twice that age.

"Trust me, brother," I said. "I've been luckier than most." I gestured to Baine and Jebido where they knelt on the deck with

Fanrissen, playing dice. "Without people like them and your mother and father, I would have been dead long ago, believe me."

I looked away wistfully as water sprayed along the longboat's hull, thinking of those I'd lost over the years. What would have become of me if not for the support of people like my father, my sister Jeanna, Ania, Eriz, Aenor, Flora, and good old, faithful Sim? Not to mention Niko, whose death was still so fresh in my mind. I couldn't imagine what my life would have looked like without them.

I turned back to Einrack. "Our lives don't just belong to us or the gods, brother," I said. "They also belong to all those we meet, befriend, and love during our time in this world. Some of those people go, and some stay, but each one adds something that wouldn't have been there without them. They might make you stronger or weaker, but either way, they change who you are in small ways. The trick is to take what each one offers, both the good and the bad, and use it to try and mold yourself into something better than you were before you met them. Do you understand?"

Einrack shrugged before folding his arms over his chest. I could tell he didn't really know what I was talking about. The truth was, I wouldn't have at his age, either. I realized with a start that I was starting to sound a lot like Jebido and I wondered if maybe I was starting to get old.

"What could someone like Lorgen Three-Fingers have possibly given you?" Einrack asked, cutting into my thoughts.

"Besides a headache and pain in my ass?" I asked with a chuckle. Einrack laughed, looking genuinely amused. "Some of the best and most needed lessons come from our enemies, Einrack. Remember that. Lorgen was no different and, in the end, I learned something very valuable from him."

"What was that, brother?"

"That the moment you lose your honor, you lose everything," I said gravely. "Lorgen Three-Fingers tried to cheat during the Tribal Challenge, and even if he had killed me, he would have been finished as chieftain of the Amenti. His own people would have turned on him."

"But you killed him despite what he tried," Einrack said, looking thoughtful. "Along with his Blood Guard. Not many survive a challenge, brother."

"That's true. I got lucky that day."

"I doubt luck had much to do with it," Einrack replied. He looked over at Saldor where the Pith warrior was dozing in the bow. "Yet, after all that, you gave up what you'd rightfully earned with your blood and sweat, handing it to Saldor instead for nothing. Why?"

"Because I was not suited to rule the Amenti," I explained patiently. "I never was. But I knew Saldor would be a perfect choice, and as time has proven, it was the right decision to make."

"What about me?" Einrack asked.

"What about you?"

"Do you think I'm suited to rule?"

I shrugged. "I don't know, Einrack. Time will be your answer. Being a good leader isn't just about being strong and ruthless. There's more to it than just that."

"I know that, brother."

"Yes," I agreed with a nod, convinced that the boy really did understand. "I believe you do. You're smart just like your father was before you, and I'd wager you'll be as good a warrior as he was, maybe even better."

"I plan to be Chieftain of the Peshwin before my eighteenth birthday," Einrack announced loftily. He lifted his chin as if daring me to disagree.

"I don't doubt it," I said, believing him. No one that young had ever risen to be a Pith chieftain before, not even Einhard, but something told me that this boy would do just as he said. I raised an eyebrow. "Why not become king instead?"

"Because we have a strong and wise queen right now and there is no need," Einrack answered seriously. I'd been joking, but apparently the boy hadn't realized that. "When the time for succession does come, the tribes must vote on who shall lead them next. That is the rule my grandfather insisted on when he became our first king, and that is why my mother is now queen because the tribes wanted her. I wish to earn my place like she did, not have it handed to me because of who my grandfather and parents were."

I pursed my lips, impressed. "I think you will make a wise chieftain," I said, "and an even wiser king someday."

Einrack looked away then, peering out over the water. After that, we sat in easy, comfortable silence, listening to the harsh shrieks of the gulls overhead and the sounds of the waves slapping against the longboat's hull. Finally, the boy turned back to me. "Does a part of you still hate my father, Wolf?"

I blinked at him in surprise. "Of course not," I said. "We were brothers."

"He thought you hated him. At least a little, anyway. I know it always bothered him."

"That's ridiculous," I said, hurt more than I cared to admit that Einhard had thought that of me. Though I knew there was some truth to it and that he'd felt the same way at times, too.

"Father told me once that there was only one man in this world that he truly feared with a blade," Einrack said. "And that was you. He told me honor and hatred lived inside you in equal parts, and that's what made you such a dangerous man to cross."

I lowered my head and swallowed, missing my friend more than words could say. "Your father meant a great deal to me, Einrack. The world is a dimmer place without him in it."

Einrack pondered that before he said, "Yet, there was a time when you would have killed each other."

"Yes," I agreed. I grimaced. "But not with any happiness. Our relationship was complicated."

"Because of the chicken scratches?"

"That and other things," I replied warily, not interested in getting into an argument over the codex right now.

"He would have beaten you, brother," Einrack said confidently. He gave me a challenging look. "If not for that silly book of yours, Ganderland would lie in ruins today."

I sighed. Even with Einhard gone these many weeks, I was still forced to engage in pissing matches with the man, only now it was through his son. "Anything is possible," I muttered noncommittedly. I had no intention of debating what might have been with a boy who was still learning to wipe his own arse when it had all happened.

I could feel darkness falling over my mood, and Einrack must have sensed that, for he changed the subject. "I have a favor to ask of you, brother."

"Which is?"

Einrack cleared his throat. "When we return to the land of the Piths, I would like to remain with you."

"No," I grunted immediately.

Einrack's eyes flashed with sudden anger. "Why not? It was my father and brothers and sisters who those bastards murdered, Wolf, not yours. I made a vow to find and kill those responsible, just as you did once, and that vow needs to be honored."

"It will be," I assured the boy. "They will all pay for what they did. You have my word."

Einrack snorted. "That's not good enough. I need to be there. I need to look into their eyes as they die. Don't you understand?"

"Better than most," I said. "But even so, you will stay with your mother."

"Would you have accepted that when you were my age?" Einrack demanded, not giving up. The boy didn't wait for me to answer. "No, of course you wouldn't have. So, why should I?"

"Because I say so," I growled, my patience at an end. "You will return home with your mother and that is final. I promised your father to bring you home safe, and I'll be damned if I intend to go back on it now."

Einrack stood and began to pace in front of me across the rolling deck, his face flushed as he opened and closed his fists. I watched him, saying nothing as I rested my hand on the rudder. I could see rage flickering along his limbs like fire, and I wouldn't have been surprised if he launched himself at me.

Finally, the anger burned out, replaced by a cold calm that seemed even more dangerous. "This isn't over, brother," Einrack grunted. "You'll see." The boy turned then, his shoulders set as he marched away, heading for the bow where his mother leaned against the railing, staring into the water below.

I watched him go, shaking my head. Einhard had told me before our fateful parting in Gasterny years ago that I had no idea what I was yet, but that the entire world would tremble when I did. I'd never really understood what he'd been trying to say back then. But now, as I looked at his son on the cusp of manhood and greatness, I knew that whatever Einhard had seen in me that day, I was now seeing in Einrack. But, no matter how impressed I was by the boy and how much I understood his need for vengeance, I swore that nothing he said or did would stop me from returning him to his homeland. The matter was settled in my mind, and whether Einrack came to accept my decision or not hardly mattered to me. He was going home, and that was final.

Unfortunately, my plans for him and everyone else under my protection were about to be upended in a very unpleasant way.

We reached the Fivefingers River the next day, and just as before, we had to carefully navigate our way around the sand bars that guarded the entrance like sentries. Nothing seemed to have changed since the last time we'd been there, with even a single albatross flying high above our mast just like before as we slipped past the mud-covered fingers into the heart of the river. I could feel my anticipation building as each hour went by after that, with either the wind or, when necessary, the oars drawing me ever closer to a reunion with Shana. It seemed like months since I'd last seen her, though, in truth, it had only been three weeks.

The morning of our second day up the river began humid and sticky, with no wind to be found. I stripped to my waist and took an oar along with all the others except for Demee, who steered for us since he couldn't do much else with his mutilated hand. Einrack, Saldor, Baine, and Alesia rowed on the portside, while Fanrissen, Jebido, and I did the same on the starboard. It was tough, grueling work with the sun beating down on us, made more so because there were so few of us. But, despite that, I enjoyed the physical activity as I called out the beat stroke after stroke, glad to stretch my muscles after doing so little for the last few days.

Jebido sat on a bench in front of me, and after half an hour of relentless rowing, he turned to glance back at me, his face looking red, sweaty, and annoyed. "Hey, do you think maybe you could slow it down just a little?" he puffed. "I want to get there as much as you do, Hadrack, but I'd also like to arrive alive. I'm not a young man anymore, you know."

"Oh," I said, unaware that I'd been pushing the others so hard. "Sorry."

I could see Einrack fighting for air as he rowed, though his face was set in a knot of determination. Alesia was covered in sweat on the bench behind her son, her eyes fixated on his bare back as she worked. I hadn't noticed that she'd removed her tunic along with everyone else on the benches, though no one seemed to care all that much. We'd been sharing the confines of a small ship for many days now and there was no modesty left between any of us anymore.

I slowed the call of the beat, realizing that Jebido was right. Wearing out my crew so we could arrive an hour or two sooner would change nothing in the end. I let Jebido set the pace after that, and we rowed for half an hour at a more sedate rate, then took a short break to rest and drink some ale before starting again.

By the time midday arrived, the wind had begun to rise, allowing us to gratefully stow the oars and relax. I moved to the bow, holding onto a stay line as I watched the water ahead. Finally, after more than an hour, the trees to either side of the river began to thin out noticeably. I leaned forward in anticipation as the longboat approached the bend in the river that hid the rocky shore where we'd anchored *Sea-Wolf*, ready with a welcome smile on my lips. But that smile quickly fell away moments later when we swept around the bend and I saw nothing but empty water and shoreline waiting for us. *Sea-Wolf* was gone.

    I stared for a moment in shocked disbelief, while behind me I heard Jebido cursing softly. Saldor and Fanrissen hurried to haul in the sail as we glided toward the rock-strewn shore while I studied the area with wary eyes. I saw nothing to indicate that there were any threats close by. I could hear hundreds of birds singing from the trees around us and the higher fields ahead, which surely meant no one was around.

    "Maybe they went upriver to fish," Jebido said as he came to join me. He didn't sound very convincing to me.

    "Maybe," I grunted doubtfully, unable to hide the worry in my voice. I'd ordered Putt not to move from this spot until I returned, and I knew the former outlaw would never have disobeyed my wishes unless he'd had no choice.

    We were almost ten feet out from shore when the longboat's bow scraped against the sandy river bottom with a soft squelching sound. I immediately sprung over the gunwale before we'd come to a complete stop, landing with a splash in the water before wading forward onto dry land. I climbed the bank to get a better view of our surroundings, dislodging stones with every step while the others used ropes to pull the longboat up onto the shoreline where she'd be secure.

    I reached the top of the river's embankment to find the fields empty in all directions. There was no one in sight. I paused as I looked west toward a small stand of trees, feeling a sharp thud in my gut when I saw what appeared to be five mounds of dirt with markers overlooking them in the shadows there. They looked very much like fresh graves to me. I shouted to the others, then began to run, my heart thudding in my ears as dread filled my being. I reached the first grave moments later, my chest heaving from the sprint as I stared in dismay at the roughly scratched-out words on the wooden marker.

Here lies Walcott Parest—killed by Cardian scum

I cursed, moving to the next marker, which showed the name of another member of my crew, as did the third one as well. I shuffled my feet sideways, trying not to think about what those final two markers might say. I paused over the graves and a small moan escaped my lips when I read the names scratched there. I noticed almost as an afterthought that one of the mounds of dirt was much smaller than the other. I closed my eyes, saying a whispered prayer to The Mother.

"No!" I heard Fanrissen suddenly cry out in horror from behind me. I silently cursed myself, realizing that I should have thought to warn him of what was coming. I stepped aside as the pirate brushed his way past me, his face a twisted mask of agony. The damage was done now, anyway, and there was little I could do to ease the man's pain, much as I wished otherwise. Fanrissen stood for a moment in disbelief over the two graves, and then he sagged like a man suddenly poleaxed, dropping to his knees between the earthen mounds where his wife and daughter had been laid to rest. "No! No! Dear Mother, no! It can't be! No!"

I shook my head as I retreated backward several steps, saddened for the man, though a part of me was selfishly relieved that Shana's name wasn't among those of the dead.

"What happened here?" Jebido asked as he joined me. My friend looked just as stunned and upset as I felt.

I took a deep breath while the gut-wrenching sounds of Fanrissen's grief filled the air. The birds in the fields and trees had abruptly stopped their songs to listen as if they were ashamed to feel joy when such misery was so close. "I don't know," I told my friend helplessly.

We stood in respectful silence after that until Alesia finally called out to me, "Brother!" The Pith Queen had moved off a hundred paces to the north, searching the ground. Alesia held up the broken shaft of an arrow. "It's one of ours." She motioned around her. "There were rains recently and most of the tracks are washed away, but it looks like a running battle was fought here." She pointed further north in the direction of the Swail village, Evrar. "The trail is old. I'd guess at least a week or more, but it comes from that direction."

I sighed, stepping forward to put my hand on Fanrissen's shoulder. "I am sorry, my friend," I said softly to the man before turning and making my way over to Alesia. "Are you sure they came from the village?" I asked once I reached her. "Not the river?"

"No question, brother," Alesia said. "By the looks of it, I'd say there were a lot of the bastards, too."

"It couldn't have been the Swails," Baine said as he, Saldor, and Jebido joined us. "They wouldn't have attacked the ship."

"It wasn't," I replied. "The markers say Cardians killed our people."

"But what happened to *Sea-Wolf*?" Saldor asked. "Where did she go?"

"I don't know," I growled. "But I'm damn well going to find out." I headed back to Fanrissen, who was leaning forward with his forehead pressed to the earth of his wife's grave, his body wracked by sobs. I motioned to Demee, who had remained with the pirate. "Take care of him," I said to the old man. "Whatever he needs. The rest of us are going on to the village."

"I understand, lord," Demee said. I could see deep sympathy in his eyes as he flicked his gaze to the grieving man. "I will do what

I can for him. But this loss, sadly, will take time to heal, if it ever does."

I clapped the older man gently on the shoulder in silent commiseration, then turned back to the others. "Let's move," I grunted, feeling a wave of dark anger filling my soul. Woe to the Cardians if they were still at Dagric's old village, I vowed.

Two hours later, I saw the remnants of the chieftain's *aestrand* where it stood, jutting above the small woodland that surrounded the village. The building had been majestic-looking the last time I'd been there, constructed out of oak, straw, woven plants, and thatch. But all that was gone now, with only four withered, blackened poles remaining, each reaching up to the sky like an accusing skeletal finger. I motioned for Alesia to circle the village to my right and Baine to head to my left. I waited then in silence with Saldor, Jebido, and Einrack until I heard Baine's bird whistle that he was in position, then a second one from him that told me the village was free of the enemy. Moments later, I heard the harsh cry of a jay, letting me know Alesia was ready, too.

"All right," I told the others. "Baine just signaled that there's no one around, but stay alert. The bastards might be hiding inside some of the houses." Most of the Swails lived in buildings called *tuftstrands*, which were dug out of the ground and walled with dirt and grass. They were odd dwellings that I'd found stuffy and damp, but I knew you could hide plenty of men inside them if needed. I hoped that was the case, for I badly needed to shed some stinking Cardian blood after what I'd seen this day. "We go in hard and fast," I told the others. "If you see anything in a red cape, kill it and ask questions afterward." I glanced at Einrack. "Stay close to Saldor, and don't do anything stupid. You hear me?"

"Yes, brother," Einrack said. He was trying to appear calm, but I could see the excitement building in him. All Piths loved a good fight, even the children.

I led the way through the dense trees toward the village, pausing every five feet to listen, but no sounds were coming from ahead that appeared suspicious to me. We reached a thorned barrier the Swails had erected around the small town, and I frowned at the gaping, singed hole in it. The Cardians had clearly made short work of the wall. I stepped through the breach cautiously, clamping my teeth in frustration when a twig snapped with startling clarity beneath my right boot. I waited while those behind me froze, but no movement came from inside the compound at the harsh sound.

My eyes fell on a large post pounded into the ground at the base of the *aestrand,* and I cautiously made my way in that direction. A board was tacked to the post with a crude drawing on it and I slowly relaxed when I saw it, understanding what the message meant.

"You can lower your weapons," I grunted, feeling a steely cold resolve coming over me. "They're gone."

Saldor moved to the board and examined the drawings in puzzlement. Finally, he looked at me. "What does it mean, Chieftain?"

"It means the Cardians have Shana," I growled, fighting to get the words out around the rage I felt. "And we're going back to Blood Ring Isle."

Chapter 20: The Hundred Knives

"Somebody sure thinks they're clever," Jebido grunted with distaste.

There were actually three separate drawings on the board. The first two were done in black paint and the last one in red. I ran my hand over the top drawing, which depicted a howling wolf's head. The paint was long dried, not that I'd expected it to be anything else. It was obvious the Cardians hadn't been here in some time. Next, I moved my hand to a drawing of a lamb. This one wasn't as well done as the wolf, but it was still identifiable. Below the lamb was a large red circle with a black dot painted in the center. Some of the red paint at the bottom had run down the board in streaks, but there was no mistaking it meant Blood Ring Isle.

I took my sword and pried the board free without saying anything, then tucked it under my arm. I was going to find whoever had left this message for me and make them regret painting it no matter how long it took.

"Stop! You there, stop!"

I looked up just as a figure broke out from one of the *tuftstrands* to the west, with Baine's dark form in close pursuit. The two disappeared among the trees while the rest of us automatically spread out, anticipating an attack.

Einrack started to head after Baine and I called him back. "Wait and listen," I grunted to the boy as I let my eyes roam over the deserted village. "You'll live longer that way."

Moments later, I heard a high-pitched cry, followed by a curse from Baine. "I've got her, Hadrack!" my friend called out. He reappeared, dragging a struggling young girl along with him. I could see Alesia peering around the charred remnants of a *tuftstrand* wall forty yards away, waiting and watching with an arrow nocked to her bow. If this was a ploy, she would be well-positioned to deal with whatever came our way. "The little she-wolf bit me," Baine grumbled as he drew closer with his prisoner. He stopped in front of me, his right hand clamped around the girl's left wrist while she struggled ineffectively to escape.

I sheathed my sword, certain there was no danger now, for the captive was clearly a Swail. I guessed the girl to be perhaps ten years old, with torn clothing and ragged, dark black hair. I thought she would have been pretty if not for the filth covering her from head to toe and a nasty, scabbed-over cut on her chin.

"My friend is going to let you go now," I told the girl gently. "Don't run. We're not Cardians, we're friends. All right?" The girl nodded slowly, having relaxed somewhat as she got a good look at us, though I could still see a hint of fear in her eyes. I motioned for Baine to release her. "My name is Lord Hadrack," I said. "What's yours?"

"Bottra, lord," the girl replied in a low voice as she rubbed her wrist gingerly where Baine's iron grip had held her.

"Bottra," I repeated with a friendly nod. I remembered her now from the last time we'd been here. She'd spent an hour hovering in the background while Evrar's Chieftain, Olffur, took us on a tour of the village. The girl had been curious about us but relaxed and at ease back then, which was very different from her appearance now. "You're the Chieftain's daughter, is that right?"

"Yes, lord," the girl managed to mumble. I could see she was fighting tears.

I tapped my chest. "Do you remember me? I came here a while ago in the big ship with Dagric, who used to be chieftain here."

"Yes, lord, I remember you."

"Then why in the name of The Mother did you run, girl?" Baine said with a snort. He flexed his left hand, which I could see had puncture marks oozing blood along the thumb and meat of his outer palm.

Bottra looked down at the ground. "I saw men with weapons and I ran. I was afraid."

"Perfectly understandable," I said. I glanced around the deserted compound. "Where is everyone?"

"Many are dead, lord," Bottra said. She pointed south. "Buried in the Sleeping Fields after the invaders left."

"Your father?"

"Gone to lie in the fields as well, lord," Bottra replied with a catch in her voice.

I took a deep breath, saddened to hear of Olffur's death. I'd liked the man, respecting him greatly after he'd pledged to step aside so Dagric could resume his place as Chieftain of Evrar. Dagric had declined, though, stating that there was nothing he could offer the village anymore that Olffur could not do just as well if not better. "And the survivors?" I asked.

"We have a campsite to the east, lord," Bottra said. "Many are injured from the battle, but we are still too afraid to return here in case the Cardians come back."

"Why are you here all alone, then?" Baine asked.

"My dog ran away from the camp last night," the girl replied. "I've been searching the forest all day for him and had hoped maybe he'd come back here."

I put my hands on the Swail's shoulders, careful not to hurt her in my anxiety. "What happened to the Gander ship in the river, Bottra?" I asked. "Where did it go?"

Bottra looked up at me, her deep brown eyes filled with misery. "I do not know, lord. One of the women from my village says she saw it sailing northwest upriver. It was on fire and the *Panwa* were attacking it."

"*Panwa*?"

Bottra paused for a moment while she thought. "The spirit people, lord. I believe you call them Shadow Pirates."

I cursed. Captain Bear and his damn pirates again. I should have dealt with the bastard when I'd had the chance. "How far away is your camp?" I asked the girl.

"A few miles, lord."

I pointed to the ground. "Can you draw a map for me so we can find it later?"

"A what, lord?"

"A picture," I said. I showed the girl the board with its drawings. "Like this, only it shows me where your camp is located from here." I could tell the girl still didn't understand, so I squatted, indicating she should do the same. "Baine," I grunted. "Give me a knife." I had his knife in my hand moments later, and I drew a wiggly line with it in the dirt. "This is the Fivefingers," I said to the girl. Do you understand?"

"Yes, lord."

I could see I'd piqued her interest as I made a mark on the line. "And this is where *Sea-Wolf*—my ship, was anchored." I drew a circle some distance away. "And this is where we are right now. Your village." I flipped the knife in my palm, handing it to her by the leather hilt. "Now, can you show me where your camp is from Evrar?"

Bottra took the weapon, her lower lip jutting out in concentration as she peered at the ground. "There is a trail here," she said, making a barely discernible path from the village, heading northeast. She frowned, then started over, digging the blade deeper into the ground this time. "You must walk until you reach a stream that runs across the trail," she said, looking up at me. "Follow the water east," Bottra continued, drawing a line, "until you see a tree with bark that looks like the face of an old man. Then go north again until you reach Golmark Pond. You will find my people there."

"Good," I said. I stood and the girl shyly handed the knife back to Baine. I could tell that the child was quite taken by him despite how they'd first met. "We're going back to the river to find my missing ship," I told Bottra. "But after that, I'll return and bring food and whatever else your people need to the campsite."

"Thank you, lord," Bottra said unenthusiastically. I could tell by her expression that she didn't believe me.

A dog suddenly began to bark from somewhere in the trees to the west, and the girl's expression lit up with joy. "Tazwa!" she cried. Bottra began to run toward the sounds while waving her arms in excitement. "Tazwa! Oh, Tazwa!" She disappeared moments later, followed almost immediately by the sounds of giggling and happy laughter along with the dog's excited yelps of greeting.

I almost smiled as I imagined the reunion, but then I remembered Shana was gone, taken by Cardians, and whatever momentary pleasure I'd been feeling slipped away. "Come on," I growled at my men. "We've got a long run back to the ship."

The distance between Evrar and the river was roughly eight miles, and it took my men and me just over an hour to return at a dead run to where we'd left Fanrissen and Demee. Jebido had fallen behind almost immediately, but he kept on running gamely, always just managing to stay within sight of us. Einrack, Saldor, and Alesia held the lead easily, with Baine and me bringing up the middle as best we could. Fanrissen was still where we'd left him when we arrived, though now he was sitting cross-legged between the graves, one hand on each with his head lowered. The pirate was so still that he might have been sleeping, but I knew with certainty that he wasn't. Demee sat beneath the shade of the trees not far away from the graves, and he stood stiffly at our approach.

"Is everything all right, lord?" the tavern keeper asked in alarm.

I came to a weary halt in front of him, trying to catch my breath as I leaned over with my hands on my knees, blowing hard. "The Swail village has been razed," I finally managed to gasp out. "We spoke to someone there that claims *Sea-Wolf* was under attack and headed upriver." I glanced at the three Piths, who looked unfazed by the long run. Baine was crouched down beside me on one knee, fighting for air. I put my hand on his shoulder. "You and the others get the ship ready to sail. I'm going to talk to the pirate."

I motioned to Demee as Baine, Saldor, Einrack, and Alesia headed toward the river. "Go with them. I want to get moving as soon as possible."

I made my way toward Fanrissen, nodding to Jebido, who stumbled past me, his face red and covered in sweat as he headed after the others. I stood behind the pirate for a moment, wondering what I could possibly say to the man. Finally, I knew. "I was eight years old when men came to my village," I said. Fanrissen didn't move, but I could tell he was listening. "They took everything from me that day. My home, my father, my sister, and my friends." I took a deep breath, remembering the flames and the screams. "I couldn't bury everyone," I continued. "I was too small. But I carried my sister to this stream I knew in the woods, then went back for my father." I chose not to mention that I'd only brought his head. It was irrelevant to my point, anyway. "I buried them both near that stream, and then I sat between them for hours, much like you are doing right now. I remember I cried and cried and cried."

Fanrissen finally stirred, and he twisted his neck to look back at me, his features torn by heartache and suffering. "But you stopped crying eventually, didn't you, lord?"

"I did," I agreed. "The tears had all run out after a while, you see, and all I had left inside was hatred and the need for vengeance." I touched my chest. "But in here, the tears still flow to this day. Silent and unseen, but always there. I expect that will continue until my last breath in this world." I stooped to put my hand on his arm. "Your wife and child are gone now, my friend, which greatly saddens me. But you still live, and every moment you sit here grieving and doing nothing is one more moment that their killers get to breathe." I shook my head regretfully. "I cannot bring back your family, Pirate, but what I can offer you is vengeance against those who murdered them. Come with me now, and together, I swear we will exact payment for what they did here."

Fanrissen turned to look back at the graves and his shoulders sagged. "But they will still be dead, lord." He shuddered slightly as he stroked the mounds. "No matter what happens now, they will always be dead. Until the end of time itself, they will be dead."

"That's true," I said. "But you have to remember that this isn't the end of your journey together. You will meet them again, just like I will see my family again someday. But ask yourself this, Pirate. What do you want to say to your wife and child when you finally meet in the next world? Will it be that you did nothing other than sit and weep at their loss? Or will you be able to look them in the eyes and say those men who took their lives paid for it in blood and pain?"

I straightened then and waited, not knowing which way the pendulum would swing. Finally, Fanrissen stood and he turned to me. His eyes were red-rimmed and stained dark with loss, though I thought I could see determination burning there, too. "I choose blood and pain, lord," he said in a tortured voice. "Lots and lots of blood and pain." He shifted his sword in its scabbard. "But after that, I shall join my family in the next world. For I cannot bear the thought of life without them in this one."

I almost protested his words before I thought better of it. Each man must walk his own path in this life, and Fanrissen's choice was clearly made. Who was I to tell him differently? The pirate walked past me, moving stiffly as he headed for the river. I followed moments later. I thought about blood and pain as I approached the Fivefingers and worked my way down the rocky embankment overlooking the water. I knew blood and pain were coming for the Cardians and I relished the idea, but I could also hear a small, annoying voice in my head whispering, *but at what cost*? I chose to ignore that voice, for everything we do in life has a price attached to it. As long as I got Shana back alive, I was willing to pay whatever the gods demanded, even if I had to die to make that happen.

We located *Sea-Wolf* thirty miles upriver, where she lay partially on her side on a giant sandbar that jutted out from the shore. Her great hull was scorched and blackened, and I could see several holes and fresh planking on the bow and keel. A small group of Pith warriors stood knee-deep in the water as they worked to position a beam on the keel. Tyris was with them; his tall form bent over as he used the head of a war-hammer to bang the beam in place. One of the warriors looked back and saw us approaching and he shouted in alarm, which sent the others scurrying for their weapons on the shore.

I stood at the bow of the longboat and cupped my hands to my mouth. "It's Lord Hadrack!" I cried. "It's Lord Hadrack!" I waved my arms as we drew closer, shouting along with the rest of my men until finally, the Piths realized who we were and began to cheer.

I heard, "Wolf! Wolf! Wolf!" floating over the water and I raised a fist in the air, grateful to find my men still alive and the ship relatively intact. It was truly more than I had hoped for. Ten minutes later, the longboat was beached on the grassy shore and I embraced Tyris heartily.

"I knew you would come, lord," Tyris said with obvious relief. His face was drawn and haggard-looking, and I saw he walked with a limp. "It's nothing, lord," Tyris said, seeing where my eyes had gone. "One of those pirate bastards got lucky." He hesitated, his face suddenly filled with a mixture of sorrow and dread. "Lord, I am so sorry to have to tell you this, but Lady Shana was—"

I held up a hand. "I know, Tyris. The Cardians have her. There's no need to say more. I'm sure everyone did all they could, but now we need to get her back."

"Yes, lord," Tyris said, looking surprised. "How did you know?"

I hooked a thumb the way we'd come. "The Cardians left me a message in Evrar."

"Lord! Lord Hadrack!" I looked up as Haf came racing down the bank, the boy almost tripping and falling over a clump of grass in his eagerness to get to me. Haf reached the shore and flung his arms around my waist, hugging me tightly. "I prayed every day that you would return, lord!"

I rifled Haf's hair, relieved to see that he was all right. "The gods favored us," I said, motioning to Einrack. "And here is the proof." I glanced at Tyris as Haf stared at Einrack curiously. "Where's Putt?" I asked.

"In camp, lord," the tall archer said, motioning in the direction Haf had come. "He's in a bad way. Took a sword thrust in the gut from that big bastard Captain Bear. We're doing what we can for him." Tyris hesitated. "It was Captain Bear that took Lady Shana, lord. Putt did everything he could to stop him. We all did."

I nodded and glanced around. I counted only four Pith warriors, one of whom I was happy to see was Gislea. "How many men did we lose?"

Tyris took a deep breath. "Five, lord, with four wounded." His eyes flashed. "But we made the bastards pay dearly. It was only when they retreated to their ships and broke away that I realized Captain Bear had Lady Shana thrown over his shoulder." He hesitated. "The ship was on fire, lord, and there was little we could do to stop them. I am sorry."

"I know you are," I said, picturing the desperate scene. "Thank you, Tyris. Trust me when I say Captain Bear will pay soon enough. But for that to happen, we need to get *Sea-Wolf* back on her feet as quickly as possible." I motioned to the Cardian longboat. "We have plenty of supplies and extra planks. Take whatever you need to get the job done. Tear the damn ship apart if you have to."

"Yes, lord!" Tyris said before he began shouting orders to the Piths.

I climbed the embankment with Haf, one arm around the boy's thin shoulders as I headed toward the camp to check on Putt and the other wounded. I'd ordered Baine, Jebido, and the others to stay behind to help Tyris with the ship. I looked back to see Fanrissen talking intently with Tyris and Gislea, his face set in serious concentration. I knew exactly what he was asking them—how did my wife and child die, and who killed them? It would have been the first question out of my mouth, too.

Putt was sitting up and drinking water from a skin when I arrived in the crude camp, and his eyes lit up with joy at my appearance. His face was whiter than I'd ever seen, with dark circles of pain and exhaustion under his eyes.

"Thank The Mother, lord!" Putt said. He shifted, then winced as he clutched at his side.

Several other wounded Piths were lying close by, including Finja. Hamon the Pathfinder was busy changing a bandage on her leg. "It's good to see you back, Wolf," the priest said as he worked. He paused to look at me. "Did you find the boy?"

"We did," I said. "He's safe and sound."

"Praise the Master for that," Hanon grunted. "Now we can go home and forget all about this cursed place."

I didn't respond to the Pathfinder as I dropped to one knee beside Putt. "How are you?" I asked the former outlaw.

Putt started to shrug, then stopped as he hissed in pain. He smiled weakly. "It's just a scratch, lord. I've had worse."

"Captain Bear did this?"

"Yes, lord." Putt lowered his eyes. "I'm sorry I failed you."

I pointed to Putt's wound. "You tried to stop him from taking Shana. What more could I ask for than that? I'm just glad you're alive."

"I'm too mean to die, lord," Putt grunted. "Besides, I still have a score to settle with that bastard."

"That's the spirit," I said. I went on to tell him about the message left for me in Evrar and how our successful mission to rescue Einrack had gone.

"Getting into Blood Ring Isle a second time won't be easy, lord," Putt said when I was done. He looked very worried at the idea, which I couldn't blame him for, because so was I.

"I know," I agreed. "But we'll find a way."

The words came out of my mouth easily and confidently, though, in truth, I felt nothing but doubt inside. Blood Ring Isle's defenses were formidable and deadly, and though we'd passed through them safely once, I knew it wasn't likely to happen again. I also knew we wouldn't be able to use the same ploy to gain entry like we had at Ravenhold, either. They'd be watching for that. I glanced around at the other wounded. Those awake were listening intently to our conversation, including Hanon, who looked annoyed that our ordeal wasn't over yet. I hardly cared what the man thought about it. The Pathfinder answered to his queen in all things other than faith, and I knew Alesia would never turn back now with Shana in the Cardians' clutches.

"We don't have that many able-bodied men left, lord," Putt said with a sigh. "Without more fighters, I don't see how we can do this."

"I'll think of something," I said as the germ of an idea began to grow in my mind. Excluding the wounded, I had less than twenty men left who could be counted on to fight. It wasn't nearly enough if we had any chance of success. Putt was right. We needed help, and I knew just where to find it.

Two days later, *Sea-Wolf* was back on the water, with her sails mended and her hull repaired. The work wasn't pretty, but it seemed to be holding up just fine. I prayed it continued that way. Tyris had taken what he'd needed from the Cardian longboat, but not enough to make her unseaworthy, which I was thankful for, since I would need her too if my plan was to work. Putt had insisted on resuming command of *Sea-Wolf*, and nothing I or anyone else could say would dissuade him from it. I'd finally given up arguing with the man and instead had a chair fashioned from poplar saplings so that he could at least be off his feet. Now, Putt sat upon that chair like a triumphant king, counting out the beat to the rest of us with relish as we worked the oars, propelling us back toward *Sea-Wolf's* original anchorage.

We arrived at that anchorage just before midday, two days after we'd left it, this time in a better frame of mind. Tyris was in command of the Cardian longboat, and I had him continue downriver around the bend to act as a lookout. I thought it highly unlikely that the Shadow Pirates would return for another crack at us, but if they did, then at least we'd have some warning first. But, as certain as I was that Captain Bear wouldn't return, I was still reluctant to leave *Sea-Wolf* unprotected, so I only took Baine, Jebido, and Alesia with me back to Evrar.

We brought as much food and supplies with us as we could carry on our backs. I didn't know what the situation would be when we finally reached the Swail encampment, though I was sure that what we were carrying wouldn't do much to help in the long run. But I'd promised Bottra that I would bring something on my return, and I was sticking to my word. It would just have to suffice for now. I still had a fair amount of gold and silver on me, and I planned on giving them some, though my generosity wasn't all due to good-heartedness. The truth was I needed the Swails' help desperately if I hoped to get Shana back and, hopefully, the gold coupled with a desire for revenge would be enough to ensure I got it.

We reached Evrar and quickly found the trail Bottra had told us about, and after about ten minutes of walking, we came across a trickling stream. We turned right, following the streambed east for another twenty minutes. Baine was the first to notice the old cottonwood tree, and he nudged my arm, pointing it out. The tree sat back fifty feet from the stream, with the thick bark of the trunk gnarled, twisted, and gray. Someone had carved out a man's face in the tree's center, with fierce eyes, a wide, flared nose, and a flowing beard that ran down the length of the trunk to the ground. It was both impressive and intimidating at the same time.

I led the others across the stream, heading north along a well-beaten trail. The trees were thick here, with the canopy above blocking a good deal of the light, leaving behind shifting shadows that played tricks on the eyes. Twice as we progressed I thought I saw movement ahead, only to reach those spots to find nothing there. I started to get the uneasy feeling that we were being watched, and I glanced at my companions, all of whom looked like they were experiencing the same thing. I heard a rustling sound off to my left and I paused, the feeling of being watched having grown even stronger.

"It's all right," I called out. "We're friends. Bottra told us how to get here."

I waited then, trying not to show how startled I was when a man stepped out from behind a tree less than six feet away from me. He was dressed in animal skins dyed different shades of brown and green, helping him blend in with his surroundings. He had a bow in his hands and it was drawn, with the arrow pointed at my midsection.

"Who are you?" the man asked suspiciously.

I smiled and lifted my hands. "Lord Hadrack," I said. "We're Ganders." I gestured behind me. "The Cardians attacked our ship just like they did your village."

The bowman's stance relaxed somewhat, though he only eased up on his bow a little. "What do you want?"

I turned so he could see the pack on my back. "To bring you food and other supplies. Bottra told me you have many injured."

"This is true," the man said. He finally lowered his bow and emitted a low whistle. Six more men immediately appeared around us, all similarly dressed, though none had their bows drawn. "My name is Aarav," the first man said. "You will come with us."

Aarav turned then and headed down the trail while the others just watched us silently. The Swails' expressions weren't hostile, but they weren't exactly friendly either. After what they'd been through recently, I could hardly blame them. I glanced at my companions and shrugged, then followed after Aarav. We walked for another twenty minutes, with Aarav leading and the rest of the Swails following at a distance behind us. We eventually broke through the trees into a wide glade of soft grass and wildflowers that led down to a sparkling blue lake shaped like a three-quarter moon. It appeared that Golmark Pond had either grown considerably since the body of water had first been named, or the person doing the naming hadn't fully understood what a pond was.

"Wait here," Aarav grunted. "If you move, you die." The Swail gave us all a baleful glance before he headed off to the west with his men, where I could see campfires and tents along the shore of the lake.

"Friendly fellow," Jebido muttered sarcastically.

I barely heard him as my focus fell on three Swail children playing and swimming in the lake. One by one they disappeared below the water, with only a strange, stick-like apparatus poking out from the lake to show where they'd been. I waited and watched, expecting them to resurface at any moment, but long minutes went by with no sign of them. I started to move forward, alarmed that maybe they'd drowned, but then a girlchild broke the surface, laughing as she removed the strange stick from her mouth. I realized with a shock that she'd been using it to breathe underwater all that time. I shook my head and started to laugh.

"What's so funny?" Baine asked me.

"I think I just found our way into Blood Ring Isle," I said.

Chapter 21: Return to Blood Ring Isle

 The Swails surprised me. As it turned out, they didn't want my gold or my silver in exchange for their help. All they wanted was a chance to exact revenge for what had happened to their village. But it went even deeper than just that it seemed, for there was also a burning desire in these people to make the Shadow Pirates and Cardians finally pay for all the misery they'd caused over the years. The promise of vengeance and payback that the Swails desperately sought was something that I could certainly understand, and it was a promise that I was more than happy to give them. When I'd first decided to ask for the villagers' help, I'd hoped to get maybe ten men to join us, though even that had seemed optimistic at the time. But what I got, in the end, turned out to be far, far more than I could have ever expected.

 Jebido, Baine, and Alesia, along with Saldor, Einrack, and me, stayed in the camp by the lake to help with the wounded while the bulk of my men remained with the ships, guarding them with the help of some of the Swails. We'd made a second trip back to the river that first day and returned with more food and supplies, which the Swails were extremely grateful to have. My plan on how to assault Blood Ring Isle had initially been met with incredulity from Jebido and the others. But, once I'd explained it to them in greater detail and pointed out that there really wasn't much of an alternative for getting past the isle's defenses, they'd eventually come around. Even Jebido, who always pecked away at any perceived flaws with the intensity of a cat stalking a mouse, quickly got over his initial pessimism and declared it a bold, innovative plan that had a good chance of success. I almost fell off the rock I'd been sitting on when he'd said that.

But, as innovative and bold as the plan might be, we still needed time to prepare before it could be set into proper motion. I was chomping at the bit to leave and rescue Shana, but I knew the extra days we would have to spend at Golmark Pond were necessary and might mean the difference between success or failure. Jebido insisted that I needed to be patient and focused, having correctly surmised where my head was at. I knew he was right, of course, but even so, it wasn't easy to keep my mind from wandering, wondering what foul things the Cardian scum might be doing to my wife. It was maddening and frustrating to think such thoughts, and the only way I managed to get through the long days and nights of planning and training was by concentrating on the task at hand with an almost religious fervor that at times seemed to frighten even my closest friends. It was either that or go mad with worry.

As each day passed and word continued to spread about our mission, more and more Swail warriors appeared in the glade, arriving from nearby villages in the hopes of joining in the fight. But unfortunately, I only had so much room on my two ships and couldn't take them all, so the Swails organized a combat tournament, with the top one hundred warriors earning the right to go with us. The idea had been Aarav's, and I thought it a savvy move by the man, for it ensured we got the best fighters that the Swails could offer without causing anger and resentment among those who were rejected.

I spent much of my time alongside Saldor and a chosen group of twelve Swails, who took hours training us to use the hollow reed stalks that I'd seen the children breathing with underwater. The fourteen of us would be the ones tasked with subduing the towers overlooking the island's inlet so that *Sea-Wolf* and the longboat could safely enter with the rest of my force. Saldor and I quickly learned, though, that using the reeds wasn't as easy as it seemed. We both ended up with more than our share of cold lake water filling our lungs before we finally became fairly proficient at breathing through the tubes.

The reeds were called *Caporto Fungana* in the Swail language, which translated simply meant giant grass. The plants could be found all along the waterways in Swailand, growing, I was told, at an astonishing rate each year, with some even reaching thirty or forty feet in height in a single season. The Swails used the reeds everywhere in their day-to-day lives, from thatching roofs and constructing frames for *tuftstrands* and *aestrands* to weaving baskets, making spears and fishing poles, or as fodder for their livestock. The Swails even made musical instruments out of them that looked and sounded very similar to the flutes that I'd seen minstrels playing in Ganderland.

Turning the reed stalks into functioning breathing tubes took a great deal of time and patience, for they could only be used for that purpose once the grass had fully matured. The stalks were cut to size and soaked in water for a month or more. Then, as soon as they were deemed pliable enough, the tubes were carefully bent to form a curvature so the diver could insert one end in his mouth while the other jutted above his head, enabling him to swim facedown below the surface. The newly formed stalks were then tied in that position so the bend didn't lose its curve before being left to dry in the sun. Sometimes the process took two or three tries before an effective breathing tube was produced, but once completed, they would have a simple yet sturdy tool for hunting sponges, fish, lobsters, clams, and oysters. I found it remarkable and incredibly inventive, though a part of me wondered what Hanley could do to improve the design if he was given half the chance.

It was our fifth and last day at the campsite, and I sat by a fire fifty feet back from the lake, watching as a group of Swail children—including Bottra—played and laughed in the water as dusk slowly fell. It was heartening to see the joy on their faces after the horrific events that had so recently upended their lives.

Watching the Swails playing in such a carefree manner had made me think of my own children, and I wondered how they were doing back in Corwick with the spinster twins watching over them.

"What are you so lost in thought about?" Jebido asked, startling me. I hadn't seen him approach. My friend sat down with a grunt opposite me on a faded rock worn smooth over the years by the rain and wind.

I held one of the three-foot-long breathing tubes in my hand, having rarely let it out of my sight over the last few days. I lifted it to him. "I was just wondering what Hanley could do with these to make them better."

Jebido shrugged. "What's wrong with them as they are? It seems to me the damn things get the job done just fine."

I grinned. "I'm betting Hanley would disagree with that."

Jebido waved a hand. "That lad spends too much time inside his own head if you ask me."

"Maybe so," I grunted in acknowledgment. "But he also sees things in ways that the rest of us don't. It's a skill, Jebido. One which is just as valuable as a strong sword arm or an accurate bow. Maybe more so in some ways."

"I'll stick with a good shield and a sharp sword," Jebido grumbled. "Half the time when that boy talks, my head starts to hurt."

I laughed, knowing exactly what he meant. "So, how is the training going?" I asked.

Jebido snorted and threw several dry branches on the fire. "Not so good. The Swails are damn fine warriors and brave as anything, Hadrack, but they're nearly useless in a shield wall. They have no discipline at all." He sat back and stretched his legs closer to the flames. "And as bad as the Cardians are in a fight, they'll still have no trouble crushing these poor bastards if it comes to a battle of shield against shield." Jebido sighed. "Maybe if we had more time, I could do something with them."

"We've already used up more time here than I wanted," I grunted.

"I know," Jebido agreed. "But if I had another week, then maybe—"

"No," I said with a shake of my head, cutting him off. "Shana doesn't have another week. We leave tomorrow morning, just as planned. You can keep drilling the Swails on board the ships if you need to."

Jebido grimaced. "That's not very practical, and you know it."

"No, it's not," I admitted. My ships would be crowded with men and supplies, not to mention rolling precariously on the waves. Not exactly the ideal place to try teaching the finer arts of fighting as a unit in a shield wall. *Sea-Wolf* was bigger and steadier than the Cardian longboat, so there was a chance Jebido could find some success there. But, either way, I wasn't willing to wait any longer. "You're just going to have to make the best of it, my friend," I added firmly. "We leave in the morning, no matter what."

The next day began cloudy and cool, with a steady breeze coming from the north that turned the lake waters choppy. But, despite the cold wind, every single Swail, from swaddled infant to the old and infirm, rose early to see us off. Their cheering filled the glade as light fog swirled around our legs while we marched away from Golmark Pond in a long procession. As we left the camp behind, I wondered how many of the warriors coming with us would live to see their homeland again. Aarav had taken the lead on our way back to the Fivefingers River, having easily won a place for himself in the Hundred Knives, which was what the Swails who'd earned the right to join us were now calling themselves. The name seemed fitting enough since each man carried an oversized knife in their belt called a seaxe and was just as proficient with them as Baine was with his assortment of knives.

Aarav was a ferocious fighter with either knife, spear, or bow, and he was greatly admired and respected by the other

Swails. I'd quickly realized the man's value and had made him the leader of the Hundred Knives, which seemed to be a welcome and popular move. One thing I'd learned in my many years of warfare was how to recognize a born leader of men when I saw one. Aarav was smart, decisive, and clear-headed, all of which I knew would make him worth his weight in gold on the battlefield when the time came to fight.

We did have one unforeseen incident that almost ruined our mission before it had even begun. That moment came when we reached the Fivefingers and the Hundred Knives saw the Cardian longboat anchored there alongside *Sea-Wolf*. The Swails were a highly intelligent people, but they were also incredibly superstitious, believing in various spirit walkers that roamed the world at night, searching for the souls of the wicked. And though they'd come to warily accept my reassurances that the *Panwa* were simply men of flesh and blood, the sight of the leering figurehead on the prow of the longboat sent the normally fearless warriors into moaning fits of terror.

The creature was not a *Matanga*, for it seemed only the Shadow Pirates used those, but was instead a fearsome-looking dragon with two heads. With some quick thinking on Jebido's part, we managed to avert disaster when he suggested I use my father's axe to chop the damn creature's heads and body away. The Swails had still been reluctant to board the Cardian ship when I was done, but after talking patiently to Aarav for over an hour and insisting that there was nothing to fear, they had finally relented. However, I could tell many of the warriors were still uneasy about it, and all I could hope for was they eventually overcame their fear.

I placed half the Hundred Knives on the Cardian ship with Tyris while the rest joined my men on *Sea-Wolf*. It was a tight fit for us all, but by and large, people managed to get along without too many altercations. The Swail women did not fight like their Pith counterparts did, so seeing Gislea, Finja, and Alesia carrying weapons and being treated as equals by us was something of a novelty to the Swail warriors. In truth, I don't think they took the women seriously at first. But that quickly changed halfway through our first day heading downriver when a Swail warrior made a joke about Gislea's prowess with the bow, stating that he thought she'd be more useful on her back servicing men who could actually fight. That, of course, did not go over well with Gislea, and if not for a timely intervention by Baine, we probably would have had to change the name of the Swails to the Ninety-Nine Knives.

It took us two and a half days to finally reach the mouth of the Fivefingers. But when we got there, we were forced to anchor in a small cove half a mile back from the entrance to wait out a storm that hovered just off the coast to the west. I waited the rest of that day for the storm to move away, watching in frustration as it just hung there, raging like a vengeful god while lightning flashes sizzled across the dark sky and high winds turned the water into a churning maelstrom. I knew only a fool would venture out in that, and even as impatient as I was to reach Shana, waiting where we were was clearly preferable to chancing death out on the Western Sea.

The delay may have been incredibly frustrating for me, but not for Jebido, who used the opportunity to move the Swails onto the mainland and drill them incessantly with shields and spears. The bulk of the storm stayed well out to sea, though the rain that reached the shore was still heavy at times, bringing with it a raw, biting wind. Jebido was a tough taskmaster and didn't seem bothered in the least by the weather, though I could tell the Swails didn't quite share his enthusiasm. I don't think Jebido stopped shouting from the moment he and the Hundred Knives made it ashore until they finally returned to the ship long after darkness had fallen, looking wet, miserable, and exhausted.

"Feel better?" I grunted to my friend when he finally came to join me on the forecastle once his charges were back on board. The wind and rain had lessened considerably, though I could still see flashes in the sky miles away to the west and hear the occasional distant rumbling of thunder.

"A little," Jebido admitted. His voice was hoarse from all the yelling.

"Any improvement with your prized pupils?"

"A glimmer of progress," Jebido grunted without much enthusiasm. "If I had enough time and patience, maybe I could polish some of these lumps of coal you've given me into something resembling jewels—maybe."

I nodded and took a deep breath, not saying anything as I stared at the receding storm. I knew it was too dangerous now to try and navigate around the sandbars in the darkness, so here we'd have to stay until dawn finally arrived. I closed my eyes, picturing Shana just before I'd headed out to search for Einrack in Bahyrst. I remembered she'd seemed so worried that day, still fretting about that old seer from Camwick and his infernal prophecy that had caused me so many problems. I'd assured her that I'd be fine and would find Einrack, which time had proven to be true, but now I'd lost my wife to the damn Cardians instead. It was beyond maddening that we'd sacrificed so much to get first Alesia back and then Einrack, only to lose Shana as a result. All of which, I knew, lay at the feet of that seer. If not for that lying bastard preying off the hopes and fears of others with his false prophecies, none of this would have ever happened. I swore as I watched the waning storm finally move away that if the Cardians hurt even one hair on her head, that old bastard would pay for it in blood just the same as they would.

I felt a hand rest on my left shoulder, and I turned to glance at Jebido. "She'll be all right, Hadrack," he said kindly as he faced me. "The gods will make sure of it. I promise."

"I know she will be," I growled. "But I'm not depending on any help from the gods. They're the ones who allowed her to be taken in the first place, so I'll do this without them."

"Everything has a purpose," Jebido said, keeping his right hand firmly on my shoulder. He gave me a gentle shake for emphasis. "Even this. You know that."

"What I know!" I snapped, suddenly irritated by his soothing tone, "is that my wife is gone, Jebido! She's gone because I failed to protect her when it mattered most. So don't talk to me about the gods and their scheming ways. I don't want to hear about it."

"I understand," Jebido said. He sighed and squeezed my shoulder. "It hurts me to see you like this, Hadrack. I know words are easy, but that's all I can offer you right now. But once we reach Blood Ring Isle, things will be different. We won't need words then, just actions, and I'll be with you every step of the way with a sword in my hand and vengeance in my heart. We will free Lady Shana from these bastards and make them suffer for laying their hands on her. You have my oath on that."

"Thank you, old friend," I said, feeling shame that I'd yelled at Jebido the way I had. The man was only trying to help. I put my right hand on his shoulder the same way he had his on mine. "Forgive me for being a fool. Shana is my life, and not knowing if she's all right is worse than any torture imaginable." I drew my hand away and let it drop to my side. "I need my girl back, Jebido. I'm just an empty shell of a man without her."

Jebido took a deep breath before he patted my shoulder in commiseration. "I know, lad. I know. This will all be over soon, and when it is, the two of you can finally go home to those four glorious children of yours and live a life of happiness."

Ah, if only his words had been true.

It took us more than a week of sailing before the first faint outlines of Blood Ring Isle rose once again on the horizon. I'd had no idea what to expect the first time I'd been to the island. But this time around, I was determined to finish what we'd started and ensure the Cardians never used the place as a base again. My two-ship fleet pressed onward, heading through choppy seas doggedly while making no effort to hide our presence. There was no way to get close to the island without being seen anyway, and besides—being seen was something that I was counting on.

The Cardians would feel overly confident when they realized that I was here, knowing that if I dared attack, my ships would be pummeled by tons of rock waiting above on the cliffs overlooking the inlet. They didn't know about my alternate plans, of course, which was something that I was going to take full advantage of once night finally fell.

"Are you sure he'll come?" Baine asked me. It was still mid-morning, and we were standing on the forecastle with the others of my inner circle, which now included Aarav.

"Maybe not him," I grunted. "Not yet, anyway. But I'm betting somebody will."

It took another hour for my ships to reach a suitable distance from the island—not too close, but not too far away, either. I signaled for Putt to reef the sails and drop the anchor. Now, all we had to do was wait. And, as expected, that wait didn't last long, as less than half an hour later, a sleek, black longboat slipped out from the inlet, cutting across the water nimbly toward us. I could see a gigantic figure standing in the prow watching us, and I nodded to myself in satisfaction. The bastard had come after all.

My men were lined up along the railings and on both castles with weapons ready, hoping for a glimpse of the infamous pirate, though I didn't expect to see any aggression coming from the approaching craft. I guessed this meeting would be nothing more than a feeling-out, with terms given that I'd pretend to consider and perhaps the odd threat and insult thrown in for good measure. That suited me just fine. I could play that game.

The pirate ship dropped its black sail as it drew closer, with the crew maneuvering the vessel alongside us expertly using the ship's oars. A white *Matanga* with a red-painted face and leering mouth was carved into the prow, and I could hear the Swails muttering to themselves when they saw it. I just prayed the warriors kept their heads and courage as the hull of the smaller boat nestled against ours with a gentle thud. Several ropes were thrown up and over the railing by the pirates and two Piths secured their ship to ours, then dropped a rope ladder over the side. I waited with my hands clasped behind my back, keeping my face neutral, though inside, my heart was pounding as the huge figure of Captain Bear appeared at the railing. He smiled when he saw me, pausing with one leg swung over the gunwale to study me.

"So, it seems we meet at last, Lord Hadrack."

The pirate leader dropped lightly to the deck, looking amused when several Swails standing close to him automatically drew back. I studied the man that I'd sworn to kill with professional curiosity. It was said that he was named Captain Bear because of his size, and now that I'd gotten a closer look at him, I knew that the name was fitting. The man was, without question, the largest person that I'd ever encountered. The pirate leader wore tight-fitting trousers and a mail coat, with a monstrous sword strapped across his back that looked as tall as I was. I stood almost six feet four inches in height and weighed two hundred and twenty pounds, but Captain Bear easily topped me by close to eight inches. I guessed he probably outweighed me by at least sixty pounds, too. The pirate leader was a formidable, dangerous-looking man—and probably the strongest warrior that I'd ever faced or ever would—but even so, I couldn't wait to cross swords with him. But I knew that glorious moment would have to wait, for this clearly was not the time nor the place for it. My opportunity would come.

I stepped forward several paces until we were less than three feet apart. I couldn't remember ever having to look up at another man since I was a boy, and it was an experience that I was not particularly enjoying. "Where's my wife, you bastard?" I growled by way of greeting.

"Ah, right to business, then?" Captain Bear said with a chuckle. He glanced around at my men, assessing them with the air of someone who knew their business. I was gratified to see he looked suitably impressed at what he saw. He noticed Fanrissen standing off to one side and his face darkened momentarily before he focused back on me. "I wasn't expecting you to come with so many extra fighters. I had anticipated twenty or so at the most. I should have realized you might gain the help of the Swails."

"I guess you're not as smart as you think you are," I grunted.

Captain Bear laughed, looking completely relaxed and at ease. "Yes, well, be it twenty men or twenty thousand, we both know there's only one way onto that island, and if you try to use it, we'll easily sink your ships. So, Lord Hadrack, let's stop pretending they're actually going to make a difference."

"Then, if things are so bad for us," I said with a sneer. "Why are you here with your tail between your legs?"

"Why, to talk with you, of course, lord," Captain Bear said with a grin. "We Wentile's are great talkers, you see." I frowned. It had slipped my mind that this man was the Overseer's brother. The two men were so unalike that it seemed almost impossible. The pirate leader motioned toward the cabin beneath the aftercastle with a massive hand. "In private, though, if you don't mind." I hesitated, and the big man chuckled. "Fear not, Lord Hadrack. I promise when I kill you that it won't be behind closed doors with an assassin's knife." His eyes hardened. "It will be face to face like a man."

I glanced at Jebido, who gave me a worried look and a shake of his head. I ignored my friend and turned back to the pirate. "All right," I said in agreement. "If that's what it takes to be rid of you." I turned and headed for the cabin that Shana and I had shared, then waited by the open door for the pirate leader to enter. The big man had to stoop to get through the entrance. "So," I said once I'd entered and closed the door behind me. "Say your piece, and then get off my ship. I don't want your foul stench soaking into the wood any longer than necessary."

Captain Bear didn't respond to my jibe, letting his eyes roam around the small room with interest instead. He moved to the desk and glanced at my wife's book about the Raybold family, rifling through the pages. "Lady Shana is a uniquely charming woman, lord," the pirate leader finally said. He glanced at me and smiled. "I find that surprising for a Raybold. I've found the entire lot to be quite unsavory up until now. But she's something different—beautiful, smart, and courageous, all at the same time. A rare combination in a woman. I can certainly see why you are so enamored with her."

I waited, not allowing the man's obvious goading to get to me. Losing my temper now would do nothing to help Shana, though I was dearly tempted to introduce Captain Bear's throat to Wolf's Head anyway.

The pirate leader flipped the book closed with a snap when I didn't say anything before turning to face me. "As you may have guessed, Lord Hadrack, I'm rather annoyed with you." He leaned on the desk and folded his arms over his barrel-like chest as he studied me. "You destroyed my fortress at Ravenhold. An unforgivable act, that. One which demands restitution."

"You should have thought of that before you attacked the Piths," I grunted with little sympathy. "There's always a price when you make war on innocent people, you bastard."

"War?" Captain Bear said in surprise. "Don't you think that's a little extreme, lord? I'm just a simple businessman making transactions authorized by the Emperor himself. Everyone knows the Piths aren't much better than animals, so why should you or anyone else care if we take a few here and there?" He looked at me in mock wonder. "Do you make war on farmers every time a sheep is sheered, or a cow slaughtered as well, Lord Hadrack?"

"You're like a woman jabbering on about nothing," I muttered, not hiding my impatience. "Do you have a point for being here? Because if not, then I think you should just crawl back to your island and wait there for me to come and kill you." I leaned forward, glaring at him. "Because I am coming for you, you ugly bastard. And trust me when I say you're not going to enjoy it when our paths cross next."

Captain Bear's face hardened. "I always have a point in everything I do, Lord Hadrack," he said as he stood. He dropped his hands to his sides, and I could see his big fists clenching and unclenching. I could tell the man wanted to fight me right here, but something held him back.

"Then get to it," I grunted. "I've got an attack to prepare for."

Captain Bear forced his hands behind his back, clasping them together as he smoothed his features. "I'm here to offer you a deal, Lord Hadrack. One which will return your wife to her home unharmed if successful. That's why I've come."

"What kind of a deal?" I asked, trying to hide my surprise.

"Simply put," the pirate leader said. "A duel. You against me. If you win, you get your wife back. If you lose, your men agree to surrender to me and be sold off as slaves while Lady Shana goes to the Seven Rings."

I shook my head, trying to assimilate what I'd just heard. "You're not serious?"

"I'm always serious, lord," Captain Bear said. "The entire world has heard endless talk of your prowess with that wonderful sword of yours. So, let's put your skills to the test and see who the better man really is."

"You want to fight me?"

"More than anything in this life, lord," Captain Bear growled as his eyes glittered with hatred. "But in a setting that is fair and impartial." I saw the man smirk at that, knowing what that meant.

"What do the Seven Rings have to do with any of this?" I asked, feeling hope rise in my breast. With one fight, I could save my men from a long and costly assault on Blood Ring Isle and rescue my wife at the same time. It seemed too good to be true.

"They have everything to do with it," Captain Bear said. He snorted. "The Emperor and his pets have some silly notion that they can use your wife as leverage against your king and Ganderland. They also believe they can use her against you as well."

"Leverage how?"

The pirate shrugged with disinterest. "That I don't know. What I do know is my brother and I were offered a great deal of gold to capture Lady Shana and hand her over to them."

"But you haven't done that," I pointed out.

"*Not yet*," Captain Bear stressed. "The Rings seem preoccupied with the idea that you should live for some reason, Lord Hadrack." The pirate leader smiled, but his eyes stayed hard and focused. "I, on the other hand, have no such reservations. So, once I kill you and get my restitution for Ravenhold, I can then collect the bounty on your wife. As for the Emperor and the Seven Rings, well, since you'll be fodder for the hogs by the time they learn of your death, there won't be much they can do about it. Now, will there?"

"And if I refuse this offer of yours?"

The pirate shrugged. "Then I'll just wait until you foolishly try to attack us. Because we both know you'll never leave here without Lady Shana. One way or another, Lord Hadrack, your destiny is to die in this place. The gods have assured it."

I dropped my hand to Wolf's Head. "Then, if you're so sure of yourself, why don't we just do this thing right here and now and be done with it?"

Captain Bear laughed. "Don't be ridiculous. The place and time will be of my choosing, not yours. And that place will be Blood Ring Isle." The big man held out his hand. "So, what do you say, lord? Do we have a deal, or are you afraid?"

I hesitated for just a moment, then locked arms with the massive pirate. "We have a deal, you bastard," I said.

For truly, how could I have said no?

Chapter 22: Underwater Siege

"Absolutely not!" Jebido thundered. "You are not sticking your head in that lion's mouth, Hadrack! I won't let you!"

I was standing on the aftercastle with my inner circle, all of whom were protesting just as loudly as Jebido about my agreement with Captain Bear. Even Fanrissen, who had been reserved and moody ever since the death of his wife and child, was visibly upset at my revelation.

I held up my hands and waited patiently until everyone had calmed down and stopped talking. "I'm just telling you what I spoke about with that bastard because you needed to hear it," I told them. "I never said anything about actually going through with it."

"Oh, thank The Mother!" Jebido muttered, his entire body sagging with relief. "For a moment there I thought you'd lost your mind, Hadrack."

Captain Bear's terms had been clear; only three of my men and I would be allowed to enter Blood Ring Isle—taken there on one of his boats. He'd given his word that we'd be allowed to leave with Shana if I won. But, the word of a man like that was worth less than dog shit scraped off the bottom of a boot. I'd quickly realized after the man had left that if I did what the pirate leader wanted, none of us would ever leave Blood Ring Isle alive, no matter how well the fight turned out for me. I was certain Captain Bear's even more treacherous brother would see to that. I knew the Overseer had a seething hatred for me after what I'd done to his island only a few short weeks ago, so even when I killed Captain Bear, Shana's safety would still not be guaranteed. In fact, it would be even less so, which left me only one recourse—to break my word. Normally doing so would have bothered me, but I barely gave it a second thought after all the crimes committed by the Shadow Pirates and their ruthless leader.

"So, what's the plan, then, Hadrack?" Baine asked.

"The same as it always was," I grunted. I started to pace. "Captain Bear and his brother expect me to arrive for the duel at midday tomorrow. Which means our advantage has just increased, since his men likely won't be as alert tonight as they might have been otherwise." I looked around me and smiled. "So, you see, this is actually a good thing."

"Don't count on his men being less alert, lord," Fanrissen cut in. "That bastard takes nothing for granted. They'll be watching us from the cliffs like hawks."

I frowned at that, then shrugged. "Regardless, he won't be expecting an attack from beneath the water in the middle of the night."

"True enough, lord," Fanrissen agreed. "But I warn you, men who've underestimated Captain Bear in the past have come to regret it. My advice is to assume the worst."

"Duly noted, Pirate," I said with a quick nod. "Now, I suggest you all try to get some rest if you can. It's going to be a long night."

Twelve hours later, I stood once again on the forecastle, having tried to take my own advice and sleep only to fail at it miserably. The night sky was dark, lit only by the occasional glow of the moon as it slipped in and out from behind banks of heavy clouds moving west. Our captured Cardian longboat was lashed to *Sea-Wolf*'s starboard side, with both ships sitting in almost pitch darkness as they rolled in unison with the gentle tide. Not a single lantern was lit on board either vessel, for I didn't want the Cardian lookouts watching from the towers to see what we were doing. Not yet, anyway.

I was completely naked except for a black loincloth and tight leather wrappings on my feet that were extremely light and maneuverable in the water. I also wore a simple belt with a tied-down seaxe that had a compartment to hold my breathing tube securely along my thigh until I needed it. The only other attire I had on was a weighted pouch of dark leather strapped to my back to help keep me from floating to the surface of the water. Saldor and the other twelve Swails who would be making the assault on the towers were similarly dressed as I was.

"Stop fidgeting," Alesia scolded me.

She was busy slathering my upper torso and legs with a bluish-black concoction that the Swails made from a weed called woad. It looked very similar to what the Shadow Pirates used to paint their faces, though it was apparently used to keep divers warm in colder water. The woad was ground up and mixed with limestone powder and water, creating a thin, paint-like dye that Aarav guaranteed me would last long enough for us to reach the harbor and shore. I wasn't entirely convinced of that, but I saw no reason not to give it a try anyway.

My biggest fear was having my men discovered by some sharp-eyed pirate or Cardian who happened to notice a flash of white skin moving below the water. The dye—if it stayed on our skin as the Swails claimed it would—should help to prevent that from happening. We'd also painted our breathing tubes the same color as our skin. Coupled with the dark water and night sky, the eight inches or so of reed sticking out from the surface would be almost invisible.

"You ready for this?" Jebido asked me when Alesia was finally done her work.

"I'm ready," I growled. I looked around at my small force, whose faces were barely recognizable with the dye and the darkness. All the men I'd selected had dark hair except for Saldor, who had run the woad mixture through his blond locks and beard. I found the Pith looked older and strangely less intimidating that way for some odd reason. "What about you?" I asked the Swails. "Are you ready to finally get some revenge for Evrar?" The warriors all nodded enthusiastically, with only the whites of their eyes showing in the moonlight. They'd been ordered not to make any loud sounds and they were heeding that, though I could see the fierce determination in their body language. I nodded, satisfied. "Then let's go."

Jebido stuck out his hand to me as the Swails headed down to the main deck. "We'll see you soon, Hadrack. May The Mother watch over you all."

I locked forearms with my friend. "And you."

A small Swail fishing boat that we'd towed behind *Sea-Wolf* from Swailand rocked gently against the big cog's hull on the portside, and one by one, the Swail warriors climbed down to it.

I glanced at Baine, who was leaning against the railing nearby. "Don't kill all of them before we get there," he said. "Leave some for us, you selfish bastard."

I couldn't help but smile. "No promises," I grunted.

I started to head for the ladder, but Alesia stopped me. She put her hands on my cheeks and stood on her toes to kiss me on the lips. "You find her, Wolf," the Pith Queen said firmly after the kiss. "You find your girl and get her out of there. Let us worry about the Cardians. Shana comes first."

"Don't worry," I promised. "I'll find her."

I kissed Alesia on the cheek, then went down the ladder. Haf was waiting for me at the bottom, looking anxious and biting at his fingernails. "Don't look so worried, lad," I said, rifling his hair. "This will be over before you know it. Just be sure you stay on the ship with Einrack and Putt." I wagged a finger at him. "And don't do anything stupid, or I'll tan your hide when I get back."

Haf swallowed and lowered his eyes. "Yes, my lord," he mumbled.

I stepped past the boy and used a knotted rope to lower myself hand over hand into the waiting fishing vessel while eager hands reached up to help me down. I was the last man in, and the little boat was now dangerously overcrowded, with fourteen men crammed together, reeking from the woad's heady scent and the pungent aroma of sweat. The tight confines hardly mattered to me, though, since I knew we wouldn't be stuck that way for very long.

Two Swails in the center of the boat began to paddle us away from the bigger ships the moment I was settled in at the back beside Saldor. We headed west toward the reef-riddled shore of Blood Ring Isle, where I hoped the jagged and inhospitable cliffs would help hide us from any sentries that might be around.

We traveled for almost two hundred yards in the darkness, with only the gentle plip-plop of the paddles dipping in the water cutting through the stillness before the first of the lanterns was finally lit along *Sea-Wolf's* stern. That lantern was quickly followed moments later by several more on the bow and main deck, then a fourth one burst into brilliant light on the longboat, swinging back and forth from where it hung from the mast. Both ships were now lit up in bold relief, and moments later, I heard someone start to play a flute. The shrill, haunting notes drifted easily across the water to us as we continued toward the island while a deep, male voice began singing, filled with a raucous enthusiasm that I could tell was only half theatrics. I smiled to myself as many more eager voices joined with the first, though the original singer could still be plainly heard above all the others. Good old Putt might not be all that steady on his feet just yet, but despite his wound, the man could still belt out a tune that would wake up the dead even in the middle of a thunderstorm.

I knew there was no way the Cardians watching from the cliffs wouldn't hear the bawdy song and see the ships so brightly lit, which meant their attention should stay focused there and nowhere else, exactly how I wanted it. Despite what Fanrissen had told me about Captain Bear, I knew his men would inevitably relax their guard once they were satisfied we were staying put for the night and not planning anything. It was simply human nature for them to do so. I was well aware that didn't guarantee there wouldn't be more sentries along the waterway, though, which was something that we'd just have to deal with when the time came.

Luckily, Fanrissen knew the island well, and he'd drawn us intricate maps of the harbor and inlet, showing us where we'd have the best chance to exit the water without being seen. The wharves that ringed the port would be the key to our success, and I hoped most, if not all of them, had been rebuilt after the fire we'd caused there. If not, then I knew we could be in serious trouble.

We paddled on in silence for another five minutes until finally, I could hear the steady *clap-clap-clap* of the surf rolling against Blood Ring Isle's rocky shores and smell the overpowering stench of rotting vegetation. We were getting close. The moon overhead that had stayed hidden for our entire journey suddenly chose that moment to slip out from the clouds, winking down at us almost in amusement before another bank hid it from view. One of the Swail warriors sitting at the prow abruptly hissed low under his breath just as darkness fell over the boat again, motioning for us to get down. The two men with the paddles instantly froze, leaning forward with their blades halfway in the water. I pressed my face into the back of the Swail in front of me, trying to make myself as small as possible in the cramped space. The warrior's name was Ratin, and I ignored the strong odor coming from him as I strained my ears, certain now that I could hear the faint murmuring of voices coming from my left.

"What is it?" I whispered.

My words were passed on in a low murmur from one man to the other up the line until the reply from the Swail in front came back to Ratin. The warrior turned as best he could in the tight confines. "*Panwa*, lord," he said.

I cursed under my breath. "How many of the bastards?" I waited, my heart racing in my ears for the reply. If Captain Bear had sent out a full complement of Shadow Pirates to guard the coast here, then we were sunk.

It seemed like forever before the answer was finally passed back down the line. "Apologies, lord. Not *Panwa*, *hecterfin*."

"What's a damn *hecterfin*?" I asked Ratin, unsure if I'd just been given good news or bad.

"Fishermen, lord," the Swail whispered. "Two of them hunting for reef lobsters," he added. "Night is the best time to catch the lobsters searching for food on the rocks."

I sighed with relief. "All right," I said to Ratin. I motioned to him and a hulking beast of a man sitting beside him named Arginto. "You two go take care of them. But be damn quiet about it."

"Yes, lord," Ratin whispered.

The two men fought to get their legs over the sides of the boat, moving slowly and carefully until they finally slid down into the water with a slight splash. I waited, peering in the direction the voices had come from but could see nothing. Ten minutes went by without a sound, then another five before suddenly the water near me was displaced and a shadowy head appeared.

"All clear, lord," Ratin said.

We helped the two Swails back into the boat, and then I signaled for the paddlers to carry on. The fishing boat's wooden hull scraped against a coral reef with a noticeable screech less than ten minutes later. I winced, for the sound had seemed ear-splitting to me. But after we waited in silence for a time without an alarm being raised, I finally sighed in relief.

"This is it," I grunted, keeping my voice low. "Everybody tie off."

Each man except for the two in the front—twin brothers named Newdel and Nindel—grabbed a length of thin, precut rope from the bottom of the boat. We worked quickly and efficiently to tie the lines around our waists, just like we'd trained to do at Golmark Pond. The free end went around the waist of the man directly in front, and when we were done less than five minutes later, we had two separate teams of seven tethered together by ten-foot lengths of rope. Both Sandor and I were very good swimmers, but nothing compared to the Swails, so we would take up the rear on each team where the going would be the easiest.

Newdel was to lead my team to the northern side of the harbor, which gave access to the tower there, while Nindel would lead Saldor's to the southern side. Once on land, the Pith warrior and I would take over command of our teams. The twin brothers were natural-born swimmers, nicknamed *The Owls* for their uncanny ability to see at night, even beneath the water. It was a skill that I knew we would dearly need, as the rest of us were depending on those two men to get us through without the need to surface and get our bearings.

"Plugs in," I grunted.

We each had a finely-crafted pair of nose plugs made from deer bones that had been shaped and smoothed over many hours. I inserted mine, not relishing the feel as they closed off my nasal passages. I'd worn the plugs countless times in the lake while training, and though they had worked efficiently to keep the water out, I still couldn't say I enjoyed it. The Swails had insisted the plugs were vital to our success if we wanted to stay submerged the entire way, and I agreed with them despite the discomfort. It seemed a small price to pay to get Shana back.

"Over the side now," I said, aware of how strange my voice sounded with my nose blocked.

The Swails lowered themselves into the water one by one, careful not to get their tethers tangled. I was the last one over the side, and once I was in the water, I dove beneath the boat, fumbling along the hull until I found the wooden bung that we'd hammered into a hole that had been cut in the center. I twisted it out, then hurriedly swam back out from under the vessel as it began to take on water rapidly. Ratin was close by me, making sure my rope connected to him didn't snag on anything. We all treaded water then, waiting until the fishing craft had sunk completely beneath the waves before the twin Swails led us away.

We swam overhand slowly and carefully along the shore in two lines, heading east while trying to make as little noise as possible. I didn't want to risk swimming underwater on this leg of the journey because of the coral below that could tear open a man's flesh as easily as a knife. I was sure no one could hear us over the sound of the surf, but it was better to be cautious just in case. It was also highly unlikely that anyone standing on the cliffs above could see us swimming in the darkness. They'd need to lean over and look straight down two hundred feet or more, which was an unenviable task to attempt on the slick, jagged rock formations. I doubted anyone would dare try it, especially since our ships were in plain sight a quarter mile away and obviously offering no threat.

The swim took us fifteen minutes, and despite the coolness of the water, by the time we finally approached the yawning mouth of the inlet, my muscles felt warm and loose. I was feeling good and breathing easily through my mouth, though the plugs were still an annoyance. Both Newdel and Nindel raised their right hands in a fist at the same time, signaling a stop. Moments later, Newdel undid his rope, then slipped below the waves. I waited, treading water with the others for a long time until he eventually returned, popping up beside me with no warning. He blew water out of his breathing tube, then removed it from his mouth and leaned close to me.

"There's a ship blocking the entrance, lord," Newdel whispered in my ear. "They've dropped fishing nets around it, too."

I felt my eyebrows automatically lifting in surprise. Captain Bear was a cautious and resourceful bastard, just like Fanrissen had warned me. "Can we get past them?"

I sensed Newdel grin. "Easily, lord. I've already cut us a path."

"Good," I grunted. "Tell your brother about the nets, then you lead us through first, then him."

"It will be done, lord," Newdel said.

The Swail swam away from me with relaxed, easy strokes, pausing to whisper in his brother's ear before he tied his tether around his waist again. Moments later, the twins lifted their right hands, motioning downward. I fumbled for my breathing tube and inserted it in my mouth, using my teeth to hold it in place along ridges that had been painstakingly carved there by the Swail women. I took a few practice breaths in and out, then slid below the waves. I opened my eyes, barely able to discern anything other than pitch darkness just as I felt a tug on my rope. I started to swim, careful to keep the breathing tube above the water like I'd been taught and my arms in front of me with one hand clasped over the other as I kicked my legs. As the last man in line, that's all I was required to do, since the six far-superior swimmers ahead of me were essentially towing me along.

I saw points of faint light coming from ahead as we approached the inlet, winking through the water, and I realized with sudden clarity that it was flames from torches burning on the Cardian ship. The entire inlet entrance was lit up. I could just make out the dark mass of the vessel sitting low in the water and actually see a man walking the deck before suddenly my rope started to angle downward without warning, dragging me with it. I hurriedly sucked in a lungful of air, understanding that Newdel was going deeper to ensure there was no chance we would be seen. We went down and down and down until the light from the torches was lost from view and all was darkness again.

Finally, we leveled out and moved forward. I could feel the pressure building in my chest now from the lack of oxygen, and I fought panic as my body was whisked helplessly along. Something rubbed against my shoulder, then snagged for the briefest of moments on the hilt of my seaxe, holding me back before the pressure abruptly let go. I realized that it had been one of the fishing nets the Cardians had placed in the water as a barrier. Once I was through safely, I started to count in my head, closing my eyes and concentrating on not giving in to the growing need for air. Finally, I felt us beginning to rise until, eventually, there came three sharp tugs on the rope. I prayed to The Mother that those tugs meant what I thought and breathed outward forcefully, sending whatever water was trapped in the tube up and out. I sucked in greedily afterward, half expecting to taste cold saltwater and overjoyed when I drew in wonderful, sweet-tasting air instead. We'd made it through.

The Swails continued onward without a break, dragging me along with them. I tried once to look behind me to see how close Nindel and his team were, but I could see nothing other than murky blackness. I closed my eyes since they were starting to feel irritated from the saltwater and I couldn't see anything anyway. I envisioned the inlet in my mind from the last time I'd been there. I remembered it was long and narrow, with high cliff walls to either side broken only by a few stubborn trees and bushes. Eventually, that inlet would break out into an enormous bay, with the entire length from the entrance to the shore being slightly less than half a mile long. I did the math in my head. A mile was 5,280 feet, so half that would be 2,640 feet. I didn't know how fast we were traveling in the water but assuming it was something like three miles an hour, then it should take us roughly ten more minutes or so to reach the shore. I couldn't wait to get there.

I had no idea how Newdel and Nindel could know which direction to take underwater, but having seen their uncanny abilities demonstrated for me in Golmark Pond more than once, I had little reason to doubt them. I spent the time after that rhythmically kicking my legs and counting each second off in my head. I reached a hundred and ten before I felt the rope rubbing along my chest suddenly slacken. I started to flounder, unsure of what to do just as my tether grew taut again. I could tell that our direction had just changed and I resumed my counting, focusing on taking long, even breaths like the Swails had taught me. Finally, after counting to five hundred and seventy, I felt a rough hand on my arm dragging me upwards. My head broke the surface and I fought the urge not to gasp as I spit out the breathing tube. I could feel an ache in my jaw from my teeth having been clenched for so long.

"We're here, lord," Ratin whispered.

The Swail warrior was treading water, with his head and upper shoulders lit up faintly by several torches on poles that I could see burning a hundred yards away along the shoreline. There were many more of them lit all along the harbor. Captain Bear was taking no chances, it seemed. I saw with approval that Newdel had led us unerringly underneath a narrow pier that jutted straight out into the bay. Ten or so small fishing vessels were moored in some of the berths on both sides, but I could see no one around. I could smell the scent of fresh lumber mixed with the underlying odor of charcoal, mud, and seaweed. The pier had clearly just been rebuilt recently. It was perfect.

    I smiled and latched on to one of the thick pilings that had survived the flames as my team surrounded me. "Good work, lads," I said. I nodded to Newdel. "Especially you, my friend." The Swail actually looked embarrassed by my praise as Arginto rubbed at his wet hair playfully with a massive hand. "I'm going to take a look around," I added. "Stay here until I call for you."

    I let go of the piling and fumbled to untie my tether, then swam toward the shore until I felt ground beneath my feet. Crouching low, I cautiously waded out from the pier, using the solid supports to steady me over the uneven, muddy soil. Once I was out of the water, I glanced around but could see no movement anywhere. Two lengths of thick logs led from the shore in front of me up the bank to a black pirate longboat fifty feet away that was lifted three feet off the sandy soil on a wooden frame. It was clear the ship had been dry-docked to scrape the hull free of barnacles, mussels, and seaweed. I'd had the same thing done to my boats more than once over the years.

    I undid the weighted pack from my back and let it drop to the ground, then, bent over double, I scampered up the bank to the ship and crouched down beneath it in the shadows. I glanced out across the bay behind me, but there were no vessels or threats to worry about. I could see the longboat lit up in the inlet mouth to the east, but they were too far away to notice us. I thought I saw a hint of movement out of the corner of my eye along the shoreline to the south, but when I focused there, I couldn't see anything. Had it been Nindel and his team? I dearly hoped it had been and that they'd arrived just as safely as we had, for without them taking over the second tower, our mission was as good as doomed.

I unsheathed my seaxe and crawled further beneath the dry-docked ship until I could peer out the other side. Several darkened and burned-out buildings rose ahead of me sixty feet away, with a stone Holy House missing its roof sitting back from the buildings on a hill. A burning brazier filled with wood lit up a small grassy courtyard in front of the place of worship's entrance. I knew by Fanrissen's map that a narrow road wound past the rear of the Holy House and up the cliff to the tower that was our target. The pirate had warned me that there was a guard station that we would need to deal with first at the cliff's base. Unfortunately, there were also two soldiers wearing red capes warming their hands over the brazier in the courtyard. I headed back under the boat until the Swails could see me and lifted two fingers to them, motioning for just a pair of warriors to join me. I waited while two shadowy forms appeared from underneath the pier and ran up the slope toward me in a crouch.

"Lord," Ratin said with a nod as he knelt beside me. The huge Swail, Arginto, was the second man.

"We've got a couple of sentries blocking our way." I pointed to the stern of the raised ship. "I'm going to draw them over that way. You two stay under the boat and hit them from behind. Understood?" Both men nodded. "Remember, not a sound. Make sure you end their lives quickly and silently."

"*Betherik wer naustrim*," Arginto rumbled with a grin, revealing a row of dark teeth.

I blinked at him in confusion.

"It means death to the enemy, lord," Ratin explained.

I grinned, liking it. "*Betherik wer naustrim*, indeed."

I made my way to the back of the boat while the two Swails slipped into the darkness beneath the bow, waiting to pounce. I almost tripped over a discarded wooden mallet lying in the sand, and I picked it up before dropping to my knees and crawling under the stern. The two Cardians were still standing over the fire, talking. I could hear the murmur of their voices but couldn't make out what they were saying. I tapped the mallet lightly against the boat's keel several times to get their attention, careful not to make it too loud. The Cardians stopped talking and looked my way, though they quickly lost interest and resumed their conversation moments later. I tapped again, only to have the whole scenario repeated a second time.

I cursed under my breath and dropped the mallet, then slid out from beneath the hull. The bastards clearly needed a little more prodding than just a couple of dull thuds to make them leave the warmth of that fire. I cupped my hands to my mouth and mimicked the cry of a stricken animal, keeping it low but sounding urgent. I waited, then did it again. I heard Ratin's hiss of warning moments later, and I tensed at the unmistakable tread of the Cardians' pointed boots getting closer. I made the cry one last time, fainter this time, then leaped up and grabbed the railing of the dry-docked ship and pulled myself up. I dropped silently down inside just as I heard the Cardians come around the hull.

"It's just a damn cat," one of the soldiers said in a bored voice. "Probably caught himself a rat or something. It's nothing, Karis."

"Maybe," Karis grunted. This Cardian sounded a little more alert and suspicious to me than his companion. "But if it isn't, do you want to be the one that tells that big bastard we missed something afterward?"

"No," the second man said sulkily. "I guess not."

I could tell the two soldiers were standing right below me by the smell of them, and after a few moments of silence, Karis said, "There's nothing here."

"I could have told you that," the second man grumbled. "Aw, Karis, what are you doing now?"

A hand suddenly appeared on the railing, followed by its mate less than a heartbeat later. "Just being thorough," the Cardian soldier grunted as he hauled himself up.

I pressed myself into the curved side of the hull beneath a bench, making myself as small as I could in the shadows just as a helmeted head appeared over the gunwale. I angled my blade upward around the plank shielding me. If the bastard looked down and saw me, I'd have no choice but to strike. Come on, I thought, wondering what was taking the Swails so long. The Cardian soldier peered around suspiciously while his companion continued to complain below him. I couldn't believe the man hadn't noticed me yet. I knew he was about to any moment now, though, and just as I was preparing to strike, I heard a strangled gurgle from below, followed seconds later by Karis disappearing with a soft exclamation that was quickly stifled. I counted to ten, waiting and listening.

"Lord?" Ratin's voice drifted up to me in a whisper.

I stood up and rolled over the side, landing easily on my feet beside the Swails. I glanced at the dead Cardians, who both had their throats cut. "Good work," I grunted to Ratin and Arginto. "Get the others."

Five minutes later, the seven of us were crouched in a grove of apple trees, staring at a small stone guardhouse built against a solid granite wall. I now had a decent sword in my hand and a shield on my arm that I'd taken from Karis. I felt much better with the weapons, though neither of the men had been large enough for their armor to fit me. I wasn't complaining. None of the Swails had opted for the other dead man's sword and shield, being more comfortable with their seaxes, which was fine with me.

I studied the guardhouse critically, guessing it could probably house three or four men comfortably at the most. Tall cypress trees ringed both sides of the road around the small building before being suddenly cut off as the pathway continued upward at a steep angle through solid rock. I could see lantern light filtering through a shuttered window, though no one was standing guard outside the structure. I shook my head, my gut telling me something wasn't right.

"Ratin," I finally grunted. "Go scout it out. By my way of thinking, there should be at least one man outside. Find out why there isn't."

"Yes, lord," Ratin said.

The Swail was gone less than ten minutes, and when he returned, I saw fresh blood splattered across his dyed chest.

"What happened?"

"The fool was taking a shit," Ratin said with a chuckle. "He still had a turd hanging out of his ass when I cut his throat." The Swail waved a hand in front of his face. "Stunk bad, too."

The other warriors all laughed softly in appreciation.

"See anybody else around?" I asked.

"No, lord," Ratin said with a shake of his head. "Just him."

"All right," I grunted, coming to a decision. "We go in hard and fast." I glanced at Arginto. "*Betherik wer naustrim*, eh?"

"By The Father's balls, yes, lord," Arginto said with a smile. "The more we kill, the better."

I clapped the big man on the back, then motioned for the Swails to follow. We moved quickly and quietly, staying hidden in the trees until we reached the building before spreading out and surrounding the door. When we were in position, I grasped the handle and pushed the door open, then rushed inside. Two men sat at a table on benches playing chatrang, and before they could react, my sword was in motion, severing the head of the man on the right clean off. Hot blood sprayed in the air and across the chatrang board as the headless corpse flopped sideways and fell off the bench. I tossed my shield aside and wrapped my left hand around the second man's neck just as he started to stand and draw his sword. I dragged the soldier over the table with him kicking and screaming as game pieces flew in all directions before smashing him hard against the floor. The Cardian tried to fight off my grip on his throat, gasping and wheezing, but my hand was like iron on his flesh. The soldier's face turned deep red, then purple as he struggled futilely while my men watched dispassionately as he died. Finally, the soldier's struggles ceased and I released him, motioning the warriors back outside. Now all we had left was to take the tower.

It took us fifteen minutes to make our way to the cliff's summit, moving quietly and staying in the shadows as best we could. The road began to level out at the top, and I paused behind an outcrop to peer cautiously around the massive granite. Torches on wooden poles lit a large, flat plateau in front of us, with five soldiers holding spears standing at attention near the tower's base. Several more men stood above on the battlements, leaning against the stone as they stared off to the east where my ships lay. A man and woman stood alone along the cliff edge with their backs to me, also staring east. I growled low in my chest.

The man was Quilfor Wentile, and the woman standing next to him was Shana.

Chapter 23: The Fury Of The Lamb

My first instinct was to rush ahead, sword swinging. When I was a younger man, that's probably what I would have done. Now, though, I hesitated, letting my eyes roam over every inch of the plateau. Wentile and Shana remained where they were, not moving, with the Overseer holding onto her upper arm with his left hand. I couldn't see what his right was doing, but the way they were standing seemed unnatural to me for some reason. A large stock of rocks was piled along the cliff edge a hundred feet away from them, but I saw no threats anywhere there. The Swails were all bunched behind me, waiting, and I moved backward carefully, motioning for Ratin to take my place and look.

"The girl is your Lady, Lord?" the Swail warrior asked once he'd seen enough. I nodded, not saying anything. He grimaced. "The spears are not so good."

"I know," I replied. "Any ideas?"

"How many spears?" Newdel asked from behind us in a hushed tone.

"Five outside the tower," I replied. "Maybe more inside. I don't know. Two soldiers on the battlements. They might have bows. I can't tell."

"Bah," Arginto grunted, waving a hand. "Five spears is easy. We kill now?"

I hesitated as I took another peek around the rock. Nothing had changed. The spearmen were all turned away from us, staring east and presenting their backs as tempting targets. I knew if we were careful and moved silently enough, we could probably get close to them before they realized we were there. It seemed relatively easy and straightforward, and I wondered why I was holding back.

I slipped back from the rock a second time and turned to the Swails. "Does something feel wrong about any of this to you?" I asked no one in particular.

Ratin shook his head. "No, lord."

Arginto just stared at me blankly, and Newdel shrugged noncommittedly. I took a deep breath, knowing we couldn't delay much longer. Saldor could have secured the south tower by now and might be about to light the signal fire at any moment. I needed to capture this tower right now before the soldiers saw the flames and became suspicious. Finding Shana and Wentile with the Cardians had both complicated and simplified things for me at the same time, but I needed to focus on the threats out there first before I could worry about my wife. Without the tower, we couldn't control the inlet, and without the inlet, I couldn't bring in my men to get Shana away from here.

"All right," I said, coming to a decision. I squatted, motioning for the others to do likewise as I made five circles with my finger in the dust that covered the rocky floor. "The spearmen are all lined up like so. I want each of you except for Arginto to pick a man and kill him as quickly and as silently as possible." I glanced at the big Swail. "Arginto, you will guard the tower doors until your brothers join you. Don't let anybody inside get past you." I looked around at the dye-darkened faces that I could just make out in the weak moonlight. "Be sure to pick up the Cardian spears and shields," I warned. "Then use them to clear out that tower. I'll deal with the old man and my wife. Any questions?" Six heads just shook back and forth in unison. "Good," I said. "Let's go." I lifted my left fist in the air. *"Betherik wer naustrim,"* I growled.

"Betherik wer naustrim," the six Swails responded, raising their fists.

Arginto and I held back while the rest of the Swails crowded against the rock blocking our view of the plateau. Ratin was in the lead, and he glanced at me. I tensed, gripping my shield and sword tighter, then nodded. The five Swails immediately raced out from cover, hurtling across the solid ground as quickly and silently as possible with their seaxes ready to strike.

Arginto and I followed, with the big man moving surprisingly fast ahead of me toward the tower while I sprinted toward Shana and Wentile, the leather on my feet whispering across the ground. My five Swail warriors were halfway across the distance to the spearmen, who still seemed oblivious to them. I felt my heart soar—it was going to work! Then, with a quarter of the distance left, a sharp command rang out and the battlements on the tower that had held only two men were suddenly filled with archers. I didn't even have time to cry out a warning before a wave of spinning shafts slammed into the charging Swail warriors, plucking them off their feet or spinning them around to collapse in the dust. The five spearmen twisted around together smartly in a practiced motion, ready with pikes balanced on shields. At least fifty more heavily armored soldiers in red capes burst out from the tower doors and from around the back of the building, with some of them taking up defensive positions in front of Shana and Wentile.

Of the five Swails, only Ratin was somehow still on his feet, though his body was peppered with arrows. The warrior shouted in defiance and threw himself at the wall of spearmen, but was easily cut down before he could land even a single blow. I cried out in anger, helpless to do anything but watch the slaughter in horror. Arginto kept running at full speed, ignoring the odd arrow that smacked into the ground around him as he bulled his way through the line of spearmen with sheer brute strength. The Swail warrior screamed like a madman, flailing left and right with his seaxe while I shifted directions to help him, adding my voice to his.

I killed one, then a second Cardian who tried to cut me off while Arginto headed with single-minded purpose for the tower doors just like I'd told him to, knocking men out of his way like they were paper dolls. The big warrior almost made it to the steps of the building before he was brought down to one knee by a well-aimed spear that caught him in the back. The Swail bellowed, spitting in anger and swinging his seaxe wildly around him as at least ten Cardian soldiers surrounded him, stabbing over and over again with their pikes and swords until the warrior finally collapsed dead in a bloody pool.

I could hear Shana calling out my name in despair as men with spears converged on me from all sides, forming an impenetrable barrier three lines deep. I spun around and around, cursing the bastards and swinging at their bristling spearheads as the soldiers began to taunt me. I cried out in pain and helpless frustration as they poked and prodded at my unprotected, naked back, drawing blood, though none chose to land a fatal blow. I wondered why not.

"That's enough!" I heard a deep voice finally boom.

The spearmen immediately stepped back ten paces, forming a rough rectangle around me as the huge figure of Captain Bear strode out from the tower. I glanced at Shana, who still stood with Wentile holding her arm. I could tell she was crying, and I tore my tortured gaze away from her to focus on the pirate leader as several soldiers stepped aside to let him pass. The big man strode up to me, his hands empty of weapons. The bastard was smiling smugly, and I tensed, preparing to leap forward and skewer him before his men could stop me. At least I'd have that satisfaction before I died.

"Ah, Lord Hadrack," Captain Bear said. He paused ten paces from me and motioned with a hand. "Please put the weapon down, Wolf. I would hate it if my men were forced to kill you for trying something foolish."

"You want my sword, you bastard!" I hissed, breathing heavily. "Then come over here and take it."

Captain Bear chuckled. He gestured to Shana and his brother, who still hadn't moved. "Please take notice, lord, of the manacle on your wife's right ankle." I looked that way, feeling a lurch in my stomach when I saw the cold steel encircling her flesh. It was attached to a ten-foot length of chain, with the other end connected to a metal pin driven into a large rock that sat frighteningly close to the edge of the cliff near the Overseer's feet. One kick and the stone would plummet over the side, taking my wife with it. "It's a long way down, lord," Captain Bear said with a sigh. "A fall that I would rather the Lady not have to endure. Drop your weapons, or you give me no choice."

I threw down the sword and shield without a moment's thought, then unsheathed the seaxe and tossed it to the ground.

"That's better," Captain Bear said with satisfaction. "Now, we can talk like gentlemen without the threat of violence." He grinned mockingly. "At least for the time being, anyway."

"If you hurt her," I growled, "I'll make you wish—"

"Yes, yes," Captain Bear said, cutting me off with an impatient wave of his hand. "Fear not, lord. Lady Shana has been treated according to her station during her stay with us. I assure you she has not been hurt. I wouldn't dream of it." His face hardened. "Unless you force me to do something that I would rather not."

"How did you know?" I asked, each word leaving my lips feeling like unbearable torture. The bitterness I could taste in my mouth was worse than anything I had ever felt before. "How did you know that I would come here tonight?"

"I didn't," Captain Bear said with a shrug. "Not for certain, anyway. I had this feeling after we talked that I couldn't depend on you to honor our agreement. I've learned to trust that feeling."

I thought of Fanrissen, wishing now that I'd listened closer to his warnings. "You knew we'd go for the towers," I said, more statement of fact than a question.

"Of course I did," the pirate leader agreed.

"How?"

"Because if it were me," Captain Bear said. "That's exactly what I would have done. It's the only logical recourse." The big man shook his head in admiration. "We're very much alike, you and me,

Lord Hadrack. Though I must admit using the breathing tubes was pure genius. I doubt even I would have thought of that."

"Yet you figured it out anyway," I said grudgingly.

Captain Bear grinned. "Yes, that's true. I saw one of your pet Swails holding a tube when I visited your wonderful ship. I didn't think much of it at the time, and it was only later, once I'd returned to the island, that I remembered I'd used some Swail slaves to dive and clear the channel of rocks at Ravenhold. They used breathing tubes to do it. That's when I guessed what kind of mischief you were up to. Pure brilliance, my friend. I'm hugely impressed."

"But why the fishing nets, then?"

The pirate grinned modestly. "Just some theatrics to make things a little more interesting. I didn't want your assault to be too easy, you see."

I could feel my jaw aching as I ground my teeth, trying to contain the rage I felt inside. I had been outfoxed by this bastard at every turn like a novice chatrang player pitted against a master. It was beyond humiliating. A sudden flare of light caught my attention to the south and I stared at it in surprise. Someone had just lit a fire on top of the south tower, which was the signal that the mission there had succeeded. I glanced at Captain Bear and he just grinned back at me infuriatingly. What did it mean? Had my men won through despite the pirate leader's preparations against them? If they had, then Saldor's team and my men on board the ships would all be staring toward this tower, waiting for a similar signal of success from me—a signal that would now never come. I felt confusion and crushing defeat wash over me again.

"Ah," Captain Bear said in commiseration. "I understand it's a lot to take in all at once, lord. Perhaps I can assist you with that." The pirate leader looked up at the northern tower and whistled shrilly. I gaped in astonishment when an answering fire roared into life there moments later.

"What are you doing?" I stammered, even more confused than ever now.

"My dear Lord Hadrack," Captain Bear said. "Please come with me." He motioned me closer, and in a daze, I walked over to him as he put his muscular arm around my shoulders. He directed me toward the cliff edge like an old friend, careful to keep me well away from Shana and the Overseer. I could feel the older man's eyes boring into me with hatred, and I latched onto Shana's grief-stricken face. I mouthed the words, *I'm sorry*, feeling a lump in my throat when she moaned out loud. Shana took an involuntary step forward, trying to reach out to me before Wentile dragged her roughly back, causing her to cry out in pain. It took everything for me not to rush over there and tear the bastard apart.

"Very good, Lord Hadrack," Captain Bear said in approval. "Your ability to restrain yourself is impressive, though I can see the beast inside you just itching to roar. You've correctly realized that the longer you remain alive, the better the chances are that you'll find a way out of this predicament. Taking vengeance on my brother for his actions, while undoubtedly satisfying, would likely only result in the deaths of both you and your lovely wife. Well done. Perhaps you will be a worthy opponent after all."

"You still want to fight me?" I asked, startled.

Captain Bear chuckled. "But of course," he said. "Why else would I have gone to such elaborate lengths to ensure you were captured alive? I could have had you killed easily at any time if I'd wanted to." We reached the cliff edge, and the big man pointed down to the Cardian longboat guarding the entrance. "So tell me, lord. Had you been successful in your little scheme, what would you have done about that little inconvenience?" I just glowered at the man, not saying anything. "Now, now, lord, don't be shy. Impress me."

"I would have dropped some big rocks on it and sunk the damn thing," I grunted.

"Indeed," Captain Bear said with a thoughtful nod. He snapped his fingers, the sound unnaturally loud on the clifftop.

A group of soldiers hurried forward at the signal toward the pile of stones, then, without any fanfare, began rolling them over the side of the cliff. I stared in disbelief as the missiles hurtled downward, striking the Cardian ship amidships and in the bow as the sounds of wood snapping and men screaming drifted up to us. I glanced at Captain Bear, who was staring down at the devastation with rapt attention. I realized it would take but a simple push to knock him over the side, but I knew if I did that, Shana would quickly follow. I remained where I was, helplessly frozen, watching as the stricken vessel began to list to one side before it capsized and quickly sunk. I could hear faint cheering coming from the east where my ships lay, and I groaned as the two vessels moved apart and began to head our way.

I looked at Captain Bear in confusion. "Why?"

The big man turned to face me. "Because, lord, we had an agreement, and I am a man of my word, even if you are not. Your men will enter the bay, and when they do, you will be there to greet them and ensure that they lay down their arms. Then, once they have done that, those close to you will witness your death at my hands. After that, they will all be sold into slavery as per our pact, and I will gain a spectacular new ship and immeasurable fame for killing the Wolf." He winked, looking very pleased with himself. "Unless you manage to defeat me instead, of course, in which case, you, they, and your charming wife will be free to leave here unharmed."

I blinked at the man in astonishment, feeling hope rising in my breast. "You plan to honor our deal?"

"Of course I do," Captain Bear said. "Why wouldn't I?"

I looked over at Shana and her captor, the Overseer, who was glowering at me with little love in his eyes. "What about your brother? How do I know he'll follow through when I kill you?"

Captain Bear laughed in genuine amusement. "Ah, such confidence, lord. You continue to impress." He flicked his eyes to Wentile. "As for my older brother, while I agree his dislike for you is, shall we say, rather profound, you have my word that he will abide by the agreement."

"What if he doesn't?" I prodded. "You'll be burning in The Father's pits by then and won't have much of a say in anything."

The big man chuckled and shrugged. "Admittedly, I suppose there is a small risk that he might disobey my wishes, should you somehow triumph. But in truth, lord, what choice do you have in the matter?"

I didn't say anything to that as Captain Bear led me away from the cliff's edge. What was there to say? The bastard was right. There really was no choice.

The sun had risen almost halfway in the sky when I finally returned to the plateau where Captain Bear and my wife awaited me. The pirate leader had refused to release Shana from her bonds, though he did allow me to speak to her before sending me down to meet my forces. Our reunion had been brief and filled with mainly tears and professions of love for one another. I was actually relieved when the pirate had grown impatient with us and had grunted that it was enough. Holding my shaking and weeping wife in my arms only added fuel to my doubts and fears that I had about failing her and everyone else. I needed my mind focused on only one thing right now—killing Captain Bear.

Perhaps one of the hardest things that I'd ever had to do in my life was explaining to Jebido, Alesia, and the others how badly I'd underestimated Captain Bear and had been so thoroughly outmaneuvered by him. My friends were stunned by the news that we'd failed and had taken it badly, which I could hardly blame them for. What had seemed like a good chance at victory and revenge had been cruelly snatched away from them before a single warrior had even set foot on Blood Ring Isle's shore. Some of the Swails had initially refused to surrender, but after I'd talked to Aarav and guaranteed him that I would win the duel and all of our freedom along with it, they had reluctantly agreed.

Now, most of those Swails remained below in the bay, confined to the ships and watched over by several hundred soldiers, many of whom carried the dreaded Cardian longbows. The Piths, along with Jebido, Baine, Putt, Tyris, Haf, Demee, and Fanrissen, had all been herded up to the plateau to bear witness to the fight. They were there, I was told by Captain Bear, to ensure my defeat, humiliation, and death would be remembered long after they'd all been sold off as slaves.

We'd damn well see about that.

Only Saldor had survived the attack and subsequent ambush on the southern tower, and though he'd been wounded in several places, none of his injuries were life-threatening. The Cardians had been careful to keep him alive just as they had been with me, since Captain Bear hadn't actually known for certain which tower I would personally choose to attack. The pirate leader had gambled that I'd select the northern one and so had waited there with Shana as bait, which had only helped to add to the bastard's smugness when he was proven right. Now, Saldor stood with Alesia, Einrack, and the other Piths, still looking stunned by the turn of events as he clutched at his wounds, refusing to show any weakness by sitting or kneeling.

"How are you feeling?" Jebido asked me. My friend looked tired, I thought—tired and old and filled with despair. Baine stood beside him, his eyes dark with fury and the need to kill as he clenched and unclenched his hands, clearly missing his knives and bow. I'd never seen the man look more dangerous.

"Ready to make some bear stew out of that bastard," I grunted.

I was still dressed in just a loincloth, though at least now I had the familiar grip of Wolf's Head in my hand again. Alesia and Gislea had scrubbed most of the dye from my skin, though some still stubbornly remained in the crooks of my elbows, knees, and at the base of my neck.

Baine motioned to the Overseer. "Do you really think we can trust him to let us go after the fight?" he asked me skeptically.

I glanced at Wentile, who had resumed his position near Shana, though at least now he no longer had his filthy hands on her. Captain Bear had gotten Shana a small bench so she could sit, although he still refused to remove the chain around her ankle or move her away from the cliff edge. I could see my wife staring at me anxiously, her hands clasped together against her breasts. I gave her a confident smile, which she bravely tried to return.

"Probably not," I grunted.

"Then I guess you'll just have to do something about that, Hadrack," my friend said.

"Like what?" Jebido asked.

Baine just looked at me as a silent message passed between us. I knew what he was suggesting, and I nodded in approval. "That doesn't mean things won't go bad for us afterward anyway," I pointed out.

"True," Baine agreed. "But it should increase our chances." His eyes hardened even more. "Either way, Hadrack, we'll be ready to move whatever happens. You just make sure to get us there first."

I nodded as Jebido suddenly stiffened, looking past me. "Here we go," he whispered.

I turned away from my friends and watched as Captain Bear exited the tower with long, confident strides. The pirate leader was dressed in only a white loincloth and heavy boots, and he carried his incredibly long sword in his right hand. It was without question the biggest sword that I'd ever seen, yet somehow the weapon still managed to look almost toylike in his giant fist. I couldn't help but be impressed by the massiveness of the man's muscular upper torso, which had been oiled until his skin gleamed.

"Mother Above," I heard Jebido whisper in awe as he studied the big man.

"Lord Hadrack," Captain Bear said to me with a smile. "Shall we get on with it?"

I could hear mutterings of doubt coming from some of the Piths watching, which I could hardly fault them for. Captain Bear looked like a god as he made his way through his cheering men toward the center of the plateau. A giant, glittering, unstoppable god. But the difference was that unlike actual gods—this one could be killed.

"Listen to me," Captain Bear called out, lifting his sword and free hand in the air. He waited until there was relative quiet, then pointed at me. "Lord Hadrack and I have a gentlemen's agreement regarding this match. If he wins—" The big man had to stop there as the Cardians and Shadow Pirates began to boo and protest loudly. He waited until they'd quieted down again. "Like I said," the pirate continued with a laugh. "Should I accidentally slip and fall on my sword, enabling Lord Hadrack to actually win this duel." There was laughter coming from the Cardians now. "Then he and those that came here with him are free to go." The pirate's face turned hard as he pointed around at the soldiers. "I have given my word on this, and I expect it to be kept. No matter what happens here today, should I die, these people must be freed unharmed." He paused then to glower at his brother. "Do you understand me, Quilfor?"

"Of course I do, brother," the Overseer said through clenched teeth. He bowed his head to avoid the younger man's gaze, staring at the ground. "I will do as you wish. You have my word." I could tell the bastard was lying through those clenched teeth and that he had no intention of honoring his brother's last request. Baine was right.

"Good," Captain Bear said, looking pleased. He gestured to me. "Shall we begin, then, Lord Hadrack?"

"Don't worry, Hadrack," Baine said as he clapped me firmly on the back. "Big bastards like him just make a louder noise when they fall down."

I nodded to my friend, then strode toward the pirate leader until we were less than a foot apart. I smiled up at him. "I'm going to enjoy killing you," I said.

Captain Bear pursed his lips. "It's always nice to have aspirations, Lord Hadrack, no matter how futile they might be. I wish you the best of luck in that lofty goal. You're going to need it."

We stood like that for a moment, staring into each other's eyes, searching for weaknesses like two bulls about to lock horns. Then, moving faster than I would have thought possible, the pirate lashed out with his balled left fist without warning, catching me with a staggering blow on the jaw that snapped my head back. I stumbled backward three steps in surprise, stunned and shaking my head to clear the sudden ringing in my ears. Never in my life had I been hit as hard as that. I regained my composure quickly, though, fighting off the cobwebs with determination buttressed by hatred of the man in front of me. I crouched, left hand up and sword extended out across my chest.

I smiled at the pirate with contempt while ignoring the taste of blood in my mouth. "Is that all you have?"

"Impressive, lord," Captain Bear said, looking somewhat disappointed. "That little move of mine usually ends a fight before it even gets started."

"Oh, this fight has a long way to go," I promised with a growl. "And I bet you won't like the ending."

I could hear my men chanting, "Wolf! Wolf! Wolf!" behind me while the Cardians and Shadow Pirates whistled and shouted encouragement to their champion. I pushed all the sounds from my mind, focusing only on the huge, gleaming figure in front of me. Find his pattern, I told myself. Remember the lessons Jebido drilled into you. Captain Bear was enormously strong and fit, but that didn't mean he was automatically good with a sword. Maybe a man like him didn't need to be, I reasoned, for who in their right mind would willingly want to fight him?

I stalked to my right, keeping my eyes on the pirate as he matched my move with easy grace for such a big man. I feinted with a quick jab that Captain Bear swatted away easily like an annoying insect. The man was fast, I had to admit. Incredibly so. His reach with his oversized sword and long arms was much greater than mine, too, so I needed to be careful and pick my moments. I feinted a second time, trying to see a pattern to his movements, but again the pirate slapped my blade aside with what appeared to be casual indifference. But it wasn't indifference, for this time, he charged forward and smashed his shoulder into me—hard. I felt the wind gush from my lungs with a whoosh, and I backpedaled, slashing Wolf's Head back and forth in front of me in anticipation of an attack. But the big man pulled back, looking amused. I could feel rage building in me at the expression of contempt on the pirate's face and I stoked it, taking my time as I regained my breath.

I could feel a pinch in one of my ribs on the right side with each intake of air, guessing it was either badly bruised or broken. The man's brute strength was staggering. I pushed the discomfort from my mind and advanced again, this time wary of the other man's speed.

"But you're fast, too," I heard Jebido's voice in my head. "Fast and strong. Give the bastard a taste and see how he likes it."

I approached the pirate and made as if to feint once more, but as soon as the big man's blade came around to block mine as before, I spun and dropped low to one knee, bringing my left fist around in a blinding punch to the pirate's midsection. My fist impacted with a solid smack, feeling like I'd just stuck iron. But even so, I was gratified to hear the big man grunt in surprise, though his great sword was already coming for me just the same. I rolled out of the way just in time, feeling the swish of the long blade above me before I sprung nimbly back to my feet.

"Not bad," Captain Bear said grudgingly. He glanced down at his lower torso, where I could see a clear imprint of my knuckles appearing on the muscles of his rippled stomach. "You've got some power there."

"I'm just getting warmed up," I grunted.

Captain Bear smiled, though there was nothing but the promise of death in it as he advanced on me. I backtracked, angling my way toward Quilfor Wentile, who had moved closer to the battle in his enthusiasm. The Overseer's face was red with blood lust, and he was shouting at his brother to finish me. Captain Bear came on, moving frighteningly fast as he slashed without warning at my legs. I had no choice but to leap upward or risk a crippling injury. I lunged outward with Wolf's Head in mid-air, trying to catch the pirate off-balance. I'd aimed for the notch at the base of Captain Bear's neck, but the big man shifted his head and shoulders aside at the last moment and I missed, taking part of his right earlobe instead. The pirate grunted and retreated ten feet, then another ten, as wild cheers arose from my men amid shouts of anger from the Cardians and pirates.

Captain Bear finally paused to wipe at his ear with his left hand as bright red blood pumped freely from it. He glowered at me, his great chest heaving, while behind me, the Overseer rained curses down on me in a fit of rage. I saw the older man was less than half the distance away from me as his brother was, and I realized I might never get a better opportunity than this. I glanced quickly at Baine, who nodded, then turned and rushed at the Overseer and rammed Wolf's Head into his belly. Wentile gasped, his eyes bulging in shock as warm blood rolled down my sword's blade to pool on the grinning wolf's head hilt.

I leaned forward and looked the Overseer in the eyes. "This is for putting your filthy hands on my wife, you piece of shit!"

I pushed the Overseer backward then and he cried out in pain and fear, unable to resist the pressure of my blade. We reached the cliff's edge and I held him there, tottering on the precipice as he blubbered in terror, begging me to spare his life. I just laughed and shoved against Wentile's chest, sending him slipping off my sword and tumbling out into empty space. The man wailed all the way down until the water and rocks below ended his cries. I glanced over my shoulder at Captain Bear, who, like all his men, stood frozen in shock and disbelief at what I'd just done.

"Hadrack!"

I turned to Shana, ignoring the fear, love, and tears in her eyes, much as it pained me, for I knew I didn't have time to acknowledge it. I dashed toward my wife even as I heard Captain Bear roar like his namesake. I swung Wolf's Head downward with all my strength, severing the chain holding Shana's ankle halfway between her and the rock. I pulled her off the bench and shoved her toward Jebido and Baine. "Get away from here!" I shouted.

Captain Bear was coming fast, his face twisted in fury and his sword raised over his head. I saw Shana dash away, dragging the chain behind her as it bumped and rattled across the rocky ground. Then the furious pirate leader was on me. I raised my sword, feeling the shock in my shoulders as Captain Bear's blade pounded into mine with a force that set my teeth on edge. He struck again, bellowing, and it was all I could do to fend him off. Then a third time before his left fist suddenly shot out again, catching me on the cheek. I felt the skin there split open like an overripe fruit as blood sprayed.

I ignored the pain and switched to offense, letting the beast out as I roared, using everything I'd learned in my many years of battle to hack and smash at the bigger man. Captain Bear began to give ground beneath my furious onslaught foot by foot. I saw his left shoulder suddenly start to droop like before, aware of what was about to happen. His big fist clenched, then shot out and I let it come, willing to take the shot to land one of my own as I swung my fist. We hit each other simultaneously, both screaming in fury and battle lust. I felt the pirate's nose crumple beneath the power of my blow, with hot blood spurting out both sides while his punch caught me on the collar bone and deflected away—but not before I heard something crack. I felt a sharp pain shoot down from my right shoulder to my hand and knew immediately that the bone was broken.

I staggered backward in desperation, barely able to lift my sword past my waist as Captain Bear came on, his teeth bared and bloodstained and his eyes mad with killing fever. He swung at me, grinning in triumph when my reaction was slow. I managed to bring up Wolf's Head and deflect him away, but the cost was unbearable pain that made my head swim and my eyes water. I was in trouble, and I could tell by the wild cheering coming from the Cardians and pirates and silence from my men that everyone else knew it, too.

"Now what, Wolf?" Captain Bear sneered.

His face was a mess of blood, his broken nose turning purple even as I watched. But for a man as dangerous as the pirate leader, I was certain it wouldn't do much to slow him down. Captain Bear began to circle me cautiously, still a little unsure, I think, about whether I was really hurt or just feigning an injury. I knew if he could feel the excruciating pain I felt every time I moved my right arm even slightly, whatever doubts he had would be gone.

"You haven't disappointed me, Wolf," the pirate rumbled. He glanced toward the cliff where his brother had fallen, then frowned. "Though I think after what you did to Quilfor, we need an amendment to our agreement."

Now it was my time to frown. What did that mean?

"The old man," Captain Bear grunted. "The one with the silver hair and bushy eyebrows."

"What about him?" I said, feeling alarm rise in my chest.

"An eye for an eye, Wolf," the pirate replied. He attacked suddenly with a quick overhand slash and I had no choice but to parry, crying out at the pain. The pirate leader smiled and retreated, looking more relaxed now. He'd realized that I wasn't pretending. "I see how you look at that old man. Is he your father, perhaps?" I didn't say anything as we continued to circle each other. I could tell Captain Bear was taking his time now, enjoying himself. He grinned and shook his head. "No, not a father, something else, I think. A dear friend, at any rate."

"You talk too much," I growled.

Captain Bear laughed. "Only when I'm having fun, lord." He nodded his head toward Jebido. "And I promise, once I kill you, I'm going to have a great deal of fun making that old man scream."

"We had an agreement," I said, more to buy time than anything else. I wasn't expecting any sympathy from my opponent.

The pirate snorted. "Which you voided when you killed my brother. But don't worry, lord. I'll only kill that one man in retribution. The others will be sold as promised." He chuckled then. "Well, maybe some of those pretty Pith women with the nice tits can stay to amuse my men. We'll see. As for your wife, the Seven Rings may have paid me to capture her, but they never said she couldn't share my bed first before I hand her over. After all, she'll be a widow by then and no doubt will need consoling."

I felt instant rage explode at the man's words, and moving in a blur, I tossed Wolf's Head into my left hand, then slashed upward with the blade, catching the pirate by surprise. He tried to block me, but it was too late, for the razor-sharp tip of my weapon had already torn open his flesh from his stomach to his right nipple. Unfortunately, the cut wasn't that deep, though. The pirate cried out in pain and shock, but rather than back away like any other man would have, he lunged toward me with both arms outstretched, wrapping them around me. I cried out in agony as the big man lifted me in the air and shook me, with both my arms pinioned to my sides and my sword useless.

"I have enjoyed this," Captain Bear said with his face pressed close to mine like two star-crossed lovers. "You have more than exceeded my expectations. But a bear always beats a wolf one on one, and the time has come to end this little game of ours."

I glared at him, as helpless in his iron grip as captured prey was in the coils of a giant python. I did the only thing that I could think of and reared back my head, then smashed my forehead into his broken nose. Captain Bear cried out, his hold on me loosening just enough for me to twist my wrist, pointing Wolf's Head downward. I stabbed for the pirate's foot, gratified when the tip sliced into the man's boot, eliciting another howl of pain. The pirate flung me aside with a bellow and I landed hard, unable to suppress a scream as searing agony burned across my shoulder and down my arm.

    I heard voices calling out my name in warning, and I rolled away just in time as Captain Bear's great sword clanged off the rock beneath me. Despite the big man's wounds, it was clear that the pirate wasn't even close to being defeated yet. He pounced on me, growling and using his knees and weight to pin my arms as he raised his sword for the killing blow. I bucked like a wild stallion, unseating him, then twisted away as he landed in the dust. I was back on my feet in an instant, crouched low with Wolf's Head in my left hand as the pirate slowly forced himself back to his feet.

    We faced each other then, both of us bloody, battered, and breathing heavily. Gone now was Captain Bear's smug confidence, replaced with growing fatigue, wary respect, and pain. I could see him favoring his wounded right foot, while I knew he could see me favoring my injured right arm. Both of us were now crippled to some degree, but at least I still had reasonable mobility, which he did not. I knew all I had to do now was stay out of the man's reach and wear him down, then move in for the kill. I started to make a series of quick attacks, stabbing with my sword and forcing him to counter me before dancing away. The movements didn't feel natural to me since I'd rarely practiced fighting lefthanded, but regardless, it was still effective. Captain Bear had no choice but to block me as I skipped around him, and twice his right foot almost gave out from underneath him. Sooner or later, it would go, and when it did, I would have him.

    I started to gain more confidence, dodging and darting around the pirate as he cursed at me helplessly and swung his sword wildly in frustration. The weapon he held would have been devastating on a battlefield and truly terrifying to behold, but it was also heavy and would eventually wear down even the most powerful of men. I kept at him, always just out of reach. Finally, after one such attack, Captain Bear suddenly stumbled and almost fell. I dashed forward into the opening, only realizing it had been a ploy when the big man swung at me again with his hammer-like left fist. I managed to duck back just in time as his fist grazed my chin, aware that I'd almost made a costly mistake. Had the powerful blow connected, I'm sure it would have sent me on my ass and ended the fight right there.

"I'm going to hang your head from the bow of my ship," I growled as I circled Captain Bear. "Right beside that of your worthless brother."

"Is that right?" Captain Bear wheezed. He steadied himself, gritting his teeth as he ignored the pain and planted his feet firmly on the ground. The big man lifted his sword with both hands, resting the huge blade on his right shoulder like a pike. He glared at me, his eyes glittering with hatred. "Then all you have to do is come and get it."

I smiled. "Gladly."

Our battle had raged across the plateau from one end to the other, and I saw we were now close to the bench where Shana had sat earlier. I realized the pirate was hoping that I'd charge him and he could use my momentum to fling me off the cliff. I smirked, then shifted away until my back was to the precipice, forcing him to counter me. I laughed then at the look of disappointment on the man's face. Did he really believe I was that foolish? I started to move forward just as the pirate's features changed, turning to triumph. He suddenly moved, flinging his sword toward me two-handed like an axe. I'd been focused on the cliff and what I'd supposed Captain Bear's strategy was, so I was completely unprepared as the monstrous sword twirled once in the air before catching me squarely in the stomach with the point bursting out my back. I gasped in astonishment, feeling the strength in my body instantly slip away. I dropped Wolf's Head and fell to my knees, desperately trying to yank out the sword as Captain Bear limped toward me.

He stooped down on his bad leg, taking the weight off his foot as he stared into my face. "It was a good fight, lord," he said.

I could only stare at him in disbelief, my hands cut and bloody now from the blade as I continued to try to extract it. Captain Bear shook his head almost regretfully. He saw my sword lying in the dirt and he picked it up, examining it. I could hear rival voices crying out in dismay and happiness across the plateau, but I couldn't focus my eyes properly. All I could see was the pirate.

"A fine weapon, lord," Captain Bear said. He glanced at me and smiled, then flung it with casual indifference over the cliff. I watched in horror as Wolf's Head twirled end over end, its fabulous, gilded hilt winking in the sunlight before the weapon disappeared from view forever. The pirate clucked his tongue. "A shame, really. But as you can see, I have a much better sword." Captain Bear put his hand on the hilt of his monstrous weapon, then, with a quick tug, he yanked it free from my body with a horrible sucking sound. Dark blood instantly gushed out of me like a river and I groaned, wobbling on my knees. I heard a shout breaking through the fog in my brain and looked past the pirate to see Jebido fighting to get to me. Several Cardians pulled him to the ground and began pounding him with their fists, while still more soldiers had my men surrounded, weapons at their throats. I could see Baine on his knees, weeping as he stared at me in disbelief.

I reached out a hand to him. "I am sorry, my friend. So sorry."

"Well, Lord Hadrack," Captain Bear said with a weary sigh. He stood shakily, then used the hilt of his sword to push against my chest. I had no strength to resist him, and I fell on my back, staring up at the blue sky as the pirate stood straddling me. He lifted his sword for the killing blow. "Despite what you may think, lord," the pirate whispered as the blade began to descend. "It has been an honor."

"Wait! Stop! In the name of The Mother, stop!"

Captain Bear hesitated, and he looked behind him. "Lady Shana, I insist that you get back. Your man fought a noble fight, but he has lost. Death is the penalty."

I fought to lift my head and see my wife. Two Cardians had their hands on her, dragging her away as she tried to tear herself free. I growled low in my chest, trying to make my body obey and go to her. But I couldn't move.

"Please!" Shana pleaded to the pirate leader. "Let me say goodbye to the father of my children! I beg of you! That's all I ask!"

Captain Bear sighed, then lowered his sword and motioned with a hand. "Very well. Let Lady Shana go." He glared at my wife. "You have one minute, then this ends."

The pirate limped over to the bench and sat while Shana dropped to her knees beside me, her face wet with tears.

"I am so sorry," I croaked. "I failed you."

"Don't you ever say that, my lord," Shana said, her voice cracking. She put a hand over both of mine where I had them pressed to my wound. "You could never fail me. Never."

I blinked away tears, staring past her at the deep blue sky. I tried to speak, but my tongue felt swollen and unresponsive.

"It's all right, my love," Shana whispered as warm tears dripped from her cheeks onto my face, mixing with mine. I realized that it was the last thing we would ever share, and I felt heartache like I'd never felt before at the thought. There was so much more I wanted to say to her. So many things that I'd hoped we'd do together. Shana pressed her face to mine, her mouth close to my ear. "You will not die here today, my lord. The gods will see to that. You will live a long and prosperous life and provide for our children. It has been foretold."

"What?" I managed to gasp out in confusion. I couldn't understand what she was saying. I could hear the words, but my mind was filled with fog and pain, and none of them made any sense.

Shana sat up, her eyes gleaming now with love and something else—something that I couldn't interpret. "I understand the prophecy now, my lord," she said. "It's all crystal clear to me." I just blinked up at her, still struggling to understand as darkness swirled around me. Shana smiled sadly, then leaned forward and kissed me on the forehead and each cheek, then finally on the mouth. "Otmar was right all along, my lord," she said when the kiss was done. She stroked my hair lovingly. "There was a reason why I needed to be by your side all this time, just as he foretold. That reason is this moment."

I blinked in sudden, horrified understanding and started to shake my head. "No!" I pleaded in desperation. "No, Shana! No!"

"Yes, my love," Shana said with a sigh. "This is the way that it was always meant to be. Do not fight it." She closed her eyes for a moment, squeezing out one final tear before opening them again and staring down at me. "I will love you until the end of time itself, Hadrack Corwick. And I promise you that someday we will meet again. You have my word. But now it's time for us to say goodbye until that day comes. Farewell, love of my life, farewell."

I reached out to Shana weakly, unable to stop her as she stood with determination and turned away from me without looking back.

"No!" I whispered, helpless to do anything other than watch as my wife suddenly started running, with the chain attached to her ankle jingling like music across the stone.

Captain Bear saw Shana coming, but he was so shocked by her actions that he remained frozen on the bench, gaping at her in astonishment. Shana screamed her hatred for the pirate, launching herself at him like a mother bear protecting her cub. Captain Bear was a huge, powerful man, but at that moment, my wife was an irresistible force filled with love, devotion, fury, and determination. I don't think anything could have stopped her that day. Shana and the pirate collided like a thunderclap, sending their entwined bodies careening backward off the bench. I can still hear the pirate's scream of despair in my mind as he and my wife rolled to the cliff edge, then plummeted over the side and disappeared. Shana never made a sound.

I lay where I was in stunned disbelief, unable to comprehend what had just happened. Then, somehow, unaware that I was doing it, I was on my feet. All I could think of was that I had to be with my wife. I had to find her. I staggered toward the cliff, fighting nausea, pain, and dizziness as I called out Shana's name over and over. I was only a few feet away from the edge when I felt hands on me, pulling me back from the brink. I fought those hands, crying and pleading for them to let me go, but I had no strength left and was like a helpless baby in their arms. I looked around to see Baine and Tyris holding me, with Jebido hovering behind them, his face a battered mess.

"Please," I whispered to Jebido.

"I can't let you do it, Hadrack," Jebido replied, his voice catching in his throat. "The gods know I don't blame you for wanting to be with her, but your friends and family need you now more than ever."

I sagged then, defeated as mercifully the darkness came for me and I knew nothing more.

Chapter 24: The Watching Hill

They said that it was the biggest funeral that Ganderland had ever seen. Bigger even than when King Jorquin had been laid to rest almost ten years before. Tyden, our current king, had come all the way from Gandertown to attend, arriving with his new bride and two hundred or so members of his entourage that always followed after him like stray dogs hoping for table scraps. All the lords and ladies from across the realm came as well, for Shana had been universally liked and respected by all. The First Son had even put in an appearance, although he'd been sensible enough not to come anywhere near me. Son Oriell and I had a mutual hatred for each other, and in my current frame of mind, he'd correctly determined that it wouldn't be wise to try and offer his condolences to me.

The First Daughter had come as well, arriving on horseback at the head of a solemn procession of one hundred Daughters and two hundred Daughters-In-Waiting, all dressed in black mourning robes and chanting. It had been a truly inspiring sight. Jin had been with them, too, and I'd broken down when I'd seen her, for she and I were as close to family as you can get—perhaps closer. We shared a special bond, her and I, forged by fire and death during the Corwick massacre so many years ago. I knew Jin had loved Shana almost as much as I had, and having her there by my side had given me the strength to make it through the lengthy ceremony filled with flowery speeches and touching reminisces about my wife. I doubt I could have done so otherwise.

A week had already gone by since the funeral, and now, thankfully, the last of the well-wishers and hangers-on had finally gone home, leaving me alone to mourn in peace. I was sitting in my customary place on a stool in front of Shana's grave marker at the top of a great hill that I'd built in the fields east of Corwick Castle. I called it, The Watching Hill, a place where Shana would be able to look out across our lands and watch the sunrise each morning for all eternity. I'd had fifty chaste trees—Shana's favorite—planted all around the top of the hill in homage to her. And though the trees were small still, the scent of the already budding purple flowers that bloomed all summer long was already almost overpowering, with both bees and hummingbirds signaling their approval as they buzzed and flitted happily among the petals. I knew Shana would be pleased.

    A month and a half had passed since my wife had taken that fateful plunge over the cliff on Blood Ring Isle. It seemed to me like a lifetime already. My friends still considered it a miracle that I'd survived the long journey back to Ganderland afterward—but I knew it had been no miracle. No, the fact that I'd somehow recovered and was still breathing was just a cruel joke foisted on me by the gods. I'd spent every day in *Sea-Wolf's* cabin lying in the bed that I'd shared with Shana and praying for those gods to take me and let me be with her. But those who pull at the strings of our lives are mischievous, conniving creatures, and they refused to let me die despite my prayers. It seemed the gods weren't done with tormenting me just yet.

    As each day of the journey home turned into the next and it became more and more apparent that I would not die, I spiraled deeper and deeper into my grief and guilt, refusing even to eat or drink. Jebido and Baine tried to force-feed me at one point, but I fought them off like a wildcat, spitting and hissing and ultimately tearing open my wound. After that, other than changing my bandages, they left me alone to my own devices. The horrible injury I'd taken from Captain Bear would have killed any other man, everyone agreed on that. But since it had somehow failed to get the job done with me, I figured starvation and dehydration were the next best things. Surely one of them would do the job.

    It was only after we'd finally returned home to Corwick weeks later, with me nothing more than skin and bones by then, that I'd finally relented and started eating after my four children had given an emotional plea that I stop trying to destroy myself. It's hard not to react when those you've fathered profess their love for you and beg you to eat and grow stronger so that you won't abandon them. But though they succeeded in getting me to eat out of guilt, not even seeing my children could bring any joy back to my life, for every time I looked at their innocent faces, all I saw was my failure reflected in their eyes.

The children knew their mother was dead, of course, but not the circumstances behind how she'd died. I intended to keep it that way until they were older. No one in the castle was to speak of what had happened to Shana on penalty of death. It was harsh, I know, but I could barely bring myself to think about the events on that island, let alone try to explain it to four young children who were bound to ask questions that would hurt me more than Captain Bear's sword ever had. I would tell them about their mother's death when they were older and better prepared, I'd promised myself. I just didn't realize at the time that it wasn't they who needed to be prepared but me, and that it would be more than forty years before that time would actually arrive.

A lot had happened in the month and a half since Shana had died, with the Emperor of Cardia accusing King Tyden of an act of war after my attack on his outpost at Blood Ring Isle. The Cardian soldiers and Shadow Pirates on the island had surrendered to my men and the Swails immediately following the deaths of the Wentile brothers, despite outnumbering them four to one. Cardians were forever cowards, it seemed. Now, the Swails had claimed Blood Ring Isle as their own, and there was little that Cardia could do about it without risking losing many ships to the inlet's defenses. Somehow, it seemed fitting considering how the bastards had been raping Swailand of its people and resources over the last few years.

The king had rightly scoffed at the emperor's claim and had instead accused him of being responsible for Shana's death, which Tyden had asserted was, in fact, the true act of war since she was of royal blood. Ganderland had been at peace for seven long years, but now it seemed that peace was about to be broken, as the rhetoric going back and forth between the two kingdoms was becoming more and more threatening by the day. I, for one, didn't care one way or the other what happened. I was done with war and killing for good, for all it had ever brought me was misery and heartache. Corwick was where I belonged—Corwick and The Watching Hill.

I heard a sound behind me and turned, not surprised to see Jebido and Baine striding up the brick pathway that led to the hilltop and Shana's grave. Baine carried something wrapped loosely in canvas, though I barely glanced at it. I turned back to the stone marker that bore my wife's name and stared at the words chiseled across the smooth face. I'd put them there myself. I'd sat in this very spot every day on the hill with Shana since her burial, stewing in guilt and self-loathing from before sunrise to long after sundown. I'd vowed that this day and every day after it would be no different until I took my last breath in this world. It was my penance, I knew, for failing her.

I heard my friends come to a stop directly behind me. "How are you feeling?" Baine asked after a moment.

I didn't bother to respond. Every day it was the same thing with these two. Hopefully, they'd eventually give up and stop coming here.

"Alesia and Einrack are getting set to leave, Hadrack," Jebido added.

He waited then, and I heard him shifting his feet on the ground. I just stared at the marker.

"Don't you want to say goodbye?"

"I already said goodbye to them this morning," I grunted.

There was an awkward pause, then Jebido cleared his throat. "Alesia told me she hasn't talked to you in days."

"Well, she's wrong," I said, feeling sudden anger. "Now go away."

"You can't spend the rest of your life up here, Hadrack."

"Why not?" I muttered.

Jebido let out a long-suffering sigh, then moved to my side and put a hand on my shoulder. "Because you have things to do, my friend."

I looked up at him, feeling hopelessness weighing me down. "Like what?"

"Taking care of your children, for one," Jebido said. "There's going to be a war, too, Hadrack. A long and bloody one."

"What has that to do with me?"

"Ganderland needs a man like you to lead them."

I snorted. "I'm the last person this kingdom can depend on." I gestured bitterly to the marker. "Just ask Shana about that."

Jebido crouched down until we were eye to eye. His face from the beating he'd taken had mostly healed, though there was a four-inch purple scar along his right temple and another, smaller one below his right eye left behind as a reminder. I knew he'd been lucky not to lose that eye. "Now you listen to me, boy," Jebido growled. I could see the anger burning in his features, but it just washed over me. "I'm getting sick and tired of watching you mope around like a lost puppy. What happened to Lady Shana is beyond tragic, but she saved your life for a reason, and I'm damn sure it wasn't just so you could sit here every day crying about the past."

"What did you just say to me?" I grunted in sudden anger. I stood in one smooth motion, towering over Jebido.

"I said that it's enough, Hadrack," Jebido replied evenly, not backing down. He prodded my chest with a finger. "The time has come for you to move on. Feeling sorry for yourself is a waste of time. The castle is in shambles, and no one knows what to do. People are whispering that you've lost your mind."

"So let them whisper," I grunted. "If they don't like it here, then they're free to leave. I won't stop them." I glanced at Baine, then back to Jebido. "And that includes the both of you."

"You're being an ass," Baine grunted.

I glared at him. "I'm the Lord of Corwick," I said. "And I can be whatever I want. Now go away."

"Why don't you make me," Baine said with a flash of challenge in his eyes. I stepped toward him, feeling an almost uncontrollable rage building inside.

"That's enough!" Jebido snapped, stepping between us and putting a hand on my chest.

I hesitated, picturing Baine and me down in Father's Arse as boys, teasing and fighting with each other almost every day until Jebido finally had to break it up—just like he was doing now. It seemed some things never changed regardless of the passing years. But, despite how angry we'd get with each other back then, Baine and I were like brothers, and it would always blow over and we'd be friends again in no time. I knew this moment would be no different. I lowered my head, feeling shame that I had even considered desecrating this sacred place with violence against someone who had always meant so much to me.

"Forgive me," I said. I rubbed a hand down my face, feeling incredibly weary and alone. "I'm not myself these days."

"We know that," Jebido said kindly. "You've been walking in the land of the dead ever since you got home, Hadrack. But that walk has got to end." He motioned to Baine, who began unwrapping the canvas in his hands. "I think this will bring you the purpose you need to walk among the living again."

I watched Baine unravel the object, curious despite myself. Then, as it came free and bright sunlight glinted off hard steel, I gasped in surprise. It was Wolf's Head.

"The Swails found it," Baine explained, unable to stop himself from smiling. He tossed the canvas aside, then, balancing the sword by the hilt and blade, he offered it to me reverently.

"They've been searching for it ever since the fight," Jebido said as I took the weapon in my shaking hands.

I looked at Wolf's Head in wonder, feeling a closeness and love for the sword that I couldn't have expressed in words.

"It must have hit the rocks first before going into the water," Baine added with a regretful shrug. "But I'm sure Smithy can fix it."

I nodded, studying the many scratches and dents along the blade. One of the ruby eyes was missing from one side of the wolf's head, too, and one arm of the crossguard was broken off. But even so, I'd never seen anything more beautiful. Finally, I turned to my friends. "Thank you," I said, feeling emotion welling up in my breast. "I can't tell you what having this back means to me."

Jebido and Baine shared a look that I couldn't interpret before Jebido cleared his throat. "I think you should know, Hadrack, that the king has summoned all the lords to meet with him in Halhaven, including you."

I frowned. "Why?"

Jebido shrugged. "Who am I to say what a king might want?" He tapped his nose with a forefinger. "But if I were a betting man, which I am, I would say it's to announce war on Cardia and that he wants you to lead his army."

I sighed, letting Wolf's Head dangle at my side. "Well, he's going to be disappointed because I'm not going."

"You would disobey a king's summons?" Baine asked, looking surprised.

"Yes," I grunted stubbornly. I turned to face my wife's grave, leaning heavily on the sword. "There's nothing for me in Halhaven. My place is here with Shana."

"Are you sure about that?" Jebido asked. "What about what she wants?"

I looked over my shoulder in annoyance as Jebido and Baine exchanged another one of their odd looks. "What's that supposed to mean?"

"Look at the sword, Hadrack," Baine whispered.

I glanced down at Wolf's Head, then shrugged. "What about it?"

Baine took the weapon and held it by the blade with the hilt at my eye level. "Look there," he said, pointing to a spot just below the remaining half of the crossguard.

I took the sword from him in both hands, holding it higher and peering at the odd scratches and dents that had formed an almost perfect ring of small circles interjoined. I'd never seen anything like it. "What could have done that?" I asked in wonder. "Surely not a rock?"

Jebido approached me on my other side and he put his hand on my arm. "How many rings are there, Hadrack?"

I counted them. "Seven," I answered even as I felt a superstitious tingling run up and down my spine.

"It's the Seven Rings, Hadrack," Baine whispered from my other side. "This is clearly a sign from the World Beyond. One that can't be ignored. Lady Shana has spoken to you from the grave, demanding vengeance. You must heed it!"

I gaped at my friends in astonishment just as a green and blue hummingbird appeared above me, its little wings beating far too fast to see. It hovered over my head for a moment, then zipped down until it was level with the sword's hilt as the sun glinted off it. I held my breath, knowing this was yet another sign from the gods as the hummingbird flitted to the wolf's head, zooming back and forth while it studied the remaining ruby eye. Finally, in a blur of motion, the hummingbird darted away and I let out a stream of air, unaware that I'd been holding my breath. I stared after the tiny creature in awe, then turned my gaze back to the seven rings etched on my blade—seven rings that I knew had just changed my fate in an instant.

"So, what are you going to do about it?" Jebido asked me. I could tell by his hushed tone that he wasn't sure what I was about to say.

"I'm going to find the Seven Rings," I stated firmly. "I'm going to find them, and I'm going to kill every one of the bastards. Then I'm going to burn Cardia to the ground until there's nothing left of that foul place but a bad memory. That's what I'm going to do."

I knelt in front of my wife's grave and rested the tip of my sword's battered and tarnished blade on the head of her marker, then bowed and pressed my forehead to the broken hilt. There were no tears of loss coming from me now. No doubts, fears, or recriminations, either. All I felt was a deep resolve and sense of purpose. My wife had given me the gift of life by giving up her own for me, and now she was reaching out again to ensure that my life continued to have meaning. I vowed I wouldn't let her down.

I was heading back on the vengeance trail once more, but this time I wasn't a boy chasing a rabble of soldiers scattered across a vast kingdom. The Seven Rings were some of the most powerful men in the known world, with enormous wealth, vast resources, and large armies at their disposal, as well as an even more powerful Emperor behind them pulling their strings. But I was the Lord of Corwick now, the second-most powerful man in Ganderland next to the king, and I had my own wealth and resources. I also had a burning need for retribution, fueled by a message of love from another realm—a message that could not be ignored.

"I have heard you, love of my life," I whispered to the grave marker. "And I swear that what you ask of me shall be done." I put my left hand on the stone, feeling the sun's warmth beating on it. "I will not fail you again, Shana Corwick," I pledged. "You have my word."

I stood then with finality and turned to my friends. "Well, what are you two waiting for?" I grunted as I strode past them and headed down the pathway with long, purposeful strides. "We have a King's summons to attend and a war to win."

EPILOGUE

It had taken me almost two full days to tell my story to my three children and granddaughter. I waited in silence when I was finally done, with my chambers filled only by the sobs of Kalidia and Lillia. My eldest son, Hughe, stood near the door against the wall as far from me as possible, his face hard and unreadable as he stared at the floor. He'd been like that ever since I'd described what had happened to his mother on Blood Ring Isle. My other son, Taren, who was younger and slimmer than Hughe yet just as tall, stood staring out the window at the courtyard below. I truly didn't know what their reactions would be, but I was prepared for the worst.

Taren was the first to move, and he turned from the window and strode toward me. I could stand for longer periods now, as my strength had grown exponentially hour by hour. I was thankful for that strength now as I looked Taren in the eye, man to man. My son stopped in front of me, his features bruised by loss and pain. Hughe had always been the tougher and more ruthless of the two brothers, for Taren, though a deadly fighter when riled, was tempered by a sensitivity that he'd inherited from his mother. If things went badly for me now with this one, then I knew I'd lost them all.

"Why didn't you tell us, Father?" Taren asked. His tone wasn't aggressive, though, just curious and resigned. "Did you think us all so weak that we couldn't deal with it?"

I put a hand on his shoulder. "Not you, my son," I said. I glanced around. "Not any of you. I'm the weak one. I should have told this to you long ago, and for that, I will always be sorry."

"We had a right to know," Hughe rumbled angrily—the first words he'd said in a long time. My son opened and closed his huge fists over and over, looking as if he'd dearly like to lash out at something or someone.

"You did have that right," I agreed. "And I took it from you because of my selfish failings." I sighed. "I cannot change what I did in the past and only ask for your forgiveness here in the present. But I do understand if none of you can give me that. I've never been able to forgive myself for what happened, so why should any of you?" I turned my eyes to my daughter. "What about you, my sweet Kalidia? What do you say, child?"

Kalidia was far from being a child, of course, with several sons and a husband of her own. She was by far the smartest and most level-headed of my children, and her opinion and thoughts were widely sought after by everyone in the castle, myself included. Kalidia dabbed at her tear-streaked cheeks with a handkerchief where she sat beside Lillia on my bed, then stood without saying anything.

She came to me then as Taren moved aside for her, and she put her arms around my waist before resting her head against my chest. "I think that might be the most tragic story I have ever heard, Father," my daughter whispered sadly.

I put my hand on her chin and lifted it to see her face. There were creases around her eyes and alongside her nose that I couldn't recall seeing before, and I realized with a start that all my children were getting old. It seemed hard to imagine. "Yes, it is tragic, child," I said. "Your mother's death was a terrible thing that has haunted me from the day it happened."

"I don't mean her death, my lord," Kalidia said as more tears rolled out from the corners of her eyes. "Tragic as it was. I mean that you had to bear the weight of this guilt inside you by yourself for all these years. That is the true tragedy."

I frowned at that as both Taren and Lillia nodded in silent agreement, though Hughe did not. My eldest son finally snorted, then stalked out of the room, slamming the door behind him.

"He'll come around, Father," Kalidia assured me after Hughe was gone. "I'll speak with him. All he needs is a little time."

"I'm not sure I have a lot of that left," I said.

"Nonsense," Lillia admonished me from the bed. "You're healthy as a horse, my lord. Kieran says now that you've fully recovered, you could live for many more years to come."

"Perish the thought, child," I grumbled.

"What happened to the pirate, Father?" Taren asked. "Did he get his revenge in the end?"

"Sadly, he did not," I said regretfully. "Saldor killed the man who murdered his wife and daughter during the battle for the southern tower."

"Ah," Taren said. "What became of him after that?"

"The last anyone saw of Fanrissen," I replied, "he was sailing away from the island in a fishing boat all by himself."

"He went to join his family in the World Beyond, then?" Lillia asked.

I shook my head. "No. The Pirate was a man lost and he needed to find himself." I smiled sadly, remembering. "Eventually, he would find his purpose in life, and when he did, he and I would be fated to meet again." I shook myself out of my reverie. "But that is a story for another time."

Taren moved to the fireplace, staring up at Wolf's Head where the weapon hung in its usual place of honor. He reached out, tracing the black etchings of the seven rings that I'd had enhanced years ago after they'd begun to fade. "I asked you about these once, Father, remember?" my son said in wonder. "Years ago." He glanced at me reproachfully. "You told me they represented the seven realms of the United Kingdom of Ganderland."

I moved to stand beside him, limping on my bad foot as I stared up at the sword. "A necessary lie at the time," I said. I shrugged. "Or at least I believed it to be, at any rate."

"Do you really think that it was our mother who reached out to you from the World Beyond, my lord?" Kalidia asked, coming to stand beside us, her voice filled with awe.

I hesitated for the briefest of moments. "Of course I do," I lied.

The truth was, Jebido and Baine had scratched the rings on the blade themselves before bringing it to me that day so long ago on The Watching Hill. They had figured out that it was the only way to get me to stop feeling sorry for myself, and they'd been right. Baine had confessed to me what he and Jebido had done on his deathbed—the sneaky bastards. I thought that last bit with nothing but affection, though, for in truth, if not for my friends and their trickery, the world my children and grandchildren now lived in might be a far, far darker place than it was.

"What will you do now, my lord?" Lillia asked me, breaking into my thoughts.

"Do?" I asked, raising an eyebrow.

"Now that you're healthy again."

I chuckled and raised my right arm, holding my hand out flat. There was no hint of a shake now, nothing at all. It had been a very long time since I'd felt so strong and alive, and I was still finding it hard to get used to my new reality. I'd grown accustomed to being weak and infirm with death constantly hovering over me like a cloud in recent years, and I hadn't given much thought to what came next. But, hearing the question from my granddaughter had produced an immediate answer in my head. One which I knew was the right path to take.

"I'm going to finish writing my story," I announced. "I'm going to keep writing until it's all down for the world to see, and then, maybe then, the gods will finally say that it's enough and take me."

Hours later, I sat alone at my desk as the night winds beat against the implacable stone walls of Corwick Castle. I had quill and parchment in front of me, and I paused, looking down at the blank pages. There were still so many things that my family didn't know yet—dark, horrible things—and I wondered if I really should bring them to light. For truthfully, what good would it do anyone in the end to dredge up these long-forgotten memories? But then I glanced at Wolf's Head and the seven rings on it placed there by a long-ago lie. That little lie had ultimately set half the known world on fire and had brought great men and powerful kingdoms to their knees. But maybe that was how it had always been meant to be, I thought. Maybe Jebido and Baine had just been mere instruments of the gods all along when they'd made those marks. Who was I to say? And more to the point, who was I to try and rewrite history, anyway?

    No, I thought firmly. It was my duty to all the generations coming behind to write down the words exactly as they had happened, regardless of how it made me or anyone else look in the end. I began to write almost feverishly then, working well into the night—for there was still so much of this story left to tell.

THE END

Author's Note

Thank you, dear reader, for your incredible support and kind words regarding this series. When I finished writing The Wolf At War, I was hesitant at first to dive into another Hadrack book, simply because I felt that I couldn't write anything better than book 4 in this series. Instead, I switched to the Past Lives Chronicles, needing to test my creative juices on something other than Hadrack's many troubles. I was worried at the time about turning into a one-series author who just keeps churning out book after book using the same old, tired format and taking his readers for granted. That is something that I promise you I will never do. If I can't keep this series fresh and inventive, then it will end—though I'm pleased to say that with what I have planned for Hadrack, I don't think that ending will be anytime soon.

Writing Past Lives and then Jack the Ripper—which at almost 600 pages is my biggest book yet—opened up a whole new world of creativity for me, and I am so glad that I wrote them. Those books have given me greater confidence in my writing and my ability to do in-depth historical research. As for Hadrack, while the events that unfolded in this book were tragic at times, it now lays to rest the question about what happened to Lady Shana and opens up a whole new world of opportunities for the storyline. As a sidenote, killing off Einhard was a tough decision for me to make, but I couldn't see any other way to push the narrative along without it. I will miss the tough warrior, though, for he was one of my favorite characters to write about.

I wrote the first draft for The Wolf And The Lamb in just 79 days, which is a record for me. After I'd finished Jack the Ripper, I had promised myself that I'd take a month off before starting back with Hadrack. However, that promise lasted exactly one day, for I just couldn't wait to jump back into the Wolf's head. But, now that the book is finished, I will be taking some time away from writing to get to the many, many other things that I've been neglecting these past eight months. Hadrack, Baine, and Jebido will return soon, and I look forward to having you, dear reader, along for the ride. It's going to be fun!

    Terry Cloutier
    May 2nd, 2022